THE
Collected
Short Fiction
OF
Bruce Jay Friedman

Also by Bruce Jay Friedman

Novels

STERN
A MOTHER'S KISSES
THE DICK
ABOUT HARRY TOWNS
TOKYO WOES
THE CURRENT CLIMATE

Non-fiction

THE LONELY GUY'S BOOK OF LIFE
THE SLIGHTLY OLDER GUY

Plays

SCUBA DUBA
STEAMBATH
HAVE YOU SPOKEN TO ANY JEWS LATELY?

Screenplays

SPLASH!
STIR CRAZY
DR. DETROIT

Collections

FAR FROM THE CITY OF CLASS
BLACK ANGELS
LET'S HEAR IT FOR A BEAUTIFUL GUY
BLACK HUMOR

THE
Collected Short Fiction
OF
Bruce Jay Friedman

DONALD I. FINE, INC.

NEW YORK

Library of Congress Catalogue Card Number: 95-060939
ISBN: 1-55611-462-1

Manufactured in the United States of America

10   9   8   7   6   5   4   3   2

Designed by Irving Perkins Associates, Inc.

For Pat and Molly

CONTENTS

Foreword by Bruce Jay Friedman

By Way of Introduction

The Subversive   3
Brazzaville Teen-ager   9
Far from the City of Class   16
The Partners (featuring Harry Towns)   27

Crazed Youth

Black Angels   47
The Man They Threw Out of Jets   52
Detroit Abe   61
A Change of Plan   74
The Mourner   80
Lady (featuring Harry Towns)   87

Halcyon Days (Family Life and The Service)

When You're Excused, You're Excused   105
The Hero   115
The Good Time   123
The Mission   136
The Enemy   142
23 Pat O'Brien Movies   151
The Icing on the Cake   156
Wonderful Golden Rule Days   162
The Humiliation   167
Back to Back (featuring Harry Towns)   174

Mother

Post Time   195
An Ironic Yetta Montana   198
Mr. Prinzo's Breakthrough   207
Our Lady of the Lockers   218

Business Is Business   244
Living Together   251
The Trip   256
Marching Through Delaware   264

Sex

The Gent (featuring Harry Towns)   271
The Holiday Celebrators   277
The Operator   280
The Investor   292

Death

For Your Viewing Entertainment   301
The Canning of Mother Dean   308
Show Biz Connections   316
The Night Boxing Ended   324
The Interview   328
The Death Table   332
The Little Ball   336
Yes, We Have No Ritchard   344
The Neighbors   351

The Family Man

Let's Hear It for a Beautiful Guy   357
The Scientist   363
The Gentle Revolutionaries   367
The Golden Years   379
The War Criminal   384
Pitched Out (featuring Harry Towns)   391

FOREWORD

IN HER LATE YEARS, my mother confessed to me that she had dropped me on my head when I was two. As I've grown older, I've come to believe that her presumably innocent mistake resulted in the "tilted" quality I've been accused of having in my work. And I have grown older. The first of the stories in this collection was published in 1953, the last one in 1995, proving that I'm a lot older than I'd realized.

An agent who read the first one I tried said she knew my type. I'd write some stories and drift off, but I would always drift back. And that's the way it's happened. Or maybe it was because she'd said it would happen.

Along with everyone else, I've celebrated Dr. Johnson's celebrated observation that no one but a blockhead wrote for anything but money. But I wonder if it applies to my case. I don't recall sending back any publication checks, but most of these stories were written to puzzle things out for myself. The first one I tried had to do with a troubling experience I'd had in the Air Force. When I finished the story—complete with lies and other adornments—I wasn't quite as troubled. My second effort dealt with an upsetting experience in junior high school. Writing the story made me feel a little lighter. This is not to argue for stories as self-therapy—but that's one of the things a story can accomplish. I've also written stories just to show off a little, to put brackets around an experience or an intriguing person, to put in boldface what I thought of as something ridiculous or unfair in the culture. I've written some just because I thought I could. Most probably came out of unhappiness, either vague or specific. I can't recall ever whistling happily to the typewriter and I'm suspicious of writers who do. None of the stories were written either to or for anyone, although obviously I've been happy when someone else came along.

My birthdays generally slide by with no particular clangor—but I noticed the last one—my sixty-fifth. The drill was—no parties, no gifts —just a dinner with my wife and daughter, which is always remarkable and celebration enough for me. Then I realized I'd already been given an exquisite gift by Donald I. Fine, the publisher of this book—a chance to have all or most of my stories in one place, proof that they exist and that I got them written.

Once in a while, and certainly not every twenty minutes, an interested but busy person asks to read something of mine and could I please recommend the work that best represents me. My favorite. I've never known what to say in that instance until the publication of this collection.

—BJF

WATER MILL, N.Y.

1995

By Way of Introduction

The Subversive

My friend ed stamm was the most all-American person I've ever met. It came out when he brushed his teeth and shaved. He did both at the same time, using enormous quantities of toothpaste and shaving cream. When you approached him in the morning, he looked like a white, foaming symbol of Free World cleanliness.

I knew him in the Air Force when he was waiting to get into jet fighter training, and I was waiting to get into something small and inconspicuous where my general lack of military know-how would do the least amount of damage. He looked like a recruiting poster, with clear blue eyes and perfect profile and a sweet countryness about his mouth. Audie Murphy is the Hollywood star he most resembled, although next to him, Murphy would have seemed swarthy. He had wonderful manners and said to me at the base swimming pool when we met, "I'd certainly enjoy your compny this evening." I've known people who wouldn't have minded hanging around with me for a few hours, but the idea of anyone wanting my "compny" was something else again. It was a phony kind of line, but he said it with such all-American sweetness it actually became disarming. I worked it into my repertoire and even *I* was able to get away with it, although I used "company" instead of "compny." He also fell right on top of little children, getting right down on the ground when one came along, his face scrubbed and beaming, and then saying, "Hello, little boy (or girl)," which came out more like "Heddo, lidder booey." He wasn't trying to impress anyone. He did it when people were around or when rooms were empty. He just felt like hugging and kissing little children. I do that one too, now. I felt kind of pretentious the first few times, but then I swung into it and now I get right down there with children just as naturally as I'd check my watch for the time.

I understand that Hollywood puts its new screenwriters into categories such as "adventure," "comedy," "suspense," "war," a typecasting, incidentally, from which I'm told they never escape. Ed's background might have been concocted by one of the lesser lights in "homespun." He came from a small town in the Midwest, lived with his family in a two-story frame house (mortgage just about paid up), had a kid sister with freckles, earned enough working part-time at a gas station to get

3

through the local college, won four letters in sports. His dad: football and track coach at the high school. His Girl Back Home: the bank president's daughter, cheerleader at the college, voted "Prettiest" in her senior class. Tennis wasn't one of his sports, although when we played at the air base, he picked it up quickly, performing with the instinctive grace he would have brought to anything from jai alai to hammer throwing. I was better than him, though. I'd been playing for years and I beat him, not overwhelmingly, but consistently.

One day I wrapped him up pretty solidly and teased him about it and he said, "Do you want to play for money? Forty bucks." He picked just the right amount of money to get me nervous. In all our playing he'd never won a single set. Yet he looked at me in a funny way and made me back down. I said, "You can't play for money without a referee. Anyway, I'm not taking your money." I knew that in some crazy way, even though he never had before, he'd outlast me, or outgut me, or outheart me, or do whatever special thing it is that all-Americans do, and beat me no matter how much better a player I was.

I automatically gave up in all competitions with him. Where girls were concerned, we'd run neck and neck for a few minutes, but then I'd begin to peter out self-consciously and Ed would say, "We certainly would enjoy your compny in my car," whereupon I would stand by while he hooked arms with the cuter of the two and I fell in behind with the bomb. Even when a rare, offtrail girl made it perfectly plain she preferred my swarthiness to his clean-cut wholesomeness, I would begin to do a lot of staring down at the ground until she disgustedly marched off to join Ed's "compny," leaving me to guard her heavily acned friend. Once, with Ed along, I completely mastered a girl. It was at a bar in Illinois, and the girl was serving drinks to the tables. I'd come in after a Bogart movie at the base, spit something out at her through clenched teeth, and she had loved it. Through sheer accident, I'd evidently found myself a pretty little masochist. "Did I do anything wrong?" she asked, and, catching on, I spit out another line, twice as hard. "Could I call you somewhere?" she asked me, and this time, giddy in the role, I said the liquor was rotgut and knocked the shotglass off the table. "What did I do?" she asked Ed, who looked on in fascination. "For Christ's sakes, she's yours," he said to me. "Do you know what I'd do if she was giving me invitations like that?" I stared off into the distance, not really sure of what to do next, and said, "I don't go for that." She kept coming up to me, beseechingly, practically purring with hurt, and then finally I said, "All right. You can call me at Base Operations, extension 976. Any night except Wednesdays when I'm on duty."

"I see," she said, the fire dying in her eyes. Later, I saw her dancing with Ed.

This is not one of those stories in which one guy is better than his friend in a million things, and then at the end there's this one thing the friend is able to win out in, proving it's really better to be a terrible fellow with just one talent. As a matter of fact, there were quite a few things at which I was able to top him. Tennis is one I mentioned and then there is singing (he had no voice at all), general smartness (he had read very few books), and jokes. There was one girl I was sure I'd have the edge with because of the jokes and general routines I did, a new singer at the base club. As the welcoming committee that week, we were to meet her at the club and be her escorts for the evening. We sat with her awhile, Ed assuring her it was swell to be in her compny. I thought I'd work my routines in naturally, rather than announce, "Now I'll do some routines." But before I knew it, Ed was doing them, all of the best ones: Joe Louis commenting on the Ezzard Charles–Marciano fight, a Durante thing I do with a few variations of my own, and a short take from an old Fred Allen script in which two potatoes are the only characters in an avant-garde play. His Joe Louis was too Midwestern, his Durante came out Jimmy Stewart, and he blew the punchline on the Allen skit. His timing was awful, too, but the girl was giggling away just the same. After a while he said, "Now you do one, Tony," forcing me to serve up an Edward Everett Horton imitation I'd far from perfected. The singer listened patiently and in a short while was, inevitably, walking to the jukebox with Ed, nibbling at his ear.

The other all-American things I remember about him are sort of scattered and don't really sound *that* all-American when you set them down. He got the snuggest fit out of his jockey underwear of anyone I've ever known. He drove a new Nash, and instead of making out payment checks to the bank, he was paying off someone named "Old Man Bagley" in a combination of money and chores he was to do during his furloughs. In driving the Nash, long before he came to stops, his brake foot would begin to fidget on the pedal, caressing it, pumping it a little, testing it, until, if you were a passenger, you had ridiculous amounts of confidence that he would be able to pull off the stop. He called everyone "old buddy" and it was a thrilling and special thing to have him pat you on the back and say, "Old buddy, what'll we do tonight?"

One night, a short colonel with a twisted body and a reputation for being touchy about his youth and the quick promotions he'd received, announced he was going off to the flight line to shoot landings in jets. Ed heard him and said, "I'd certainly consider it a great privilege to go along with you, sir." It meant he was willing to squat on the floor of the

plane while the colonel took off and landed and took off and landed
long hours into the night. It really wasn't necessary for him to do all
this and he'd be getting plenty of it in pilot training. But it was something like sweeping floors in grocery stores and doing lowly things in
banks and walking several miles to school each morning, and if you're
an all-American worth your salt, you don't miss chances to do these
things. The colonel explained that it was going to be a pretty miserable
kind of evening, but Ed said if the colonel didn't mind his compny,
he'd like to go up with him. The colonel, a sour man, melted before
Ed's sweetness and said okay.

I'm not entirely sure how this last thing fits into the all-American
picture. It has something to do with it. In any case, I did discover that
for all his pretenses of all-Americanism, the freckled sister, the gas
station job, the chores for Old Man Bagley, my friend Ed Stamm was a
subversive.

I found this out during a weekend in which Ed invited me and a
mutual "old buddy" of ours named Rig to his home in Iowa for the
weekend. We made a perfect movie combat trio with Ed, the hero; Rig,
the slow-talker from Texas; and me, the Brooklyn boy, telling jokes
about my mother's potato pancakes. We drove in shifts, with Ed, by
silent agreement, taking over my turn, since my driving was uneven and
I was obviously unable to do those confidence-inspiring pumps with my
brake foot. Our first stop in Ed's town was at his girl's house; she came
running out the way they do in Andy Hardy movies, predictably and
agonizingly pretty, filling the car with a minty Seventeen freshness,
kissing Ed's head like a puppy, and then flouncing herself around and
teasing with Ed's "Old buddies" while Ed drove to the—you guessed it
—tree-lined street on which he lived. Ed's father and sister were on the
lawn waiting for us, his dad a slender, slightly taller and gray-haired
Ed, his sister freckled, and surprisingly (rather disappointingly, since
she was to be my date) broad-shouldered. Mr. Stamm took to Rig
immediately, regarding me with a hint of suspicion. He had heard that
Rig was in charge of painting at the air base and said to us all, "Now
don't forget, boys. You're going to work for your meals. I've got a fence
back there could use a good coat of paint."

Not much more that night. We all ate dinner together, with Mr.
Stamm, after donning apron and cook's hat, fixing and serving the
meal. Later, when Ed's girl had gone home, Mr. Stamm turned down
our beds and said good night to us. The following day, Ed went off
early to do one of those chores for Mr. Bagley. Rig and I ate breakfast
with Mr. Stamm and then we really did paint the fence. I thought the
idea was wholesome and everything, but I could have done without it.
In the afternoon, we all went to a roadside place and danced, Rig and

Ed taking turns with Ed's girl. I danced with Ed's sister. A female version of Ed should have been wonderful, and she certainly was healthy looking, but when you analyzed her, she turned out to be all back and no bosom. It was that night at dinner that Ed was unmasked as a subversive.

We had all decided to wear our dress uniforms at the dance that night, and were sitting around the table with Ed's sister, as though we were at a festive NATO conference. Mr. Stamm, in apron and cook's hat, once again was serving platters of food. Ed had just done a George Sanders takeoff of mine, poorly, and then, as though to sell me to his father, said, "That one was made up by my old buddy here, Tony."

"That Rig can certainly paint a fence," said Mr. Stamm. "I could use a boy like that around here. I'd keep him jumping." Rig said, "Yes, I believe you would, too," drawling out the line, and Mr. Stamm slapped him on the back and said, "Oh that Rig, he's a corker."

Ed said, "I know how to pick my old buddies," and then a wheelchair came into the room carrying a shriveled woman in a bathrobe with deep crevasses in her face and beautiful blue eyes. Her bathrobe went flat below her waist, concealing either withered legs or none at all.

Ed stood up at the table, his eyes shut and his fists clenched, screaming in a monotone, "SON OF A BITCH. SON OF A BITCH. GET IT OUT OF HERE. DIRTY. DIRTY. SON OF A BITCH. OH, DIRTY, DIRTY BITCH."

The woman said, sweetly, "Now Ed. Now Ed," and he screamed, "YAAH, YAAH, YAAH."

Mr. Stamm came over quickly and said, "Now Ed," spinning the wheelchair around and taking it out the door, with the woman saying, "Now Ed, now Ed," patiently and sweetly, and giving off an odor of camphor.

When Mr. Stamm got back, we continued the meal, the chatter starting up again, with Mr. Stamm teasing Rig about getting a bargain on some Air Force paint, Ed telling Mr. Stamm about the books I'd read, and Mr. Stamm finally succumbing and saying to me, "We had a Brooklyn boy at school here once. Got along just fine." Later, we went to the dance on schedule and I got in several dances with Ed's girl, her sharp, pointed bosoms a fine relief from my date's vague ones. We started back for the base around noon the following day, after shoveling a little coal for Mr. Stamm, who'd jokingly suggested we do it to work off our meals.

Weeks later, Ed and I drifted apart, or possibly got wrenched apart. My assignment came through before he got into jet pilot training. In the first weeks of getting oriented in my new job in base information, I didn't call him at all, and once, when I did see him, I failed to introduce him to my new friends. They were flip and waspish and, for one brief second, I was a little ashamed of Ed. He must have sensed it. In any case, I violated some crazy all-American code of his for friendship. When I saw him later, there was a flatness between us, and we were never to be close again. This was much to my regret, because many times I longed for his compny and for his arm around my shoulder and for him saying, "What are we doing tonight, old buddy?"

In any case, I think of him as the most all-American person I ever knew (or perhaps I should drop the all-American part—because that's sarcastic and I don't mean to be—and just say "American"), his looks, his manners, his sweetness, the bit with the little boys and girls. Or at least I *would* think of him that way if I could forget that one subversive thing he pulled at dinner that night. It proved to me that you probably can't trust a goddamned soul in this country.

Brazzaville
Teen-ager

HE HAD ALWAYS FELT that perhaps a deathbed scene would unite them; he and his father would clutch at each other in a sicklied fusion of sweetness and truth, the older man dropping his lifelong cool, finally spilling the beans, telling Gunther what it was all about, philosophy, stories of extramarital rascality, the straight dope on how much dough he had to the penny, was Mom any good in the hay. Did it hurt to be old? Was death a breeze?

This may or may not have been a deathbed scene. You could not tell and perhaps that was the trouble. His father hung before him in harnesses and nettings, elaborate pullied contraptions. Two weeks before, the old man had suddenly collapsed into himself, accordion-style, pinching off nerves. Undreamed of pain. A classic new high. He had to be kept stretched out indefinitely. Later, they would see. Gunther pulled up a chair, not too close.

"How's it feel, Dad?"

His father faced the ceiling, chin high, as though he wore the world's tightest collar, a steel ascot.

"It's no picnic."

"What do they say?" asked Gunther.

"What do they know? This one gives you one kind of pill. Then you get another. They're nice guys. You should see how young they are these days. Clean-cut, you know. Not wise guys. And you'd be surprised. They think nothing of treating a man much older than they are. Way older. I'd say I'm a good thirty, thirty-five years older than one fellow they had working on me. I told him and he laughed, but it didn't bother him."

Did you ever make it with an actress, Gunther wanted to ask. Ever catch a dose? What's the worst thing you ever pulled? Let him dare ask one of these; his father would somehow get out of the contraptions and smack him in the mouth.

"You'll be out of there in no time," said Gunther.

"I'll tell you one thing about this," said the old man. "It's bad, very bad. It's one of those things where they don't know. Don't ever get this,

9

kid. You're a hundred per cent better off without it. To tell you the truth, I think I'm finished."

"Don't say that, Dad. You'll get better."

Later that night, Gunther thought of his father's enlarged knuckles. The contraptions had not bothered him quite that much. Somehow you could get free of them. The old man's body had been whittled all the way down, but there were force-feedings. You could get back the weight. The knuckles were the tip-off, though. Once knuckles got out of hand, you were washed up. Still later that night, the idea came to him that only if he, Gunther, were to debase himself, to do something painful beyond belief, the most embarrassing act he could imagine, only then would his dad recover. Grimly, he shopped along the noisy streets of his mind. The instant his plan formed, he wanted to tear it from his head.

The following day, Gunther, a voucher clerk, was summoned to the office of his boss, Hartman, a tall gray-haired man with steady bomber-pilot eyes. Although Hartman had never scolded him, Gunther feared the man, came to work an hour early each morning so there would be no chance of a time-clock slipup. The boss's quiet gaze had sent others in the office writhing into colitis attacks.

Before Hartman could speak, Gunther himself raced into words. "Sir, if you don't mind, I've got this thing going on. My father's very sick, I've never really asked you for anything, but I've got this thing to ask."

"I'm sorry," said Hartman. "All right, go ahead."

Gunther took a deep breath, as though about to swim a pool under-water. Perhaps if he just asked, just said it, that alone would keep his father's fever down.

"The only thing that can possibly save him is if you make a recording with Little Sigmund and the Flipouts, three kids, doing the background doo-wah, doo-wahs and the second-chorus yeh, yeh, yehs."

"I'm not following any of this," said Hartman, his calm reaction throwing Gunther into panic.

"The recording is called 'Brazzaville Teen-ager.' It's about a young boy whose father is a mercenary and gets sent to the Congo. The boy goes along and writes this letter back to his girl in the States, talking about how great it was surfing and holding hands and now here he is in Brazzaville. Little Sigmund and the Flipouts are a new group, with only one other recording to their credit, 'Berlin Wall Teen-ager.' If this goes, the idea is to come up with an album of teen-agers at the world's trouble spots. In any case, you're involved in only one record, Mr. Hartman."

"You're still not coming through," said Hartman, throwing his legs up on his desk, a movement that terrified Gunther, as did most of Hartman's movements. "What's the connection between all this and your father's sickness?"

"I can't explain it," said Gunther, amazed he was still talking. "There is just one. I've learned that if I can get you to do this thing, which of course is way out of your line, the bottling business and everything, Dad will recover."

"What do you mean, you've learned?" said Hartman.

"I know it," said Gunther. "I don't know much, but I do know this. Can we forget the logic part for just a second? I'm asking you to do this thing. It's no fun asking, believe me. I wish I could tell you what I feel like. But will you please do it? I figure I've got one no-questions-asked favor coming."

"Do *me* a favor," said Hartman, taking his legs down.

"Anything," said Gunther.

"Go back inside and forget you ever made this little speech. You forget it and I promise I'll try to forget it."

At least I came out with it, Gunther thought, as he drove his car aimlessly through Manhattan. For no special reason, he owned a car in the city and had to pay a huge monthly garage bill for it. To get his money's worth, he took it out for pointless drives at night.

If I got myself to say something like that to a boss, there's no limit to what I can do.

His contentment lasted only momentarily and before long, he was stifled, out of breath. Hands other than his seemed to sweep the car into a U-turn and out he drove to Westchester. As he entered the Hartman estate, platoons of dogs, signifying great wealth, yipped at his tires. Gunther had heard that worthless brothers-in-law, other no-goods and hangers-on lived in cottages on the grounds; he strained to see them in the darkness. At the main house, Gunther was ushered into the dining room where Hartman and his guests were completing their dinner. "Well, what is it?" said Hartman, pushing back from the table. "He works for me."

"One would think the poor fellow had driven all the way from Nairobi," said a bushy-haired man in a witty Viennese accent, to which the other guests tumbled back with laughter.

"You'll have to forgive Mr. Ortberg," said Mrs. Hartman, a charming woman with many jeweled coils at her neck. "He has trouble keeping his untrammeled sense of humor in tow."

Leaving the table, Hartman took Gunther off to a side room. "They're going to press the platter at five P.M. tomorrow," said Gunther. "Look, I don't know how it would be if my father died. Maybe I'd be casual. Maybe I'd really fly off my cork. All I know is that I saw him, I don't think he weighs a hundred pounds, and I really want to have him around. Not that we ever exchanged two words that meant a goddamned thing in all our lives. Hell, I've talked more intimately with you, Mr. Hartman, and you know how I've kept my distance in the last eight years. Anyway, I really don't want to lose him. You should see the way they've got him rigged up. There's nothing left of him."

"Gunther, look, I've been in the bottling business for thirty-three years. Anyone will tell you I've never fired a man on the spot . . ."

"Why don't you go along with him, darling," said Mrs. Hartman, who had slipped into the room. "The poor fellow's obviously quite upset. It will cost you very little and it might be fun. My husband told me about it this morning, Mr. Gunther."

Hartman's jaw bunched up, then softened as he put his arm around his wife's waist, embarrassing Gunther. "Now what is it you want me to do again?" he asked.

"The doo-wah, doo-wah and yeh, yeh, yeh backgrounds, Mr. Hartman," said Gunther. "The A and R man at the studio will clue you in. Oh, Christ, thanks a lot, the both of you. Thank you, Mrs. Hartman. Sometimes you just meet someone out of the clear blue sky and they'll go along with you, no matter how crazy you sound."

In the handsomely paneled penthouse office of Conrad Jaggers, lunch hour the following day, Gunther momentarily lost his nerve. Meeting the young president of Dirty Bird Recordings at a bar the previous week, Gunther had no idea Jaggers headed such an elaborate operation. The pimpled young fellow sat on a fanback chair in a blizzard of phone calls, memos, stenographers; there seemed no way for Gunther to get back on the footing they had so quickly established at the bar, three in the morning, two fellows drifting quickly into a kind of cabaret intimacy, sliding capsule wisdoms back and forth across the table.

"Fantastic to see you, Gunther," said the young man when he had finally cleared his office.

"Nice to see you, Mr. Jaggers. I mean Conrad. Look, I'll go right into it. It would be easier to say this if we were back at the bar. My dad's dying and I need a favor. It's got to be on trust alone, one of those things that guys at a bar do for each other. You know that recording you told me about, 'Brazzaville Teen-ager.' You hummed it in my ear."

"We go on that this afternoon."

"Well, I want you to let a friend of mine work in with the Flipouts, you know the doo-wahs and yeh, yehs."

"You mean a singer buddy of yours just needs a fast credit, doesn't want to monkey around, that it?"

"Something like that," said Gunther. "What do you say."

"Let me meditate," said Jaggers, putting his head on the table. "Yogi." Thirty seconds later, he lifted his head. "Done," he said. "Like you say, two guys at a bar, one asks the other a favor. Operate that way and you never go wrong."

Later in the day, Gunther arrived at the recording studio with Hartman, who was introduced to Little Sigmund and the Flipouts, sullen, empty-eyed boys with patched, beginning beards.

"You stand in here, Hartman baby," said Jaggers, "between Raymond and Alfredo. You know about the doo-wahs. Now listen, can you girl it at all?"

"He hasn't done that much work," said Gunther.

"What do you mean?" asked Hartman.

"You know, the falsetto thing. If we can get that working in the record, we can cut through all the strings I plan to use. Anyway, try it on the first press, you know, do a high-pitched little-boy thing and if it works, we'll keep it. Ready Sigmund, ready kids?"

> *I'm writing you my darling,*
> *From war-torn Brazzaville . . .*

"I do hope it wasn't too much of an inconvenience," said Gunther, driving his boss to the railroad station.

"I'd rather not go into it," said Hartman. "The music does get to you, though, in a way I can't quite explain." Gunther drove carefully, his back stiff. How would it be to crack up with a boss inside your car. Cruising along Broadway, he passed a small restaurant with a crowd gathered out front, their eyes on a man in the window tossing flapjacks. Gunther suddenly began to perspire as though vaulted into the middle of a tropical sickness. Pulling on the brakes, he double-parked and then ran round to open his boss's door. "Sir, look," he said. "I know this is unforgivable after what I've put you through, but you've got to go into that store with me."

"Not on your life," said Hartman. "I think I've been jackass enough for one day. Not only that, but if you don't get right back into this car . . ."

"Where do you want me, on my knees?" said Gunther. "It just came to me that maybe the record wasn't enough. And just one more thing would put over the deal, get my dad out of there clean. I swear to Christ I'll work for a month, no salary. You've just got to go into that window and flip a batch."

"Your job's not worth a plugged nickel," said Hartman, but some people in the crowd had turned toward the car and Hartman began to ease out of his seat. "I think I'm doing this for my wife," he said as Gunther took his arm and led him through the crowd into the restaurant.

"Christ, this is difficult for me to do," said Gunther, leading Hartman into the window-cooking area. "All right, all right," he said to the performing chef, taking out some new bills he had somehow anticipated he would need, "here's fifty if you let my man toss the next round."

"What have you got, a publicity thing?"

"Never mind," said Gunther, helping Hartman off with his jacket. "What's the matter with this town, doesn't money talk any more?"

A week later, Gunther arrived at the hospital to help his father pack. The old man walked cautiously, with a slight limp, but color had appeared in his cheeks and he had put on a few pounds.

"You know what I like about this place," the old man said. "They do all these things for you and they don't charge a cent. Isn't that a laugh. Not much they don't. Well, what the hell, they got to get paid. Otherwise, how would they run the place. Somebody's got to pay them, am I right?"

"Right, Dad. The important thing is you're back on your feet."

In the car, the old man said, "I'll take it easy at first. No sense rushing into things. Otherwise you're right back where you started and what was the good."

Gunther spun the car into Central Park, a few miles from where his dad had his apartment. More than ever, Gunther wanted something from the old man, anything. Had he ever stolen anything? Could he still get it up at his age? What about broads? Was Mom the first he'd ever slept with? Had he ever gone to a cathouse? Which way did he like it best, straight or tricky stuff?

"Dad," said Gunther.

"What's that?" the old man said, whirling suddenly as though he had guessed Gunther's dirty thoughts and might throw a decrepit punch.

"Nothing," said Gunther.

"I thought you wanted something. For a second there it sounded like it, but what the hell, everyone's wrong sometimes. The top men in the country."

Gunther double-parked, then helped his father to the apartment. Half an hour later, his father settled, Gunther entered the elevator and pressed the lobby button. But midway between floors, he pulled the emergency switch and screamed up the shaft, "You son of a bitch, do you know what I had to go through to get you on your goddamned feet?"

Far from the City of Class

FOR A TIME THERE, during my freshman year at college, it seemed no one was going to invite me home for the long weekend during mid-semester recess. This bothered me since it was customary for boys who lived near the Middle Western college to invite us Easterners home with them during holidays. I had no idea what you did when you weren't invited home with someone. The town would be deserted, and it seemed to me the only thing to do would be to walk around and wait until people came back to school.

An invitation finally came through, however, for me and another Eastern boy named Hank. It came from a Kansas City sophomore who generally didn't invite people home with him but was taking a crack at it this once. He was very unsure about the idea and was careful to lay down specific terms for the visit. His father owned a grocery store in Kansas City called the Save-A-Dime, and it was understood we would help out on deliveries during the day in return for which we would get to eat at his house and be fixed up with girls.

There was a cold tang to the air and snow flurries dusted about as Hank and I took our seats on the bus to Kansas City. Hank was a short boy with a broad nose and thick glasses who talked endlessly in a low, mournful voice about New York.

"New York," he said as the bus droned away from town. "Man, how Hanky remembers it. Toots Shor's. Lindy's. Oh, man, what's Hanky doing here—on a bus to Kansas City? Remember this, boss, when you're out of New York, you're out of town."

"Why do you talk so much about New York?" I asked. "You're from Newark."

"Yes, boss, but what other city is there, I ask you?" he said, as though I'd asked him a completely different question. "What can compare with tearing into a hunk of cherry cheese at Lindy's, midnight after the hockey game. Sashaying through Central Park with a class broad on your arm. Getting two quick ducats down front for a Porter show. It's a class town, I'm telling you."

"I'm not arguing with you on that," I said. "I just don't understand how you can get so excited about it when you're from New Jersey."

16

"Oh, boss, what are we doing here?" he asked, ignoring my question again. "On a one-way ride to Cornville, U.S.A."

I'd known Hank for several months now. The first time I saw him was at a sorority dance. He had walked over to me, glanced down for a second and then whispered, "Get some class in your shoes." My shoes, as it turned out, were scuffed and needed a shine. They were a little worn down at the heels, too, but it was because I never paid attention to shoes—I just wore them until they had holes in them and then got a new pair. I got very angry at him right then and there and said, "Mind your own business."

It flustered him and he said, "Man, don't get excited. Hanky apologizes. The way you get excited I can tell you're a class guy." He introduced himself then and told me about his eyes. He was very close to being blind, but it never stopped him from being a football star. In high school they had called him "Eagle." They practically had to lead him out on the field, but once the ball was in his hands, he was somehow able to hit ends with forty-yard passes. We became friendly then, and after a month or so, out of the clear blue sky, he suddenly began calling me "boss."

Now, as the bus pushed through the snow on its way to Kansas City, I asked him, "Why do you call me 'boss' all the time?"

"Cut it out," he said. "You know you love it. Hanky and the boss. The boss and Hanky. That's the cutest thing Hanky's ever heard."

"It's not cute to me," I said. "I wish you'd cut it out."

"Oh, boss," he said. "Take it easy on Hanky. Hanky's on your team."

He looked at me, let out a mournful sound and then put his arms behind his head and stared at the top of the bus. "The boss and Hanky," he moaned. "In Lindy's. Then over to Shor's. A fast mambo at La Martinique." He began to sing a chorus from "On the Town." I was drowsy and the song didn't keep me from going to sleep.

The next morning, Butz, the fellow who had invited us to Kansas City, greeted us at the bus terminal. He was short, with hair that couldn't recede much farther. I can never remember seeing him when he wasn't perspiring. He was driving a truck with the lettering, "Save-A-Dime," on the outside and he looked very nervous.

"Throw your things in the back," he said, "and then we'll go right over to the store and deliver a few orders. That'll square things with my mother and father. About your staying over tonight, I mean."

"Oh, well, that's very classy," said Hank.

"All right," I said.

We were still sluggish from the trip. Inside the truck, Butz started the motor and began to drive. I'd never seen anyone drive so hard. He gripped the wheel so tight the veins on his hands bulged out. Then he began to clutch and brake and spin the wheels furiously, his shoulders hunched way over the wheel, his eyes popping out nervously at the road.

After a while, Hank began to announce. He lifted one fist to his mouth, as though it were a microphone, and announced, "Ladies and gentlemen, we are now passing through Cornville, U.S.A., home of cornballs who've never heard of Gotham. Never heard of the Empire State Building. Ladies and gentlemen, take a good look at Cornville, U.S.A. This is so far Off Broadway, ladies and gentlemen, it might as well be Minsk or Pinsk."

"Don't tell me we're going to hear that New York routine all day," said Butz, clutching, braking, steering, his eyes bulging.

"I'll smack you right in the mouth, brother," said Hank, his face suddenly red, drawing back his fist to hit Butz.

"Quit," I said, grabbing his hand.

He sat back now, breathing hard, and adjusted his collar. "All right, boss," he said, quieting down. "I won't slug him, if you want it that way. But Hanky's been around. Hanky doesn't take stuff like that sitting down."

"Hell," said Butz, clutching and braking and perspiring. "What did I do? Insult your mother or something? What's wrong with you?"

Hank paid no attention. In a little while he leaned back, raised his fist to his mouth and began to announce once more: "Ladies and gentlemen, I regret this little break due to technical difficulties. We continue with our broadcast from the heart of Nowhere, U.S.A. . . ."

When we arrived at the grocery store, Butz wiped his perspiring hands on a handkerchief and said we should leave our luggage in the truck. We would just meet his father, deliver a few orders and then go to the house and begin the actual visit. I said "How do you do" to Butz's father and he told me his shoulder was killing him. "My one arm is so numb," he said, "I don't know whether I'm coming or going."

Hank said, "It's a pleasure to know you, Mr. Butz. I know a shipper in Jersey who'll get you a good break on canned goods. You might as well. He carries first-class merchandise and you'll never regret it."

"We do all our business local," said Butz's father. "Well, I suppose you boys want to get started." He laughed a little. "You know when you visit us we make you work for your board."

"That's very classy of you," said Hank.

"Butz told us about it," I said. "We'll do whatever you like."

First Butz's father loaded the truck with orders for Butz to deliver and then he gave Hank and me ours, which were within walking distance. Hank got a big basket of fruit that was to go to a poor section of town. He hefted it to his shoulder and said mournfully, "If my mother could see me now, she'd have a heart attack." I got some mineral water that was to go to a fourth-floor walk-up.

When I got to the apartment and made the delivery, the old woman who had ordered it gave me a fifteen-cent tip which I threw at her.

"That's a good tip," she said. "Why are you throwing it at me?"

"I don't know," I said as I walked down the landing. Actually, I'd always wanted to throw a tip in someone's face. My brother did it once and I'd been aching to try it ever since. But I had to admit fifteen cents really wasn't sufficient provocation for hurling it back in the lady's face, and I felt a little funny as I went back to the store. Hank was waiting for me when I got back, slumped over on a vegetable carton. "It's a lucky thing my poor mother doesn't know what's going on. She *really* sent me to college to be a delivery boy."

It took several hours for us to get out the rest of the deliveries, and then we joined Butz in the truck and he drove us to his house. It was a duplex in a pleasantly wooded section of town. The house itself smelled of cooking, and as Hank came in he inhaled deeply in a pleased way and said, "New York. It's a New York smell. I knew it the second I got in here."

Butz's mother took her son aside and asked in a loud whisper, "Did they make the deliveries all right?"

"Yes," he said. "They worked for three hours."

"Why shouldn't they?" she said to no one in particular. "They come in like strangers. I don't see what's wrong with doing a little work."

Hank came toward her then. "Darling," he said, "do you know what this means to Hanky? Away from home the way he is. And to just walk into a New York home like this. So help me, your cooking smells just like Lindy's."

"He's very charming," said Butz's mother.

"Yes, he is," I said.

"New York," said Hank, walking with his arms stretched out like a tenor at the Met, his eyes open wide behind his thick glasses. "I'm in New York."

The dinner was very heavy, most of the dishes having been prepared with potatoes and bread crumbs. Butz's brother, who was around twelve, said he wanted to sing a song before dinner and Hank insisted upon bringing him on stage.

"Ladies and gentlemen," said Hank, lifting his fist to his mouth, "from the Starlight Roof of the Waldorf-Astoria in midtown Manhattan, we bring you the romantic voice of little Butz singing 'Swanee River.' " Butz's brother then began his song and, before he was halfway through, Hank pounded his fist on the table and said, "What's wrong with you people? New York-type people like you. You ought to be

ashamed of yourselves. The kid's got talent. Get the kid an agent before he loses his voice. Hanky's surprised at you."

"He sings at the church," said Butz's mother.

"Go on," said Hank, shaking his head hopelessly. "I'm really surprised at you. New York-type people."

After dinner, I thanked Butz's mother for the meal and said it was
very tasty.

Hank said, "I want to thank you for a New York-type evening, for
giving Hanky a little taste of New York in old Kansas City. On behalf
of the boss and myself I'm very thankful."

Hank and I then went up to Butz's room and Butz took out a manila
folder of Japanese pornography.

"What are you showing Hanky that for on a full stomach? Put it
away."

"I thought you might like to see them," said Butz, perspiring. "I'll
put them away."

"Did you get us dates for tonight?" I asked.

"I couldn't really get them because I didn't know you were coming
here until the last minute."

Hank leaped up from his chair and grabbed Butz by the collar. "You
didn't get Hanky a date? I'll slap you in the mouth. What about
Hanky's reputation? What about the boss? Hanky and the boss don't
go without dates on Saturday night."

"Get your hands off him," I said, pushing him away from Butz.
"That isn't going to help."

"What's *wrong* with you?" said Butz. "Did I really do anything that
bad? You're always acting like I've just insulted your mother." He was
really afraid of Hank.

"My poor mother," said Hank, moaning. "If she only knew Hanky
was in a strange town without a date on Saturday night."

"You never give me a chance to even say anything," said Butz. "I *do*
have a girl for tonight. We have a date with her later on."

"I'm sure she's really a class girl," said Hank. "If *you* know her and
she lives in this town, I'm sure she's very classy."

"One girl for the three of us?" I asked.

"Wait till you see her," said Butz, "then you won't be so smart."

We got dressed a little later. In the middle of tying his bow tie in
front of the mirror, Hank threw his hands down and said, "I don't like
this, boss. I'm a New York operator. I'd be laughed off Broadway if this
ever got around. One girl for three guys. In fact, this whole weekend
has been *very* classy when you think about it."

"Can't you cut out the New York stuff for a minute?" asked Butz.

"I'll belt you right in the head," said Hank, charging across the room and grabbing him by the collar.

"All *right,*" said Butz. "Can't you even take a joke? Hell, I didn't insult your religion, you know."

Hank went back to the mirror. "Hanky may not be handsome," he said to the mirror, "but ask any New York girl who knows how to treat a girl best. When it comes to class, Hanky's your man."

On the way out, Butz's mother said to Hank and me, "I've packed up some of the extra bread puddings we had for dinner. I thought you might want some for the ride home."

"That's very nice of you," I said to her.

Then she took Butz aside and said, "Why do you have to use the truck? I don't understand why you don't take a cab. They just come right in like this, perfect strangers, and they have to use our truck."

"It's all right, Mother," said Butz. "We're splitting the gas and it's not so terrible."

"Maybe I'm wrong," she said.

She turned to Hank and me and said, "In case I don't see you in the morning before you leave, we enjoyed having you, and I hope you like the bread puddings on the way back."

Hank put his arm around her waist and said, "You know what you are, darling?"

"What?" she asked.

"A New York girl," said Hank.

In the truck, Butz began to drive furiously. It was snowing and he did more braking, clutching, wheel-spinning and wiping than before. He pulled up in front of a poolroom and we followed him inside. He walked up to a thin fellow with a cigarette hanging from his mouth who seemed unable to stop bowing. It must have been a nerve condition. Butz said something to him and the fellow bowed his way over to the telephone and dialed a number. "Hello, Gale," we heard him say. "Listen, honey, I've got some talent agents from out of town here, very big men in the East. You know how bad you want to make out in show business. Well, anyhow, be very nice to these gentlemen and I'll see you soon, honey. They'll be over in ten minutes, so look pretty, baby. This might be your chance."

He hung up the phone, shook hands with Butz and then bowed back to the pool table. Hank went over to the table and said, "Hanky likes the way you handle yourself. You're a smooth guy and Hanky would like to shake your hand."

In the truck once again, Butz said to Hank, "You see. You wanted to belt me and look how nicely things are running."

"Hanky likes the way that guy handles himself," said Hank.

"How are we supposed to pass ourselves off as talent agents?" I asked. "I don't see how this thing can work."

"If we just do what Sheik says—that's that fellow's name—we'll be okay," said Butz. "He never steers you wrong."

"I like the way he handles himself," said Hank. "If Hanky had the dough, he'd send that guy to Palm Springs for his back condition."

It got very cold in the truck. I asked Butz to turn on his heater and he said there wasn't one. We all blew on our hands.

"If it ever got around I was riding in a cold truck on Saturday night," said Hank, "my reputation would be wiped out on the Eastern seaboard. Finished. Hanky and the boss in a cold truck in Nowheresville."

Butz stopped the truck and dimmed his lights at what seemed to be the doorway of a basement apartment with one bleak light over the doorway. A little more light came from behind some Venetian blinds. "These things scare the hell out of me," I said. It was bitter cold in the truck.

"You let Hanky lead the way, boss," said Hank.

"I don't understand how she's going to believe we're talent agents," I said. "We're too damn young to pass for them."

"If Sheik says it's all right, it's all right," said Butz. He started to get out of the truck.

Hank stopped him and said, "The boss and Hanky will call you when we're ready. We've got to feed this girl a little class before you come in."

"I'll stay awhile," said Butz, "but I'm not going to freeze my tail off in this truck."

Hank and I got out and knocked on the door. "No real names, boss," Hank whispered. "I've been on these excursions before."

A girl who seemed to be in her late twenties opened the door. In the shadow of the doorway, she had beautiful features. Her hair was long and hung casually over her shoulders. Some of it fell upon her bosom which seemed full beneath the dressing gown she wore. "Good evening, gentlemen," she said. "I'm terribly sorry to be caught this way. You people never seem to give a girl much time, the way you breeze in and out of town." Her voice seemed musical and pretty.

Hank introduced me as Mr. Tyler and himself as Mr. Wood. He took out cigars for the two of us. She ushered us in and then turned to face us in the light. One of her eyes floated in its socket and seemed to be on the brink of disappearing. She cocked her head at an odd angle whenever we spoke and listened as though our voices were coming from outside the apartment.

"Mr. Tyler and myself are out-of-town agents," said Hank, "actually

New York operators. We have several spots open in our revues in New York and have heard some very nice things about you."

"Mr. Wood is one of the foremost agents on the Eastern seaboard," I said.

"Well, I'm delighted to meet you nice gentlemen," she said, her eye floating unevenly. "May I ask you some questions?"

"Why, of course, darling," said Hank. "But first," he said, reaching for his checkbook, "do you need a little advance? A little something on account?"

"Nothing," she said, cocking her head as though Hank's voice came from a secret place.

"We insist," I said, uncertainly. Hank was much better than I was at this.

"Not a thing," she said, oddly, crossing her handsome legs.

"All right, sweetheart," said Hank, "but if you change your mind, just name your price."

"Can you go from the chorus line to a star position?" she asked neither of us in particular. She seemed to ask it to a private person we couldn't see.

There was a knock at the door and Hank went to answer it. It was Butz. Hank opened the door partway and said, "Get some class, will you, moron."

"I'm freezing my tail off," said Butz. "Can I come in at least?"

"In a minute," Hank hissed. "Hanky's handling this deal for all of us." He closed the door on Butz and came back. "It was someone had the wrong address," he said. "Mr. Tyler, would you say our chorus girls are rising to star positions regularly?"

"I would say so," I said, not looking at the girl.

"Does a girl have to let producers get into her pants in order for her to get starring roles in show business?" she asked.

"Not class producers," said Hank. "You deal with a class producer and you don't get any of that."

"I agree with that," I said. "I really do."

"All right, gentlemen," she said. "Those are my questions. I suppose you'll want to see me perform."

"It's the way we do business," said Hank.

"We really have to," I said.

She took off her dressing gown and stood nude in front of us. Then she got some make-up and began to dab it on. Her body was faultless. "I look a sight," she said. "I'm sorry I didn't have a chance to prepare for you gentlemen. I think I'll do 'A Pretty Girl Is Like a Melody.' Do either of you gentlemen know that?"

Hank began to stroke chords on an imaginary piano and sing, "Da da da dum . . ."

"That's it," she said. "Give me the opening again." She cocked her head to one side, and when she heard what she wanted she began to sing in a pretty, soft voice while she walked around the room. "These are tables," she said. "As I sing, I walk in and out of them. It makes my act more interesting, don't you think?"

"I would say so," I said.

She ended up on a high note, and then she said, "Now would you like to see my legs?"

"We never look at legs," I said. "It's one of our rules."

"I see," she said. "Well, perhaps I'll just go on with my repertoire. I think I'll do 'J'Attendrai,' which I know by ear. It won't be necessary for either of you gentlemen to accompany me."

She cocked her head to one side again, leaned back on a chair and began to sing.

Hank said to me, "You hop on first and Hanky will wait in the john."

"Why don't you hop on first," I said. "It really isn't important to me."

"For Christ's sake," he said. "You're the *Boss*. Hanky'd cut his arm off for you. The trouble with you is you don't let anyone get close to you. It was true when I first spotted you as a naïve kid from New York with no class in his shoes and it's true now. For Christ's sake, let your defenses down. Hanky'll be waiting in the wings. Only don't take too long. Hanky's always been known as a hot guy."

He excused himself and went into the bathroom. The girl finished her song, curtsied and turned down the lights. She sat in my lap and then her eye began to bother me. I wondered if it hurt. I turned the lights off completely and mussed her hair, saying, "You're a funny kid," but I kept worrying about her eye. It was worse without the lights since there was no accounting for it in the dark, so I turned the lights on again and shoved her aside, saying, "You get tired of this, town after town. You'd be surprised. Let me see you do something."

She cocked her head and began to dance gracefully through the imaginary tables, performing with a make-believe top hat and cane, her eye playing to some audience no one would ever see. I pulled her down to me and thought I'd get it over with very fast and reckon with the eye later, but I was very awkward and she perched on her knees next to me and said, "Are you sure you've done a lot of this?"

"Of course," I said. "But it isn't any fun when you do as much of it as I have to."

Hank came out of the bathroom and said to the girl, "The boss knows how to treat a class girl. He's very cute with girls. He has that little-boy way. If I was a broad I wouldn't be able to keep my hands off him."

Then he said to me, quietly, "For Christ's sake, what kept you, boss? Hanky was burning up in there. I thought they'd have to pull me out of there in a box. But that's okay, boss. Hanky's not mad. The boss has given Hanky everything he's got."

He encircled the girl's waist and as I opened the door to leave, he winked and whispered to me, "Hanky's always been known around town as a very hot guy."

"Producers are always anxious to get into one's pants, aren't they?" asked the girl.

Butz came lunging into the room then, blowing on his hands and saying, "You want me to freeze my tail off completely? It's below zero out there."

The young girl turned to examine Butz and then reached for her robe and held it in front of her. "The grocer!" she screamed. "What is he doing here?"

"I'm not a grocer," said Butz.

"Oh, yes you are," she said. "I'd know you anywhere. You delivered an order here once. And if there's anything I won't do it's perform in front of grocers."

"He really knows how to operate," said Hank. "He *really* knows his way around."

"Why don't you wait outside for a minute," I said to Butz, ushering him out the door.

"You know how freezing it is out there? What do you want? I'm letting you stay with me this weekend, you want me to freeze on top of it all?"

"Just wait a little while," I said, pushing him outside.

"That's show biz for you," said Hank. "Surprise, suspense, excitement, crazy things, all of which go toward making it the greatest business on earth."

"I don't think I'm going to perform any more," the girl said, slipping into her robe. "I'm out of the mood."

"There's no business like it," said Hank. "Broadway at night, lights over Gotham, the hustle and bustle . . ."

"I really never *was* that interested in chorus work anyway. I think I'd much prefer the legitimate stage."

"The overture," said Hank. "The hush that falls over the opening-night crowd in their tuxes. The curtain rises . . ."

"And besides, I have to go to the bathroom," she said, ushering us out the door.

"If you change your mind about an advance," said Hank, "it's all right with us, baby, anytime."

She closed the door.

Outside in the truck, Butz said, "You certainly took your time. I wanted to have a little fun, too, you know."

"I'll punch you right in your grocer's mouth," said Hank, lunging for Butz. I stopped him again and said, "There's no point in doing that now. It's too late."

"Why don't you keep your hands to yourself," said Butz.

"If this ever leaks out, Hanky's a dead man on the Eastern seaboard. Hanky can't show his face in Shor's, do you know that, boss?"

The snow was coming down heavily now. We drove along in the cold truck, and on the way back, we came to a girls' seminary. Butz stopped the truck and wiped some frost from the truck windshield until we could see lights on in the women's dormitory windows. Then he said, suddenly, "Look, there's one with nothing on."

"Where?" said Hank, straining forward to the window. "Too late," said Butz. "She just slipped into her bathrobe and you can't see anything any more."

"That did it," said Hank. He chopped Butz sharply in the chest with the side of his fist as though he were an infuriated speaker pounding a gavel. I'd seen Butz in the shower and remembered he had soft breasts like a woman. When Hank caught him there, drops of water shot up through his collar as though he'd been a wet sponge.

Butz groaned, holding his smashed breast. "What kind of a place is that to hit someone?" He couldn't catch his breath for a while, and we just sat there in the cold truck.

I reached back and picked up some of the bread puddings I'd taken along, given to us by Butz's mother. I gave one to Hank. They seemed to taste better cold. By the time they were gone, Butz had caught his breath and started the truck. We drove along through the snow, and in a little while Hank began to announce.

"Ladies and gentlemen," he said, "we are now concluding an evening in Hicksville, U.S.A., in the middle of nowhere. Far from the bright lights, from the glamorous main stem of New York City, far from Lindy's, far from the Metropolitan Opera House and the famed Madison Square Garden . . . far from the city of class. . . ."

The Partners

(featuring Harry Towns)

WHEN THE PLANE STOPPED, the man and the boy got off and were holding each other around the waist, as though one or perhaps both of them had just recovered from diseases that made it hard to take deep breaths. Back home, the boy would not have been caught dead holding his dad in that manner, but this was out West where none of his friends could see him, and it seemed all right to do so. The man was Harry Towns at a sad time in his life; he had been living apart from his family for a while, making up all kinds of stories for the boy as to why he had to do so. Except that now it looked as though a divorce might be in the picture and he had told this to his young son, straight out. So the boy kept giving him looks every few minutes and saying, "You all right, Dad?" as though the impending divorce might suddenly show up in his face as a rash. Towns would say, "Sure, how about you?" The boy would answer, "Fine." They kept reassuring themselves in that way but holding onto each other all the same. Towns did not really know the boy very well. He had taken him for granted, as he might have a fine, reliable watch that would inevitably be right there on his wrist whenever he wanted it. Now that it looked as though the family would break up officially, he had moved forward in a clumsy rush to spend more time with the boy, some of it playacting, some of it an honest attempt to savor the child and store up moments with him as though building a secret bank account. He had asked the boy where he would like to go for a trip and the boy had picked Las Vegas, aware of the gambling, but probably mixing it up a little with Los Angeles although he would never admit this to his father. Towns could have straightened him out on this, but he didn't, figuring he could sneak in a little gambling himself, and at the same time, see to it that the boy had a terrific time. There were some slot machines in the terminal, but a sign said you couldn't play them unless you were twenty-one or over. The boy was disappointed and wondered whether he could slip a few coins in anyway when no one was looking. His father said all right, that he would act as a lookout, but after the boy had played three quarters, Towns got

27

nervous about it and stopped him. "I think they mean it," he said. "I think they can lose their license."

"That's too bad," said the boy. "Because I know those are lucky ones. I can tell those are the best in Las Vegas."

"It's too risky," said Towns. "Right at the airport. Maybe when we get deeper in."

The reservation story had been dismal, but a friend of Towns had gotten them fixed up in a small, little-known hotel on the edge of town, saying that a famous bandleader always stayed there when the Sands was overbooked. It was called the Regent; they took a cab to it and found it to be a noisy, rugged little place, one with a half-dozen slots and two blackjack tables in the lobby. An Indian with coveralls and a great perspired shine on his face was the only blackjack player. "That fellow's an Indian," Towns whispered to the boy as they approached the desk. "So what," said the boy. He was always quick to spot it whenever Towns passed on formally educational little bits.

The room was quite small and Towns was embarrassed about the size of it, feeling that he had let the boy down. But the boy said he loved it; he got into his pajamas and leapt into bed with miracle speed. "It's my favorite hotel in the world," he said.

"We're going to have a great time," said Towns, tucking in the boy and clearing back his hair so that he could kiss his forehead. "I'll kill myself to see to it."

"You don't have to kill yourself," said the boy.

Towns turned out the lights and then went into the bathroom to treat his crabs. He had gotten a case of them a week before he had left for Las Vegas and felt terribly degraded about it, mostly because his new girlfriend was from Bryn Mawr and there was a chance he had passed them along to her just before he had left. There was also a distant possibility he had gotten them from her, but he didn't want to think about that. The thing he hated most was the name: crabs. The medicine bottle referred to them as body lice and that was a little better but still didn't do the trick. The doctor said that if he shampooed his body, they would go away in nine out of ten cases, but he couldn't imagine that happening. "Once you have them on the run," an adventurous friend had told Harry Towns, "they can be amusing." Maybe that was true if you were bogged down in trench warfare at the Marne, but to Harry Towns they didn't have a single delightful aspect. He just wanted to see them on their way. He soaped himself up with the medicine, stood around for ten minutes, in accordance with the directions, and then hopped into the shower and soaped himself some more. He got the feeling somehow that he was spreading them to other parts of his body, the hair on top of his head, for example. When he got out of the shower, the boy, hollering through the door, asked him why he was taking so long. "I'm just relaxing in here," he said.

The doctor had told him to get rid of all clothing that had come into contact with the crabs and he did that, throwing away his underwear. He was reminded of a fellow at college who threw away suits of underwear after a single day's wear. And that was without crabs. At the time, Towns couldn't imagine anyone rich enough to toss away underwear after one use; years later, he came to the conclusion that the fellow was unhappy and was trying to catch his unloving parents' attention. Meanwhile, Towns had to figure out how to deal with his suit. He decided to hang onto it and keep his fingers crossed that a stray crab hadn't wandered onto the fabric. He carefully hid the medicine bottle so that the boy wouldn't accidentally come across it and ask what it was. Then he got into a pair of fresh pajamas and slid into bed; the boy was sleeping, and it seemed to Towns that he itched more than ever and that he had roused the crabs to a fury, and sent them scurrying far and wide. He went into the bathroom and, not knowing whether he was awake or dreaming, began to shave off his pubic hair, being very cautious and tentative at first and then warming to the task and slashing it off with great verve. He took some off his stomach, too, and began his chest but then stopped and said the hell with it. He looked at himself in the mirror, standing on a chair so that he could see the shaved areas, and decided he looked very new and young and unusual. It was a little exciting. But then he realized there was no way to get the hair back on; indeed, he had no idea how quickly it would grow back or if it would grow back at all. It still itched like hell, but he knew it couldn't have been the crabs that were doing it and this was comforting. In bed, he realized that he would have to tell his Bryn Mawr girl he had them and wondered how she would react to that. It made him sick to think about it. He decided to tell her he had "body lice" but then changed his mind and went over to straight "crabs." He would simply hit her with it— "I've got the crabs"—and if she ran away, he would get along without her, even though she was quite gentle and extraordinary. He would then have to find a girl who had these qualities and was also tough-minded enough to accept crabs.

In the morning, the boy was dressed and ready to roll by the time Towns opened his eyes. The itching had kept him awake most of the night, leaving him tired and irritable. It seemed to Towns that getting out of bed and being easy and kind to the boy was going to be the single hardest thing he had ever done in his life. He felt inside his pajamas on the slim chance that he had only dreamed about the shaving, but he was clean as a whistle. "Do you think we can play the slots before breakfast or shall we wait till afterward?" asked the boy. When

Towns reminded him that you had to be twenty-one to play them, the boy fell back in astonishment and slapped his head, saying "What?" as though Towns were giving him the information for the first time. All through their trip, the boy was to pretend it was all right for him to play the slots and fall back in amazement when Towns reminded him that he couldn't. Towns didn't know whether to be irritated or pleased by this stunt and decided finally that it was a good thing for the boy to keep trying in the face of ridiculous odds. On the way downstairs, Towns told the boy he was going to be scratching himself a lot on the trip. "That's because I've picked up a skin condition," he told the boy. "It can drive you nuts."

"I hope it clears up, Dad," said the boy.

As soon as they hit the street, Towns realized there wasn't going to be much you could do with a young boy in Las Vegas. Gambling was the name of the game; Los Angeles, of course, with Disneyland, would have been the correct choice. To compensate for this, Towns made a big fuss over every little thing they did. When their breakfast eggs were served to them at a small diner, Towns said, "Well, there they are, Las Vegas eggs." The boy went along with Towns, saying, "Las Vegas eggs, that's great." But when they went out to the main street and Towns said, "Look at this place, isn't it something?" the boy said, "I don't see what's so wonderful about it. Maybe it is, but it's hard to tell so far." Towns wondered if they ought to rent a car and drive to Los Angeles after all; but then he decided that the important thing was that they be together and draw very close. He put his arm around the boy's shoulders and the boy, pretending they were the same height, reached way up and got his arm around his father's shoulder. They walked lopsidedly through the main street of Las Vegas that way. The boy was something of a coin collector and when they got to a shop that sold them, Towns took twenty dollars of the money he had more or less set aside for gambling and gave it to the boy so he could buy some special ones.

"I don't know whether I should be taking this away from you, Dad," said the boy.

"It's all right," said Towns. "I want to give it to you."

"But I feel it will hurt you if I take it," said the boy, looking very sad and sick.

"You'll be making me happy," said Towns. "My own folks made me feel guilty when they gave me things and I don't want that to happen to you." Hearing his own words, it seemed to Towns that he was trying to be a wonderful parent in a big hurry, leaping at every opportunity to get across slices of wisdom. So he promised himself he would try to be a little more natural. Towns waited for the boy outside the coin shop,

feeling restless about being that close to all the gambling and not having gotten to it quite yet. It would be obscene to make a trip to Las
Vegas and not get in any gambling, but he knew he had to feed the boy
a certain number of good times before he thought about the tables.
The boy came out after a bit and said, "Let's get out of here, Dad. I
think I just got a coin that's worth thousands and the man hasn't
caught on to it yet. Is there any way he can trace us back to our hotel?"
    Towns told the boy he was kidding himself and that it was a lot
harder than that to make money in life. "That man's been in the coin
business for a long time," said Towns. "He knows more about it than
you and doesn't give away thousands that easily." More wisdom. The
boy said he was sure the coin was worth a fortune, but he said it with
little conviction and Towns felt like digging a ditch for himself. Why
couldn't he just go along with the kid and let him dream? "Maybe
you're right," he said. "Hell, I don't know much about coins." But he
said it much too late for it to do any good.
    That afternoon, Towns, desperate for young-boy activities, signed up
for a bus visit to a dam that bridged two states, Nevada and Arizona.
When the boy found out they were going to a dam, he said, "I'm not
sure I'd love to do that," and Towns, short with him for the first time,
said, "Cut it out. We're going. You don't come all the way out here and
not go to their dam." On the bus, the itching got the best of him and
he was sure he had come up with a type of crab that actually ducked
down beneath the skin and couldn't be shaved off. He felt sorry for
himself, an about-to-be-divorced guy, riding out to a dam with crabs
and a young boy. At the dam site, the guide lectured the group about
hardships involved in the building of the dam and Towns said to the
boy, "They must have had some job. Imagine, coming out here, starting with nothing and having to put up a dam."
    The boy said, "Dad, I'm not enjoying this. I just came out here be-
cause you wanted to. I don't want to hurt your feelings, but I'm not
having that great a time."
    "You can't always have a great time," said Towns. "Not every second
of your life."
    When the guide led the tour group through the bottom of the dam
and into Arizona, the boy perked up considerably. "That's great," said
the boy, running around in the small area. "I'm in Arizona. It's great
here and that means I've been to another state." He kept careful track
of all the states he'd been to and even counted ones he had just nicked
the edges of on car rides.
    That night, Towns told the boy to dress up and he would take him to
one of the big shows at a hotel on the Strip. He found out the name of
one that admitted kids and when they got to it, he gave the headwaiter

a huge tip to make sure they were put at a fine table. The headwaiter led them into the dining room, through a labyrinth of tables, getting closer and closer to the stage, the boy turning back to his father several times to say, "Look how close we're getting. How come he's taking us to such a great table?" The headwaiter put them at ringside right up against the stage, and the boy said, "This is fabulous. He must think we're famous or something." Towns smiled and said, "He must." He didn't mention anything about the tip, but after they had eaten shrimp cocktails, he told the boy he had given the headwaiter some money, trampling on the dream again. "Oh," said the boy, a little forlorn. There was just nothing Towns could do to control himself. On the other hand, maybe it was wise to fill the boy in on tipping behavior. Otherwise, he might wonder, later on, why he wasn't getting fabulous tables on his own hook. Towns had been to Las Vegas several years back and he remembered the women being a lot prettier. "The girls look a little hard, don't they?" he said to the boy, realizing he was trying to draw his son out on his feelings about women. "They're okay," said the boy, who didn't seem to want to dig into the subject.

The show was a huge, awkward one with plenty of razzle-dazzle. When it was over, the boy said it was the greatest show he had ever seen and wondered why they didn't bring a show like that to New York. "They might," said Towns, "and you'd be able to say you'd seen it first out here." The casino was bulging with activity, Towns feeling the lure and magnetism of it. "I wouldn't mind doing a little gambling," he said to the boy and saw that he was asking his permission. He did that often and wondered if it was proper behavior. Once, they had gone "mountain climbing" on a giant slag heap in their town. The boy was great at it, shooting right to the top, but Towns looked back over his shoulder, got panicky, and the boy had to reach back and grab him. Were you allowed to have your son take over, even momentarily, and become your dad? Towns decided that you were, much later on, but he was getting into it a bit early.

"What if you gambled and lost your money?" the boy asked.

"It doesn't make any difference," said Towns. "You just play for pleasure and never gamble more than you can afford. That way you don't feel bad if you lose." Towns was actually the kind of gambler who fell into deep depressions when he lost a quarter and even got depressed when he won. It wasn't that wonderful for him when he broke even either. Once and for all, he had to stop telling the boy things that seemed nice but that he really didn't believe.

"I couldn't stand it if I lost anything," said the boy. "Therefore I don't think you should gamble."

Towns asked him if he thought he could keep busy for a while and the boy said, "Sure, Dad," with great cheerfulness, but then he asked Towns exactly how long he would be.

"About an hour," said Towns.

"That long, eh?" said the boy.

He went off to roam around the lobby and Towns sat down to play blackjack with a dealer named Bunny. The dealer was slow, and Towns liked that, but he was aware of having to keep an eye on the boy and felt as though only half of him was sitting at the table. The boy would disappear and then bob up between a couple of slots or behind a plant, a duck in a shooting gallery. Towns was edgy as he made his bets, as though some tea was boiling and any second he would have to run out and turn off the gas. He told himself it didn't matter, all that counted was whether the cards came or not, but he didn't believe that for a second. He felt that the boy, running around the lobby, had a strong effect on the cards he was drawing. A dark-haired, hard-looking woman played at the seat on his right; she was attractive, although Towns felt she was just a fraction over the line and into hooker territory. He wondered whether it would be possible to dash up to a room with her and still nip back to the tables before the hour was up. That arrangement would be just fine for a Las Vegas hooker. Then he remembered the shaving and knew it wouldn't work out. Hooker or not, she would be experienced enough to know something wasn't exactly right. Towns forgot whether he was winning or losing. The boy called him away from the tables at one point and said, "Dad, I don't want to disturb your game, but a man wants to kill me." Towns knew that the boy had a way of dramatizing routine events, but he followed him nevertheless to a Spanish busboy who leaned against the wall of the dining room and didn't back up for a second when he saw Towns coming. "You bothering the kid?" said Towns, standing very close to the man. "That's right," said the busboy, "he spoiling the rhythm of the place."

"Just lay off him," said Towns, pushing a finger up against the man's face. He had planned to do just that no matter what the man said.

"Tell him to behave then," said the busboy, not backing up an inch.

"I'll take care of him and you lay off him," said Towns, breaking away from the man, as though in victory.

"Do you think you could have taken him?" asked the boy as they walked back to the casino.

"I don't know," said Towns. "I wasn't thinking about that."

"I've never seen you really fight a guy," said the boy. "I think I'd like that."

"I've had some fights," said Towns. "The trick is to get what you want without fighting. Any animal can fight. Any time you do, you automatically lose."

"I think I'd like to see you do it once," said the boy, and Towns realized that once again he was saying things to the boy that he hated. If someone had given him the kind of advice he was passing along to the child, he would have vomited. He was feeding him stuff he felt he was expected to feed him. But who expected it?

"Are you going to gamble some more?" asked the boy. "Your hour's up."

"It's a little hard when you have someone along," said Towns.

"Do you understand why they don't let children gamble?" the boy asked. Towns started to tell him it led to other things like missing school and crime, but then he said, "Strike that. It's garbage. I don't know why they don't let kids gamble. It would probably be all right." Towns felt proud of his honesty, but the boy didn't seem to care for it much and said, "I thought you knew the answer to things like that."

It suddenly occurred to Towns that it might be a good idea for them to spend their two remaining days at the giant plush Strip hotel. On a hunch, he asked the clerk whether there were rooms available and the clerk said yes, there had been a few checkouts. Towns and the boy made a dash back to their small hotel in town where they packed quickly, the boy saying, "I don't know about this. I liked it here. And I don't want to hurt this hotel's feelings."

"You can't hurt a hotel's feelings," Towns told him. They checked into an enormous, heavily gadgeted room in the Strip hotel and the boy said, "I admit this is great, but the other one was great, too."

The hotel was bigger and cleaner and noisier than the other one, but when you took a careful look at it there wasn't that much more for boys to do at it. Towns checked on some saddle horses the next day, but nobody knew where the stable was or how to get to it. He heard about a college nearby and made a feeble attempt to sell it to the boy, saying, "Imagine, a Las Vegas college. I wonder what it would be like," but the boy didn't even nibble at that one. Towns knew that the swimming pool was closed, but he led the boy out to it anyway; they took off their shirts and sat in chairs alongside the empty concrete pool.

"Is this what you want to do?" asked the boy.

"Just for a while."

"What good's a suntan?"

"They're great," said Towns. "You've forgotten that it's cold back East. It's good to take advantage of things like this."

"I'll get one if you say so, Dad," said the boy. "I don't really want one, but I'll get one."

They ate dinner at a Chinese restaurant that night. On the way to it, Towns took a wistful look at the casino and his son did, too. "Maybe I can play the slots at this one," said the boy.

"You won't quit, will you?"

"I thought maybe since this was a big hotel on the Strip they let boys play."

"They don't," said Towns. He thought of a tough friend of his who had four little girls and almost died because he didn't have a son; he had the feeling that somehow his friend would see to it, if he had a son, that the boy got to play the slots. And Towns wasn't able to pull it off. At the Chinese restaurant, Towns told the boy he loved Chinese food so much that he often thought he could eat it every night of the week. The boy took hold of that, saying, *"Every* night? For the rest of your life?"

"That's right," said Towns. "I think I've had enough at the end of each meal, but the next day I'm ready to have some more."

"That's amazing," said the boy, who was thoroughly pleased by the thought. "I never knew that about you."

The Chinese restaurant had a girl singer who did old Jerome Kern tunes. After she went offstage, Towns, who knew his boy had a singing voice, said to him, "Why don't you get up there and sing a few songs?"

"Are you kidding?" said the boy. "Are you crazy? Are you out of your mind? I'd rather be shot dead than get up there."

"You're a singer, aren't you?" said Towns.

"I sing," said the boy, "but are you kidding? You must be crazy, Dad."

Towns said he had a mother who pulled that kind of stuff on him—so he was pulling a little on his son. Only his mother really meant it, whereas Harry Towns was just goofing. The boy loved hearing things about the way it had been for Towns when *he* was young.

On the way back to their hotel, Towns spotted a bowling alley and he suggested they try a few games. It was midnight and he wanted to get at the gambling, but he thought it was the right thing to do and he was proud of himself for the way he was putting himself out for the child.

"I'll bowl with you," said the boy, "but only if you promise it's what you really want to do."

"I promise," said Towns.

The alley was a giant one, completely deserted, and Towns asked the proprietor if anybody ever bowled in Las Vegas. "Not too many," said the proprietor. While they were selecting their balls, the boy said, "How come you just walk up to people and ask them questions?" and Towns answered, "It's a style of mine. I like to find out things. So I figure that's the best way." "I could never do that," said the boy. "That'll change," Towns assured him.

The boy tried several of the balls for size, and after a while declared that there was no ball just right for him in the entire alley and that he probably wouldn't be able to do any great bowling. Towns did not know how to keep score and neither did the boy, so he asked the proprietor to help them out; but even after the old man explained it with great care he still didn't know how to keep score. It was one of those things he knew he would never learn as long as he lived. So he kept a sort of rough score. Towns went over a hundred, by rough count, in the first game, topping the boy, who was amazed and said, "You never told me you were a great bowler. Incredible. And you probably haven't bowled in years either. If you kept it up, you could win thousands of prizes." Towns didn't want to win any prizes. All he wanted to do was get back to the casino and take a try at the tables. He planned to go easy and let the boy beat him in the second game, but when they got into it, he abandoned his plan and tried as hard as he could and wound up beating the kid again. He always did that with the boy, even in checkers. He just wasn't easygoing enough to let the boy win a few. He told himself it was all right, because when the boy really beat him legitimately, it would mean something. But that was bullshit. It would be better to take it easy once in a while. Of course, it was no picnic finding just the right level—when you had a son. Towns had a feeling he was working too hard at it.

"I'll never be able to beat you as long as I live," said the boy. "Yes, you will," said Towns. "One day you'll go past me and you'll stay ahead forever. All I ask, is that when I become a bent-over old man you won't come along and kick me in the head." He meant it as a joke, but the boy didn't see it that way and said, "Are you kidding, Dad? When I'm older I'll give you every cent I have."

"Just be a good kid," said Towns, "and that's all I'll ever ask."

After the third game, the boy seemed to be settling in for an all-night session. Towns took him by the shoulders and said, "Son, I really would like to do some gambling." The boy took it very well, saying, "Why didn't you say so, Dad? I thought you loved it here."

"I did," said Towns, "but I think I've had my fill."

They returned to the hotel and when the boy was undressed, he said, "What do I do if someone smashes down the door and gets me?"

"Someone won't," said Towns.

"What if you lose?" asked the boy, with real terror in his eyes. It was as though his father was going off to war.

"Then I lose," said Towns. "Meanwhile I've had a lot of fun."

He closed the door and even though he knew it was a sure sign he was going to lose he actually found himself trotting down the hall to the casino. He looked for the slow dealer named Bunny and when he found him, he sat down at the table, got some chips, and, with all the exhilaration of a new thief with his hands on some jewelry, began to gamble. Bunny gave him plenty of time to think and he began to win and at the same time to dispense advice to a fellow next to him who wasn't doing that well.

"Blackjack is the only game where you've got a break. The casino gets its edge from people who really don't know the game, women, for example, who just throw their money away and will split pictures every time they get them."

"Fine," said the man next to him.

Towns played for about three hours, winning four hundred dollars and then stopping, with the idea that he would return on the following night, his last one, and try to bump his winnings into some significant money. He had pulled that off once, in Europe, probably the only time he could think of when he had had no pressing need for the money. He won at roulette, not knowing much about the game, and with no particular system. He won thousands of dollars, a lifetime of luck seemingly crowded into those few weeks of playing in French casinos. He bought a German car-boat with the money, one you could drive up to the edge of the water and then drive in and have it become a boat so that you were driving through the water. And then he sold it. There just weren't enough places where you could drive off a highway and into the water. You had to be living in Canada somewhere, not around New York City.

Before Towns left the table, he told the man next to him that the trick in gambling is to get some of the casino's money and play on that. The man seemed relieved to see him go. Towns cashed in his winnings and when he got back to the hotel he woke the boy at four in the morning. It was one of those things he knew was wrong to do, but he couldn't resist it.

"How'd you do?" asked the boy.

"Won four hundred," said Towns. "And fifty of it is yours, for coins."

"That's not fair," said the boy. "It's your winnings."

"I want to do it for you," said Towns. "You were my partner."

"What if you'd lost?"

"That's different," said Towns.

"I'll take it," said the boy, "but I don't think it's right. I didn't do anything."

"You're my son," said Towns.

They slept late their last full day in Las Vegas and when they awakened in the early afternoon, Towns felt compelled to tell the boy a little about what had happened between the boy's father and mother. "Sometimes people get married young and maybe they shouldn't have and then all of a sudden they're not getting along at all." Of course that wasn't telling him much. He wanted to tell the boy about the Bryn Mawr girl, but if he knew anything he knew that was the wrong thing to do although he was certain the boy would like her. If not on the first meeting, then on the second for sure.

"I'd want to stay with you," said the boy.

"No, you wouldn't," said Towns, but he was pleased the boy had said that. How could he not be?

Towns discovered a gym in the hotel, and after lunch they went into it for a workout. When the boy had stripped down and gone into the workout room, the owner said, "That's terrific the way the kid comes in here. When he grows up he'll have a helluva build on him because he's starting now." Because of the crab situation, Towns was careful to keep himself wrapped in a towel. The gym had some unfamiliar apparatus and he was scared out of his wits that the boy would get tangled up in it and kill himself, or at best hurt his trick knees. All he wanted was for them to work out and get the hell out of there, safe and sound. He hardly did any exercise and spent most of his time warning the boy about the apparatus. A massive black fighter skipped rope in the middle of the floor, Towns recognizing him immediately as a main-eventer who had suffered an important reversal in recent months. Towns moved protectively toward his son, and when the fighter left, he told the child he had been working out right next to a famous fighter. "Why didn't you say so?" said the boy. "I would have asked him what happened in that last fight." Everyone in the gym got a kick out of that, and the owner said, "That's all you would have needed." Towns went in to take a shower, and after a moment, heard a loud noise and then some unnatural stillness. Without looking, he knew what had happened. He walked into the gym and saw his son's body stretched out with a heavy weight over his face. The owner and the masseur were kneeling beside him, the owner saying, "See what happens," and the masseur adding, "Don't move him, you never move them." Towns took his time walking over to the boy, aware that it would look good if he came off as a calm, clear-thinking father. He picked the plate off the boy's face, expecting to see only half a head under there. The boy's eyes were closed and his right cheekbone had an unnatural color, but there was no blood. The boy opened his eyes and asked, "Am I all right? I can't tell. I think I was unconscious for a while, my first time." Towns said he had probably overloaded one side of a barbell with the result that the heavy side tipped over on his head. "It happens to every fellow in a gym," said Towns, "except that the weight doesn't always hit them the way it did you. It'll probably never happen to you again." The boy was delighted that he had been unconscious. "In all my years that never happened to me," he told the owner. The owner said the boy had just been shaken up and that he would be fine, but Towns wasn't so sure and figured the owner was making light of it to fend off a possible lawsuit. He asked for the name of a doctor and when the owner gave him one he called the fellow who said, "Listen, I'm eating dinner thirty miles away." Towns said it was an emergency and the doctor asked, "Were any bones driven into the skull?" When Towns told him he couldn't tell, the doctor said he would meet them in the hotel room. Towns carried the boy up to the room, feeling terrible about what had happened; here he'd watched his son like a hawk and then just two seconds after he'd turned away the boy wound up with weights on his head. Why was he taking his boy to gyms and casinos? Didn't other fathers take their sons camping and duck-hunting? Next thing you knew they'd be passing hookers back and forth. Wait till a judge got wind of the way Towns was bringing up the kid. They'd let him see his son once a year, if he was lucky. "I'm dizzy," said the boy, as Towns put him on the bed, "but I think I'll be all right, except that maybe I won't be." When the doctor arrived, he looked at the boy and said, "The bone hasn't been driven into the skull. He'll be okay, except for the banged-up place." It was a terrible thing to think, but Towns felt guilty about the injury not being a little more serious—to justify taking the doctor away from his dinner on a thirty-mile trip. "I'm positive I'm going into a coma," said the boy. The doctor laughed and when Towns tried to pay him, he put up the palm of his hand in a negative gesture and said, "That's all right, I've got a boy." When the doctor left, the boy said, "I'm sorry to be spoiling your good time," to which Towns replied, "Are you kidding? I'm just thrilled you're all right." Towns packed his face down with ice and sat with the boy while he dozed on and off. If the bone had indeed been tucked back in the boy's skull it would have entailed staying in Las Vegas for days, maybe weeks, or possibly some special kind of plane to get him back East; he was re-lieved they weren't going to get into that. The boy was good-looking, but in a curious, unconventional way; Towns decided the banged-up cheekbone wasn't going to hold him back much. It would be just an-other curious feature adding to his curious good looks. The boy said he was a little dizzy and had no appetite so Towns simply sat with him until long after the dinner hour. They were leaving the next morning and Towns wondered if he could get in one last session at the tables and try to boost his winnings to an important level, like that time in France. Only this go-round, he wouldn't buy a German car-boat. He would salt it away, about half for his son. Towns would hand it over to him when he was twenty-one and say, "Here you are, kid, five grand—do anything you like with it." And that would include gambling and hookers, if the boy wanted to go that way. The important thing was not to put any strings on it. When it was close to midnight, he suggested to the kid that he might like to take one last shot at the tables. Appearing to be startled, the boy said, "You would do that? Don't do it, Dad. I was unconscious for a while, the first time in my life." Towns said okay, okay, he wouldn't leave him, and the boy dozed off again. When he awakened, a fraction after midnight, Towns brought it up again. "And don't forget, you're my partner," he said. "If I win, I'll give you a lot of it for coins."

"Okay," said the boy, "but you've got to use some of my money." He sat up a little, reached into his wallet, and took out twenty-five dollars of the fifty his father had given him. Towns took it, putting it in a separate pocket so as to make sure not to gamble it at any cost. They had to get up at six in the morning to make their plane and Towns promised to be back by two at the latest. He gave the boy a fresh icepack and went off to look for Bunny. He had always said that he could either take gambling or leave it, but now, for the first time in his life, he wasn't so confident about it. When he was in the area of a casino, there was no stopping him. He made sure to be in the area of one some four or five times a year. To a certain extent, when he was alone, he did get some pure pleasure out of gambling. He could sit down at a blackjack table at eight in the evening, get up at four in the morning, and not know what had happened to the time. Sipping brandies and pulling on a delicious cigar or two. Sometimes, when he was ahead, he would slip in a quick hooker and then saunter back to the tables. They had a new kind of semihooker in Vegas, dazed girls from Northern California who would straggle through Vegas on weekends to pick up some cash and then push on. Some were startling in their beauty and almost all were junkies. They were both better and worse than your normal Vegas hooks. They didn't hold you up on the price. It depended on whether you liked dazed and beautiful Northern California junkies or your dyed-in-the-wool Vegas showgirl types. This was at a time of his life when Harry Towns didn't think much about hookers. He just more or less took them on. That would change later. Of course, none of this applied if you had a son along. Ideally, it was not a good idea to have anyone along when you were gambling. Even a supportive girlfriend. It was a private thing to do and you had to concentrate. Besides, you had all the company you needed, right there at the table. And don't forget the dealer. And the cards.

As on all other nights when he was to win, Harry Towns started off dropping some. But then he made it back and when he went ahead, he began slowly to convert his five-dollar chips into twenty-fives until he was playing exclusively with the expensive chips. Half the fun of the twenty-fives was the extra attention you got from the other players; often you got a little crowd around you. By one in the morning, Harry Towns had a good stack of the high-priced chips; he counted them on the sly, considering it bush league to do it openly, and saw that he was ahead eleven hundred dollars. Anything over a thousand started to be "significant money" to Towns, who began to think of going ahead as much as five or even ten thousand. A comedian started to tell jokes to the crowd in a lounge behind Towns's table; he was sure this would throw him off, but it was one of those nights and he kept winning all the same. And he wasn't that good a player. For example, he never went out of his way to wait for the "anchor" seat where you could survey the board and have a somewhat better chance of predicting the next card to come up. He always took insurance which, statistically, was a bad bet. He just liked the idea of being insured. And he was too interested in the other players. If he saw a man with terrific hands, he would say, "I'll bet you work with your hands," and find out that the fellow was a champion three-wall handball player. So he would know that, but his attention would have been diverted for a split second, and that tended to widen the casino's edge.

He heard his name paged over the loudspeaker. He thought of leaving his chips where they were and telling the dealer to hold his place— in the style of the real gamblers—but when it came down to it he didn't trust the people at the table not to snatch some; so he gathered them up in his pockets and went to take the call. It was the boy on the hotel phone saying his father had promised to come back to the room at two. "I did, but it's only one-thirty," said Towns.

"No, it isn't," said the boy, starting to cry. "It's later than that. It's almost morning. Look what you're doing to me." Towns said it really wasn't two yet, and could he please hold out until it was. "I know what I promised and I'm sticking to it. I'm winning a lot now." When he got back to the table, someone had taken his seat and he had to sit a few spots over on the end. Bunny smiled at him, as though he knew all about the boy with icepacks in the room. Towns bet heavily and indeed shocked himself by winning a few hundred more; but then, like a veteran fighter coming on in the late rounds, the dealer, with slow, kind, almost remorseful fingers, began inevitably to grind Towns down and take it all back. He took Towns's first-night winnings, the money he was ahead for the night, and five hundred more that he needed badly. When Towns's last chip had been cleared, the dealer said, "One of those nights. I thought you had me there for a while."

"I didn't," said Towns. "The thing with me is that I need a lot of time. When I rush I get killed."

When he got back to the room, the boy was cranky and irritable and said his head was killing him. Towns easily matched him in irritability. "I was winning a bundle until you called me," he said. He tossed the boy his twenty-five dollars and said, "Anyway, here's your money. I didn't lose that."

"Yes, you did," said the boy. "And I don't want it." The boy started to cry and said, "I was dying in here and you were out there." Towns said he was sorry and that he would stay with him now. When the boy had cried himself to sleep, Towns smoked a cigarette in the dark, feeling very dramatic about it, and then went into the bathroom to see if his hair had grown back. There was a little shadow around his groin, but he could see that it was going to be a long haul. He checked to make sure the boy was sleeping and then went into the bathroom again where he made a long-distance call to the Bryn Mawr girl, paying no attention to what time of day or night it was in New York. She was drowsily awake and he told her about losing the money and what had happened to the boy. "And I've got body lice," he said. The girl laughed hysterically and when she had recovered for a moment she said, "You've got crabs. That's the funniest thing I've ever heard in my life." He knew it was going to be all right with her and that made him feel better; but when he came out of the bathroom and looked at the sleeping boy, he felt like a thief for having made a call to the girl when the kid was probably hoping and praying he would get back together with his mother. Towns couldn't sleep at all and decided the trip had been a bust. The dam, the bowling alley, dropping five hundred, and now bringing the kid back with a broken face.

The boy evidently didn't see it that way. He was cheerful when he awakened and said, "Do we have to go back today? I think I love Las Vegas more than anyplace in the world." That helped Towns out a little, but not much. "How come you loved it?" he asked. "We hardly did anything. And look what happened to your face."

"I can't explain it," said the boy, hugging his father. "I just loved it. And I wish we didn't have to go home."

Towns saw that the boy was really saying he had loved being away with his father, eating together, going places with him, anyplace at all, sleeping in the same hotel room. All that did was make Towns feel worse; he hated himself for not having shown the boy a better time, for having the crabs, for calling up Bryn Mawr girls in the middle of the night, for not knowing how to get back with the boy's mother. When they were packed, Towns settled his account at the front desk and noticed that the doctor's bill had been tacked onto it. They got a cab in front of the hotel and Towns told the driver to take them to the airport. "Oh hell," said the driver, his shoulders slumping. "I don't want to go to the airport." The boy looked at his father with a dumbfounded expression and then began to laugh so hard that Towns got worried about his cheekbone. "Where *would* you like to go?" Towns asked the driver, playing along for the boy's benefit. This time the child laughed so hard he had to hold his face which must have pained him. Towns knew the boy was on to a story he would talk about for years, a driver who only liked to go to places *he* wanted to go to. Towns and his son shared a whole bunch of those. The driver finally turned on the ignition and started off along the Strip. Towns put his arm around the child and asked him how he felt, and the boy said not too bad, but that the day he turned twenty-one he was going to come out to Las Vegas, maybe with a friend or two, so he could gamble. "That's a ways off," said Towns, but when he said it he realized it wasn't that far off after all. And that there wasn't too much time. Before he turned around, the boy would be in his teens, away at college, maybe in the service, and God knows what after that. With a divorce coming up, the time with the boy would probably be lumped into weekends and maybe a little bit of the summer. He wished, at that moment, he could start the Vegas trip all over again. If he could only do that, he would forget about the casino entirely and spend every second with the boy, and really show him a time. Maybe they *would* go camping. He'd buy a couple of sleeping bags and figure out a way to put up one of those fucking tents. When they got to the center of town and began to drive past some of the cheaper casinos, Towns suddenly told the driver to stop in front of one of them. "What for?" asked the driver. "Just stop," said Towns. He made sure to say it in a measured way so the driver would make no mistake about how serious he was. When the cab stopped, Towns got out with the boy and walked up to the cashier of a corner casino where he changed the boy's twenty-five dollars into quarters and halves.

"What's that for?" asked the boy.

"For you," said Towns. "To play the slots."

"I thought I wasn't allowed to," said the boy, standing in front of a quarter machine.

"Just play," said Towns.

"I don't know, Dad," said the boy. "What about him?"
He pointed to a uniformed man approaching them from the rear of the casino.

"I see him," said Towns.

"I don't feel right, Dad," said the boy, putting in his first quarter and pulling the lever.

"It's all right," said Towns. "Play." And he took a position with his back to the boy, his legs a fraction bent, his elbows close to his sides, as though he were cradling a machine gun and would kill any sonofabitch that dared to come within ten feet of the two of them.

Crazed Youth

Black Angels

SMOTHERED BY DEBT, his wife and child in flight, Stefano held fast to his old house in the country, a life buoy in a sea of despair. Let him but keep up the house, return to it each day; before long, his wife would come to her senses, fly back to him. Yet he dreaded the approach of spring, which meant large teams of gardeners who would charge him killing prices to keep the place in shape. Cheapest of all had been the Angeluzzi Brothers, who had gotten him off the ground with a two-hundred-and-fifty-dollar cleanup, then followed through with ninety dollars a month for maintenance, April through October, a hundred extra for the leaf-raking fall windup. Meticulous in April, the four Angeluzzis soon began to dog it; for his ninety, Stefano got only a few brisk lawn cuts and a swipe or two at his flower beds. This spring, unable to work, his life in shreds, Stefano held off on the grounds as long as he could. The grass grew to his shins until one day Swansdowne, a next-door neighbor who had won marigold contests, called on another subject, but with much lawn-mowing and fertilizing in his voice. Stefano dialed the Angeluzzis; then, on an impulse, he dropped the phone and reached for the local paper, running his finger along Home Services. A gardener named Please Try Us caught his fancy. He called the number, asked the deep voice at the other end to come by soon and give him an estimate. The following night, a return call came through.

"I have seen and checked out the place," said the voice, the tones heavy, resonant, solid.

"What'll you take for a cleanup?" asked Stefano. "We'll start there."

Long pause. Lip smack. Then, "Thutty dollars."

"Which address did you go to? I'm at 42 Spring. Big old place on the corner of Spring and Rooter."

"That's correct. For fertilizing, that'll be eight extra, making thutty-eight."

"Awful lot of work here," said Stefano, confused, tingling with both guilt and relief. "All right, when can you get at it?"

"Tomorrow morning. Eight o'clock."

"You're on."

Stefano watched them arrive the next day, Sunday, a quartet of massive Negroes in two trucks and two sleek private cars. In stifling heat, they worked in checkered shirts and heavy pants, two with fedoras impossibly balanced on the backs of their great shaved heads. Stefano, a free-lance writer of technical manuals, went back to his work, stopping now and then to check the Negroes through the window. How could they possibly get by on thirty-eight dollars, he wondered. Divided four ways it came to nothing. Gas alone for their fleet of cars would kill their nine-fifty each. He'd give them forty-five dollars to salve his conscience, but still, what about their groceries, rent? Late in the afternoon, he ran out with beers for each. "Plenty of leaves, eh?" he said to Cotten, largest of them, the leader, expressionless in dainty steel-rimmed glasses.

"Take about two and a half days," said the Negro.

"I'm giving you forty-five dollars," said Stefano. "What the hell."

The job actually took three full days, two for the cleanup, a third for the lawn and fertilizing the beds. The last day was a bad one for Stefano. Through his window, he watched the black giants trim the lawn, then kneel in winter clothes and lovingly collect what seemed to be each blade of grass so there'd be no mess. He wanted to run out and tell them to do less work; certainly not at those prices. Yet he loved the prices, too. He could take it all out of expense money, not even bother his regular free-lance payments. At the end of the day, he walked up to Cotten, took out his wallet and said, "I'm giving you cash. So you won't have to fool with a check." It had occurred to him that perhaps the Negroes only did cleanups, no maintenance. By doing enough of them, thousands, perhaps they could sneak by, somehow make a living. "What about maintenance?" he asked the head gardener.

The man scratched his ear, shook his head, finally said, "Can't do your place for less than eighteen dollars a month."

"You guys do some work," said Stefano, shivering with glee. "Best I've seen. I think you're too low. I'll give you twenty-two."

The Negroes came back twice a week, turned Stefano's home into a showplace, hacking down dead trees, planting new ones, filling in dead spots, keeping the earth black and loamy. Swansdowne, who usually let Stefano test-run new gardeners and then swooped down to sign them up if they were good, looked on with envy, yet called one day and said, "I would never let a colored guy touch my place."

"They're doing a great job on mine," said Stefano.

Maybe that explains it, he thought. All of the Swansdownes who won't have Negro gardeners. That's why their rates are low. Otherwise they'd starve. He felt good, a liberal. Why shouldn't he get a slight break on money?

At the end of May, Stefano paid them their twenty-two dollars and distributed four American-cheese sandwiches. The three assistants took them back to a truck where one had mayonnaise. "You guys do other kinds of work?" Stefano asked Cotten, who leaned on a hoe. "What about painting? A house?"

The gardener looked up at Stefano's colonial. "We do," he said.

"How much would you charge?" The best estimate on the massive ten-roomer had been seven hundred dollars.

"Fifty-eight dollars," said the huge Negro, neutral in his steel-rims.

"I'll pay for half the paint," said Stefano.

The following day, when Stefano awakened, the four Negroes, on high, buckling ladders, had half the house done, the paint deep brown, rich and gurgling in the sun. Their gardening clothes were wildly spattered. He'd pick up the cleaning bill, thought Stefano. It was only fair.

"It looks great!" he hollered up to Cotten, swaying massively in the wind.

"She'll shape up time we get the fourth coat on."

By mid-June, the four Negroes had cleaned out Stefano's attic for three dollars, waterproofed his basement for another sixteen; an elaborate network of drainage pipes went in for twelve-fifty. One day he came home to find the floors mopped, sanded, shellacked, his cabinets scrubbed, linen closets dizzying in their cleanliness. Irritated for the first time—I didn't order this—he melted quickly when he saw the bill. A slip on the bread box read: "You owes us $2.80." Loving the breaks he was getting, Stefano threw them bonuses, plenty of sandwiches, all his old sports jackets, venetian blinds that had come out of the attic and books of fairly recent vintage on Nova Scotia tourism. Never in the thick of marriage had his place been so immaculate; cars slowed down to admire his dramatically painted home, his shrubs bursting with fertility. Enter any room; its cleanliness would tear your head off. With all these ridiculously cheap home services going for him, Stefano felt at times his luck had turned. Still, a cloak of loneliness rode his shoulders, aggravation clogged his throat. If only to hate her, he missed his wife, a young, pretty woman, circling the globe with her lover, an assistant director of daytime TV. He saw pictures of her, tumbling with lust, in staterooms, inns, the backs of small foreign cars. He missed his son, too, a boy of ten, needing braces. God only knows what shockers he was being exposed to. The pair had fled in haste, leaving behind mementos, toys lined up on shelves, dresses spilling out of chests. Aging quickly, his confidence riddled, Stefano failed in his quest for dates with young girls, speechless and uncertain on the phone. What could he do with himself. At these prices, he could keep his home spotless. But would that make everything all right. Would that haul back a disgruntled wife and son. One night, his heart weighing a ton, he returned from an "Over 28" dance to find the burly Negroes winding up their work. Sweating long into the night, they had rigged up an elaborate network of gas lamps, the better to show off a brilliantly laid out thicket of tea roses and dwarf fruit trees. Total cost for the lighting: five dollars and fifty cents.

"Really lovely," said Stefano, inspecting his grounds, counting out some bills. "Here," he said to the head gardener "take another deuce. In my condition, money means nothing." The huge Negro toweled down his forehead, gathered up his equipment. "Hey," said Stefano. "Come on in for a beer. If I don't talk to someone I'll bust."

"Got to get on," said Cotten. "We got work to do."

"Come on, come on," said Stefano. "What can you do at this hour. Give a guy a break."

The Negro shook his head in doubt, then moved massively toward the house, Stefano clapping him on the back in a show of brotherhood.

Inside, Stefano went for flip-top beers. The gardener sat down in the living room, his great bulk caving deeply into the sofa. For a moment, Stefano worried about gardening clothes, in contact with living-room furniture, then figured the hell with it, who'd complain.

"I've got the worst kind of trouble," said Stefano, leaning back on a Danish modern slat bench. "Sometimes I don't think I'm going to make it through the night. My wife's checked out on me. You probably figured that out already."

The Negro crossed his great legs, sipped his beer. The steel-rimmed glasses had a shimmer to them and Stefano could not make out his eyes.

"She took the kid with her," said Stefano. "That may be the worst part. You don't know what it's like to have a kid tearing around your house for ten years and then not to hear anything. Or maybe you do?" Stefano asked hopefully. "You probably have a lot of trouble of your own."

Silent, the Negro sat forward and shoved a cloth inside his flannel shirt to mop his chest.

"Anyway, I'll be goddamned if I know what to do. Wait around? Pretend she's never coming back? I don't know what in the hell to do with myself. Where do I go from here?"

"How long she gone?" asked the guest, working on the back of his neck now.

"What's that got to do with it?" asked Stefano. "About four months, I guess. Just before you guys came. Oh, I see what you mean. If she hasn't come back in four months, she's probably gone for good. I might as well start building a new life. That's a good point."

The Negro put away the cloth and folded his legs again, crossing his heavy, blunted fingers, arranging them on the point of one knee.

"It just happened out of the clear blue sky," said Stefano. "Oh, why kid around. It was never any good." He told the Negro about their courtship, the false pregnancy, how he had been "forced" to get married. Then he really started in on his wife, the constant primping, the thousands of ways she had made him jealous, the in-laws to support. He let it all come out of him, like air from a tire, talking with heat and fury; until he realized he had been talking nonstop for maybe twenty minutes, half an hour. The Negro listened to him patiently, not bothering with his beer. Finally, when Stefano sank back to catch his breath, the gardener asked a question: "You think you any good?"

"What do you mean?" said Stefano. "Of course I do. Oh, I get what you're driving at. If I thought I was worth anything, I wouldn't let all of this kill me. I'd just kind of brace myself, dig out and really build something fine for myself. Funny how you make just the right remark. It's really amazing. You know I've done the analysis bit. Never meant a damned thing to me. I've had nice analysts, tough ones, all kinds. But the way you just let me sound off and then asked that one thing. This is going to sound crazy, but what if we just talked this way, couple of times a week. I just sound off and then you come in with the haymaker, the way you just did. Just for fun, what would you charge me? An hour?"

"Fo' hunnid," said the Negro.

"Four hundred. That's really a laugh. You must be out of your head. What are you, crazy? Don't you know I was just kidding around?"

The Negro took a sip of the beer and rose to leave. "All right, wait a second," said Stefano. "Hold on a minute. Let's just finish up this hour, all right. Then we'll see about other times. This one doesn't count, does it?"

"It do," said the Negro, sinking into the couch and snapping out a pad and pencil.

"That's not really fair, you know," said Stefano. "To count this one. Anyway, we'll see. Maybe we'll try it for a while. That's some price. Where was I? Whew, all that money. To get back to what I was saying, this girl has been a bitch ever since the day I laid eyes on her. You made me see it tonight. In many ways, I think she's a lot like my mom . . ."

The Man They Threw
Out of Jets

HIGH ABOVE GILA BEND, in the middle of Arizona, with the desert floor pushing hot blasts of air against the belly of his tiny plane, the Major's mind fell apart. He screamed, shook his sunburned fists, and swore that he would beat the jets in a race across the sky. From the rear seat of the plane I watched and listened, yet I never said a word.

I was going to. I had made up my mind that I would tell the Air Force that one of their fliers was insane and something ought to be done about him. Yet when the day was over, I never said a word. I couldn't.

The man who first told me about the Major was a Negro jet pilot who flew me to the desert gunnery range from a nearby air base. The Air Force had assigned me to take some pictures of the jet gunnery ranges, and when I asked the name of the man who was in charge of the ranges, he began to talk about the Major. We were at 30,000 feet, and I was being lulled to sleep by the soft, even whistle inside the plane.

"When they took him out of jets," the pilot said, "they should've taken him far away from here where he could never hear the sound of one. That was the real crime. You take a piece out of a man when you take him out of jets."

"Why did they take him out of jets?" I asked.

"His ears," the pilot said. "He gets up high in a jet and he can't hear anything. His ears pop. I'm not saying he should still be flying them. All I'm saying is they did a foolish thing keeping him here on the ranges. Everything is jets here. Everywhere you look."

The desert range on which he dropped me was the nerve center for the other ranges. It had no jet targets, just a short runway and a wooden control tower which directed jets to the gunnery ranges spotted around the desert. I walked along the runway, feeling the heat from the desert, and watching the sky. The jets were all over the place. They traveled overhead in straight lines as if someone very big was pulling them on thin, powerful strings. And they filled the air with the mixture of sad cries and terrible gliding screams the jets had brought to

52

the air age. On the desert, there was no hiding from them, and, as the pilot had said, they were everything.

The single plane on the runway was not a jet. It had a propeller. A Chinese mechanic circled the T-6 nervously, moving in under the wings, climbing up on the fuselage, tightening, rubbing, polishing, smoothing. He seemed very afraid someone would come and find he hadn't done a good job. The little plane sparkled in the sun, sleek and scrubbed down like a fine racehorse, yet it made me think of a shiny Model T Ford I had once seen parked between two late model Oldsmobiles. At another time, in another place, it might have seemed beautiful, but the jets overhead had a way of making all other flying machines appear spindly.

I asked the Chinese mechanic where I could find the Major, and he told me that the little T-6 was the Major's plane. The Major would be along soon. I stood beside the little plane and waited, watching the packs of jets as they passed overhead on their way to the targets. Four at a time would come over, and then one would pitch out to the side and the others would follow it into a giant circle of violence.

In a little while, a squat, charred-looking man with Major's leaves drove up in a jeep. The Chinese mechanic came down from the fuselage to open the door for him, and the Major walked out carrying bundles of money in his arms. He piled them into the rear baggage compartment of the small plane.

"You refueled, chopsticks?" he asked the mechanic, completely ignoring me.

"All refueled, Major," the mechanic said.

"Then I'm shoving," the Major said, wriggling into a seat parachute.

I stood up and introduced myself. "The Air Force said when I came out here there'd be someone to fly me over the ranges," I said. "For my pictures."

He made the chute comfortable around his crotch and asked, "What are you? A first or second balloon?" He still hadn't looked at me.

"First lieutenant," I said.

"First balloon," he said. "All right, first balloon. You're a first balloon, you been around long enough to know today's payday. I got 150 bastardos waiting out there to be paid."

"I just know what they told me," I said.

He looked up now, as if he'd begun to smell something sour. "All you know is what they told you?" he repeated unbelievingly. "You're quite a balloon. That's all I can say. You're really something. Get in."

His neck got very red, and I was amazed at how quickly he had gotten mad. He made it seem as if he had known me for a long time and had a thousand reasons for hating me.

In one motion, he swung his squat body up on the wing and into the front seat of the plane. He started the engine. The Chinese mechanic told me a chute was in the back seat of the plane and that I should put my hat in the rear baggage compartment. I opened the flap of the compartment and it came off in my hand. I stood there, holding it above my head, not really knowing what to do with it. The wind from the propeller blew my hair over my face. It also blew some of the money out of the baggage compartment. Dollar bills came flying out along the runway. The Chinese mechanic wrung his hands and chased after them. The Major turned around and saw me holding the flap.

"You broke my plane," he said. "Why did you break my plane?" His voice was low like people who are too incensed to shout.

"I didn't break anything that wasn't broken before."

"Get in my plane," he said, a little louder. "Get off the ground and get in my plane. You broke my goddamned plane, now get in. *Get in!*"

I got into the rear seat and put my legs around the dual control stick, fumbling for the safety harness. The Chinese mechanic stood clear, his khakis flapping in the prop wash, and the Major, after a short taxi run down the field, wrenched the plane off the ground into a steep, shuddering bank. It was a weird takeoff that made my head ache. The wings trembled dangerously in the desert wind until the little plane righted itself. I held the bottom of the seat with my hands and inhaled some of the sweet-smelling gasoline that washed back over me. The Major flew low over the barren desert, shifting his head from side to side. When the jets whined overhead toward the ranges, the Major looked the other way, ignoring them. He was completely silent as if he were alone in the plane, and we flew that way, not speaking, for about fifteen minutes until we reached the target range. From the sky, it looked like a giant buzzard. I had a brief flash of some jets diving down upon it, and then the Major brought the plane into the same kind of insane bank he had used on the takeoff. Without circling the field, he bent the plane backward as if it were his body and thrust it straight down toward the target range, pulling out at the last possible second. It made the top of my head throb, and throughout it, I had the feeling there was no plane and I was alone on a man's back through a perfect highboard jackknife.

On the ground, seven men, bare to the waist, their backs an angry red from the sun, were standing in a loose line on the target range. In back of them were rows of skull-like automobile targets, shot through with black holes from the jet rockets. Off in the distance were other targets, ragged circles of tires and huge bull's-eyes you could see through. When the Major's plane rode up, the wet bodies of the men became rigid in the position of attention. The landing had shaken me up and I stayed in the cockpit while the Major vaulted to the ground. Then he paid the men and dismissed them, catching the sergeant in charge by the arm.

"You find out who took the tire from the pickup truck?" he asked.

"No, Major."

"Nobody knows, huh?"

"Yes, sir."

"All right, ask them again. Next time I come round I want the tire out here. The tire isn't here and I'll make it your ass. One thing I don't hack is a man stealing. You steal from trucks, soon you're stealing from each other. The tire isn't here, it'll be your ass. Then I'll line every bastardo you got up in the sun till they drop."

"I asked everyone," the sergeant said. "I . . ."

The Major didn't wait for him to finish. He came back to the plane and looked at me briefly and bitterly as if to say his words were as much for my benefit as that of the range troops. He swung into the cockpit. The range troops had turned around and were squatting in front of the targets watching the Major's takeoff. It seemed to be a ritual that they had witnessed many times. I had fastened the safety harness and clamped on my parachute, but when the takeoff came I wasn't ready. He pulled the plane off the ground, forcing it into the air almost straight up, like a helicopter. The desert heat was much stronger than when I had first come to the main range. I had kept the cockpit closed during the takeoff, and little globes of moisture were forming on the inside of the plastic canopy. I opened my collar and tried to swallow the thickness that was starting in my throat. The Major lurched off sharply in the direction of another range, keeping low as if to avoid the jets that flew by in packs overhead. He flew with short, twisting motions as if he were the plane and he was not sure where he was supposed to go.

At each of the remaining three ranges, he paid the barebacked men who stood in the sun and told them there were several things he just didn't like. "One of them is stealing," he said. "Anyone who knows me knows I treat a man fair. I got a swimming pool for the men on week-ends. I can't hack something like stealing, though. I catch a man stealing and it's his ass." And at each of the ranges, he took off and landed in the same spinning, writhing manner. When we left the final range, my clothes were all wet and tight, and I was getting sick. Instead of turning back toward the main range where we had started, he twisted off in the opposite direction. He flew even closer to the ground than before, and the plane began to buffet and shake from the steady blankets of heat that came up from the desert. The jets kept sweeping by us overhead and disappearing into the clouds far ahead of us, making it seem as though we were going very slow. He kept on the same course, brushing along on top of the desert, going farther away from our starting point. I wanted him to go back to the main range. I had long given up on any pictures and my head hurt very much. It annoyed me most of all that he hadn't said a word since I had broken his plane. All through paying the troops and the landings and takeoffs.

In a little while, the desert began to change. There were patches of shrubbery here and there and not so much barrenness. On the rim of the horizon were some small, sloping mountains and one slightly larger one toward which the Major seemed headed. The jets began to taper off in number until there were none at all in sight. We flew silently across the desert. The only noise was a clop-chopping one that came from the engine. When he began to talk, he sounded very old over the intercom and what he said was like a chant.

"I can think better out here," the chant said. "The one thing I can't do around jets is think. Did you read that, balloon?"

I held the talking piece of the intercom in my hand, pushed the little button and said, "Yes, I read it."

"I can think better out here," the chant continued. "I want you to get the picture. When anybody comes out here, all they see is jets. Nobody looks at the ground. Nobody looks at what we have here, what we're doing. They take one look at the jets and anything else is garbage. I like to take people out here and give them the picture. Did you read that?"

I said "Yes" over the intercom. I was thinking of saying "Roger," and changed my mind. I always felt silly saying it, for one thing. And I was beginning to dislike the Major. I felt very sick and he could have told me all this on the ground when we got back to the range. Or he didn't have to tell it to me at all.

"This is the picture, balloon," the chant continued. "I got 150 bastardos working out there on the desert for me. They work for me. They don't fly a jet. They don't touch a jet. When people come out here to the ranges, they don't even *see* my men until I give them the picture. They stick their nose in the air and all they see is jets. Anything else, forget it. My men work for me and they have to work. I work their ass. I worked on a construction gang before the Air Force and that's where *I* learned to work. They work Saturday if I want them to work, and Sunday. They'll work for me and they won't bitch because I treat a man fair. Rough, too. I mean I'll kick a man in the ass, but then I'll turn around and let him have a swimming pool if he'll move his tail and build it. I'm sorry for before. The reason I got sore at you is I've had two balloons working for me I had to get rid of. They didn't hack working. They watched the jets too much. I caught them and got rid of them."

He kept the plane close to the desert. It shuddered continually from the thermal waves. Whenever he wanted to make a point, he would do something sharp and violent with the plane. My headache came back, and the intercom began to pinch my skin. We were coming pretty close to the mountain.

"What we got here, balloon, is Russia and China. I been to China and shot down Chinks and I know the Chink ground. There's a fellow comes by here who knows the ground in Russia. We build up the ranges to look like China and Russia and then the jets come over and bomb the ranges just like they're fighting the next war. Then you know what we do? We take what they bombed and we build it up again to look like China and Russia. Did you read all that?"

"Uh-huh," I said. I was beginning to worry about the mountain. It wasn't very high, but it was there, and the Major wasn't paying much attention to it.

"We take the little pieces of tanks and guns and trenches and we build them up again so the jets can do the same thing again. We're always picking up after the jets. Sometimes I send my bastardos out on Saturday and Sunday to build up the ranges."

He saw the mountain and began slowly to gain altitude.

"That's important, balloon. If that isn't as important as the jets I don't know what is. I mean picking up after them. Anything they break up, we go and build up again. That's why it eats me when people come out here to the ranges and all they see is the jets. All the Air Force sees is the jets, too. We got to steal wood and paint out from their behind for the target ranges. Once I paid for some paint myself so the jets could have a tank and blow the ass off it."

He leaned over the side, looking out at the mountain, and then he looked back at me. When he began talking, his voice had a note of urgency to it.

"You're pretty young, balloon," he said. "Young balloons come into the Air Force, all they know is jets. They don't remember anything else flying in the air. Everywhere they look, they see jets, jets, jets. When I get hold of a young balloon, I like to take him out and show him what another kind of airplane can do. That's why I land and take off like that. Did you ever see a jet fly like that?"

"No," I said. "I never did." He was rougher on the controls now, and he seemed to be getting drunk with his own words.

"Did you know a T-6 can pull G's? Tell me when you feel the G's."

There was still some space between us and the mountain, but not much. He pulled back on the stick until the plane slowed down and almost stalled. Then he thrust the stick forward and pushed the little plane into a spin. The sky passed over my head, and then the wing, and the little plane pitched forward like a broken glider. We whipped downward quietly, with the wind washing against the wings. "Tell me when you feel them," he hollered. "Tell me when you feel them."

He spun the other way. It made my eyes bulge and it hurt in places where I never dreamed it would hurt. In my wrists and in back of my knees and on my elbows. We went down further and I yelled, "I feel them. I feel them." I would have said it earlier, but I forgot.

He leveled off and looked back at me. His eyes were wide and his lips were wet in the corners. His words came fast. "That's what I mean," he said. "If anyone told you a T-6 could pull G's you'd bust a gut laughing. There's more."

He did a slow roll. "A T-6 can fly, balloon," he said, raising his voice. He did a barrel roll. "A T-6 can fly." Then he stood the plane on one wing and held it there as if he was trying to decide what to do next. He looked back at me and probably saw the four dots before I did. They were miles behind us, and suddenly they weren't. The sun caught the four dots on their wings and turned them into jets. They flew together with little threads of black fuel smoke streaming from their tails and came forward inevitably in that straight line until they were close.

"They're not even supposed to be here," the Major said. "I'm glad you're here. This is the first time I ever had a balloon here to see how they can mess you up. Everywhere you go around here they turn up. There's no place you can go."

He hunched over the controls and gunned the plane forward. "Watch while I beat them to the mountain. I'll beat them in a T-6." When the plane reached its maximum speed, it began to shake and I held tight to the seat. The Major was standing up a little at the controls, and as he flew, he yelled, *"Let's see how fast you can go. I'm only in a T-6."* We were too close and too low to go over the top of the mountain. The Major turned the plane over on its side, and we crept along the edges of the mountain slope like a fly on a wall. I saw the jets speed by over our heads and take the mountain easily. They became four dots again and finally disappeared. The Major shook his fist at them once more and yelled, *"You weren't even supposed to be here."*

On the other side of the mountain, he sat back in his seat and headed the plane in the direction of the main range. "I'm really glad you were here, balloon," he said, quietly. "I always wanted to show someone what they can do to you." He didn't say anything else, and when we came in over the main range, he set the plane down with one of his landings. The sun had gone down, and it was cooler now. We had been flying for about three hours. I was sore all over my body and nauseated from all the flying. I didn't want to look at another plane. When the Chinese mechanic came over and asked me whether I'd lost my cookies, I kidded with him for a while, but in the back of my mind I knew I wanted to talk to someone about the Major and tell them how he had carried on over the desert. I didn't know exactly how I would present it or what I would say. All I knew is I wanted to tell someone about him. But as I say, something came up and I never did. The whole thing took about ten minutes. After the Major had jumped out of his plane and the mechanic come over to talk to me, a siren rang on the range and everyone sprinted to the tower and climbed to the top. I ran over, too, with the mechanic. Everyone who worked on the main range was gathered around an airman with earphones who sat next to a radio set. From the top of the tower I saw the little Major running toward his T-6 which couldn't have had much fuel left in it. From what I could make out, a French pilot had misjudged a target on one of the gunnery ranges and nosed right into the ground in a jet. Since the other jets couldn't land in the desert, his squadron leader was radioing in for some help. The mechanic said that crash rescue was part of the Major's job. Everyone watched the Major take off, in the same rough way, and a very young man said, "He gets off the ground, doesn't he?"

The Major took off in the direction of Range 2, the scene of the accident. The fellow with the radio picked up the Major on the radio and stayed with him until the Major landed on the desert. There was radio silence then for a while, and then the tower man said the Major had scooped the Frenchman out of the cockpit and taken off for the main base with him. The Frenchman's safety harness had come undone in the crash and he had gotten it in the face when he fell forward on the instrument panel. The Major said over the radio he had the Frenchman in the back seat of the plane and the foreign pilot was unconscious. You couldn't get every single detail sitting there in the tower, listening to it second-hand from the radio man. But there was quite a bit of excitement when the radio man said that the Major couldn't land because each time he circled the field and made his approach, the unconscious Frenchman in the back fell over on the controls forcing the plane into a spin. It was difficult to land, too, because of the jets. Since they burn up so much fuel and can't stay up long, they take priority in landing. The Major had to circle the field seven times before he got in. Once he touched down, the Frenchman died immediately on the runway, and that's about all there is to the story. Except that, as I say, I never told anyone about the screaming or the race with the jets. Not because I was suddenly convinced the Major was a big man and a hero. And not because I suddenly changed my mind about him and saw the light—that he was really important and very sane and that everyone else was crazy. There were no impressive reasons for it. I just thought it over and decided I wasn't going to say anything.

Detroit Abe

ALONE, FRIGHTENED, POUNDED ON the head by alimony, the IRS circling closer, Abrahamowitz almost considered going back to the synagogue. Once in a while he would walk by one, take a peek inside, and keep going. They weren't going to get him just yet. The ground was crumbling beneath his feet. If the roof ever collapsed, he would barge in, perhaps during the High Holidays, and say, "How about taking me back?" To the best of his knowledge they would have to, unless it was an expensive one that could keep him out with prohibitive dues. Once it had been his dream to end his days as an aging boulevardier at the Gritti Hotel in Venice, staring at the Canal.

"Who is he?" a tourist would ask the maître d'.

"The American," would be the reply. "They say he was once a literary fellow, an intimate of both Roths, Henry and Philip. Now he just orders a Negroni and sits and stares at the Canal. I think he is waiting for the contessa, but she will not come."

But at the rate he was going, Abrahamowitz was not going to make it to Venice. Where would he get the fare? How could he calm down enough to make the trip over? The chances were strong that it would be the synagogue after all, his ace in the hole.

He taught irony to a group of students in a heavily ethnic division of a city university. And he taught a lot of it, too, three separate courses: Classical Irony, Eighteenth-Century Irony, and Contemporary Irony. Why did they need so much irony? And why Abrahamowitz to teach it, when his real strength was in War Fiction, a course he could not get approved by the department because of the Vietnam experience? He was sturdy in contemporary irony, held his own in the eighteenth century, and, by his own admission, disgraced himself in the classics. His classes were packed with students, the overflow spilling out into the halls. Weeks into the semester, a half-dozen more would transfer from Spenser seminars. He couldn't figure out why everyone wanted to get into irony. They were poor kids; shouldn't they be learning how to run small businesses—or at least mastering the fundamentals of hospital supply? Exactly where were they going with *Candide* and *A Tale of a Tub*? How were they going to throw *A Vindication of Isaac Bickerstaff, Esq.* into practical application?

Abrahamowitz was afraid of his students. Even though great armies of them poured into his classes, once installed, they would sit and stare blankly at him. What were they thinking? That he was an idiot? He had no way of knowing. He would ask a question—"Is literary irony a positive or negative force?"—then sit back, arms folded, determined to sweat them out. But after a few beats he would become terrified and push on with the answer, which was that he wasn't sure—it could be either.

Outside, an elevated train—one of the few remaining in the city—roared by every five minutes, invariably drowning out his best material. Also, the seats in the classroom were arranged in maddeningly straight, geometrically precise lines and riveted to the floor. Abrahamowitz yearned to yank them free and scatter them about—but the dean said that an expensive departmental study had advocated neat rows (as a pathway to neat thinking) and that he wasn't allowed to.

He taught four days a week and spent the other three getting ready for the four. He lived alone in a one-room apartment, his only luxury a huge Sony television set that he never turned on. Often he sat and stared at the blank screen, which was somewhat relaxing. He used this as an example of irony to one of his classes, the staring at a blank set. Their reaction was to stare back blankly at him. Maybe it wasn't ironic enough for them. He lived alone because women had always deserted him at critical junctures in his life. His wife told him she wanted a divorce as he was being wheeled in for a hemorrhoid operation. A longtime girl friend walked out just as he was leaving to deliver the most important lecture of his life, at Notre Dame, replacing a Polish novelist who had gone through the windshield of an Alfa Romeo. His delivery was shaky, and when he got back, the lecture bureau struck his name from the catalog. (He had to admit there had been one good moment, when an old poet cried out to him as he boarded the train: "You've got something fine. Hold on to it. I never could.") So he had little to do with women. His sex came to him through magazines, lately ones in which women were tied to brooms.

Each night, drained from teaching, Abrahamowitz would take a little nap and then eat dinner alone at a restaurant, usually one of the city's colorful ethnic ones—since, amazingly, in spite of leading what he saw as a harsh, nervous life, he was blessed with an iron stomach. So, in the event he went wrong on a Filipino delicacy, he didn't suffer as much as the next man. One particular night he selected a new and somewhat high-priced establishment that featured the foods of north India. Plushly decorated, boasting authentic clay ovens, and highly recommended by a leading restaurant guide, the place had quickly caught fire. Since the dining room on this particular occasion was overflowing with customers, Abrahamowitz, a single, was asked by the management if he would mind having his dinner in the lounge.

"It's all right with me," he said, and was led to a small table in the corner. Seated in a booth next to him was a pleasant-looking young black man with a jeweled pendant around his neck and a smashingly lovely, though somewhat vacant-looking, young white girl at his side. She had long, black hair, and when she got up to go to the ladies' room, Abrahamowitz noticed that she was just a fraction too plump around the bottom—in other words, his favorite physical type if he had been interested in women, which he wasn't. Possibly he had been more aware of the couple than he realized; otherwise he would never have noticed the long pause that followed when the waiter asked them what they would like for dinner. Not thinking much of this, and feeling a little buzz from his second J & B Scotch sour on the rocks, Abrahamowitz abandoned his normal reticence to lean over and say, "I hear the tandoori chicken is marvelous." The black man glanced neutrally in his direction but did not respond. Yet when Abrahamowitz turned away he heard the fellow say, "I believe we'll both have the tandoori chicken." Roughly an hour later, the black man sent his girl friend off with a light tap on that terrific behind; then, with an appealing shyness, he asked Abrahamowitz to join him for a drink.

"Delighted," said Abrahamowitz.

"I'm Smooth," said the fellow, extending a gentle hand.

"Irwin Abrahamowitz. How do you do?"

Both men, strangely enough, loved the same drink, sombreros—Kahlúa with a little white "hat" of sweet cream on top—and this is what they ordered.

"First off," said Smooth, "I want to thank you for saving my ass."

"For what?" said Abrahamowitz. "Telling you about the chicken? That's ridiculous."

But it wasn't so ridiculous to Smooth, who explained that he was involved in pimping, that his companion was the number-one girl in his stable, and that the moment after the waiter had asked for his order had been one of the most terrifying ones of his life.

"How come?" asked Abrahamowitz.

"My cool was in danger. If I had said something dumb, Diane would have picked up on it. Next morning she'd be over working with my archrival, French Fries."

By way of further explanation, Smooth told Abrahamowitz that "cool" was the most important element in his profession. This was particularly true in his case, since he never smacked his girls around or razor-marked them in the style of French Fries, his competitor. On the contrary, he treated them with kindness and had even set up a retirement plan in which over-the-hill ones were given boutiques. Hence the nickname Smooth.

"So I'm very grateful to you," said Abrahamowitz's new friend.

"Glad I was able to help."

"What profession are you in, may I ask?"

Abrahamowitz said that he was the visiting irony professor at Monrose College, adding, reflexively, that he was underpaid and that in spite of it they were working him like a dog.

"A way to spot irony," he explained to Smooth, who hadn't asked, "is when you can't quite make out the intentions of the author and when the hero ends up in puzzled defeat." Smooth considered this momentarily, then said that he himself was trying to shift over to the recording business as a hedge against his middle years and the possibility of the pimping business going sour.

"Would you care to step out to my car and listen to one of my tunes?"

Abrahamowitz, slightly edgy, with an eight-in-the-morning class coming up the next day, said all right but that he couldn't stay long. Smooth got up quickly and led the way, Abrahamowitz dropping a few dollars on the table to pay for the sombreros. The mild-mannered young man then escorted Abrahamowitz to an old Dodge, explaining that his real car, a forty-five-thousand-dollar reconverted Bentley pimpmobile, was in the shop for repairs. In the front seat of the Dodge the two listened to a tape of "Checkin' My Birds," which had been written and produced by Smooth. The number was catchy and melodious. Abrahamowitz admired particularly the falsetto of the lead singer, who turned out to be Smooth himself. Smooth explained that for a brief period he had been one of the Milk Duds, a group doing club dates out of South Philly.

"Do you have any connections in the recording business?"

It seemed a strange question to be asking Abrahamowitz, an irony man whose life was bounded on the one side by Juvenal, on the other by *The Cankered Muse*. Abrahamowitz shared a desk in the faculty lounge with Ostrow, a Dryden man and a cellist who, as a favor to the music section, occasionally covered Harmonics I; but he was hardly the man Smooth was after. Besides, they fought bitterly over the desk, Ostrow continually trying to get extra drawer space.

"Frankly, nobody comes to mind," said Abrahamowitz.

"That's perfectly all right," said Smooth, who certainly did have a sweet disposition. "May I give you a lift home?"

"That would be lovely."

As they drove along Abrahamowitz found himself humming the infectiously catchy "Checkin' My Birds." Fleetingly, he wondered why—if Smooth was so grateful to him—he didn't offer to send over the girl with the slightly heavy behind, even for half an hour, which was the absolute limit on time he could spare from his classroom preparation. As they reached the front door of Abrahamowitz's West Side apartment they shook hands, Smooth once again thanking him for bailing him out of a tight spot. Abrahamowitz got out of the car.

"Incidentally," said Smooth, leaning out of the window, "did you notice how I didn't offer to send over the girl, even though you did me a big turn?"

"Yes, frankly, I noticed that."

"Another thing. I have a whole pile of money in here with me. Did you wonder why I let you spring for the drinks?"

"That crossed my mind, too."

"Well, let me ask you a question," said Smooth, his brows furrowed in thought.

"Go right ahead."

"Is that what you mean by irony?"

And that was the last he had seen or heard of Smooth, even though he occasionally found himself humming the damnably catchy "Checkin' My Birds." One morning several weeks later, Abrahamowitz was rushing through a second cup of coffee at the Delicatessen Elegante when his eye fell upon a *Times* news story that told of the roundup and indictment of seven of the city's leading pimps. There were photographs of each of these fellows, and the one that registered immediately was that of Arthur Taylor, age twenty-seven, who resided at Henry's Motor Lodge in midtown Manhattan. There was no doubt that this was the person Abrahamowitz knew as Smooth, his friend from the Indian restaurant. According to the *Times* crime blotter, the mild-mannered fellow, along with the others, was under criminal indictment on the grounds of income tax evasion. Staring him in the face: A sentence of three to seven years in a federal penitentiary. Further along, the story said that Arthur Taylor had first come under suspicion as a result of a radio interview in which he let slip that he earned a quarter of a million dollars a year and hardly lifted a finger to get it, rising each day at noon. What an idiotic thing to admit to on the public airwaves! Some downtrodden, overworked IRS sleuth earning fourteen thousand nine hundred ninety-nine dollars per annum (Abrahamowitz's salary to the penny, incidentally) must have been tuned in and gotten infuriated. The last line of the story indicated that one of Arthur Taylor's girls was ready to testify that she handed over fifteen thousand dollars in cash to the pimp, the IRS insisting there wasn't a penny of tax paid on this amount.

It was late, and Abrahamowitz would have to race to the subway to make it out to Monrose College on time. He had no irony to teach on this particular day, but he was expected to show up at a meeting to discuss faculty dental benefits. As he took a last sip of coffee Abrahamowitz wondered if Smooth would be able to sweet-talk his way past the homosexuality that was so rampant in the prison system, or if he would be turned briskly into a fairy. Noting with irritation that juice had gone up a dime, he paid his check to Seitz, the owner, a ferocious reader of bestsellers who knew Abrahamowitz was in literature. "What'd you think of *Princess Daisy*?" asked Seitz, ringing up the $2.85 for juice, eggs, and coffee. What was Abrahamowitz supposed to do—give him a quick critique with forty people listening in, not to mention the countermen? "I didn't read it," Abrahamowitz lied. "Wait till you do," said Seitz. "You'll piss." Abrahamowitz ducked out, not allowing Seitz to get started on his daughter, who was an artist in Los Angeles and designed drapes. "If you're ever in L.A.," Seitz would say, "I want you to see those drapes." That's just what Abrahamowitz wanted to do—look at Gloria Seitz's drapes in L.A.

On the subway out to Monrose, guarding his briefcase so that no one could snatch it, Abrahamowitz decided that the girl who had ratted on Smooth was probably the one with the lazy, magnificent behind. After all the nice things Smooth had done for her, coldly and perversely she had gone to the tax boys and turned him in. Exactly Abrahamowitz's experience with the fair sex.

Later in the day, Abrahamowitz sat in his tiny English department office, filling out a long dental-care form. Actually, it wasn't that great a plan. The first twenty fillings were on the subscriber; after that the insurance company took over. Only if you came into the plan with a smashed mouth or teeth decayed by long periods of malnutrition did it make any sense. Still, it was on the house, so he filled out the form anyway. In the back of his mind he was thinking about the three students who had spent a month in one of his irony courses under the impression that they were in Intermediate Logic. Whose fault was it? Were they really paying attention? Not only had they petitioned out of the class, but they had complained to Dean Kiltar that their sense of logic had been thrown off. If that was the case, why didn't they stay in irony? Who asked them to leave? These were his thoughts as the phone rang and he received, not with total surprise, a call from his troubled acquaintance.

"Abrim . . ."

"Yes?"

"This is Smooth."

"Nice to hear from you," said Abrahamowitz. "How are things going?" he asked, knowing full well they were going lousy.

"Just fine. I wonder if you could spare me a few moments of your time."

"Of course," said Abrahamowitz. "How about drinks and dinner at the Punjab again. I haven't been there in a long time and I could use a little Indian food."

"Actually, I'm a little pressed for time. I'm in your neighborhood and I wonder if I could drop by in the next hour."

Abrahamowitz was more or less free, but he was not thrilled by the prospect of the indicted pimp showing up in the English department. So he named a restaurant six blocks away. "The food isn't so hot in this neighborhood," he said, "but this particular place is first rate, because it's right near the courthouse, and you know lawyers. They won't stand for anything but the best."

"Half an hour," said Smooth.

As he walked past row upon row of cut-rate furniture stores, religious-medallion stores, and pizza parlors Abrahamowitz felt a drumming of both excitement and apprehension at the prospect of meeting Smooth. He had never spent time with an indicted fellow. What did Smooth want from him? Money? That was ridiculous, since by his own admission the industrious young flesh peddler had tons of it. Legal counsel? Abrahamowitz, in his divorce, had been represented by a firm that was so exalted and dignified that he himself was afraid to call them up or visit them. Billings, Cohen and Le Tournier represented corporations, retired diplomats, entire western states that were in boundary disputes with adjoining territories. How would it look to show up at their offices with Smooth, even though he wasn't exactly ashamed of him? Abrahamowitz felt the reason he was always in such hot water in the alimony department was that he was too embarrassed to take up any of the law firm's time. What if he asked them a lowly question about alimony reduction, threw off their rhythm and as a result a northern county of Oklahoma lost its natural gas rights to a greedy neighbor. So he couldn't help the troubled pimp in this department. Maybe Smooth simply wanted the comfort of being with an older-brother type and a friend, which, of course, was preposterous. With his street-wise intelligence, surely he had grasped the fact that Abrahamowitz was a loner, temporarily—perhaps permanently—sealed off from the world, unable to give help or solace to any other human being except perhaps a tiny little bit to his ex-family.

At the Jury Box Restaurant, Smooth wasted little time in getting to the point. Before the waiter arrived to take their lunch order, the soft-spoken pimp said that he was going to be taking a little vacation in the near future.

"I'll be going away for from three to seven . . ."

"So I've heard," said Abrahamowitz.

"What do you mean?" said Smooth, with a sharpness Abrahamowitz hadn't seen before. Apparently he was touchy about his legal situation. Abrahamowitz saw that he would have to tread softly. He also decided Smooth would be able to take care of himself in prison.

"I hadn't exactly *heard,*" said Abrahamowitz. "I just figured you fellows get a lot of leisure time."

Smooth cocked his head quizzically, making a judgment. After a few beats he relaxed and offered his proposal.

"How'd you like to take over the operation for a while? During the period I'm in absentia?"

"I don't follow you," said Abrahamowitz, who was actually following him very closely. "What do you mean?"

"You know, run the game. Take care of the birds, check the traps, do the collecting. Half goes to you and you hold my half till I return from resting up."

"I don't know anything about such things," said Abrahamowitz, sneaking a hand over to his chest to check his heartbeat. "I've got my teaching—"

"There's not much to it," said Smooth. "I can go into the details later. I just wanted to get a sense of your general reaction."

"I hardly know what to say," said Abrahamowitz, who, as Smooth must have noted, did not give him a flat-out no. "How would it be for a college professor to be a pimp? Incidentally, I hope you don't mind my use of the word."

"That's perfectly all right," said Smooth. "You see, that's why I figured you'd be effective. Nobody would be quick to put you together with the game."

"The last thing I am is smooth," said Abrahamowitz, a bit weakly.

"You're smoother than you think, Abrim." With that, Smooth picked up a shoe box he had brought along and gestured discreetly toward the men's room.

"Come along inside there with me," said Smooth. "I'd like to show you something."

"What have you got, a hot watch?" said Abrahamowitz, a nervously lame joke that Smooth beat back with a cool glance. The pimp then led the way to the restroom; Abrahamowitz followed, eyes on the mysterious shoe box, recalling for an instant Abrahamowitz & Sons, the medium-huge empire of his forebears that had ruled the Lower East Side hosiery game until the four shiftless and lazy Abrahamowitz brothers (his uncles and his own dad) let it go to seed. Inside, Smooth peered around to make sure there were no eavesdropping lawyers in the stalls. Satisfied they were alone, he lifted the lid of the box and showed Abrahamowitz the contents: bills, in individual stacks, tied together with string. They were weathered and tragic-looking bills, indeed, but Abrahamowitz spotted batches of fifties, not to mention a thick border of hundreds along the sides.

"Now, this here is the type of money the operation gets involved with," said Smooth. He might have been a salesman showing Abrahamowitz slacks. "What you're looking at, for example, is fifty thousand dollars, which is the take for the bimonthly period." Outside of the movies, it was the most cash Abrahamowitz had ever seen. His own yearly full-time-professor's salary? It could have filled a matchbox. He had to restrain an impulse to reach in, take a fistful and worry about the consequences later. A lawyer came in to use the urinal and Smooth quickly snapped the box shut. "I've secreted the widow in a remote section of Long Island," Smooth said, adopting a barrister's tone, "while the battle over trustees ensues." Smooth certainly did think with lightning speed. Abrahamowitz tried desperately to think of something legalistic to say in reply. "Torts," he hollered out finally, causing the urinating attorney to wheel around.

"So what do you think, Abrim," said Smooth when they had returned to their table. He rocked his chair back and snapped his fingers to get the waiter's attention. "You in or you out?"

"I guess I'd better say out," said Abrahamowitz.

"I didn't ask what you'd *better* say," said Smooth, with a slight trace of contempt. "I asked what *do* you say."

"I can't handle it," said Abrahamowitz.

"Tell you what," said Smooth. "Take a couple of days to think it over. I'll be occupied with making preparations for my trip anyway. Then you let me know." He did some scribbling on a matchbook, which he then handed to Abrahamowitz. "Now here's three numbers. You can reach me at one of them. Deal?"

"Deal," said Abrahamowitz, who always leapt at a chance to put off a decision.

The waiter appeared and handed them menus.

"Don't even bother to read it," said Abrahamowitz. "I know what's good. Take the stuffed derma."

Smooth raised his head slowly and fixed Abrahamowitz with a look so terrifying that he no longer feared for the pimp but for the other prisoners. Then, not taking his eyes off Abrahamowitz for an instant, he addressed the waiter.

"I'll have the cheese blintzes, a double order of kasha varnishkes, and a diet celery tonic."

For the next several days, Abrahamowitz wrestled with the sweet-talking Smooth's proposition. Should he give him a flat-out no, or try his hand at the pimping game? On the one hand, it was preposterous—a man of letters overseeing a troupe of hookers. He would be out of business in a week. (Abrahamowitz had noted, incidentally, that Smooth's rival, the vicious French Fries, so quick to use a razor, had eluded the police roundup.) On the other hand, there was the shoe box full of money, which represented a mere taste of Smooth's annual gross receipts. Even a handful would solve so many of his problems— bring him up to date on alimony and enable him to move out of his stuffy one-room rear apartment and perhaps put a deposit down on a terrific three-roomer he had looked at wistfully, one with a charming glassed-in French dining area in a reconverted town house. And there would be money left over for that battered, windswept house he was almost positive he wanted on a deserted section of the Maine coastline.

Still, Smooth's proposition, to put it mildly, represented a minefield of dangers. If word ever leaked out, he would be finished in higher education. But to look at it another way: Where exactly was he going in higher education? For sixteen years he had kicked around on grubby little fellowships and temporary appointments. Like an idiot, he had never signed up for a pension plan—the forms were too complicated. He had put in three years at Monrose, but there wasn't a chance in hell that Dean Kiltar would allow him to achieve tenure. Anyone who had been present when Kiltar observed his Classical Irony session and listened to Abrahamowitz make a hash of Juvenal's Third Satire could have told you this.

Then there was the moral and ethical question, of which he had barely scratched the surface. Again he thought of the bills in Smooth's shoe box. Did he want to achieve financial security through money that had lonely dreams and come on it? He tried to view this in another light: the girls had presumably given pleasure, gotten some cash for themselves. If they were Smooth's girls, it was a safe guess that they had not hit their customers on the head. In the great universal scheme, who had actually suffered?

Setting aside questions of morality for the moment, there was the hard issue of criminal behavior. If a girl had ratted on the streetwise

Smooth, why wouldn't another spill the beans on the outrageously naïve Abrahamowitz? He would wind up in a cell right next to Smooth. Abrahamowitz was of two minds about prison—as he was about everything else. On the one hand, he might finally get some peace and quiet. But what if he got a sudden urge for a cheeseburger one night and found the guards unsympathetic? He knew himself. He would smash his head against the bars. Add to this the fact that if Smooth was even a marginal candidate for homosexuality, Abrahamowitz was a dead duck. They'd have him turned into a gay the second he set foot inside prison walls. He had devoted a great deal of thought to this subject and come to the conclusion that it was not his cup of tea. (Maybe years later, in Naples, with an urchin.)

On the subject of hookers in general, Abrahamowitz, were the truth to be told, was not so naïve as his professorial demeanor might have indicated. He'd had quite a little romance with them over the years, starting with a pair of teenage sisters he had encountered while on a fellowship at the University of Puerto Rico. "Fucky, fucky," the older one whispered in his left ear; "Sucky, sucky," her sister said in his other ear; and for fifty dollars he was off to the races. For ten years, every once in a while he would slip off and find a hooker, and this was not because his marriage was shaky. He liked the very coldness of the transaction. As a youngster, growing up in Queens, he often felt he would lay down his life for a single glimpse of the outer aureole of one of Kathryn Grayson's filmdom breasts. For him it remained miraculous that he could simply plunk down some money to buy a strange woman's body, getting aureoles to his heart's content—imagining, if he preferred, that they were those of the imperious Grayson herself. Some said what good was it—you couldn't buy the girl's soul. That was the whole point. What did he need her soul for? Where was he going with it? In truth, Abrahamowitz would still be going to hookers if it hadn't been for a chance remark he had overheard in a cafeteria: "Hookers don't work hard enough for their money." The truth was: Some did and some didn't. But that was a side issue. He liked the sound of the remark and stopped going to them. That's the way he was—he would change the course of his life on the basis of a stray bit of wisdom, one he had reached out and caught as if it were a fly ball. Also, giving up hookers gave him a chance to renounce another pleasure—for Abrahamowitz, a pleasure in itself.

Though he kept focusing on the shoe box loaded with soiled but tax-free fifties and hundreds, it was not so much the money that kept him toying with Smooth's proposition. In one corridor of himself, he enjoyed being hard-pressed and financially put upon. For all his complaining, he had heat and shelter and ate in ethnic restaurants that weren't exactly dirt cheap. At some point later in his life he might want to take a round-the-world cruise, but he was in no hurry. His clothes, for some mysterious reason, never wore out; vainly he waited for sweaters that were seventeen years old to get a little frayed around the sleeves. The fact that he was always behind in alimony to his wife, who had fled with his daughters to sunny California, gave him shivers of martyrdom.

It was not, finally, the dollars that made him vulnerable to Smooth's farfetched proposition. Taking a cold look at his life, Abrahamowitz could see clearly that his options were running out. He was forty-eight. One by one his dreams had been picked off at the plate. He still felt there was poetry in him, but it was too late to pry it out. At thirty-eight, yes. At forty-eight, no. When his wife had fled to the West Coast during his hemorrhoid operation, he dreamed, upon recovery, of a shy, scholarly, flaxen-haired girl who would take her place, occupying a quietly supportive corner of his life. He was still waiting—but he no longer held his breath.

Apart from certain hotly spiced ethnic foods, life no longer had any taste to it. He lacked the ambition to turn on the TV set. One by one his friends drifted away when he didn't return their calls, not that he'd had a crowd of them to begin with.

He had loved his daughters but he noticed that when the summers came he didn't rush to the West Coast to see them, even though he could have gotten a special professor's ticket discount. He was an "old" forty-eight. Like an idiot, he asked strangers how old he looked, and most guessed fifty-five. As a desperate measure he had shaved off his beard, and come out looking older. What was left for him? Walks in the park? Marriage to a middle-aged psychiatrist with a stock portfolio and a thick waistline? It was true that he enjoyed some measure of success as a teacher and that students, mysteriously, flocked from far and wide to attend his irony classes. But how could he account for their collectively hollow look while he struggled to be charming and ironic? And if they loved irony so much, why was there a groan when he sneaked an extra book into the syllabus, an Evelyn Waugh they might love?

Still and all, after weighing the pluses and minuses of Smooth's offer, he came to the only possible conclusion for a civilized man—no soap. The idea of becoming a middle-aged pimp while continuing to teach a full schedule at Monrose College was preposterous. And this is exactly what he intended to convey to the well-intentioned Smooth, when a little birdie whispered into his ear: "Abrahamowitz. Don't be a fool.

You're leading a stuffy and selfish life. Let a little air in. All you are doing is tap-dancing, waiting around to die. Time is running out. Take a shot."

It was late at night, and he had stopped at a corner pay telephone, one of the few in the neighborhood that had not been ripped out by vandals. He tried one number, then a second and finally reached Smooth at the third. Henry's Motor Lodge, room 1214. "Who's this speaking?" asked Smooth.

Abrahamowitz said nothing.

"Who is this?"

More silence while he flailed about for terminology.

And then, a beat later, with a knot at the end of his voice, Abrahamowitz spoke.

"Smooth?"

"Yes, yes, who *is* it?"

Abrahamowitz let out a long, deep sigh, hesitated one last time, then dove in.

"This is Detroit Abe."

A Change of Plan

AND SO FINALLY, after four years of drift, they had found all exits barricaded and gotten married in a sudden spurt, bombing their parents with the news. A Justice had been rounded up, also uncles in the area. After the ceremony, Cantrow's new father-in-law had taken him around and said, "It's going to be great, isn't it."

"How can you say that?" said a stray uncle, wandering by. "Which one of us knows such things? Maybe it will. Then again, maybe it won't." That night there was a need to get away, to sail as quickly as possible into the eye of the marriage, and off they went, south, driving in a frenzy, all that afternoon, all that night. Once, bleary-eyed, they had gone through a Southern town with two wheels up on a sidewalk. Later, moving through a misted patch of farmland, Cantrow spotted a monster turkey, his first live one, and gunned the motor, thinking it was a dreaded hawk. Only once had they stopped, for chocolate frosteds, Cantrow tipping his into her lap. With soaked shorts, she broke into laughter, then chuckled her way through five more towns. This is the kind of sense of humor she has, Cantrow thought. And I didn't even catch that.

Curling from side to side, as though the car itself were drunk, they were somehow blessed, missing head-on collisions; at the hotel, Cantrow told the clerk, "We're not bums," and got a room. Upstairs, zombielike, they made a feeble pass at sex, wanting to try it married, but collapsed instead into sleep. Two hours later, hardly fresh, Cantrow awoke and stared at his bride's slack form. So that's what I've got, he thought. Maybe for forty-seven years.

Down below, at poolside, the lifeguard winked and said, "Ho, ho, ho," a standard greeting to honeymooners. The pool water slapped Cantrow awake; so did a blond girl, sitting at the edge. She had a nice fleshiness, a good hundred thirty pounds to his bride's hundred four. He caught her scent, too, just like honey. He had never really smelled honey, but guessed it must be in that family.

"I didn't know they allowed big puppies in pools," she said. And now there was her voice, crushed, feminine for a change. At a club, once, he had introduced his bride to a football-star friend of his. "She's okay,"

74

the friend had said privately, "but I could never live with those pipes of hers."

Cantrow fished himself out of the water and sat by the girl's side. She was eighteen, from Minnesota, vacationing between semesters. These were her folks, at the terrace bar, the heavyset man and the handsome woman in the white silk dress. Cantrow and the girl kidded around, wound up tickling each other. Then the shadow of the hotel seemed to fall on his back like a heavy beam. "You probably know I'm married," he said. "Just since yesterday. Down here on my honeymoon."

"And what else is new," she said. Cheered on, Cantrow told her some jokes; they teased each other. But there was a whisper of difference. Before it became a roar, Cantrow suddenly panicked, took her arm and said, "Look, this is crazy, but I've got to see you one more time and find out something. I really have to." Their glances met, combined, turned soft together.

"We don't stay here," she said. "At the Regent."

"I'll be there at six," he said. "I'll work it out. For cocktails."

"Guess who I met at the pool," he told his bride, later, in the room. "Crazy guy from school, Blaum, always wore a tooth around his neck, called it the Sacred Tooth of Mickasee. Didn't care what you did to him, beat him up, anything, long as you didn't touch his tooth. 'Fool with my tooth and you're in trouble,' he'd say to you. Anyway, I told him I'd meet him later tonight for a drink. No girls, though. He's not himself when any are around and I want to see him carry on about that tooth again." He hurried on. "I'll just have a quick one with him and then I'll come back and we can really start."

In the early evening, he dressed carefully, getting his hair just right, one loop down over the eye, with feigned carelessness, for extra appeal. At the Regent, she sat with her folks at a table, but joined him immediately at the bar. He liked the size of her in heels, the weight of her, the bounce of her hair, the honeyed look. A combo began to work in a deep beat; he gathered her in, made it once around the floor, then put his nose in her hair and said, "That did it. Over to your folks we go."

The parents were pushed back from the table, comfortable, expectant, as though waiting for a curtain to part. Cantrow stood before them and began to speak, then said, "Hold it a second," and unbuckled his belt for comfort. "Okay, sir," he said, "I've just made one helluva mistake, about the biggest one a guy can make. But I met your daughter and I'm undoing it, no matter what it takes. You see, I got married yesterday and I'm down here on my honeymoon, but it was a bad idea from the beginning. There wasn't a damned thing in the world between us and I just got married because it seemed like the only way out. Anyway, I met your daughter and she's the one I want. I know it's crazy, but I could tell in a second. You should see the difference between them. There's no comparison. I just had to be with her a few minutes and I saw all the things I was really after. She's easier, more feminine, just real comfortable to be with. I don't know exactly what I expect from you. What I'd like, really, is for you to study the look in my eyes and know that I've never been more sincere in my life and that I'm not fooling around and that I'm the right guy for her. I'm getting out of the thing and then I'm coming after your daughter, but I just wanted to lay it out on the table and see how it struck you, whether you were with me or against me."

The father yawned, drummed his fingers on the table and said, "Not if they stripped me naked and dragged me four times around the world. Over the desert, through the jungle, under the seven seas."

"Okay," said Cantrow. "Long as we're clear. But you don't know me, sir. You don't know what I can do. I'm coming after her anyway. Once I make up my mind on something, that's it.

"First thing I've got to do is get out of it," he said, with a bow to the parents. "You take it easy, honey," he said, pecking her on the cheek.

"But I listen to my father," she said, as he walked to the door.

"Another thing about you that turns me on."

Pale and angular, Cantrow's bride slapped on pancake before a mirror. "Hold it, hold it," he said, tearing into the room. "Whoa. We're not going out tonight. Any night, for that matter, unless we meet some day later on as platonic friends, and I'm not even really sure of that. There was no Blaum and no tooth. That is, there *is* a Blaum and the tooth part was no lie either, but I didn't just meet him. It's a new girl I ran into at the pool. I don't see any point in describing what went on, because that would be just like waving a red flag in your face. What's important is us and how flat it's always been when you take away those first few weeks, just one, if you really want to be strict about it. Look, I'm pulling out. I admit, I shouldn't have gone this far, but I didn't see it clearly until just before at the pool. There's a whole other way. With us, it would be one long downhill ride. Get yourself someone else. I admit, I'll be a little shaky on that issue if I stop and think about it, but I can stand it. Meanwhile, I'm on my way."

"And I'm supposed to just listen to that."

"Oh, we can kick it around if you like," said Cantrow, packing, "but how'd you like to lift this hotel on your back and move it across the street. That's roughly what you'd be up against trying to talk me out of this thing I've got in my head. Look, here's three hundred dollars for openers. I'm throwing in the car and just holler if you think that's not generous. The funny thing is, as we're making this break, I'm starting to like you more already.

"Maybe," he said, slamming shut his suitcase, "years later, when the sting is out of it for both of us, we really *can* meet for dinner."

That night, Cantrow flew north and woke up Wenger, his attorney-cousin, at midnight. "Cantrow with an emergency," he said. "Remember that marriage I told you about? I've got to get out of it now. We were just hitched for the shortest time you can imagine and then the whole thing blew up. Anyway, I'm actually out of it already since there isn't anything—tornadoes, nuclear war, you name it—that could get me back in. So you just take care of the legal part. I've got five grand from the service and believe me it wasn't easy to save. Cut down on everything, meals included, to get it together. Anyway, use the whole bundle if you need to and keep the change. Just get me out."

"If we weren't cousins, you wouldn't call me at this hour."

"I'll stick around one week, in case there are papers. Then I'm getting into something else."

"Hi, Mom," said Cantrow at his folks' apartment. "The entire marriage is down the drain, but don't worry, I'm in good health and got out clean."

"I saw the whole thing coming," said Cantrow's mother. "If you'd asked me, I could have recited the entire story before it happened. Okay, how about a trip to Europe, all expenses for a month. To clear your head."

"No, Mom, I'm bunking in here for a week, then I've got to go out to the Midwest on something."

"I knew it," she said. "Another little winner. One wasn't enough for my son. I can tell you the end of this story, too, if you want to sit and listen."

With great crankiness, Wenger gave the go-ahead and Cantrow took a plane west, then tracked the girl down to a small teachers' college of Episcopal persuasion. Off-campus she lived with her folks and came home for meals. His first night in town, Cantrow announced his presence to her mother at the door. "Hi, you probably remember me from the resort hotel. I don't expect you to let me see your daughter right

off, but I thought I'd let you know I'm here and that wasn't a wild story
I'd made up when I saw you at the bar."

"My daughter's preparing for bed," said the mother, easing the door
shut. "She studies very hard and needs her sleep."

Later that night, Cantrow asked around and smoked out his one
rival, a fair-skinned fellow of strange, shifting sexuality. Sliding in beside him at a bleakly lit campus hangout, Cantrow ordered the local
special, beer and braunschweiger sandwiches, and said, "Hi, I've just
gotten down here and what I'm after is Sue Ellen Parker. Now look, we
can do this like gentlemen, you just tapering off with another date or
two to save face, or else we can go to muscle. You look pretty well set
up, but the point is, if we fight, it doesn't matter how it goes. If you
take me boxing, I'll bring in karate and if you know that I'll go to
guns."

"Would you really do all those things?" said the fellow with a wet
stare, kaleidoscopically shifting sexes before Cantrow's very eyes.

The road partially clear, Cantrow called the girl herself. "I'd be teasing
if I pretended not to be flattered, but it's just so completely out of the
question," she said. "I mean with Mother and Dad. And me, sort of."
Undismayed, driven, Cantrow hung on, peppered her with calls, nour-
ished himself on her great phone voice. One night that honeyed blond
fragrance seemed to trickle through the wire. She said she would sneak
out and meet him on the corner. Cantrow hired a car, scooped her up
and off they drove in silence to a wooded place she knew. Thin, tower-
ing Minnesota trees, crowded together, stripped and haunted. "I won't
sleep with you tonight," she said, as they left the car, "but let's take off
our clothes and run through there, as far as we can go."

"Suits me," said Cantrow, knowing instantly he'd been right about
her.

And so they began. All the things he had missed. Nude walks and
swims. Hours of savoring honeyed flesh. Sudden love, almost anywhere, under stairwells, beneath a tree. Giving everything. Wonder of
wonders. Getting back. "I knew I wasn't crazy," he told her one night,
bewitched, at some lake's edge. "It must have been a hell of a jolt to all
concerned, but I knew I was on the right track."

A month later she phoned, out of breath. "Dad's calling a truce.
From now on, it's the front door for us, darling." Legitimate now,
Cantrow arrived that night in a suit and tie. "I never thought I'd see
the day I'd be doing this," said her father. "But let's have us a handshake. You Eastern fellows sure are determined. Well, more power to
you, son."

Later that night, passion undiminished, they made love in the parlor. The next night in her very room. Pacing himself, Cantrow waited another week, then told her, "Look, I haven't been fooling around."

"I know, darling, I feel the same way. I've already said something and the folks' answer is, of course, anything we want."

With blurred speed, the wedding plans were made. Cantrow's folks declined, but Wenger, the lawyer, came west with the final papers. Soon Cantrow, who had always dreamed of tails, stood erect in them and watched strange blond people with great Scandinavian profiles mill around him at the church. Mr. Parker came over, cuffed him in friendliness and said, "Now this is one for the books, isn't it. The first time you came up to us and now here we are. I think it's great though, kind of thing you see in the movies." He disappeared in a swirl of guests. Mrs. Parker took his place. Solid, tanned gold, an easeful ripened version of her daughter. She took his arm and said, "I want you to know how warming I find all of this. And I have a confession to make. Even at the hotel I just knew. There was something so profound about the cast of your neck and shoulders."

"And how about how I feel?" said Cantrow. "I get sick when I think of how I could have let the whole thing slide and muffed the chance of a lifetime. Sue Ellen. Being here in Minnesota. The things that have happened. Mr. Parker. You. Even the way you just said that. That it was all so warming. And what was that word you used about my neck and shoulders. You know once in a while I'd check myself in mirrors and there really was something about them, although I guess I'd be the last one to say it about myself. But what was that you called them? *Profound.*

"Oh, Jesus, look," he said, covering her hand. "I wonder if we could just talk for a second. I'll talk and you don't say a word till I'm finished."

The Mourner

ONE DAY, MARTIN GANS found himself driving out to the Long Island funeral of Norbert Mandel, a total stranger. A habit of his was to take a quick check of the obit section in the New York *Times* each day, concentrating on the important deaths, then scanning the medium-famous ones and some of the also-rans. The listing that caught his eye on this particular day was that of Norbert Mandel, although Gans did not have the faintest idea why he should be interested in the passing of this obscure fellow. The item said that Mandel, of Syosset, Long Island, had died of a heart attack at the age of seventy-three, leaving behind two sisters, Rose and Sylvia, also one son, a Brooklyn optometrist named Phillip. It said, additionally, that Mandel had served on an East Coast real-estate board and many years back had been in the Coast Guard. An ordinary life, God knows, with nothing flashy about it, at least on the surface. Gans read the item in a vacant, mindless way, but suddenly found his interest stirred, a fire breaking out with no apparent source. Was it the sheer innocuousness of the item? Of Mandel's life? He traveled on to other sections of the paper, sports and even maritime, but the Mandel story now began to prick at him in a way that he could not ignore; he turned back to the modest paragraph and read it again and again, until he knew it by heart and felt a sweeping compulsion to race out to Mandel's funeral, which was being held in a memorial chapel on the south shore of Long Island.

If this had happened at some idle point in his life, it might have made some sense. But Gans was busier than ever, involved in moving his ceramics plant to a new location on Lower Fifth Avenue, after twenty years of being in the same place. It was aggravating work; even after the move, it would take six months before Gans really settled in to the new quarters. Yet you could hardly call Mandel's funeral a diversion. A trip to Puerto Rico would have been that. Nor was Gans the type of fellow who particularly enjoyed funerals. His mother and father were still living. No one terribly close to him had died up to now, just some aunts and uncles and a couple of nice friends whose deaths annoyed rather than grieved him. Gans had probably contributed to one aunt's death, come to think of it. A woman in the hospital bed next to Aunt Edna had attacked a book the visiting Gans held under his arm.

Gans struck back, defending the volume, and a debate began over poor Aunt Edna's head, as she fought a tattered intravenous battle for life.

The day of Mandel's funeral, Gans took a slow drive to the memorial chapel, allowing an extra half-hour for possible traffic problems and the chance that he might lose his way on the south shore, which had always been tricky going for him. On the way, he thought a little about Mandel. He pictured him in an overcoat, also with a beard, although a totally nonrakish one. Mandel struck him as being a tea drinker and someone who dressed carefully against the cold, owning a good stock of mufflers and galoshes. Gans did not particularly like Mandel's association with the East Coast real-estate board, but at the same time, he saw him as a small property owner, not really that much at home with the big boys and actually a decent fellow who was a soft touch. He liked the sound of Mandel's two sisters, Rose and Sylvia, envisioning them as buxom, good-natured, wonderful cooks, enjoying a good pinch on the ass, provided it remained on the hearty and non-erotic side. Phillip, the optometrist, struck Gans as being a momma's boy, into a bit of a ball-breaking marriage, but not too bad a fellow; the Army, Gans felt, had probably toughened him up a bit. There was a chance, of course, that Gans was completely wide of the mark, but these were his speculations as he breezed out to the chapel to get in on the funeral of Norbert Mandel, a fellow he didn't know from Adam.

The chapel was part of an emporium that lay just outside a shopping center and was used as well for bar mitzvahs and catered affairs of all kinds. An attendant in a chauffeur's uniform took his car, saying, "No sweat, I'll see it don't get wet." Inside the carpeted chapel, a funeral-parlor employee asked him if he was there, perchance, for Benjamin Siegal. "No, Norbert Mandel," said Gans. The attendant said they had Mandel on the second floor. Before climbing the stairs, Gans stopped to relieve himself in the chapel john and realized he always did that before going in to watch funeral services. Did this have some significance, he wondered, a quick expulsion of guilt, a swift return to a pure state? Or was it just the long drives?

There was only a small turnout for Mandel. Those on hand had not even bothered to spread out and make the place seem a little busier. Mandel's friends and relatives were all gathered together in the first half-dozen rows, giving the chapel the look of an off-Broadway show that had opened to generally poor notices. Gans estimated that he was about fifteen minutes early, but he had the feeling that few additional mourners were going to turn up and he was right about that. Somehow he had sensed that Mandel was not going to draw much of a crowd. Was that why he had come? To help the box office? Come to think of it, funeral attendance had been on his mind for some time. He had been particularly worried, for example, that his father, once the old man went under, would draw only a meager crowd. His father kept to himself, had only a sprinkling of friends. If Gans had to make up a list of mourners for his dad, he was sure he would not be able to go beyond a dozen the old man could count on to turn up, rain or shine. This was troubling to Gans; in addition, he wondered what there was a rabbi could actually say about his dad. That he was a nice man, kept his nose clean? First of all, he wasn't that nice. People see an old grandmother crossing a street and assume she's a saint. She might have been a triple ax murderer as a young girl in Poland and gotten away with it, thanks to lax Polish law enforcement. Who said old was automatically good and kind? Who said old and short meant gentle and well meaning? Gans's own funeral was an entirely different story. He wasn't worried much about that one. At least not about the turnout. He had a million friends and they would be sure to pack the place. His mother, too, could be counted on to fill at least three-quarters of any house: if you got a good rabbi, who knew something about her, who could really get her essence, there wouldn't be much of a problem in coming up with send-off anecdotes. She didn't belong to any organizations, but she had handed out plenty of laughs in her time. It would be a tremendous shame if she were handled by some rabbi who didn't know the first thing about her. He had often thought of doing his mother's eulogy himself; but wouldn't that be like a playwright composing his own notices?

Gans felt a little conspicuous, sitting in the back by himself, and didn't relax until three middle-aged ladies came in and took seats a row in front of him. He had them figured for cousins from out of town who had taken a train in from Philadelphia. They did not seem deeply pained by the loss of Mandel and might have been preparing to see a Wednesday matinee on Broadway. Their combined mood seemed to range from aloof to bitter, and Gans guessed they were on the outs with the family, probably over some long-standing quarrel involving the disposition of family jewelry and china. Gans had little difficulty picking out Rose and Sylvia, Norbert's sisters, who were seated in the front row, wearing black veils and black fur coats. They wept and blew their noses and seemed deeply troubled by Mandel's death, which had come out of the blue. Phillip, the only son, was a complete surprise to Gans. Gans assumed he was the one who was wedged between Rose and Sylvia in the front row. He was certainly no momma's boy. He was every bit of six-three and you could see beneath his clothes that he was a bodybuilder. His jaw was tight, his features absolutely perfect, and you simply wouldn't want to mess with him. Let a woman get smart with this optometrist and she'd wind up with her head in the next county. What woman would want to get smart with him? Jump through a few hoops is what a girl would prefer doing for this customer.

The rabbi came out at a little trot, a slender fellow with brown disappearing hair and rimless glasses—ideal, Gans felt, for a career in crime investigation, since he was totally inconspicuous. Gans did not know much about rabbis, but when this fellow began to speak, he could see that his was the "new style"; that is, totally unflamboyant, low-pressure, very modest, very Nixon Administration in his approach to the pulpit. As he spoke, one of the sisters, either Rose or Sylvia, cried in the background, the bursts of tears and pity coming at random, not really coinciding with any particularly poignant sections in the rabbi's address. "I regret to say that I did not know the departed one very well," he began. "However, those close to him assure me that this was, indeed, my great loss. The late Norbert Mandel, whom we are here to send to his well-earned rest this day, was, by all accounts, a decent, fair, kind, generous, charitable man who led a totally exemplary life." He went on to say that death, sorrowful as it must seem to those left behind in the valley of the living, was not a tragedy when one looked upon it as a life-filled baton being passed from one generation to another or, perhaps, as the satisfying final act of a lifetime drama, fully and truly lived. "And who can say this was not the case with the beloved Norbert Mandel, from his early service to his country in the Coast Guard, right along to his unstinting labors on behalf of the East Coast real-estate board; a life in which the unselfish social gesture was always a natural reflex, rather than something that had to be painfully extracted from him."

"Hold it right there," said Gans, rising to his feet in the rear of the chapel.

"Shame," said one of the Philadelphia women.

"What's up?" asked the rabbi.

"You didn't even know this man," said Gans.

"I recall making that point quite early in my remarks," said the rabbi.

"How can you just toss him into the ground?" said Gans. "You haven't told anything about him. That was a man there. He cut himself a lot shaving. He had pains in his stomach. Why don't you try to tell them how he felt when he lost a job? The hollowness of it. Why don't you go into things like his feelings when someone said kike to him the first time? What about all the time he clocked worrying about cancer? And then didn't even die from it. How did he feel when he had the kid, the boy who's sitting over there? What about the curious mixture of feelings toward his sisters, the tenderness on one hand and, on the

other hand, the feelings he couldn't exercise, because you're not allowed to in this society? How about some of that stuff, rabbi?"

"And they're just letting him talk?" said one of the Philadelphia
women.

"They're not throwing him out?" said another. But Rose and Sylvia
kept sobbing bitterly, so awash in sorrow the sisters appeared not to
have even realized that Gans had taken over from the rabbi. Gans was
concerned about only one person, the well-built son Phillip; but, to his
surprise, the handsome optometrist only buried his head in his hands,
as though he were a ballplayer being scolded at halftime by an angry
coach. The rabbi was silent, concerned, as though the new style was
determined to be moderate and conciliatory, no matter what went on
in the chapel. It's a big religion, the rabbi seemed to be saying by his
thoughtful silence, with plenty of room for the excessive.

Up until now, it had been a kind of exercise for Gans, but the heat
of his own words began to excite him. "Can you really say you're doing
justice to this man?" he asked. "Or are you insulting him? Do you
know how he felt? Do you know anything about his disappointments?
How he wanted to be taller? To you, he's Norbert Mandel, who led an
exemplary life. What about the women he longed for and couldn't get?
How he spent half his life sunk in grief over things like that. And the
other half picking his nose and worrying about getting caught at it. Do
you know the way he felt about yellow-haired girls and how he went
deaf, dumb and blind when one he liked came near him? Shouldn't
some of that be brought out? He wanted blondes right into his seventies; but did he ever get a taste of them? Not on your life. It was
Mediterranean types all the way. Shouldn't you take a minute of your
time to get into how he felt about his son, the pride when the kid filled
out around the shoulders and became tougher than Norbie would ever
be, and the jealousy, too, that made him so ashamed and guilty? Do
you have any idea what he went through, playing the kid a game, beating him and then wanting to cut off his arm for it? Then letting the kid
win a game and that was no good, either. You act as though you've
scratched the surface. Don't make me laugh, will you please. You know
about his vomiting when he drank too much? On the highway. How do
you think that felt? What about a little something else you're leaving
out? Those last moments when he knew something was up and he had
to look death right in the face. What was that for him, a picnic? I'll tell
you, rabbi, you ought to pull him right out of the coffin and take a look
at him and find out a little bit about who you're talking about."

"There was a time," said Phillip, the sole surviving son, as though he
had received a cue, "when he left the family for a month or so. He was
around, but he wasn't with us. He got very gray and solemn and didn't

eat. We found out it was because an insurance doctor told him he had a terrible heart and couldn't have life insurance. He called him an 'uninsurable.' That was something, having an uninsurable for a dad. It was a mistake—his heart was healthy at the time—but it was the longest month of my life. The other time that comes to mind is when he shut someone up on the el when we were going out to Coney Island. Shut him up like you never saw anyone shut up. Guy twice his size."

"Very touching," said the rabbi. "Now may I ask how you knew the deceased?"

"I used to see him around," said Gans.

"Fine," said the rabbi. "Well, I don't see why we can't have this once in a while. And all be a little richer for it. If the family doesn't object. Do you have anything else?"

"Nothing I can think of," said Gans. "Unless some of the other members of the family would like to sound off a bit."

"He had a heart of solid gold," said one of the sisters.

"He was some man," said the other.

"Sounds like he was quite a fellow," said the rabbi.

Gans had no plan to do so originally but decided now to go out to the burial grounds, using his own car instead of accepting the offered ride in one of the rented limousines. After Mandel had been put into the ground, Gans accepted an offer from one of the sisters, whom he now knew to be Rose, to come back and eat with the family in a Queens delicatessen. Gans's own mother had always been contemptuous of that particular ritual, mocking families who were able to wolf down delicatessen sandwiches half an hour after a supposedly beloved uncle or cousin had been tossed into the earth. "They're very grief-stricken," she would say, "you can tell by their appetites." Gans, as a result, had developed a slight prejudice against the custom, although the logical part of him said why not eat if you're hungry and not eat if you're not. There seemed to be a larger crowd at the delicatessen than had been at the funeral. And it wasn't delicatessen food they were eating, either; it was Rose's cooking. Evidently, the family had merely taken over the restaurant for the afternoon, but Rose had brought in her own food. Gans had some difficulty meeting young Phillip's eyes and Phillip seemed equally ill at ease with him. Gans could not get over how wrong he had been about the boy. He had had an entirely different feeling about what a Brooklyn optometrist should look like. This fellow was central casting for the dark-haired hero in Hollywood Westerns. Even the right gait, slow and sensual; Gans wondered if he had ever thought seriously about a career in show business. Gans ate a hearty meal, and there was something in his attack on the food that seemed to indicate he had earned it. He sat at the same table as Phillip, who ate dreamily, speculatively and seemed, gradually, to get comfortable with the mysterious visitor who had taken over the funeral service.

"You know," said Phillip, "a lot of people never realized this, but he was one hell of an athlete. He had two trophies for handball, and if you know the Brooklyn playground league, you know they don't fool around. And a guy once offered him a tryout with the Boston Bees." The boy paused then, as if he expected a nostalgic anecdote in return from Gans.

Instead, Gans took a deep breath, tilted his chair back slightly and said, "I have to come clean, I never met the man in my life."

"What do you mean?" said Phillip, hunching his big shoulders a bit, although he seemed more puzzled than annoyed. "I don't understand."

Gans hesitated a moment, looking around at the sisters, Rose and Sylvia, at the cousins from Philly, who seemed much more convivial, now that they were eating, at the rabbi, who had come over for a little snack, and at the other mourners. He complimented himself on how easily he had fitted into the group, and it occurred to him that most families, give or take a cousin or two, are remarkably similar, the various members more or less interchangeable.

"I don't know," he said, finally, to the blindingly handsome optometrist, sole surviving offspring of the freshly buried Norbert Mandel. "I read about your dad in the paper and I had the feeling they were just going to throw him into the ground, and that would be the end of him. Bam, kaput, just like he never lived. So I showed up.

"Now that I think of it," he said, reaching for a slice of Rose's *mohn* cake and anticipating the crunch of poppy seeds in his mouth, "I guess I just didn't think enough of a fuss was being made."

Lady

(featuring Harry Towns)

WHEN IT WAS GOOD, it was of a smooth consistency and white as Christmas snow. If Harry Towns had a slim silver-foil packet of it against his thigh—which he did two or three nights a week—he felt rich and fortified, almost as though he were carrying a gun. It was called coke, never cocaine. A dealer, one side of whose face was terrific, the other collapsed, like a bad cake, had told him it was known as "lady." That tickled Harry Towns and he was dying to call it that, but he was waiting for the right time. The nickname had to do with the fact that ladies, once they took a taste of the drug, instantly became coke lovers and could not get enough of it. Also, they never quite got the hang of how expensive it was and were known to toss it around carelessly, scattering gusts of it in the carpeting. Even though one side of his face was collapsed, the dealer claimed there were half a dozen girls who hung around him and slept with him so they could have a shot at his coke. Harry Towns could not claim to have enslaved groups of women with the drug, but it did help him along with one outrageously young girl who stayed over with him an entire night. She didn't sleep with him, but just getting her to stay over was erotic and something of an accomplishment. Wearing blue jeans and nailed to him by the sharp bones of her behind, she sat on his lap while he fed her tastes of it all night long. She lapped it up like a kitten and in the morning he drove her to her high-school math class. He wasn't sure if he was proud of this exploit—she wasn't much older than his son—but he didn't worry about it much either.

If someone asked Harry Towns to describe the effects of coke, he would say it was subtle and leave it at that. He could remember the precise moment he had first smelled and then tried grass—a party, a girl in a raincoat whose long hair literally brushed the floor, some bossa nova music that was in vogue at the time, a feeling he wanted to be rid of both his wife and the tweed suit he was wearing—but he could not for the life of him figure out when coke had come into the picture. It had to do with two friends in the beginning, and he was sure now that the running around and hunting it down was just as important as the drug itself. They would spend a long time at a bar waiting for someone to show up with a spoon, one of them leaping up at regular intervals to make a call and see if their man was on his way. It was exciting and it kept them together. While they were waiting, they would tell each other stories about coke they had either heard about or tried personally, coke that was like a blow on the head, coke that came untouched from the drug companies, coke so strong it was used in cataract eye operations. Or they would tell of rich guys who gave parties and kept flowerpots full of it for the guests to dip into at will. It was a little like sitting around and talking about great baseball catches. Sometimes they wondered how long you could keep at it before it began working on your brain. Even though they kidded about winding up years later in the back streets of Marseilles with their noses chewed away, it was a serious worry. Freud had supposedly been an addict and this buoyed them up a bit. Also, Towns had once run into a fellow who lived in Venezuela most of the year and had a gold ring in his ear. Rumor had it that he was a jungle queer. Leaning across to Towns one night, he had tapped his right nostril, saying "This one's thirty-six years old." The fellow was a bit bleary-eyed, but otherwise seemed in good health; the disclosure was comforting to Towns although he wondered why the fellow said nothing about his left nostril.

Once their contact arrived, they would each get up some money, not paying too much attention to who paid the most. Then they would go into the bathroom, secure the door, and lovingly help one another to take snorts from the little packet. One of Towns's friends was a tall stylish fellow who was terrific at wearing clothes, somehow getting the most threadbare jackets to look elegant. It was probably his disdainful attitude that brought off the old jackets. The other friend was a film cutter with a large menacing neck and a background in sports that could not quite be pinned down. They were casual about dividing up the drug, with no thought to anyone's being shortchanged, although later on, the stylish fellow would be accused of having a vacuum cleaner for a nose. But it was a sort of good-natured accusation. On each occasion, Towns's debonair friend could be counted on to introduce a new technique for getting at the coke, putting some in a little canal between two fingers, getting a dab of it at the end of a penknife, and on one occasion producing a tiny, carved monkey's paw, perfectly designed to hold a little simian scoopful. Towns's favorite approach was the penknife one. The white crystals, iced and sparkling, piled up on the edge of the blade, struck him as being dangerously beautiful. But Towns felt with some comfort that the varied techniques placed his friend farther along the road to serious addiction than he was; Towns made do with whatever was on hand, usually the edge of a book of matches, folded in half. The film cutter had a large family, and occasionally they would tease him about his children having to eat hot dogs because of his expensive coke habit. One night he gave them both a look and they abandoned that particular needle. He had been ill recently, and they had heard that four hospital attendants had been unable to hold him down and give him an injection.

After they had taken their snorts, they would each fall back against the wall of the john and let the magic drip through them, saying things like "Oh, brother," and "This has got to be the best." Towns usually capped off the dreamily appreciative remarks by saying, "I'll always have to have this." The stocky film cutter admitted one night that if it came to choosing between the drug and a beautiful girl, he would have to go with the coke. It seemed to be a painful admission for him to make, so Towns and the debonair fellow quickly assured him they both felt exactly the same way. Actually, Towns didn't see why one had to cancel out the other. He had heard that lovers would receive the world's most erotic sensation by putting dabs of coke on their genitals and then swiping it off. He tried this one night with a stewardess from an obscure and thinly publicized airline and found it all right, but nothing to write home about. As far as he could see, it was just a tricky way to get at the coke.

They would take about two tastes apiece and then bounce back into the bar with sly grins and the brisk little nose sniffs that distinguished the experienced coke user. Even if they scattered and sat with different people, the drug held them bound together in a ring. Later, when the evening took a dip, one of them would give a sign and they would return to the john to finish off the packet.

They kept their circle tightly closed, even though at least one fellow was dying to get into it. He was a writer who stood careful guard over his work and on more than one occasion had said, "I'll be damned if I'm going to let anyone monkey around with my prose." He also spoke of having "boffed" a great many girls. Towns took objection to that word "boffed" and so did his friends. They doubted that he had really done that much "boffing" and they didn't care that much for his prose either. So even though the fellow knew what they were doing in the john and gave them hungry, poignant looks, they would not let him into the group.

Sometimes, instead of waiting around at the bar, they would make forays into the night to round up some of the drug. They spent a lot of time waiting outside basement apartments in Chinatown, checking over their shoulders for the police. Towns owned the car and he had plenty of dents in the side to prove it. Somehow, tranquil and frozen by the drug, Towns felt that a little sideswipe here and there didn't matter much, but the dents were piling up and the car was pretty battered. The dapper, arrogant fellow sat in the back and seemed annoyed at having to ride around in such a disreputable-looking vehicle. He lived with his mother who supposedly did all his driving for him, after first propping him up beside her with blankets over his knees for warmth. Towns decided to have all the car dents fixed in one swipe and then start over.

Leaving his friends behind one night, Towns went on a drug-hunting foray with a hooker who had seemed beautiful in the saloon light, but turned out to be a heavy user of facial creams. He didn't object to a girl using creams in private, but felt she had an obligation to take them off when she was out and around. She said she knew of some great stuff just over the bridge in Brooklyn. Towns drove and drove and when he asked her if they were there yet, she said it was just a little bit farther. He felt he might as well be driving to Chicago. When they finally got the coke, she described herself, with some pride, as a "nose freak"—as though Towns would be thrilled to hear this. Then she got rid of most of the coke in the car, under a street lamp, leaving Towns with just a few grains. He felt it would be the right thing on his part to smack her around a little for her behavior, but he was worried about friends of hers running out of a nearby building with kitchen knives. So he let it pass. Besides, there had been something attractively illicit about snorting the drug with a heavily creamed hooker deep in the bowels of Brooklyn. And it was strong, too, even if there wasn't much of it. He would have something to say to his friends about "Brooklyn coke" and how it could tear your head off if you didn't watch it. So instead of smacking her around, he took her on a long, silent drive back to Manhattan where he let her out.

In the beginning, Towns and his friends would fool themselves into thinking that the nighttime get-togethers were for the purpose of having some dinner. They would polish off a Chinese dinner, and one of them would casually ask if the others felt like going after some coke. But after a while, they dropped all pretense, skipping the dinners and diving right into the business of getting at the drug. Towns soon discovered that he was throwing over entire evenings to phone calls, long waits, nervous foot-tapping, and great outbursts of relief when their man finally showed up with the prize. He wasn't sure if he felt the tension legitimately or if he was just playing at it. There weren't too many things in life he liked to do more than once in exactly the same way and he figured out that he was having the same kind of evening over and over. So one night he simply stopped, probably too cruelly and abruptly, the way he stopped most things. He decided to get a whole bunch of coke and have it just for himself. He invited the dealer with the collapsing face up to his apartment and told him to bring along an entire ounce. It was a very exciting and significant call for him to make, and he rated it right up there with such decisions as moving out on his wife and signing up for a preposterously expensive apartment. Both had worked out. As soon as he called the dealer, he became afraid of some vague unnameable violence. His way of handling it was to strip down to his waist and greet the dealer bare-chested. Towns had a strong body and this maneuver would indicate that he was loose and could take care of things, even stripped down that way and obviously having no weapons concealed in the folds of his clothing.

The dealer didn't notice any of this. He swept right in and began to carry on about some new moisture-proof bottles he had found for the coke. If you closed them after snorts, no moisture would get in and the drug would not cake up. He was terribly proud of the bottles and told Towns to hang on to them; when they were empty, he would come by with refills. After he had left, Towns sank back on a leather chair and didn't even try any of the coke. He just lit a cigar and richly enjoyed having bottles of it up there on the thirtieth floor with him. The idea fell into his head that if you had a lot of it, you were relieved of the pressure of always having to get it and as a result you didn't take that much. But he got on to himself in a second and knew it wasn't going to work out that way. He'd take more. The next time he saw his friends they tried to start up the coke-hunting apparatus and he excused himself by saying, "I don't think I'm in the mood for any tonight." He felt very sorry for them; they would have to go to all that trouble for just a little packet of it that would be sniffed up in an evening. Somehow they sensed he had a whole bunch of coke of his own and were snappish with him, but they stopped that quickly because they weren't that way. The stylish fellow's eyes began darting all over the place and Towns sensed he was making plans to lay in a giant supply of his own. He would be all right. But the film cutter's head drooped and when he was alone with Towns, he admitted for the first time that even though he had many children, he hated his wife. The evenings of hunting down coke had been terribly important to him. He said he always knew Towns was afraid to get close to people and amazingly he started to cry for a few seconds. At that moment, Towns would have taken him up to the apartment and given him half of the huge amount of coke. It was a close call, and the next day he was thrilled that he hadn't. As to Towns's inability to stay close to people, the fellow probably had him dead right. He had gone with a girl for three years and then brutally chopped off the affair, practically overnight. When it came to girls, if there was going to be any chopping off, he wanted to be the one to do

it. Once it had been the other way. He saw himself as a man who had
gotten off to a shaky start, then patched himself together and now had
tough scar tissue at the seams. Chopping . . . getting chopped off
. . . what he hoped for in life was to work his way back to some middle path.

Meanwhile, he had all that coke and a whole new style of evening set
up. He would spread some of the drug on a dark surface, a pretzel box
as a matter of fact, snort some, rub a little on his gums, and then take a
long time getting dressed, returning from time to time to the pretzel
box for additional sniffs. The feeling in coke circles was that your aim
in returning to the drug throughout an evening was to chase that original high. Speaking for himself, Towns saw his repeat trips to the pretzel
box as a means of making sure his feet never got back on the ground. It
may have added up to the identical thing. He had some special phono-
graph records that seemed to go with the coke, ones that he rarely
changed. They seemed to deepen the effects of the drug; cigars helped
to string out the sensation, too, and he felt he was the only one who
knew this. When he was ready to go out, he would sprinkle some coke
in tinfoil and try to figure out the best pocket to put it in, one he
wouldn't forget and the least likely one for a federal agent to suddenly
thrust his hand into and nail him on the spot. (A dealer once told him
"There's no good pocket.") He would be able to return to the tinfoil
for little tastes throughout the night and there would be enough in
there, too, for friends he might run across. Doling out coke from the
thin little packet would make him seem generous; at the same time, no
one had to know about the moisture-proof bottles lined up and waiting
for him back at his apartment.

It was amazing how little he worried about the illegality of what he
was doing. Only once did this come home to him with any force. He
was in a cocktail lounge in Vegas with two girls and for the life of him
he couldn't figure out if they were hookers. He was only fair at deter-
mining things like that. Sometimes his actions were sudden and dramatic, and on this occasion, he reached out and stuck a fingerful of
coke in each of their mouths, as if this would smoke them out and tell
him if they were joy dolls. They both sucked on the fingers and loved
what was happening, but Towns looked around the lounge and became
aware of a number of men with white socks, shaved necks, and even
expressions who appeared not to approve of his having traipsed in with
more than one girl. They probably didn't go for his beard much, either.
At least that's the impression he got. All of this shook him up. What if
one of the girls suddenly hollered out, "He shoved coke in my mouth."
Towns had a lawyer who was terrific in the civil liberties department,
but he wasn't sure he could count on the fellow dashing out to Nevada

on his behalf. He told the girls to wait for him, he had a lucky roulette hunch, and then he sneaked out of the casino and went to another one.

He didn't feel the danger much in the city, though. "Rich" is the only word to describe how he felt. When he started out of his apartment, high and immunized, he felt that nothing great had to happen. He didn't even have to wind up with a girl. The way he figured it, enough that was great had already happened. Right around the pretzel box. He knew there must be a dark side to all this, but he would worry about that later.

One of the smart things he did was not use his car. He had had enough of the sideswipes. In his new routine, going about on foot and using cabs, he would hit a few warm-up places where he knew some people and felt cozy and secure; then he would head for a drugged and adventurous bar that could always be counted on for packs of long-haired girls, each of whom for some reason had just left her "old man" or walked out on a waitressing job that very day. In the drugged atmosphere of this bar, it was possible to slip into these packs of girls and on occasion, to pick one off. All of a sudden he would be talking to one, and if her eyes looked right, asking if she would like to have a little coke in the john. If she said yes, he knew the battle was over and he was going to wind up in bed with her. The two went together. In his way, he was using the coke to push people around. One night, at one of the early bars, he stood next to two black men; one liked him, the other, whose glasses gave him the look of an abstract educational puzzle, didn't. He said that even though Towns was bigger than he was, he was positive he could take him outside and beat the shit out of him. Unlike liquor, the coke always had a defusing effect on Towns, who simply shrugged and said, "No way." Then, perhaps to teach the puzzle man a lesson, he invited the other black man into the john for some coke. They took some together and then the angry abstracted fellow appeared. Towns hesitated long enough to make his point and then gave him some, too. He put his arm around Towns and hugged him and Towns felt a little sad about how easy it had been to peel away his anger. Back at the bar, he got angry again and finally walked out in what seemed to be a flash of hot abstract lightning. His renewed fury made Towns feel a little easier. But you certainly could do things with that coke. One night, when Towns had failed to pry any of the girls loose from her pack, he went looking for a hooker and found a terrific one on the street who looked like a high-school cheerleader. She had a tough style and needled him, saying she had balled every guy in the city, so why not him? At one time this would have been a threat to Harry Towns, but it wasn't now. What did all those other guys have to do with him? She said they could go upstairs to a tragic-looking little hotel across the street and Towns said no deal, he wanted to take her to his place. She said there was no way on earth she would go to a stranger's apartment, and then he mentioned the coke. "Jesus, do you really have some?" she wanted to know. "Pounds of it," he said, "at my place." It was amazing. As tough and streetwise as she was, she jumped in a cab with him and off they went. And all he had done was *say* he'd had the coke. It was a weapon all right.

Sometimes, when he got finessed into drinking a lot, the liquor and drug combination left him shaky the next day. He had to make sure to let entire days go by without using any of the drug. On the off days, it would be like having a terrific date to look forward to. One night, a fellow with a beltful of tools walked up to Towns and said that if he ever saw him with his wife again, he would kill him in an alley. "We can do it now," said the fellow, with surprising politeness, "or at a time of your convenience." Towns could not pinpoint the wife in question, but he had a pretty good inkling of who she was. He felt weak and anesthetized, his limbs sluggish, caught in heavy syrup. He mumbled something and hoped the fellow wouldn't use the tools on him. So it wasn't all roses. He had to watch that sort of thing. Then, too, the moisture-proof bottles emptied out after a while and he had to get them filled up again. He made an appointment to go to the dealer's apartment this time, and when he got there, the fellow snatched up his money and sat him down next to a young blonde carhop-style girl who looked as though she had just given up thumb-sucking. Then he slid a huge switchblade with a capsule of amyl nitrite on it between them, and excused himself, saying he had to get the coke, which was a few blocks away. Towns knew about the capsule; it was for cracking open and sniffing. You got a quick high-voltage sexual rush out of it. He had graduated from it some time back and felt it was small potatoes next to coke. But what about having it on a switchblade with a yellow-haired teenager on the other side? It reminded Towns of a religious ceremony in which a hotly peppered herb was placed beside something delicious to remind worshippers of the hard and easy times of their forebears. But this seemed to be a kind of drug ritual, and he couldn't decide what his next move was supposed to be. Was he supposed to make a quick grab for the capsule and crack it open before she got at him with the switchblade? He decided to stick to light conversation.

A bit later, Towns excused himself to go to the john and by mistake opened the door to a closet; rifles and handguns came pouring out on him in a great metallic shower—as well as a few bullwhips. "Look what you did," said the girl, coming over in a pout, as though the cat had spilled some milk. Towns helped her to gather up the weapons; it seemed important to get them back in before the dealer returned. He showed up half an hour later, telling Towns that he was in great luck because he had come up with some pure coke rocks, much more lethal than anything Towns had been involved with before. This type of coke came in around once a year, something like softshell crabs; rich Peruvians sat around on their ranches and shaved slivers of it from a huge rock, inhaling these slivers for weeks on end and getting heart trouble in their thirties. But Towns wasn't to worry about this, since he would only be getting this one shipment and maybe never get a shot at it again. Another thing that wasn't to bother Towns was that the moisture-proof bottles would not be filled to the top this time. That was because the Peruvian coke rocks were so pure. Towns wasn't so sure about this. "Oh well," said the dealer, disdainfully, "if you want me to fluff them up." Towns thought of the weapons closet and decided to pass on this and get going. In a kind of furious between-the-acts blur of activity, the dealer and his girl whipped out armloads of equipment, and before Towns could make a move toward the door, the dealer had wound a rubber coil around his arm and was straining to make a vein pop up. Meanwhile, the girl was melting down a Peruvian rock, probably one that belonged to Towns, in a tiny pan. They were like a crack surgical team. So this was the famous shooting-up routine. Towns had never seen it and had always been curious about it. The dealer, one side of his face not only collapsing but running down, like oil on a canvas, plunged a hypodermic into his vein and went into a series of ecstatic shivers, at the same time keeping up a surprisingly sober running commentary for Towns: "What's happening is that I'm getting a rush twenty times more powerful than you get taking it up through your nose. This is really something. The only trouble is, it will stop in about five minutes and I'll have to do it again. I've gotten so I can do it ten, twenty times, all through the night." None of this was appealing to Towns. He realized that the tableau was for his benefit, to hook him into the team so that he would wind up melting rocks with them in the tiny frying pan. It wasn't going to happen. There were certain things that he could say for sure he wasn't ever going to do—like skydiving—and this was one of them. When the dealer finished up his shivers, it was time for the girl to take her turn; that's what Towns wanted to be on hand to see. She stuck some equipment under her arm and said she was going off to do it privately. Towns felt around in his bottle and pulled out a good-sized rock, saying it was hers if he could watch her in action. "No way," she said, giving him an infuriated look, "that's one thing no one in the world is ever going to see." What she seemed to want to get across was that she had been through a thousand assorted hells but was going to keep this one area stubbornly cordoned off to herself. Towns shrugged good-naturedly as if to say, "Oh well, win some, lose some," but he felt the loss sharply and didn't even wait around to see her when she got back. That wasn't what he wanted. He thanked the shivering fellow for the Peruvian rocks and sauntered out-side, deciding to hunt down another arrangement, one with less danger in the air.

He went through quite a few of these dealers. They tended to live in lofts and to have young, sluggish girlfriends; each was trying to "get something going" in the record business. The coke, according to them, was just a sideline. After Towns got his coke, he would be asked to listen to one of their tape decks. Not once did he like what he heard, even taking into account that he was not in a musical mood when he made these visits and just wanted to get the coke and get the hell out of there. It was his view that each of these fellows was going to fare much better as a coke dealer than as a musician. Towns's favorite dealer was a tall, agreeable chap who had once worked at the Mayo Clinic as a counselor. He had a healing, therapeutic style of selling the coke; after each buy, Towns would flirt with the idea of sticking around for a little counseling, although he never followed through. One day, the fellow announced that in order to kick his own coke habit, which was becoming punishingly expensive, he was making his first visit to London. That struck Towns as being on the naive side. How could you get away from coke in London? Some faraway island would seem to be more the ticket, but the fellow had his mind made up on the British Isles and there was no stopping him. Towns was convinced they would have him picked off as a user the second he stepped off the plane and be ready and waiting to sell him some.

Dealers brushed in and out of Towns's life, and he could not imagine wanting some coke and not being able to come up with it. Yet that would happen on occasion, even though he started out early in the evening trying to drum some up. He had always told himself that all he had to do in that situation was have a few drinks and he would be fine. But he wasn't that fine. He would sit around at one of his spots and drum his fingers on the bar, uneasy and unhappy. Was he hooked? He had heard that when a famed racketeer was buried, friends of his, for old time's sake, had stuck a few spoons of first-grade coke in there with him, since the racket man had been a user. Once, high and dry at four in the morning, Towns actually found himself wondering if it would be possible to dig up the fellow and get at the coke. It all depended on whether it was in the coffin with him or on the topsoil somewhere. Towns wasn't sure of the details. If he knew for sure it was in the topsoil, he might have found a shovel somewhere in the city, driven out to the cemetery and taken a try at it. That's how badly he wanted it sometimes.

One day Towns got word that his mother had died. It did not come around behind him and hit him on the head, since the death had been going on for a long time and it was just a matter of waiting for the phone call. It had always been his notion that when he got this particular news, he would drive up to a summer resort his mother used to take him to each September and hang out there for a weekend, sitting at the bar, tracing her presence, thinking through the fine times they had spent together. That would be his style of mourning. But now that he had the news, he didn't feel much like doing that. Maybe he would later. Instead, he sat in his apartment, thirty floors over the city, and tried to cry, but he could not drum up any tears. He was sure they would come later, in some oblique way, so he didn't worry too much about it. He knew himself and knew that he only cried when things sneaked up on him. Then he could cry with the best of them.

His mother was going to be put in a temporary coffin while the real one was being set up. And she would be lying in the chapel from six to eight that evening, with the family receiving close friends; the following day she would be buried. It presented a bit of a conflict for Towns. At six o'clock, he also had an appointment to meet Ramos, an old friend who had come in from California the night before. Formerly an advertising man, Ramos had now gone over entirely to an Old-West style. Long-faced, sleepy-eyed, he turned up in the city looking as though he had ridden for days through the Funeral Mountains on a burro, seeking cowpoke work. He had taken Towns into the coatroom of the bar at which they met, pulled out a leather pouch that might have contained gold dust, and given Towns a sniff of some of the purest coke he had ever run across. It rocketed back and flicked against a distant section in the back of his head that may never have been touched before. Now Harry Towns had a new story to tell his friends about Western coke, the wildest and most rambunctious of all. And he wanted that place in the back of his head to be flicked at again. So they made an appointment for six o'clock the following evening to go and get some more. Except that now Towns had to be at the chapel with his dead mother. He wondered, soon after he heard about the loss, if he would keep the appointment with Ramos, and even as he wondered, he knew he would. He didn't even have to turn it over in his mind. After all, it wasn't the funeral. That would make it an entirely different story. It was just a kind of chapel reception and if he turned up half an hour late, it would not be any great crime. And he would have the coke.

Harry Towns was at the midtown bar to meet Ramos at six on the dot, hoping to make a quick score and then hotfoot it over to the chapel. But Ramos loped in some twenty minutes late, squinty-eyed, muttering something about the sun having crossed him up on the time. He had never even heard of the sun when he was in advertising. He sat down, stretched his legs, and tried to get Towns into a talk about the essential dignity of man, even man as he existed in the big city. Towns felt he had to cut him off on that. People were already pouring into the chapel. At the same time, he didn't want to be rude to Ramos and risk blowing the transaction. He told Ramos about his mother, and the man from the West said he understood, no problem, except that he himself did not have the coke. It was just up the street a few blocks at a divorced girl's house. They would just have one drink and get going.

The divorced girl lived in a richly furnished high-rise apartment with animal skins on the floor. Towns had to walk carefully to keep from sticking his feet in their jaws. She had racks of fake bookshelves, too, suspense-novel types that whirled around when you pressed a button and had coke concealed on the other side. He was certain she was going to turn out to be his favorite dealer. Long-legged, freshly divorced, she hugged Ramos, Towns wondering how they knew each other. The animal skins may have been some sort of bridge between them. More likely, they were teammates dating back to Ramos's advertising days. She also seemed interested in Towns, handing him a powder box filled with coke, something he had always dreamed of. He got the idea that this wasn't even the coke he would be buying. It was a kind of guest coke, a getting-acquainted supply. An hors d'oeuvre. That's what he called falling into something. But what a time to be falling into it. She told him to dig in, help himself, and they could take care of their business a bit later. The girl had legs that went on and on and wouldn't quit. Why had anyone divorced her? She went over to fiddle with some elaborate stereo equipment and Towns put the powder box on his lap and took a deep snort as instructed.

"Jesus Christ," she said, pressing the palm of one hand to the side of her head, "what in the hell are you doing?"

"You told me to dig in," he said.

"Yes, but I didn't know we had a piggy here."

"Don't tell someone to dig in if you don't mean it."

Now Towns really felt foolish. There was no way to proceed from the piggy insult, which bit deep, to buying half an ounce of the drug. So he had blown at least half the chapel service and he wasn't even going to get the coke. He vowed then and there to deal only with the tape-deck boys in their lofts. Ramos tried to smooth things over by telling her, "He's a true man," but she was breathing hard and there seemed no way to calm her down. "What a toke," she said. "I've seen people take tokes, but this one, wow."

"My mother just died," said Towns. As he said it, he knew he was going to regret that remark for a long time, if not for the rest of his life. He had once seen a fellow get down on his knees to lick a few grains of coke from the bottom of a urinal. That fellow was a king compared to Harry Towns—using his mother's dead body to get him out of a jam. And it got him out, too. "Oh God," said the girl, putting a comforting arm around Towns's shoulder, "I don't know how to handle death." Towns just couldn't wait any longer. He gave Ramos the money, told him to buy some coke from the girl and he would meet him later, after the chapel service. Then he got into a cab and told the driver to please get him across town as fast as possible. It was an emergency. You could travel only so fast in city traffic, and Towns got it arranged in his mind that it was the cabbie's fault he was getting there so late. He arrived at a quarter to eight, with only fifteen minutes left to the service. Some remnants of his family were there, and a few scattered friends. Also his mother, off to one side, in the temporary coffin. Towns's aunt and his older brother were relieved to see him, but they didn't bawl him out. He would always appreciate that. They said they thought he might have been hurt and left it at that. What seemed to concern them most was the presence of a woman Towns's mother hadn't cared for. They couldn't get over how ironic it was that the disliked woman had turned up at the chapel. The few surviving members of Towns's family were very short and for the hundredth time, he wondered how he had gotten to be so tall. He chatted with some neighborhood friends of his mother, keeping a wary eye on the woman she hadn't liked. If Towns hadn't felt so low about showing up late, he might very well have chucked her out of there. A chapel official said the family's time was up. He gave out a few details about the funeral that was coming up the next day. The family filed out, and just as Towns was the last one to arrive, he was the last to leave, stopping for a moment at his mother's temporary coffin. He never should have worried about crying. Once he started, he cried like a sonofabitch. He probably set a chapel record. He cried from the tension, he cried from grief, he cried from the cab ride, from his coke habit, from the piggy insult, from his mother having to be cramped up in a temporary coffin and then shifted over to a real one when it was ready. They had a hard time getting him out of there.

That night, Ramos came by with the coke. Towns didn't weigh it, look at it, measure it. He never did. It seemed like a fat pack and he guessed that the girl had given him a good count because of the death. The main thing was that it was in there. He gave Ramos some of it, which was protocol, and told him he would see him around. "I'll stick with you, man," said Ramos, but Towns said he would rather be alone. He didn't want people saying "man" to him and telling him he had "a terrific head." All of which Ramos was capable of. The coke had a perfumed scent to it, a little like the fragrance of the divorcee. Had she rubbed some of it against herself? His guess was that she had. He took a snort of it, got into his bathrobe, and put on some Broadway show music, the kind his mother liked. The music would be the equivalent of driving up to the old summer resort. But it didn't work. It didn't go with the coke. During his mother's illness, he had put her up in his apartment and moved into a hotel, the idea being that she would get to enjoy the steel and glass and the view and the doorman service. But she didn't go with the apartment either, and they both knew it. She stayed there a few weeks, probably for his sake, to ease his mind about not having sent her away on lavish trips, and then she said she wanted to go back to her own home. She left without a trace, except for some sugar packets she had taken from a nearby restaurant and put in his sugar jar. To give him some extra and free sugar. He wondered if he should go over and take a look at the sugar. He was positive that it would start him crying again, but he didn't want to do that just then. He could always look at the sugar. Instead, he switched on some appropriate coke music, took another snort of the drug, and stared out at his view of the city, the glassed-in one that was costing him an arm and a leg each month. His mother had made a tremendous fuss over this view, but once again it was for his sake. She had been very ill and wanted to be in her own apartment. Staying in his had been a last little gift for him, allowing him to do something for her. He kept the tinfoil packet of coke open beside him and he knew that he was going to stay where he was until dawn. He was not a trees-and-sunset man, but he liked to be around for that precise time when the night crumbled and the new day got started. He liked to get ready for that moment by snorting coke, letting the drug drive him a hundred times higher than the thirtieth floor on which he lived. Once or twice, he wondered about the other people who were watching that moment, if there were any. It was probably only a few diplomats and a couple of hookers. Normally, he would take a snort, luxuriate in it, and wait for a noticeable dip in his mood before he took the next one. This time he didn't wait for the dips. Before they started, he headed them off with more snorts. He saw now that his goal was to get rid of the entire half ounce before dawn. Never mind about the problem of coming down. He would take a hot bath, some Valium. He'd punch himself in the jaw if necessary, ram his head against the bathroom tile if he had to. The main thing was to have nothing left by the time it was dawn so he could be starting out clean on the day of the funeral. Then, no matter what he was offered, he would turn it down. He didn't care what it was, Brooklyn coke, Western coke, Peruvian coke rocks, coke out of Central Harlem. If someone gave him stuff that came out of an intensive-care unit, coke that had been used for goddamn brain surgery, he would pass it right by. Because the chapel was one thing. But anyone who stuck so much as a grain of that white shit up his nose on the actual *day* of his mother's funeral had to be some new and as yet undiscovered breed of sonofabitch. The lowest.

Halcyon Days
(Family Life and the Service)

When You're Excused,
You're Excused

HAVING A GALLSTONE REMOVED at the age of thirty-seven almost frightened Mr. Kessler to death, and after he was healed up, he vowed he would get into the best shape of his life. He joined a local sports club called Vic Tanny's, and for six months took workouts every other night of the week, missing only three sessions for Asian flu. When one of his workouts came due on the eve of Yom Kippur, holiest day of the Jewish year, Mr. Kessler, who usually observed important religious holidays, said to his wife, "I've come to need these workouts and my body craves them like drugs. It's medicine and when I miss one I get edgy and feel awful. It doesn't make any difference that this is the most important holiday of all. I've got to go tonight. It's part of the religion that if you're sick you're excused from synagogue. It's in one of the psalms."

Mrs. Kessler was a woman of deep religious conviction but slender formal training. Her husband, as a result, was able to bully her around with references to obscure religious documents. Once he mentioned the psalms, rebuttal was out of the question, and she could only say, "All right, as long as it's in there."

Mr. Kessler did a great deal of aimless walking through the house for the rest of the day. His four-year-old son asked him, "Are any pirates good?" and Mr. Kessler said, "I don't feel like talking pirates." When the dark came and it was time for the gym, Mr. Kessler said to his wife, "All right, it isn't in the psalms, but it's in the religion somewhere, and it doesn't make any difference that it's such an important holiday. If you're excused, you're excused. That goes for Columbus Day and Washington's Birthday and if the Japs attack Pearl Harbor again, you're excused on that day, too. In fact, as a matter of principle, you're *especially* excused on Yom Kippur."

Mr. Kessler got his gym bundle together and his wife walked him to the driveway. "It seems dark and religious out here," she said.

"Nonsense," said Mr. Kessler.

He opened the door of his car and then said, "All right, I admit I'm not confident. I started to imagine there was a squadron of old rabbis

prowling the streets taking down the names of Jews who were going off
to gyms. When the railroad whistle sounded, I thought it was a ram's
horn, and the wind tonight is like the wail of a thousand dying ghetto
holdouts. But I've got to go there even if I just take a quick workout
and skip my steambath. It's too bad it's Yom Kippur and I admit that's
throwing me a little, but if you're excused, you're excused. On Yom
Kippur or *double* Yom Kippur."

Mr. Kessler got behind the wheel and his young son hollered down
from an open window, "Can a giant find you if you hide?"

"No giants when important things are going on," said Mr. Kessler,
swinging out of the driveway and driving into the night.

Fifteen minutes later, he parked his car outside the gym and swept
inside. He walked past the blonde receptionist who called out,
"Where's your wife?" and Mr. Kessler said, "She only came that once,
and you know damned well her hips are past help. Why do you have to
ask me that every time I come in here?"

He undressed in the locker room and gave his street clothing to
Rico, the tiny attendant, who blew his nose and said, "I've got a cold,
but I'm glad. It's good to have one. Guys come in here to lose colds
and I'm glad to have one all year round. When you have a cold, you're
always taking care of yourself and that's good."

Mr. Kessler said, "I never said anything to you before because I
know you're supposed to be a charming old character, but you're an
idiot. It's not good to have a cold. It's better not to have a cold. Any
time. I just want to take a fast workout and go home and be in the
house. I don't want to kid around."

Upstairs, in the workout room, a man with a thin body was lying on
the floor in an awkward position, lifting a barbell in an unnatural
movement. "Do you want to know this one?" the man asked. "It's the
best exercise in the gym, getting a muscle no one else bothers with. It's
right in the center of the arm and you can't see it. Its function is to
push out all the other muscles. You don't have very much of a build
while you're getting it started, but once she's going, all the other muscles shoot out and you look like an ape."

"I don't have time for any new exercises tonight," said Mr. Kessler.
"I just want to get in and get out. Besides, I don't like the kind of body
you have."

Mr. Kessler did a few warm-up exercises and then picked up a pair
of light dumbbells to work his biceps. A handsome and heavily perspired young man with large shoulders came over and said, "Whew, it
certainly is rough work. But when I was sixteen, I only weighed 110 and
I said to myself, 'I'm going to look like something.' So each night, after
working in Dad's filling station, I began to lift stuff in the family ga-

rage, getting to the point where I really had a nice build and then, in later years, joining up here. I vowed I would never again look like nothing."

"What makes you think that's such an exciting story?" said Mr. Kessler. "I've heard it a thousand times. I think *you* told it to me once and I don't want to hear it again as long as I live."

"What's eating you?" asked the handsome man.

"I just want to get in and get out and not hear any dull stories," said Mr. Kessler. He went over to a rowing machine, but a sparse-haired man who was doing vigorous waist-twisting Alpine calisthenics blocked his way. "Why don't you do those at home?" said Mr. Kessler. "You're in my way. I've seen you in here and you never use any of the equipment. You only do calisthenics and you're crazy to come here to do them. What are you, showing off?"

"I just like to do them here," said the man and let Mr. Kessler get at the rowing machine. Looking up at the clock, Mr. Kessler did half a dozen rows and then leaped up and caught the high bar, swinging back and forth a few times. A police sergeant who took clandestine workouts during duty hours came by and said, "Your lats are really coming out beautifully."

"Oh, really?" said Mr. Kessler. "Can you see the delts from back there?"

"Beauties," said the sergeant. "Both beauties."

"Thank you for saying that," said Mr. Kessler, swinging easily on the bar. "I can really feel them coming out now. I don't know why, but your saying they're coming out beautifully made me feel good for the first time tonight. I was rushing through my workout because we have this big holiday tonight and I felt guilty, but now I'm going to stay up here awhile. Six months ago I was sick with a bad gallstone and told everyone that if you're sick your only obligation is to yourself. Ahead of kids, your wife and the synagogue. Now I feel good up here and I'm not rushing. This is where I should be. I don't care if it's Yom Kippur or if the mayor's been killed by a bird turd."

"I don't say I follow all your arguments," said the sergeant, "but your lats are really coming up. I'll tell that to any man here in the gym, straight to his face."

"Thank you for feeling that way," said Mr. Kessler, dropping from the bar now and taking his place on a bench for some leg-raises. Sharing the bench with him was a tiny, dark-haired man with powerful forearms.

"It pays to work your forearms," said the little man. "You get them pumped up real good and even the big bastards will run."

"I'm one of the big bastards," said Mr. Kessler. "You can't tell because I'm sitting down."

"I couldn't see that," said the little man.

"It's all right," said Mr. Kessler. "It's just that maybe you ought to tell that story to a little bastard."

"I'm not telling it to anyone," said the little man.

Mr. Kessler did his legs and then went over to the board for some sit-ups. A man with a large head came over and said, "You look awfully familiar. From a long time ago."

"Public school," said Mr. Kessler, rising to shake hands with the man. "Your name is Block and your father was an attorney."

"Accountant," said the man. "But you're right about Block."

"You lived in the rooming house and there was something else about you. How come you're not in synagogue tonight?"

"I don't observe," said the man. "We never did. This is my first workout here."

"I do observe, but I was sick and I figure I'm excused. A long time ago I remember an old man in the temple didn't have to fast because his stomach was out of whack. That was orthodox and I figure if he was excused, I'm certainly excused. I was feeling bad for a while but not any more. If you're sick it doesn't matter if it's Yom Kippur or even if they make up a day holier than Yom Kippur. If you're excused, you're excused. What the hell *was* it about you?"

"I'd like to take off a little around the waist and pack some on the shoulders."

"I know," said Mr. Kessler. *"Blockhead.* They used to call you *Blockhead.* That's it, isn't it?"

"I don't like it now any more than I did then," said the man with the big head.

"Yes, but I just wanted to get it straight," said Mr. Kessler. "A thing like that can nag you."

Mr. Kessler did ten sets of sit-ups, and when he had worked up a good sweat, he went downstairs and showered. The massage room was empty and Mr. Kessler said to the attendant, "I want a massage. It doesn't matter that I've never had one before and that I associate it with luxury and extravagance. I want one. When I came in here I was going to get right out, but there's a principle involved. We have this big holiday, very big, but you're either excused from it or you're not. And I am. I was pretty sick."

"If I had the towel concession, I'd have it made," said the masseur, oiling up Mr. Kessler's body. "You can't make it on rubs alone. You've got to have rubs and rags."

"It's crazy that they're all sitting out there bent over in prayer and

I'm in here, but when you're proving a point, sometimes things look ridiculous."

"If you have any influence at all," said the masseur, "try to get me towels. I can't make it on rubs alone."

Music poured into the gym now, and Mr. Kessler hummed along to several early Jerome Kern tunes. His massage at an end, he got up from the table, showered, and then, as he dressed, told Rico, the locker room attendant, "I'm all tingling. I knew this was the right thing to do. Next year I'll be in the temple all bent over like they are, but I did the right thing tonight."

"All you need is a cold," said Rico.

"You know how I feel about that remark," said Mr. Kessler.

Upstairs, Mr. Kessler smiled at the blonde receptionist who grabbed him and began to lead him in a cha-cha across the front office. "I don't do this with girls," said Mr. Kessler, falling into step, "and I'm going right home. You have a ponytail and it's making me crazy."

"Where's your wife?" asked the girl, going off into a complicated cha-cha break that flustered Mr. Kessler.

"You ask me that all the time," said Mr. Kessler, picking up the beat again and doing primitive arm motions. "Look, it doesn't matter about her hips. Don't you understand a man can be in love with a woman with any size hips? Where's my wife, you ask? What do we need her for?"

"Do you want to go dancing?" asked the girl.

"I told you I don't do things with girls," said Mr. Kessler. "I shouldn't even be carrying on here in the lobby. What's your name?"

"Irish," said the girl.

"Irish?" said Mr. Kessler. "Do you have to be named the most gentile name there is? They're all out there wailing and beating their breasts for atonement and I'm with an Irish. But I've got to ask myself if it would be better if you were an Inge. I'm not doing anything wrong and even if I am it doesn't make any difference that I'm doing it tonight. I'm either excused or I'm not excused. I'm finished early and I'll go for about twenty minutes."

The girl put on a sweater and walked ahead of Mr. Kessler to his car. He started the motor and she said, "I don't want to dance just yet. I'd rather that you park somewhere and make love to me."

"I can't stand it when the girl says a thing like that," said Mr. Kessler. "That drives me out of my mind. Look, it was all right in there in the gym, but I'm feeling a little funny out here in the night air. As though I'm wandering around somewhere in the goddamned Sinai. But that's just the kind of thing I've got to fight. I don't think there'll be anyone behind the Chinese restaurant now. All we're going to do is fool around a little, though."

The lights in the Chinese restaurant's parking field were dark when they got there and Mr. Kessler stopped the car and put his head into the receptionist's blonde hair and bit her ear. "You smell young. About that ear bite, though. I just feel that as long as I'm being so honest about Yom Kippur I can't do anything dishonest at all. The ear bite isn't mine. That is, it's just something I do. A long time ago, before my wife got big-hipped, we took a Caribbean cruise and she danced on deck with a Puerto Rican public relations man named Rodriguez. She acted funny after that and finally told me it was because he'd aroused her. I got it out of her that it was because he'd bitten her ear. I can't use an ear bite on her, of course, but I've been anxious to try one out and that's why I worked it in."

"Really make love to me," the receptionist whispered, putting herself against Mr. Kessler.

"There'll only be some light fooling around," said Mr. Kessler. "Do you know what the hell night this is? Uh oh. The voice you have just heard was that of the world's worst hypocrite. Am I proving anything if I just do some elaborate kissing about the neck and shoulders? A man is either excused or he's not excused. Oh, Jesus, you're wearing boyish-type underwear. You would be wearing something along those lines. That did it," he said, and fell upon her.

After a while, she said, "Now that you've had me, I want us to dance slowly knowing that you've had me."

"You're suggesting crazy things," said Mr. Kessler. "I'm calling my wife before I do any more of them."

They drove to a filling station and Mr. Kessler dialed his number and said, "I thought I'd get in and get out, but the car's broken. It's in the differential."

"You know I don't know what that is," said Mrs. Kessler. "It's like telling me something is in the psalms."

"The garage has to run out and get some parts," he said.

"Do you feel funny about what you did?" asked Mrs. Kessler.

"I didn't do anything," he said. "Everybody forgets how sick I was. When you're sick, the religion understands."

Mr. Kessler hung up and the receptionist showed him the way to a dancing place. It was a cellar called Tiger Sam's, catering to Negroes and whites and specializing in barbecued ham hocks. They danced awhile and the receptionist said she was hungry. "I am, too," said Mr. Kessler. "It's going to be tough getting down that first bite because I know the fast isn't over until sundown tomorrow night, but it's about time I stopped thinking that way. I forget how sick I was."

The receptionist said she wanted the ham hocks, and Mr. Kessler said, "I confess I've had the urge to try them, but they're probably the most unkosher things in the world. I'm starting in again. Wouldn't I just be the most spineless man in America if I ordered eggs and told them to hold the hocks? I'll have the hocks."

When he had finished eating, Mr. Kessler began drinking double shots of bourbon until he slid off his stool and fell into the sawdust.

"I've gone past that point where I should have stopped. I only hope I don't get sentimental and run off into a synagogue. It's here where my heart starts breaking for every Jew who ever walked with a stoop and cried into a prayer book. That's just the kind of thing I've got to watch, though. It would be the best medicine in the world for me if an old Jewish refugee woman just happened to stumble in here by accident. Just so I could fail to hug and kiss her and apologize to her for all the world's crimes. And that would be that and I'd have proven that number one I was sick and number two when you're sick you're excused and number three when you're excused you're really excused."

A young Negro with a dancer's grace in his body came over, bowed to Mr. Kessler in the sawdust and said, "I'm Ben and should like to try the merengue with your lovely blonde companion. With your permission."

Mr. Kessler said it was all right and stayed in the sawdust while the two danced closely and primitively to a Haitian rhythm. Two Negro musicians sat on stools above Mr. Kessler. One handed another double bourbon down to him and said, "Like happy Yom Kippur, babe."

"I can't get to my feet," said Mr. Kessler. "You think that's funny and sort of like a jazz musician's joke, but it so happens I am Jewish. I ought to belt you one, but the point is even jokes shouldn't bother me if I'm excused from the holiday. If I got upset and belted you, it would show that I really haven't excused myself."

One of the musicians dangled a toilet bowl deodorizer in front of Mr. Kessler's nose while the other howled.

"I don't know where this fits into anything," said Mr. Kessler, "but I'm not going to get upset or start feeling sentimental."

The Negro named Ben came back now with his arm around the receptionist's waist and said, "I wonder if you two would join me at my apartment. I'm having a do there and am sure you'll love Benny's decor."

The two musicians carried Mr. Kessler out to a Sunbeam convertible and put him on the floor of the rear seat, slipping in above him. The receptionist got in alongside Ben, who drove to Harlem. The two musicians kept the deodorizer in Mr. Kessler's face. "I suppose you've got a reason for that," he said from the floor, as they howled in the night air and kept pushing it against his nose.

When the car stopped, Mr. Kessler said, "I can walk now," and stumbled along behind the four as they mounted the steps of a brownstone. Ben knocked on the door, two light raps and a hard one, and a powerful pale-skinned man in leotards opened the door quickly to a huge single room, divided by a purple curtain. It was done in the style of a cave and there were bits of African sculpture on shelves, along with campaign pictures of New York's Governor Harriman. A film flashed on one wall, demonstrating Martha Graham ballet techniques, and some forty or fifty Negro-white couples in leotards stood watching it in the haze of the room, some assuming ballet poses along with the dancers. Ben got leotards for the new arrivals and led them behind the purple curtain so they could change. There, a man in a silk dressing gown sat reading *Popular Mechanics* on a divan shaped like a giant English muffin. Ben introduced him to Mr. Kessler and the receptionist as "Tor," his roommate, a noted anthropologist. "Why do I have to get into leotards?" asked Mr. Kessler as the receptionist and the two Negro musicians began to slip into theirs and the anthropologist looked on. "I'll bet my new Vic Tanny's body won't look bad in them, though." After he had changed, there was a scuffle outside the curtain. The film had stopped suddenly, fixing Martha Graham on the screen with one leg on the practice bar. Several couples were screaming. A police officer was on the floor, and Ben said to Mr. Kessler, "Get his legs. He came up here and got stuck and we've got to get him out."

"I've never committed a crime," said Mr. Kessler, smoothing his leotards and taking the policeman's legs. Something wine-colored and wet was on the officer's breast pocket. "What do you mean he got stuck? I don't want to be carrying him if he got stuck."

They stumbled down the stairs with him and then walked several blocks in the blackness, finally propping the officer's body against an ash can.

"I don't know about leaving him against an ash can," said Mr. Kessler. "This is one thing I'm sorry I had to do tonight. Not because it's tonight especially, but because I wouldn't want to do it any night. But if I had to do it at all, I suppose I'm glad it was tonight. Why should I worry about doing this on Yom Kippur? I can see worrying about it in general, but not because it's tonight. Not if I'm supposed to be excused."

They went back to the party. The film was off now and couples were dancing wildly in the murk to a three-man combo, each of whom was beating a bongo. They were hollering out a song in which the only lyrics were, "We're a bongo combo," repeated many times. One of the

Negro musicians put a slim cigarette in Mr. Kessler's mouth and lit it. "Hey, wait a minute," said Mr. Kessler. "I know what kind of cigarette this is. I may have always had a yen to just try a puff of one, but that's one thing I'm absolutely not doing tonight. Not because it's tonight. I'd resist even more if it were just an ordinary night. In fact, the reason I haven't spit it out already is I want to show I'm not afraid of Yom Kippur. It's working already." Mr. Kessler sat down peacefully in the middle of perfumed, dancing, frenzied feet. "My senses are sharpened. I read that's what's supposed to happen." He saw the curtain part momentarily. Holding the anthropologist's purple dressing gown toreador style, the blonde receptionist, nude now, stood atop the English muffin. The noted Swede charged forward, making bull-like passes at her, one finger against each ear. A Negro girl with full lips leaned down and caught Mr. Kessler's head to her pistol-like bosoms, holding him there, senses sharpened, for what seemed like a season, and then Ben came whirling by in a series of *West Side Story* leaps, chucking him flirtatiously under the chin and then kissing him wetly in the ear. Mr. Kessler got to his knees and screamed, "J'ACCUSE. That isn't what I mean. What I mean is I'M EXCUSED, I'M EXCUSED," but no one heard him and he fell unconscious.

When he awakened, Ben and the two Negro musicians were helping him behind the wheel of his own car. Ben tapped the blonde receptionist on the behind and she slid in beside Mr. Kessler.

"We enjoyed your company terribly much," said Ben, and the two musicians howled. "Hope you enjoyed the decor and the Ivy League entertainment."

"What time is it?" Mr. Kessler asked the girl when the Negroes had driven off.

"Almost morning," said the receptionist.

"Well, at least they're out," said Mr. Kessler.

"Who's out of where?" she asked.

"The Jews are out of synagogue," said Mr. Kessler.

"I want you to meet my brothers," she said. "Maybe we can have a few beers before the sun comes up."

"The holiday is still on, but the important part is over," said Mr. Kessler. "Then tonight it's all over."

The receptionist showed Mr. Kessler the way to her white frame house. "I was divorced two years ago," she said. "Now I live with my two brothers. They're a hell of a lot of fun and I was lucky to have them."

The night was breaking when they got to the house. The receptionist introduced Mr. Kessler to the two brothers, both of whom were tall and freckled. The older brother served cans of beer for all, and when they had finished the beers, began to open a crate of grapefruits. "Our sales manager sent these back from the South," he said. "Aren't they honeys?" He picked up one of the grapefruits and rolled it to his younger brother, who fielded it like a baseball and threw it back. "You grabbed that one like Tommy Henrich," said the older brother, rolling it back. The younger brother picked it up, made a little skipping motion and flung it back again. "Hey, just like Johnny Logan," said the older one. He rolled it once again and when he got it back, said, "That was Marty Marion."

"Or 'Phumblin' Phil' Weintraub," said Mr. Kessler.

The brothers stopped a second and then the older brother rolled the grapefruit again. "George Stirnweiss," he hollered when his brother pegged it to him. He rolled it. He got it back. "Just like Bobby Richardson," he said.

"Or 'Phumblin' Phil' Weintraub," said Mr. Kessler.

"Who's that?" asked the older brother.

"That's it," said Mr. Kessler. He got to his feet with fists clenched and walked toward the older brother.

"You never should have said that," said Mr. Kessler.

"I didn't say anything," said the boy.

"Oh yes you did," said Mr. Kessler, through clenched teeth. "Maybe I went to Vic Tanny's and shacked up with a girl named Irish and got drunk and ate barbecued ham hocks. Maybe I hid a dead cop and smoked marijuana and went to a crazy party and got kissed by a Negro homosexual ballet dancer. But I'm not letting you get away with something like that."

He flew at the older brother now, knocked him down and began to tear at his ear. "He was all-hit-no-field and he played four years for the Giants in the early forties and faded when the regular players got out of service AND NO SON OF A BITCH IS GOING TO SAY ANYTHING ABOUT POOR 'PHUMBLIN' PHIL' WEINTRAUB ON YOM KIPPUR!"

The younger brother and the girl tugged at him with fury and finally dislodged him, but not before a little piece of the ear had come off. Then Mr. Kessler smoothed his leotards and went sobbing out the door.

"I may have been excused," they heard him call back in the early morning, "but I wasn't that excused."

The Hero

ON THE VERY FIRST PLAY, the new boy, younger than the others and a stranger to football, had clutched at a pair of flying feet only to have them beat against his forehead and black out his vision. In a hospital coma for half an hour, he opened his eyes finally, but one lip had already fixed itself in a strange loop above his teeth and his once handsome face had taken on a puffy Hunchback of Notre Dame quality. "Summon his kin," said the resident doctor. "I don't like the looks of this."

A stout woman with legs pared much too thinly for her bulk soon appeared; she wore a flowered dress, white anklets, and postwar "wedgies," giving her the appearance of one of those Soviet newsreel women who queue up outside stores during meat famines. "What's he pulled now?" she said, settling into a chair and crossing her legs in a great heavy-veined sweep. A horrified anesthetist turned away. "I see to it that he gets his meals and he goes and pulls things on me. If there's as much as a dime involved, you might as well keep the bugger right here with you. I'm out of it once and for all."

"There may not be much cost," said the resident, "but he'll have to be observed for a while, either here or when you have him. These things can go either way."

The boy, who had been listening vacantly, suddenly vaulted from the examination table and tore at the intern's ankles with his teeth.

"All right, get him off there," said the resident doctor. "That's what I mean. That's the kind of thing you're liable to be seeing."

"As long as I don't have to do any shelling out," said the woman. "If there's going to be any cost, you might as well check me out right now. He's not even mine, you know. My sister left him with me, went roving out on the West Coast, and hasn't been heard from since. I give him his meals, that's all anybody's getting out of me."

A week later, summoned once again to the hospital, the woman stood before the resident doctor and the boy, upright now in a discharged patient's wheelchair. His eyes seemed clear and bright, but there remained a residue of Charles Laughton-like fullness about the lips and jowls.

"Nothing much more we can do," said the doctor. "He may be all

115

right. We had two other bitings, one a nurse who was tearing along on an emergency surgery call and the other a pharmacist, nervous fellow, runs around like a headless chicken. Your boy just flew at them, really got his choppers into that prescription fellow's socks. Peculiar. He won't bother a walker. Somebody tears by at a gallop, though, and he goes for them like a bee after honey. Works right in with the football thing. I'd keep him away from any flying feet."

"You expect to bill me for this little episode, I'll show you some flying feet all right. Mine. I'm a working woman. I got just enough to keep me in beer nuts. You got a bill, send it to my sister and let me know where she's at if it ever catches up with her. I got a few items I'd like to ship her myself. This heavy-eating bugger in the chair for one."

"All right, Nonnie," she said, pulling the boy out of the wheelchair. "Let's get out of here. Before I know it, it'll be time for your meal."

An hour later, the woman, broad-nosed, of indeterminate age, took a seat at a bar called McTigue's. In the smoke-blurred, softening light, she might have been taken for just another trucker or faded merchant seaman. The boy, who had come in with her, stood opposite the juke-box, following the changing colors. He made some mewling sounds he had never made before.

"Beer, Mac," she said to the bartender. "And slide those Fritos over here where I can get a crack at them."

"Sure thing, Bertha," said the bartender. "That the kid? I never seen him in here with you before. Shouldn't he be in school?"

"He'll be coming in here with me from now on," she said. "Hurt his head. Long as it don't build up his appetite. All right, switch that TV over to bowling and let's have us some action."

Several years later, teeth bared and taking brief, huffing breaths in the manner of a short-snouted hunting dog, the boy stood as part of a crowd that had gathered in a great horseshoe to hear The Most Important Man in the Territory make a speech. He strained forward as though to wriggle free of the harnesslike contraption that laced his heavily mounded shoulders.

"Simmer down there, Nonnie," said the woman, reining him backward with much irritation. "You break another rig, and I'm cutting out Saturday treat. Stay still or I'll whip your head."

The boy craned his head backward, said "Talks" and then settled into place, still huffing.

The sun boiled down on the speaker's brow as he spoke of freedom and the richness of the land. "It don't put beans in my pocket," said the stout woman, holding tight to her reins. He spoke grandly of the nation's heritage and then a fellow in a windbreaker slipped past the guards and the guest-of-honor circle to bring his fist, in a gracefully arcing maneuver, against the Great Man's ribs. "Who let him do that?" the speaker asked and then sat down on the platform, holding his side, an enlarging spider of blood forming on his shirt.

"Christmas," said the stout woman, letting the harness reins drop to the grass. "Damned if that runt didn't slit the old man's gizzard."

The crowd, the guards, and the guests of honor all held their places in the sun as though posing for a formal portrait. They began to mill around then, groggily, as though a long film had ended. "Nail him," the chief of police said into the microphone, but the windbreakered man was nowhere in sight.

"I'm trying to hold on," said the Great Man. "It's leakin' out of me fast. Have they come up with him yet?"

"Matter of minutes," said his assistant.

"I'm not so sure," said the chief of police, kneeling in puzzlement. "I've never seen one flash away so clean in my career. Not a trace of him."

Far out on the parade grounds, beyond the last threads of the crowd, the windbreakered man dashed through some shrubbery like a flying spirochete. His feet seemed to be the only part of him that moved. They made a furious little pinwheel in the dirt and, with one exception, went unobserved.

"You get back here, Nonnie," said the stout woman, hands on her wide, flowered hips as she watched the harnessed boy race off at a humping but steady and somehow inevitable pace. "All right, chase off, you bugger, but that's the end of Saturday treat right there."

Knifing along with increased vigor, the man in the windbreaker was within sight of the railroad tracks and had begun to suck the air of freedom when he spotted the humped and snarling figure heaving along, far off in the distance. Always something, he thought. He don't seem to be getting anywhere, but I don't like his steadiness. He redoubled his speed for a while, but the vision of the steadily humping form coming along behind him added weight to his steps. Minutes later, he felt a gleaming pain at his ankles and his feet seemed to explode beneath him; he reached greedily for unconsciousness. When he awakened, the humped form was at the bottom of him, seemed to be connected.

"I wouldn't try to walk, mister," said the chief of police who stood above him. "Not much there to do it with. Anyone know the youngster?" he asked generally to the straggling crowd that had begun to form.

"Belongs to her," someone said, pointing to the stout woman who lumbered forward, adjusting the perspiration shields that soaked through her flowered dress.

"Used to," she said. "I'm giving him up after the way he broke clear and sassed me. More goddamned trouble than he's worth ever since I got stuck with him. What's he done now, and I can tell it's gonna set me back plenty."

"Bit clear through this here assassin-type's ankles," said the police chief. "Never saw anything quite like it. You don't have to worry about him, though," said the chief, stopping to cover the huddled form with a blanket. "The brave little feller's heart give out after he did his heroic act."

Late that night, a cordon of officials crowding her sides, the stout woman was led through the hospital corridors to the Great Man's side.

"Where'm I being steered?" she asked, yanking at her girdle. "Leggo of me. I was afraid of something like this. I knew I never should have taken the kid."

Eyes still fogged with coma, encased in a great vest of bandages, the Great Man had nevertheless managed to sit at a slight incline.

"My gratitude," he said, taking her plump hand. "Mine and that of a people. I suppose a boy like that would have attended a fine university."

"He had his handicap," said the woman, "but he was craftier than a lot of people thought."

"I'd like to make that dream possible," said the Great Man. "I'm depositing twenty thousand dollars in tuition fees to your account, if you'll allow me. So that the money would have been there if the brave young fellow had been around to use it."

"He'd of used it all right," the woman said, settling her great bulk into the hospital chair. "At least once a day a queer look'd come over him, like he was thinking about college."

Hours later, the stout woman stepped out of the Great Man's car, watched it race off in the darkness, and opened the crumbling door of her South Street cabin. Two middle-aged men with boutonnieres stepped out of the darkness and caught her elbows. "Oh, no, you don't," one of them said. "Right back out of there. You're coming with us."

"I knew I hadn't heard the last of it," she said as they herded her into a limousine. "You bastards start in with me and I'll sic that famous old buzzard in the hospital on your tails. I've got pull now."

They drove in silence for several miles, finally swooping beneath a marquee with a sign that said ALL SMILES ACRES and stopping before a neat, newly shrubbed ranch home with builder's chalk marks still on the windows. A group of young couples stood on the freshly seeded lawn and broke into applause as the trio got out of the car. "How do you like your new home?" asked one boutonniered man, smiling for the first time.

"Quit starching me," she said, stepping onto the porch and peering inside at the elaborately furnished kitchen. "What's the catch?"

"None," said the second man. "We just want to do our part for what happened today."

Quickly settled in her new home, the woman known·as Bertha was about to pour cream for her morning coffee when her hands were stayed by two white-uniformed delivery men. "Peh," said one, hurling her cream container into the garbage disposal. "Try this fresh stuff," he said, producing a quart of unopened cream. "There'll be a carton of dairy products each morning, ad infinitum, compliments of Seaberry Foods. You've received your first."

The TV set in the parlor had a tag on it: "With the best wishes of Eddie's Appliances." She flicked it on and watched the early news, much of which was thrown over to the previous day's tragic events at the parade grounds. A special fund, the announcer said, had been started by the station in honor of the boy who had gone to his death apprehending the would-be assassin. He said the station had kicked off the drive with a check for a thousand dollars. Finishing her coffee quickly, she dialed the station and said, "I just heard your show. Is it the boy's ma who gets the money?"

"Each Monday morning a check for the week's proceeds will be brought to her by a station official."

"Well, I'm her," said the woman, "and here's what I want to know. How about if I came over for the thousand this afternoon and we pick up the Mondays after that. Just to get the thing rolling."

Two newspapers began "Biter Funds" the following day, one announcing it would make *daily* cash presentations to the slain hero's guardian. The fully recuperated Great Man led a torchlight procession to the boy's grave. He spoke of the American way of life and announced that each day henceforth a great cascade of fresh flowers would be laid on the dead young hero's gravestone.

"He had his little sickness," the stout woman said, in an address to the crowd. "But you could tell there was this other thing simmering in him, aching to come out. It come on out, of course, the day he went for that no-good mother at the parade grounds."

The crowd applauded deliriously and a high-ranking French official, who had bypassed the nation's capital to attend the ceremony, broke forward, shouting, "La Patrie," and losing himself in her cheeks with kisses. During the solemn march back from the cemetery, the woman nudged one of the Great Man's aides who marched at her side. "Incidentally," she said, "what's it come out of?"

"What do you mean?"

"The dough for the flowers."

"Oh, he'll pick up the tab."

"Just curious," she said. "With everyone putting the bite on these days, there ain't that much left when you get down to it."

Instead of diminishing, the requests for press interviews gathered in volume. "After his injury," she said, winding up one late-night mass interview at her home, "he picked up this thing about our flag. Every time he'd see one he'd get to huffin' and carryin' on. I'd take him to parades every chance I got. Otherwise there'd be no living with the patriotic little rascal. So it come as no surprise to me the day he cut loose and tore up that no-good's ankles."

"Okay, boys," she said, scratching her armpit and beginning to roll down a stocking. "Show's over. Got to get me ten minutes' worth of beauty sleep."

There were murmurs of disappointment and then a short, goateed man of brisk movements stepped forward and announced, "Miss Gurdy regrets to announce that the interview is at an end. Please submit further requests for press interviews in writing. All such requests will receive prompt replies."

"Well, I'll be," the woman said as the reporters filed out of the door. "Look at the size of what come crawling out of the woodwork. Who give you the go-ahead to put words in my mouth?"

"I'm your new spokesman," said the diminutive fellow, drawing the blinds.

"In a pig's nostrils," she said. But with one swift movement the goateed intruder was at her side, his fingertips lightly touching a plump arm that had long gone unstroked.

"Goddamned if you're not the cutest rascal," she said. "Look at the fuzz on him, too. What's this little service going to set me back?"

"A trifle," said the bold newcomer, his tufted chin finding her neck. "One dollar out of every ten."

"No deal," she said. Arrow-swift, the short fellow went for his hat. "All right, slow down there," she said, lying back voluptuously. "Don't get so excited. Come on back here and let's see if you can sell me."

She gave frequent addresses and rare was the local gathering that did not find her on the dais, the goateed spokesman at her side. "My Nonnie would have split right open with happiness at what you're doing tonight," she told a group at an ambulance dedication.

"He'd of knelt right down on his pitiful knees and smelt every one of them," she assured a crowd that had come to receive a tulip-bearing delegation from the Netherlands.

She seemed oddly naked without her spokesman one night at a Funds for Arthritis drive. "What happened to your representative?" she was asked at the end of her remarks.

"Parting of the ways. He wasn't as good as he looked," she said. "Not at those prices."

Gradually, it became the patriotic rallies that pleaded for her appearance.

"Course he never had time to become one of you," she said, winding up her address to a large veterans' gathering, "but it's safe money he would've if he hadn't been cut down in his prime."

"Weren't but one thing in his mind when he went tearing off after that fella's feet," she told another. "Old Glory."

And then, inevitably, they came; a pair of them, corrupt Santa Claus types in overcoats. They watched her carefully and at the same time appeared to be dozing at the rear of the packed auditorium. "What do you think, Charlie?" asked one.

"You know damned well what I think, you old fossil."

Several minutes later, the pair appeared at the door of the woman's dressing room, burly types who carried their weight well, moving with the genial confidence of men who were rarely balked.

"Sorry, show's over, boys," she said, hoisting a dressing gown over her shoulders. "You fellas can catch me Memorial Day over at the Knights of Pythias."

"Won't take but a twinkling, dear," said one, pulling a stool close to her, eyes crinkling with charm.

"We've got this little proposition," said the other, snatching a second stool. "But first we'd like to get your thoughts on a few things. Vietnam, NATO, Cyprus, oil depletion . . ."

"Just where you sit on federal aid to education," the first man continued, "the integration thing? You see there's a certain senatorial someone who's been in office for twelve years. Most folks think he's a permanent fixture."

"But by golly," said his partner with a genial little fist thump on her knee, "we think the old buzzard's just about ready to be taken."

"I think you two geezers are about ready to be taken, too," she said, taking a seat at her dressing table. "And we all know where." She began to slap on some cold cream. "What's an old bitch like me supposed to know about Vietnam? I'll feel I'm lucky the day I can pronounce it. And what's the other one, NATO, where in the hell's that?

"Of course," she said, wheeling swiftly in a white mask and jabbing a finger, "that Cyprus is something else. It's the Turkish bastards you got to watch in that one. Don't trust 'em an inch and, if they get smart, let 'em have it right in the gizzard . . ."

The Good Time

THERE WAS ONCE a very bad time for me when I was in the Army and knew I was to be sent to Korea. I was in Chicago at the time, and wherever I went in that city, I couldn't seem to escape the special kind of cold Chicago had. No matter what I wore, the cold got into me and down inside my clothes and made me feel lonely and as though I would never relax for the rest of my life. It followed me into the hotel room in which I stayed and chased me as I drove along the Lake. There were other parts of Chicago to go to, and I guessed it wouldn't be so cold in them, but I never could seem to get away from the Lake. It was like a dream in which you know something good is a step away, but no matter how you fight and struggle you are unable to take the step. In any case, I felt there would be the same kind of cold and dampness in Korea; I would feel it in San Francisco, and it would be with me on the troop ship and through all the time I was overseas. The odd part is that I knew at another time, under different circumstances, I would have enjoyed the Chicago cold. It would have been not so much cold but freshness to me and would have made me feel very clean and romantic. So it was the way I felt, of course, and not the temperature that made me so cold. The very sound of the word "Korea" frightened me and there were nights when I said it over and over in my head. It began to sound then like a terrible children's disease ("Keep that child away from me. He's got Korea.") and I didn't want to go to it. I did not like the speed with which things were happening, and I felt that just because they *were* going so fast I would definitely be killed in Korea. I knew exactly how much time I would have. Eleven days of combat. Just enough to tease me into thinking I might come out alive. Then, too, there were my glasses to worry about. I had found out I was nearsighted and needed them and I was waiting now for the prescription to be filled. No one had ever told me that when you put on glasses, you saw immediately, and I was looking forward to a six-month or year period of slowly having my eyes get used to the glasses.

My furlough was a month long, and when a week had passed my mother called from Philadelphia and said she knew I must be feeling bad and that she was the only one who could cheer me up. I said I didn't think it was necessary to come all the way from Philadelphia and that, besides, I didn't think anyone could cheer me up.

"Your mother is the only one who knows how to give you a good time," she said. Then she said she'd like to have a nickel for every good time she'd shown me over the years, and I ended up saying it would be all right for her to come.

"But I don't even feel like being cheered up," I said.

Two days later, when I met her at the station, she brought over a woman of about thirty, who was carrying a small baby in her arms. My mother hugged me tight and said, "Your mother has a friend. Did you ever see it to fail?" To the woman, she said, "Meet my gorgeous son." The woman nodded to me and my mother said, "She's the sweetest thing alive. She rode with me all the way from Philadelphia and not a peep out of that baby of hers. Her husband's in the gardening business. Very interesting. He puts in gardens for people. Did you ever see such a sweet face on a girl? Look at her. That's the type I meet everywhere I go. And good? Good as gold. Her *and* the baby."

The woman, in a small voice, excused herself, and my mother squeezed her arm, kissed the baby on the cheek, and told the woman not to worry because "the real people in this world always find each other."

Then my mother came over to me and said, "Grab your mother around for a hug. It's all right. It's your mother. I came all the way from Philadelphia."

I hugged her and she said, as we walked out of the station, "The sweetest thing. Did you see her face? She has a dining room with two fold-out beds and she said to me, 'Any time you want to come and stay with me—even with your son—you just come.' That's the kind of people I meet. It's my luck. I've never had money, but I always meet real people."

"I didn't really think there was anything to her," I said. "What was she? Just another person."

"You're in quite a mood," my mother said. "I can imagine what you would have turned into if I hadn't come out here. But *you* didn't need your mother. You never do. Not much."

My mother yelled "Taxi-feller" outside the station and I said, "I could've done that. Jesus Christ." I'd moved out of my small hotel, and I gave the cabbie the name of the hotel at which I'd made a new reservation. "How're you Chicago cabbies doing?" my mother asked, and the cabdriver hesitated before answering "Fine," as though he felt some responsibility for having to answer for all Chicago cabdrivers. "They're no different here," my mother said to me. "If I gave him a quarter tip, I'd have him eating out of my hand."

The lines in my mother's face had gotten a tiny bit deeper, and her hair was recently done in a pageboy, but otherwise there hadn't been much change. Her figure was still so young and good it embarrassed me to look at it. And I have to admit I didn't feel quite so cold now with her near me.

"So, sweetheart," she said to me in the cab, "are you very heartbroken about having to go to Korea?"

"I don't care," I said. "Only I'd rather be a lieutenant." I told her about a friend of mine who'd gotten a commission and she said, "He's there and you've got to get there." I could tell by the way she said it that it had become a pet line and I would be hearing it very often when we were together. She got them and used them until she made you blue in the face. The last one I remembered had been, "You're on your way in, I'm on my way out." So I decided to nip this one immediately.

"That's where you're wrong," I said. "I don't got to get there. I don't *got* to get anywhere."

"If you want to be stubborn, be stubborn," my mother said. "See how far it gets you."

When the bellhop took our bags at the hotel, my mother took me into the cocktail lounge to get a bite to eat. "When was the last decent meal you had?" she asked. I said all I wanted was a corn beef sandwich and when the waiter came over, she pulled his sleeve and brought his head right next to her ear. "Look," she said, "I want it lean. My kid is going overseas."

"It's just a sandwich," I said. "For Christ's sake, do you have to make such a fuss?"

My mother ordered a drink, and I turned one down. "I like these guys who are afraid to order one drink," she said. "I really am crazy about that type of guy."

"Do I have to want a drink right this second?" I asked. "All I want is a sandwich."

I ate my sandwich and my mother had her drink, and then she said, "I'll bet you're feeling better already. Your mother doesn't know how to cheer you up, does she? Not much."

"I feel okay," I said.

I told my mother that later on that evening, much later, a friend from college named Chico was coming over to the hotel to join us.

"I can't think," my mother said. "I really can't worry about what's going to be. Sometimes that's your trouble. You think too much. It's not healthy."

"He'll be over around midnight, that's all," I said.

"We'll see," my mother said.

"But he *will* be over."

"I *said* we'll see," my mother said.

In our room, after the bite to eat, my mother took off her blouse and began to unpack. She had a large bosom and her brassiere seemed somehow more like an institution to me than an undergarment. I had the idea that I had seen her in her brassiere and skirt more often than I had seen her in any other costume. It made her comfortable and she walked around that way in private, just as some men seem to relax more with their sleeves rolled up. She had her suitcase almost all filled with perfume bottles and she took them out one by one saying, "Don't you worry about this baby. I've got all the perfume I need." She showed me a small green bottle and said, "What do you think of this one?" and I said, "What the hell am I supposed to think of it?"

"Someday I'll give you a little clue as to what it costs," she said. "You'll go crazy."

"I'm *very* interested," I said.

"I don't like the way you're acting," my mother said. "You better take a nap and you'll feel better. Tonight we'll get a little fun in your system."

I must have slept for about five hours, and it surprised me, because it usually took a few days for me to get used to a new and strange bed. But I woke up with that cold tremble I'd had since coming to Chicago. A bellhop came to the door with a bottle of liquor my mother had ordered and I heard her say, "Don't get any ideas. He's my son."

She opened the bottle and said, "You slept like a doll. You must have needed it like life itself."

"What a lousy taste in my mouth," I said. My mother poured me a drink and said it would make me feel more like a human being. When I took the drink and said, "Ahhhhh" and leaned back on the bed, she said, "You're really living. A hotel room, a drink, food in you, you're rested. I'd like to see what would've happened if I'd stayed in Philadelphia."

"I would have killed myself, of course," I said.

My mother took her shower and then I took mine and when I was drying myself in the bathroom she said, "I'm *sure* the bellhop believed you're my son. If he doesn't think I'm buying you, I'll eat my hat."

We had dinner in a Hawaiian-motif room, and I ate a lot, as though if I could fill up with food there would be no room for the cold to get down inside me. When I'd eaten all I could, my mother said, "I'm trying, baby. I'm doing the best I can."

"I know," I said. "I just feel lousy."

"My heart goes out to you," she said, covering my hand. "Believe me it does, darling."

We got the check and when my mother paid it, she said, "Where to now, baby? The night's yours to howl."

"Doesn't make any difference," I said.

We had seen an ad on the outside of the hotel that said Tommy Dorsey was playing in the main ballroom, and my mother asked whether I'd like to see him.

"It's all right," I said, with little enthusiasm. But then I added that it would be a good idea, because the show would run right up to the time Chico was to come and visit us.

"Well, that's something I don't know about," my mother said. "I can't think about the future."

We went into the ballroom, and although only a couple of tables were filled, the headwaiter asked if we had a reservation.

"Well, I really need that kind of crap," my mother said. "I had to come all the way from Philadelphia for that kind of crap. I mean I haven't heard this routine before. This is the first time for me."

"As you wish, madam," said the headwaiter, showing us to a table.

"I'm just in the mood for him," my mother said, as we sat down and ordered drinks. "And with his face, he can really afford to ask you for a reservation."

My mother told me some dirty jokes and I said, "Jesus, you know I don't like to hear dirty jokes from you. You're supposed to be my mother. Besides, I don't like to hear them from anyone. I like sex, but I don't like dirty jokes. That's no way to cheer me up."

"I can do without your philosophy," my mother said. "Besides, I know what's eating you. Well, you're crazy to think about it. They'll never put a gun in the hands of a college man. They'll shove you in an office."

"That isn't what's bothering me," I said. "I don't want to wear glasses."

"Then I have an idea," she said. "Kill yourself. Because no young boy ever had to wear glasses. And no one can be charming with glasses on. Dave Garroway has no charm at all. Not a drop."

"You know all about it," I said. "Thank you very much for cheering me up."

The room still had only four or five tables filled, including ours, when the bandstand began to revolve, and Tommy Dorsey and his band came into view, playing their theme song.

"Isn't he stunning?" my mother said. "You know how long I know that son of a bitch. Thirty years if it's a day."

A girl who took pictures strolled past our table with one piece of her rear end sticking out below her tights. My mother said to me, "Where are you looking?" But then she called over the girl and said, "Just this once I want to have a picture." The girl snapped off three shots of us and my mother said to her, "In case you're wondering, he's my son."

The girl made a big fuss and said, "My God, I never would have known," and my mother said, "I'll tell you a little secret, I think he could use you." Of course, after one of those introductions, there was never any possible way to make out with a girl, so I didn't even bother to check her as she swished away.

"You like a pretty shape," my mother said. "You've got your mother's taste."

In a little while, paraplegics began to file into the ballroom on wheelchairs and filled up the empty tables. I started to count them and stopped when I got to around forty. All seemed to have thick necks and upper arms. They were applauding almost from the second they got into the ballroom, and Dorsey smiled back over his shoulder as he conducted his band. "Jesus," my mother said. "I needed this to make my evening complete."

Dorsey played a waltz now, and motioned for my mother and me to come up to the bandstand. "I'll kill myself," my mother said. "He wants us to come up and dance. You know how long I know that son of a bitch."

We did the waltz and we were the only couple on the floor. The paraplegics applauded, whistled and banged on their tables.

"This is really one for the books," my mother said, as we circled the ballroom floor.

When Dorsey had completed a dozen numbers, the bandstand rotated and a rhumba group took over. Long sticks with knobs on their ends were passed around to the audience, and the idea was to beat on the tables with them in time to the music. I decided I didn't like the paraplegics. It was an awful thing to think, but I didn't care for them at all as a group, and I couldn't see why I had to love them just because they were paraplegics. Their jokes were very loud and bad, and one of them, who seemed to be a leader, said "sheeeet" all the time; they reminded me of a Rotarian bunch who had once spoiled a very smart supper club review for me in Greenwich Village. The paraplegics loved the sticks, and there was a moment when the entire ballroom seemed to roll with the thunder of a thousand sticks and I began to slide under the table to get away from the noise. Chico came in at this time, and I motioned for him to come sit with us, although I couldn't make any introductions until the beating stopped. We smiled at each other. Chico had blond hair and walked with a hunch and was a rhythmic fellow. He did a great deal of wild driving in a convertible, and he always seemed to be out of place when he wasn't behind the wheel, with a cigarette in his mouth and his hair flying. All I could ever re-

member him doing when he wasn't behind the wheel was sna
fingers rhythmically and saying, "Spat, spat. Spat, spat," all the
squinting his eyes and hunching over as if he were straining to hea
some faint band on the other side of a mountain.

"Is that the friend you were raving about?" my mother asked when
the hammering had stopped. She'd always insult someone loud enough
for them to hear it, but the funny thing is I can't think of one person
who said something back to her through all the years of her doing it.

Chico just smiled and said, "Spat, spat," and listened hard for that
faint melody in his ear.

"He's quite a bargain," my mother said.

The paraplegics began to file out at around midnight, and the one
who had kept hollering "sheeeet" wheeled over to thank us for being
such good sports and dancing for the boys. When they left, my mother
said, "I could use some air in my system." Chico took us for a drive
along the Lake then. There was some nice late music on the radio, and
my mother's perfume filled up the car. He loved to drive, and as he
held the wheel, his face and expression were quiet and numb, contrast-
ing sharply with the frantic motions through which he put his car.
"He's some crack driver," my mother said. "He can drive for me anytime." And then I knew what was coming. My mother said that she
herself would have been a wonderful driver. She had the most marvelous foot control, and of course, she had wonderful rhythm. "But I was
in deathly fear of the wheel," she said. This always annoyed me. "Then
you couldn't have been a wonderful driver," I said. "Just your feet isn't
enough, mother. Don't you understand that?"

"There are drivers who'd give their right arms to have my foot control," she said. "My rhythm."

Chico took us to a place he knew that served offbeat hamburgers. I
ordered one with banana slices on it, but I could only get down a bite
or two because even though I loved the idea of it, bananas really didn't
go with hamburgers. My mother wasn't pleased with the place and
ordered only coffee. "It must have taken some doing to find this place
out of all the restaurants in Chicago," my mother said. Chico remained
in his hunch, spat-spatting to his private concert, biding time before
getting back behind the wheel where he belonged. Driving us back to
our hotel, he skipped a red light and missed by a hair colliding with
another car at about seventy miles an hour. It took all the way back to
our hotel for my heart to stop pounding. "You get that with a crack
driver," said my mother. "He's a crack. An absolute crack. He's got
rhythm."

As he let us out at our hotel entrance, my mother asked Chico if
he'd had a good time, and I said, "For Christ's sake, do you think he's

You don't ask questions like that." Chico ...nned at us and then sped off, getting up to ...what seemed like seconds.

...p to her hotel room, and I went out to get the ...king toward the black blurriness of the Lake now ...start to come inside me again and make me tense. I c... ...cold out, but I didn't mind it quite so much because at least u... ...d quieted down a little. My mother, in spite of all the terrible tricks s..e pulled, had slowed down the march of things, and I had the feeling later, as the room filled up with her warmth and perfume, and I went inside the cold sheets, that my life had shifted around to the point where maybe I wouldn't automatically have to be killed after all. Maybe I would only have to be wounded a little.

"If you want to sleep, sleep," I heard my mother say in the morning. "It's your privilege. But you're crazy if you miss a minute. I have quite a day planned for you."

My mother had my breakfast sent up to the room, but I was too embarrassed to eat it in bed and wound up compromising, sitting in bed with my feet dangling over the side so it wasn't officially breakfast in bed. To have eaten it in bed would have made it too official that this was a last, final fling, and I didn't want it to be that way.

"You're nuts," said my mother. "Take all you can get. You'll look for these things in that goddamned country you're going to."

Before we left the hotel, I watched my mother take out a tiny little fat purse and count some money that was inside it. "Are you sure you've got enough to pay for all this?" I asked. Ever since my father died, I couldn't imagine my mother ever having anything substantial in the way of money. I could see her having a purseful, but never a penny more than that.

"Don't ever worry about your mother," she said.

"Well, how can I relax if I know that's all you've got?"

"Don't be ridiculous," she said. "I've got more money than God."

We went to see a musical comedy that had been very successful in New York and was now on tour in Chicago. It was like old home week, because Brian Aherne was doing the lead role in it. By the time I got to see musical comedies, he was always in the lead slot. Some day, I knew I'd be able to measure my success that way. When I began to see shows before Aherne took over the top spot, I'd know I had finally arrived in the big time.

Soon after the curtain was raised, two old ladies excused themselves and worked their way into our row. One of them asked my mother if this was *New Faces,* and my mother couldn't get over it for the rest of the afternoon. She said it wasn't, that *New Faces* was in New York, and when the ladies took their seats and removed their veils, my mother nudged me and said, "As far as they're concerned, they're seeing *New Faces* anyway. That's what they came to see and they're going to see it if everyone else has to choke." My mother said a little later, "You know, they're theater connoisseurs. They *really* would know the difference between *New Faces* and what they're seeing." At the end of the first act, my mother said, "Don't look now, but I think they've decided to tell everybody they saw *New Faces* after all."

My mother got hysterical with laughter over the two ladies during the second act and doubled up in her seat. Everyone turned around to look at us. "They *came* to see *New Faces* and they're *seeing New Faces,*" she said, the mascara running into her eyes. "Do them something." She continued to laugh and finally said, "I can't take too much more of this," and told me she'd wait outside. The seats were very near the stage, and although I didn't enjoy the show too much, I did get a kick out of seeing Aherne from so close.

After the show, I met my mother outside the theater and she said, "That sweetheart gave us some seats. We're going over to have dinner at his place tonight."

I asked who she meant and she said, "You remember, Monkey Lucella—the one with the crazy son you used to play with. He made a fortune of money out here and he'll kill me if we don't come over tonight for dinner."

Vaguely, I remembered a small, handsome man who rubbed his nose all the time while he talked. I remembered never being able to get over the fact that although he was handsome, he really did look like a monkey sometimes. I remembered his son, too. I once nicknamed him "the Seal" because every once in a while, as we were playing a game in our bedroom, he would suddenly fall backward on the floor and make terrible seal-like groans until his mother came to quiet him.

"What's his real name?" I asked my mother. "Not Monkey?"

"Don't ask me any nonsense," my mother said.

My mother gave Lucella's address to a taxi driver who sped off along the Lake. "He'll die when he sees how big you've gotten," my mother said.

"I don't see how it can be any fun," I said.

"Quiet," my mother said. "Did you see the seats he arranged for us? Do you want me to snub him?"

The cab drove through what seemed to be a Chicago suburb and pulled up at a handsome garden apartment. "It doesn't surprise me," my mother said, as she paid the driver. "He made a fortune of money."

Lucella came to the door, wearing an apron, and said, "Blow me down, come on in you wild Indians." He was shorter than I remembered him being, and handsomer, and his shoulders seemed wider, too. They were actually wide enough so that you'd really notice them if he walked by.

I'm sensitive about shoulders, because although the pictures I saw of my father showed him to be quite good-looking, his shoulders were round and narrow.

The apartment was done in an Oriental motif, right down to the last extension socket. It was heavily mirrored and I was not able to tell how large it was, nor how many rooms there were.

My mother looked around and said, "You must have made a fortune, Monkey. Here, let me give you a little kiss."

The house smelled of roast beef, and seated at the dining room table were "the Seal" and someone introduced to me as his teacher. The teacher had already started to eat his roast beef. It was explained that he had theater tickets that evening and would have to leave early. I could tell in one second, by the foamy look in his eyes, that "the Seal" was still making his seal-like sounds every now and then, even though ten years had passed since I'd heard them.

Inside the kitchen, at the stove, was a slender woman in a red Oriental robe who seemed quite properly dressed in it although she was obviously not an Oriental. She was quite sleek and everything about her gleamed and beamed, although you had the feeling that this was her last year of sleekness. After that, whatever terrible thing it was that happened to sleek, gleaming people who became old would happen to her. Whatever the case, she seemed, in spite of her current sleekness, to be quite subservient to Lucella.

We sat down at the table, and when for a moment it seemed no one knew what to do, Lucella said, "Look at this," and pulled out a large roll of bills with a rubber band around them and tossed them to my mother.

"The son of a bitch," my mother said, holding the money, as if she were weighing it. "The money this son of a bitch must have made here in Chicago. The *fortune* of money."

"Turn over a few," Lucella said, and my mother began to leaf through the bills. You had to go through quite a few hundreds before coming to the twenties.

"Well, blow me down," said Lucella in mock surprise. "There's real money in there."

"Fabulous," my mother said.

"Well, blow me down, we're going to have a little roast beef now," said Lucella. "Uncle Monkey is going to do the carving." He shouted into the kitchen, "Can I have a goddamned carving knife?"

"The Seal," who had not yet said hello, but who was huddled in discussion with his teacher, looked up now and began to let fly a few of the seal-like groans I knew would be coming. They were a little more mature and mellow-sounding, but they were very similar to the ones he'd done on the floor ten years before.

"You can't say a word to his mother," said Lucella. "You say a word to his mother and he'll cut you dead."

The sleek woman came out of the kitchen, her gleaming and beaming hair and teeth and eyes and skin outgleaming the carving knife she carried.

"Well, blow me down," said Lucella. "I'm getting something I want around here." He began to cut slices of the reddest, leanest roast beef I'd ever seen and put them on plates. There wasn't any bread or vegetables or salt and pepper. Just roast beef and silver.

"What do you think of this meat?" he asked.

"Fabulous," my mother said. "He must have made a mint. A mint of money."

When I finished my meat quickly, Lucella cut some more. It had a wonderful tang to it. The Seal's teacher was saying very obvious things to the Seal such as, "How do we really know we're here?" between bites of roast beef, and "Society gives us certain rules we must live by." "Society" was his biggest word, but I recall his beginning a great many lines with the phrase, "Convention dictates." I wanted to tell the Seal that the things he was saying really weren't worth the roast beef, but there didn't seem any way for me to jump into the discussion, so I just sat by and did a slow burn.

After we had all eaten enough roast beef, the sleek woman came beaming out with small glasses of a cordial she had poured. We each took one, the teacher taking his and drinking it fast as though he knew and we all knew and there was no sense denying that it was payment of some sort.

"He knows what to buy, too," my mother said, sipping her cordial. "He knows what to do with his money."

When we finished our cordials, Lucella showed us his suits. They filled two closets in what seemed to be his private bedroom. My mother said, "Now you're showing off, Monkey. You had suits when you didn't have anything else."

"Here," said Lucella, handing my mother a $100 bill. "I want you to have this." My mother took it, and when her hand touched the bill, it burst into flames. "Well, blow me down," said Lucella, once again in mock surprise.

"The son of a bitch," my mother said. "He'll tease the life out of you, too." She rubbed her finger and then said, philosophically, "Well, he's there and we've got to get there."

"I told you I hate that line," I said.

We went back into the dining room and sat in front of an artificial fire that cleverly simulated real flames by rotating a piece of metal against a battery of bulbs. There was wood that didn't burn, and a grate and andirons. When the sleek woman finished in the kitchen, she came and sat with us, taking the Seal on her lap. The combination of the flames and her gleaming and beaming was almost blinding. The teacher, who had wrapped some roast beef in a napkin, excused himself now and said good-by. The Seal got up and followed him to the door, shaking hands with a foamy look in his eyes. Then the Seal returned and sat in his mother's lap.

We hung around without talking too much; Lucella rubbed his nose and tinkered with a pair of cuff links that were made to resemble spare tires. I wanted to get going. I didn't see how this was contributing to any good time. Couldn't my mother see that I had just so many days and I needed every one of them to have fun in? I began to feel a little chilly and it struck me as being ironic that when I did finally get near a fire, it would be the kind that didn't even warm up people. The Oriental motif began to bother me, too.

My mother didn't appear to be in any hurry, and she said, after a while, "Tell the truth, Monkey. Do you miss the East Coast? Cross your heart and tell me you're happy here in Chicago. All your millions aside."

Lucella rubbed his nose and said, "There's only one Philly and only one New York. When you're in Chicago, you're strictly out of town. And don't ever forget it."

Then, in one of the few times he looked at me, he said, "You know how long I know your mother? Maybe thirty-five, forty years."

"He used to carry me into the waves at the seashore on his shoulders," my mother said.

"Let's show him how, Nora," said Lucella. He went over to my mother, put her cordial glass aside, slipped his head between her legs and then stood up with her on his shoulders. Her skirt split open and some garment showed that I never wanted to see in my whole life. It had elaborate hooks and snaps on it and it seemed you'd have to be very old before wearing it. It was just something I never wanted to see on my mother.

"The son of a bitch," my mother said, as she sat on his shoulders. She fell off them easily, and more of the garment showed when she did. When I saw the complete garment, I did something I hadn't done in perhaps fifteen or twenty years, but something I had been in the habit of doing for quite some time as a child. Starting to cry, I put my head down, closed my eyes and rammed my head into Lucella's groin.

The Seal let out an uncertain variety of groans as though he'd never before seen anything like this and hadn't had time to prepare a special groan for it. Lucella, oddly enough, didn't hold his groin where I'd gotten him, but kept rubbing his nose. Comforting me, my mother said, "I know, I know, you didn't want to see your mother carry on. You never have." I started to tell her she'd missed the point, but instead I got my coat. My mother said good-by to Lucella and his beaming wife and to the Seal. "You've got a lovely set-up here," she said to them all, and we went outside to wait for a cab.

It seemed a little colder now, but it probably *was* colder because it was later, for one thing, and we were out in the open with few houses to break the wind.

My mother put her arm around me and said, "I know. It wasn't pleasant. But it was just one of those obligations. From now on, we're going to have only good times."

But I couldn't understand why we had to fulfill even that one obligation. Why did I have to find out that my mother was once carried into the ocean on people's shoulders, and why did I have to see that garment she wore under her dress? As we stood on a dark Chicago street, my mother's arms around me, I asked her if that was her way of cheering me up. Was that her idea of giving me a good time? Was that the way you treated a son who was very cold and couldn't relax and needed glasses and was going to a place that sounded like a terrible children's disease—a disease that probably began with a rash, for all I knew, and ended by attacking your damned kidneys.

The Mission

HE WAS A SMALL, brisk-looking man whose slender form seemed crowded with power; he gave the impression of having spent much time among taller men, athletes perhaps, staying even with them by lashing his body to the utmost. He had used many conveyances to get to Central Africa: swift trains, great jets, a horse and, finally, rotted paddling things a man in good condition could easily outrun. Throughout his journey he had remained cool and dapper, but now, in the shebang, at the foot of the Limpopo Hills, his hat had slipped too far down on his ears, giving him the look of a half-shelled walnut. He ordered a native beer he would not drink and asked for Fleeger, a German with a shadowy war record, the owner of the shebang and his one lead.

At the end of the bar, barefoot girls of many shades clung to a huge beret-wearing man with a wide stumplike neck. He stood up and they began to drop like seasonal skins from a jungle animal. The man adjusted his stomach as he walked; it might have been a pillow tied to his waist. He sat down opposite the newcomer and said, "Young sausages. Blindfold me and let me touch a little sausage and I'll tell you how young she is. You like the babies, too, or you like an older pickle?" He laughed in a bellow and touched the other man with a show of camaraderie, but the laugh crumbled in his throat when he felt the steel of the visitor's arm.

"You keep in pretty good shape, eh?" said the German. "You know how many times Jacques Fleeger's been hit on the head and it didn't bother me? The Russians were the ones. I was in one of their camps, you know, in 'forty-five. They'd slip up behind and let me have it on the noggin, a game they played. Twenty-two taps I took, so now Fleeger's afraid of nothing. Not with what I been through. Anyone who doesn't behave in my place, I clean them right up. I move fast for a big man. Karate." He cut the air with some swift chops at a phantom opponent, but when he met the other man's gaze, he slapped at his wet neck with a handkerchief and whispered hoarsely, "All right, what do you want? Why are you here?"

The small man used the beer, not for thirst but as a lip-wetter. "I want to take a Sharpe's grysbok. It has to be tomorrow."

"A cape grysbok, you mean. There are no Sharpe's left."

"A Sharpe's," said the other man. "It has to be a Sharpe's."

"Well, I hope you didn't travel far, mister, because that ends the discussion. There are no Sharpe's left in Africa." The German had gotten control of his voice now and yelled, "Over here, cuties." The girls glided forward and attached themselves to him like sea anemones to a monster clam. "All I care about is my sausage," he said. "I like them in numerals, three, four, that's a good time. With one I get bored. That's what the war did. Made things complicated." He poked and jabbed at the girls, giving them swift, insectlike bites. But then, as though he had heard a telephone ring, he turned and looked across the table, his voice cracked again. "How come you wear your hat that way? Down so low."

The small man pushed the unsipped beer to the center of the table. "I want an eight-o'clock start," he said and then studied his hand with a statuelike gaze for what must have been thirty seconds. He stood up and walked briskly to the swinging doors, styled in the manner of Old West saloons.

"No, you don't," the German called after him. "They're extinct. I won't be there." And when it was too late for the small man to hear him he cried, "How many are there, three or four in all of Africa? You expect me to find one?"

At seven-thirty the following morning Fleeger heaved his great body up the stairs of the town's only hotel and entered a room on the first floor. The man in the bed slept evenly, his body hardly stirring, almost corpselike in his serenity; he wore horn-rims in bed, which robbed the huge German of any composure he had gathered overnight. He touched the sleeping man and said, "I'm not here for anything. Why should I kill myself over something foolish with what I've been through? I didn't hear you talk money either."

The small man slipped out of bed, his movements lithe, almost feminine in their economy. At the washstand he mentioned a sum, not excessive, not paltry. Fair.

"That settles it," said the German. "The deal's off. Not for that kind of dough. I'm not budging." The small man's arms were bunched with muscle, but still they appeared much more slender than they had seemed in the jacket. "You don't look that strong," Fleeger said. "What do you use, commando stuff?"

The small man dried himself and got into his clothes with dazzling speed. "Let's roll," he said, getting his hat down snugly over his ears.

"Who said anything about rolling," said the German. "I just came up here, that's all. I don't like the finances." But then he reached for his handkerchief, holding his stomach with one hand, as though it were falling off. "Jesus," he said, "I never saw anyone get dressed that fast in my life."

The trip for the most part was over water, a canoe voyage along the Siwi River, which curled like discarded thread in and out of the Limpopo Hills. The German told earthy Bavarian tavern jokes until the small man finally laughed at a weak one, a short discolored exhalation of nose breath; he showed his teeth, too, for the first time, and Fleeger's next gag went sour in his throat. Out beyond the Limpopos they came to level jungle, and the German beached the canoe. "Pafuri country," he said. "Don't get excited. It's not a whole tribe. Just a dozen guys and a few young sausages to keep them happy. They're good hunters, though. The chief'll laugh in my face when I tell him what you're after."

The other man stepped out of the canoe and stretched his arms, the German falling back as though to protect himself. "What's up?" asked the small man.

"Nothing," said the German. "Nerves. I thought you were finally coming for me. It wouldn't have surprised me a bit."

The chief of the Pafuris lived in a shack littered with dozens of old soup cans. He leaned against an antique stove, wearing GI surplus khakis and carrying a spear. "Tell him how ridiculous it is, Soko," said the German. "He wants a Sharpe's grysbok. He wouldn't believe me."

The small man had not looked once at the chief. Dapper in a business suit, he prowled around the shack like a college-grad exterminator, finally snapped open a can of beans and ate them cold.

"I like his stylishness," the chief said with resonance. "I will help that man."

"Everyone's buddies in the jungle," said Fleeger, patting the small man's back as the trio cut their way through the underbrush. The small man bristled and the German drew his hand away as though he had touched a stove. "Suit yourself," said the German and then the Pafuri chief motioned for them to get down and be quiet. They had come to the edge of a clearing where small animals ducked their snouts into a pond. "Steenboks, bonteboks, klipspringers, there's a cape grysbok," whispered the German, "but like I said, no Sharpe's grysbok. It'll be a blue moon before you see one, too."

"Shut up, kraut," said the Pafuri chief. "We'll get the man what he desires."

Hours later, a small, shy deerlike animal with an old man's thatch of white hair appeared at the pond, the other animals scattering. "Jesus," said the German. "I'll be a monkey's uncle."

"Shhhh," said the chief, raising his spear. The small man darted forward and caught his arm. "Alive," he said, "or it's no go."

"Stylish," said the chief with admiration. He narrowed his eyes and then leaped forward toward the pond, the small animal flashing away in a swirl of underbrush.

"I'm catlike for a big man," said the German and flew off after the chief. Both men returned empty-handed, the chief's head hanging.

"A Sharpe's grysbok is worse than Mr. Snake," he said. "You can't hardly hold him."

The small man put his hat even farther down over his ears, adjusted his horn-rims and disappeared into the bush. Minutes later he emerged, holding the frightened animal beneath his coat. "How do you hang on to these buggers?" he asked, looking like an amateur magician giving away his trick.

"By the ears," said the chief. "Superlative performance."

"You got him," said the German. "Where's my dough?"

With one hand, the small man took some bills out of his pocket, then put half of them back.

"Why half?" asked the German.

"That's all you earned," the brisk little fellow said and disappeared through the bush.

It was not until he reached Oran that he was able to have the frail animal properly caged. A Belgian zoologist there told him to make sure he mixed a few oribi droppings in with the grysbok's normal feedings of lettuce and young grass roots. From Oran he flew to Rome and then on to Paris, where American Express recommended a gourmet butcher shop.

"I want the tongue alone," he said in his minimal French, showing up in midafternoon with his grysbok. "Packed in ice."

Half an hour later the clerk appeared with a small package, frosty to the touch. The small man checked it and inside were heels, done up in dry ice. "I said the tongue," he cried, sticking out his own and pointing to it. He rushed into the back room, put his head in a great bin and swam through entrails until he'd retrieved the grysbok head. "All right, let's have at it again," he said, "and try to get it straight this trip."

*　*　*

That night he appeared on the doorstep of a small house in the Clichy district, two packages beneath his arm, one large, one small. A young girl with startled eyes answered his ring and said, "Oh, no, monsieur, you want four houses down. We are respectable."

"Uh-uh," he said. "I want your dad."

"He sleeps," she said. "Most of the day. He sleeps and I fear one day he will not wake." In some manner, how she could not tell, he had gotten into the house, and when she spoke to him next, the small man was in an armchair. "I cannot wake him," she said.

"A matter of great urgency," said the visitor. His hat fascinated her. She wondered why he wore it so low on his ears.

"You have a way, monsieur," she said shyly and woke her father.

In his bathrobe, her father seemed cathedral-like, ruined, a figure out of dying empires. The small man explained his proposal.

"Impossible," said the old man. "I haven't cooked in ten years. Le-Blanc will never cook again. Great men have appeared here just as you. To no avail. Food no longer has a fragrance. It is a stench in my nostrils. I am an old man and want to die."

The small man rose from his armchair and swiftly unwrapped the larger of his two packages. The old man came close, examined the contents. "Jean Sablon records," he said, his face slowly beginning to shine. He looked further. "Each one, in perfect sequence. The complete works." His ancient face gave forth a broken smile. "You have gotten around an old man. For you I will cook. What was it again?"

"*Casserole de langue de Sharpe's grysbok au champignons,*" said the visitor.

"With *beurre noir* or *en sauce béchamel?*"

"One second, papa," said the visitor, pulling a small notepaper from his wallet. He studied it, looked up and said, "*En sauce béchamel.*"

"You have the grysbok tongue?"

"On ice," said the small man, producing the second package.

"Jeannette," hollered the old chef, rolling up his bathrobe sleeves and rubbing his dried hands. "My pots."

At noon the next day, suit freshly pressed and shoes polished to a blinding shine, the small, compactly built man hopped down the ramp of his Paris-New York jet and waited several hours for another that was to whisk him from Kennedy Airport to Chicago. Six o'clock that night he stepped out of a taxicab in front of a slate-colored, monotonous-looking building in northern Illinois, tipped the driver and then walked up to giant iron gates. The guard, at first tense, relaxed when he came near, and said, "Right inside, Mr. Flick, the chief's waiting."

Minutes later, the warden of Joliet Prison charged forward to meet him, pumped his hand, then sat back and said, "How'd it go?"

"Look for yourself," said the new arrival, pointing to a neatly wrapped box alongside his luggage. "Casserole of Sharpe's-grysbok tongue with mushrooms in *béchamel* sauce."

"I'm not even going to look," said the warden. He rang for a guard, pointed to the box and said, "Okay, rush that up to the Death House and tell them to heat it up. Good work, Flick, and let's hope the next joker is a steak-and-apple-pie man."

The Enemy

For as long as Samuel could remember, Aunt Emma had been the enemy. She always looked pretty much the same to him, a large woman with an enormous but vaguely defined bosom, much white powder on her face, and skin that did a great deal of hanging, especially in the neck area and along her arms. As the years went by, all that happened to her was that her powder got a little thicker, and her skin hung some more. It was as though she were some kind of exotic tree whose age could be determined by the amount of hang added each year. She was a concert violinist, spoke with a thick Viennese accent and had great, darkening teeth which seemed a little decayed and Viennese to him; the few times she hugged Samuel he was horror-struck and held his breath so that he would not have to smell her powder, clenched his fists so that he would not somehow disappear into her great hanging folds of skin.

She was married to Uncle Rex, and presumably, before Samuel was born, she had not been the enemy at all. She and Uncle Rex lived modestly in a small Newark apartment filled with musical instruments —antique violins, lutes and strange, slender, gracefully curved, reedy things that were on the tops of lumbering, ruined pianos. Later on, when Samuel came to visit, he remembered that the walls were crowded with darkened, brooding oil paintings, each one with a little light switch above it. When he turned the little lights on, the paintings would remain dark and brooding, the only difference being that the darkness glistened a little. He remembered thick, musty Oriental rugs and music stands and things that seemed to be remnants of old, rotting Viennese fortunes. In the days before Aunt Emma became the enemy, she went out on concert tours while Uncle Rex did mysterious things involving the trading of one large batch of fabric for another.

One evening, Uncle Rex attended a concert given by Aunt Emma, and after five minutes of hearing her perform, stood up in his seat and tore at his collar, saying he couldn't breathe and that there was gas in the concert hall. He made it to the aisle and then fell down and began to roll around, gasping for breath and tearing at his clothes. Someone sat on him while the police were called, and he was taken to Bellevue where attendants found bankbooks on his person totalling two million dollars. Samuel was two years old at this time. It was about then that Aunt Emma became the enemy.

There began a twenty-year war between Uncle Rex's family on the one side and Aunt Emma and her two daughters on the other. The money, in a court transaction, had been taken from Uncle Rex and put into a trust fund, with small, regular payments being made to Aunt Emma on which she and her two daughters were to live. The war involved Aunt Emma's efforts to get the money in a few great chunks rather than to receive it in meager allotments. Uncle Rex's family, with Samuel's mother as commanding general, stood for keeping the payments modest so that Uncle Rex, once he was cured, would have a financial backlog. During the twenty-year period, he was trundled in and out of rest homes and mental institutions, both public and private. Another issue in the war involved Aunt Emma's side trying to keep him in these places and Uncle Rex's family, hence Samuel's team, getting him out of them.

Samuel's mother, as the leader of what Samuel came to know as the "good side," was a slender woman with slightly bowed legs, who never got over her bewilderment at Uncle Rex turning up with quite so much money. Uncle Rex was her oldest brother and had always been her favorite. She told Samuel that when she used to visit him before his collapse, they would sit together in his apartment watching fast new cars pass in the street below. "I told him which ones I liked," she said to Samuel. "Little did I know he could have bought the whole fleet of them." She told Samuel what a bad person Aunt Emma was; her main charge was that she was a "phony" and that she had misrepresented herself as coming from an important Viennese family. When Samuel asked where Uncle Rex had met her, his mother said, "God only knows. God only knows where he found her." Samuel's mother and Uncle Rex had been brought up in New York's Harlem section; she would say to Samuel, "There weren't enough girls in the neighborhood for him. He had to go to twenty neighborhoods away to dig up that queen of his."

Second in command on the good side, and chief lieutenant to Samuel's mother, was her sister, Aunt Ramona, a tiny, saintlike person who ran a hardware store. She was very nervous and was always rolling up things, pieces of napkin, matchbook covers, edges of menus, and sticking them in her ear for a quick shake. When she used up one ear sticker, she immediately got to work on another. Much less strident in her criticism of Aunt Emma, she would occasionally take Samuel's wrist, lead him aside and say to him, "Shall I tell you something, Samuel. Your Aunt Emma is not a nice person." The third member of the general staff was Samuel's grandmother, whose main function was the taking of suitcases of things to Uncle Rex during his stays in institutions. Samuel remembered her as always getting up very early in the morning, earlier than anyone he had ever heard of. He was quite boastful of this fact and would tell his friends, "I've got a grandmother who gets up earlier than anyone in the world." Old when the war began, she hung on for many years, her role growing smaller until senility reduced her to rising before dawn and then sitting in a rocking chair to spend the day rocking away and heaping ancient Hebraic oaths upon Aunt Emma's head. Each of the three general staffers had slightly bowed legs, although Samuel's grandmother considered hers straight and would often point at other old ladies and insult them for having crooked feet. In any case, Samuel always carried with him an image of these three frail ladies, graduated in height, marching bowlegged but unafraid—Spirit of '76 style—to do battle with giant, heavily powdered Viennese Aunt Emma of the frightening, hanging folds of flesh.

Most of the battle reports came to Samuel via frenzied, shouting telephone conversations between his mother and her two lieutenants that ate up entire evenings. It seemed to Samuel that the calls could always have been condensed if the parties had made an agreement to have first one talk and then the other. But sentences were rarely finished; almost never did either side get to string two of them together. Samuel's mother would say, "Now wait a minute . . . now let me finish . . . I want to tell you something. Wait, Ramona . . . You know what the trouble is? . . ." And at the other end (Samuel knew this because he visited his saintlike aunt on numerous occasions) Aunt Ramona would say to his mother, "Just a second . . . Shall I tell you something . . . You've got to understand one thing . . . Now hold on there . . ." The Uncle Rex calls seemed to yawn forth endlessly, taking up great sections of Samuel's youth. He lived with his parents in a small apartment, and was often hard-pressed, because of the calls, to get his homework done. When the phone rang in the evening, he would go into the bedroom he shared with his mother and father, close the door, press his hands tight over his ears and try to concentrate on his lessons. Sometimes, when he was really annoyed, he would stand in his father's bedroom closet, his head among the ties. Samuel's father, not a terribly loyal soldier in the battle, would station himself opposite Samuel's mother, and begin to make disgusted faces, crossing and uncrossing his legs, getting up and down, and occasionally, as the hours wore on, hollering out, "When in hell are you getting off the goddamned phone."

Among the phone phrases in frequent use by Samuel's mother were "The son of a bitch . . . Let her (1) Drop dead (2) Burn in hell . . . What she's done to that poor boy . . . What she's turned him into

. . . There weren't enough girls in the neighborhood . . ." and Samuel always knew these could only have to do with Aunt Emma. "The two little beauties" and "the two bargains" made reference to Aunt Emma's daughters and "that prince" and "the angel" were synonymous with Henry Howell, the family attorney, who had for twenty years gone before state mental health boards and neurological commissions to get Uncle Rex out of bad institutions and into good ones, out of *all* institutions and back to his apartment in Newark. Whenever he succeeded in the latter task, and Uncle Rex was carted back to his Jersey apartment, a new species of phone call would get under way at Samuel's house. Though equal to the other in length, they were a gentler, less frenzied variety; in these, Samuel's mother would try, and totally fail, to convince Uncle Rex that there was no gas leak in his apartment, that his fish was *not* being poisoned and that Aunt Emma hadn't bought a special kind of smothering pillow for him so that when he put his face in it, he would wake up dead one morning. "I'll come over and sleep in the pillow," she would say to him. "Is that what you want?" Or "I'll eat the fish and show you that it's all right. Would that convince you?" And then, "There's no gas leak. I'll come over to breathe in your kitchen to show you." These calls were not exactly pleasurable to Samuel, but he looked forward to them nonetheless as a form of respite. He was able to concentrate on his homework while they were being carried on and felt no need to go among the ties. But then back Uncle Rex would go to a home, and once again, the violent, warlike conferences would get under way, driving Samuel into the locked bedroom and impelling his father to take up a muttering, leg-crossing sentry duty opposite the phone.

Each time Uncle Rex checked into a new institution, Samuel would accompany his mother (and often her two lieutenants) on a visit to see that Uncle Rex was well situated and happy in his new headquarters. Most of the places Samuel could remember were sunny, flowered terraced ones that seemed just like ordinary resorts, the one difference being the people all wore bathrobes and pajamas in midday and out on the grounds. He remembered one in particular that was especially fragrant and colorful. The summer garden perfume was so balmy and unbalancing he thought it would rise up and tear his head from his body. Samuel wanted to stay at that place and just parade around in the flower beds. There was another dark one that frightened him from the start. It had tall, ominous gates and the reception rooms inside seemed too bare and high-ceilinged. Uncle Rex came out wearing a bathrobe, but this time it was the same kind that everyone else wore. His head was shaved and he looked much thinner, but it was his Adam's apple that really got Samuel. It protruded much more than it should have and Samuel thought how easy it would be for someone to just snap it off. He ran to Uncle Rex and dug his head into his waist, crying into his bathrobe and wanting to get him right out of there. For the first time he realized he had an uncle in a mental institution who couldn't just walk out and live in an apartment if he wanted to. "Can't we take him home?" he cried to the three bowlegged ladies. "I want to take him home. He can live with us. He's my uncle." Who would stop them if they just stuck him in a car and were brave enough to drive right out of there?

There was another place that seemed to be made up of a series of large empty yards where women, many of them surprisingly young, with hair cut either boyishly or allowed to flow deep down their backs, walked slowly in the sunlight, occasionally breaking into joyous dances; but his memories here were vague and most of the homes he remembered clearly were fragrant, sunny ones, where Uncle Rex would be waiting for them on a bench. Samuel always brought along a box of pralines, Uncle Rex's favorites, and for the first few minutes, his troubled uncle would make a fuss over him, saying, "How big you've gotten," just as though he were any of Samuel's uncles outside. Samuel's mother would then ask Uncle Rex a question and, before he was able to answer, say to Samuel, "We should all have his brain. Even with all he's been through, I'd like to know what he's forgotten. His mind? Don't ever sell him short." But then, after a few minutes more, a cloud would pass over Uncle Rex's face and he would begin to air small grievances, then increasingly larger ones. "They give you itchy clothes," he would say, squirming around in his bathrobe. "You want to pull your skin off." He would then ask Samuel's mother if she could have food sent in for him. "I don't like what this new doctor's having them give me. I don't like what he's having them put in my food." And then his head would tilt at a strange angle and he would say, "You smell something?" and Samuel would know it was time for the visit to end. At those head-tilting times, Samuel saw a connection between his Uncle Rex and the long-haired ladies who broke into dances.

It was only when his uncle was between institutions that Samuel got to see the perfidious Aunt Emma. Uncle Rex stayed, during these intervals, at his old, gloomy apartment in Newark and Samuel would accompany the three bowlegged warriors there, his grandmother hobbling along at the formation's rear; she carried a suitcase bulging with fine shirts that didn't itch and untainted fish. It was a strange war in that most of the guns were fired harmlessly in the air and when the opposing enemies met in the field, there would be nothing but hugs and conciliation. The princelike attorney, Henry Howell, had advised Samuel's team that Uncle Rex, despite Aunt Emma's dark nature, was

still better off with his family than without them; as a result, the visits
would commence with the three warriors lining up to kiss and hug
Aunt Emma whose name they had damned in a thousand phone calls.
Samuel's mother would say, "How have you been, darling?" and the
saintlike Aunt Ramona would take the villainous woman by her fleshy
wrists and say, "You know what, Emma. I still think you're a sweet
person." Samuel's old grandmother herself would clasp Aunt Emma's
great hands and say, "We should all live and be well, that's all," and
then look swiftly at the ceiling as though asking heaven forgiveness for
what she really felt in her heart. Samuel wasn't fooled by all the light
atmosphere, however. He hated his Aunt Emma with a purple rage.
She was bad. He hated her hanging arms and her teeth. He hated her
for being foreign. He couldn't stand her smell. Whenever he ran into
someone or something disgusting in his life, he would say, "Ugh, re-
minds me of Aunt Emma." Even the violin became a sickening instrument to him, and at concerts, he kept his eyes glued to the woodwind
section. When she hugged him during these visits, he felt as though he
were being embraced by a great powdery Viennese dead woman. On
some of the rare visits, Aunt Emma's two daughters would be present.
He considered them the enemy, too. One had black, tangled hair and a
perpetual storm on her face; she did some of the brooding paintings
with the little lights on top of them and Samuel had never seen her
smile. Her name was Mary, but he gave her the private nickname of
"Muddy." She stayed in a small, darkened half-room filled with stacks
of old sheet music, painting equipment and piano stools; she always
had charcoal smudges on her beclouded face. Aunt Emma, in a gush-
ing Viennese voice, would call her in to play a lute selection and she
would always refuse, slamming the door. The other, younger daughter
was fresh and sunny with features so lovely and a mouth so saintlike it
seemed to Samuel to be some sort of mistake. Each time he saw her he
hoped to find he had been wrong, that she had some outrageous facial
flaw he'd somehow never noticed before, but she became lovelier as
the years passed. Because she was the enemy, her beauty, of course,
did not count, and it seemed such a waste to Samuel. Her disposition
was golden and cheerful, too, and this added to Samuel's discomfort; it
took a powerful effort of will, but he managed to spread the blanket of
his hatred out far enough so that it enveloped her, too, perfect features, golden smile and all.

These visits were short. After the opening hugs and kisses, Aunt
Emma would ask Samuel if he wanted something to eat, an invitation
he always considered preposterous. He would giggle and swiftly de-
cline. Then, after a while, she would excuse herself and take the two
girls out for a walk, beckoning them in some harsh, Middle European

tongue, another sign of evildoing, Samuel always felt. As soon as Aunt Emma had left the room, Samuel's grandmother would pop open the suitcase while his mother and Aunt Ramona went inside and began testing the food in the refrigerator and smelling for gas leaks, assuring Uncle Rex finally that everything was in order. Samuel would prowl the two daughters' bedrooms then, looking in bureau drawers and always coming up with at least one book of nude sculpture, final evidence that the girls were nasty and twisted.

His last visit to the Newark apartment came when he was seventeen and about to go off to college. It was a visit totally different from the others in that Aunt Emma's living room, instead of being musty and darkened, was all aglow with floodlights. The brooding pictures had been taken down and in their place were bright, vividly colored canvases, most of them depicting religious scenes. The people in them were stiff and squarish and great-eyed as though an eight-year-old child had drawn them. In each of the paintings there stood at least one person whose hands were raised, spread-fingered and gleeful, as though he were singing out in exultation. It seemed to be a kind of artist's signature. There were some people standing around looking at the pictures, taking notes, and Aunt Emma explained to Samuel and the three warriors, each of them a little tired at this stage of the campaign, that when violin-playing had grown too strenuous for her weighty arms, she had taken up painting, which she found less physically exerting. She did twenty-five canvases and had been encouraged by a professor friend to exhibit them. This was a preview for some art magazine people. It was a little awkward to do any tasting and gas-sniffing this trip. Uncle Rex seemed remarkably placid, and so after a quick visit with him, Samuel's grandmother dropped off the suitcase and the bowlegged trio backed out of the door, calling it a day.

Samuel went off to college the following year, liberated finally from the endless nightly calls, and only via letters and visits home during intersession was he kept apprised of the war's progress. It dragged on for years, reaching no climactic moments and finally petering out uncertainly with no clear-cut victors. Uncle Rex began to spend more and more time at home in the Newark apartment and almost no time in institutions. The trust fund became depleted and reached the point where there really wasn't enough money left to fuss about; Henry Howell, the attorney, saw fit to drop all dealings with it and let it fend for itself. Samuel's grandmother died, getting up before dawn one morning and then dropping off in the middle of a rocking and oath-making session. This left only two key warriors, who didn't really seem to know where they stood, what goals to press for. Uncle Rex finally began to spend all his time in Newark, apparently liberated permanently from homes. He was seventy-seven now and seemed rather hearty, although he still craned his head around now and then and sniffed at the air. His three younger brothers had all passed away, and he admitted to Samuel's mother that he took occasional trips downtown, to "see about some fabric."

"I wouldn't be surprised if they found another million on him," Samuel's mother wrote to him at college. "Don't ever sell his head short."

Aunt Emma spent little time at the Newark apartment, finally disappearing altogether. There was a brief renewal of extended phone call attacks. The wires again began to sizzle, the main charge against Aunt Emma now being switched to licentiousness, "fooling around." The "professor friend" came in for some heavy criticism, too. But it must have seemed a little silly, even to the two hardened old veterans. They had always accused the Viennese lady of being "years older than Rex," and if this were at all true, she would have been comfortably in her eighties, certainly entitled to a little dalliance by any moral standard. Whatever the case, Aunt Emma showed up for the last time at her younger daughter's wedding. The two increasingly bowlegged warriors attended this one, but stayed away from the second daughter's wedding months later, as though unable to arrive at a clear-cut policy.

Samuel got married in his senior year of college. He did not know exactly what he was doing married. All he knew was that he had grown attached to a dark and quiet, wintry sort of girl with whom he felt terribly comfortable. Someone had pointed her out as having lots of money and that had been in the back of his mind. But it was more a case of losing his balance and saying the hell with it and turning up married six years ahead of a date he'd once jotted down on some crazy schedule he'd always planned to adhere to. He called his mother and said, "I'm coming home with a girl I'm married to."

He took her to see his mother and father and all his relatives, and she was as quiet and shy with them as she was with Samuel, sitting with her legs crossed, and for the most part, just listening to people. He felt very good with her when she did that. He took her to see saintlike Aunt Ramona, who locked onto her wrist, led her off and said, "Shall I tell you something? You've got yourself a darling boy."

He went with her to visit Uncle Rex, not exactly at the Newark apartment, but to a windy hill nearby that overlooked some water; there Uncle Rex spent his afternoons, sitting on a bench and watching boats. "This is my wife," Samuel said to Uncle Rex who held out a weak hand to her and said, "Oh, you're married. Good." The three sat silently then for a few minutes and when Uncle Rex shrugged a little and said, "I can't get a decent overcoat. This one itches me," Samuel rose and said goodbye, going off with his new wife.

The next day, Samuel went to his mother's house for dinner while his wife spent the evening with some college girl friends. Tired after the dinner, he took a nap in the bedroom and then seemed to trip in his dream, waking up suddenly, shaking his head. He heard his mother's phone voice then, lower than the old days, but still audible. "That's what you get," she was saying. "What do you expect . . . That's when they're very rich . . . That's when they've got money . . ."

He flicked on the lamp and cleared the sleep out of his eyes, taking a picture of his wife from his wallet. You'd never know it to look at her, he thought, but he had the damnedest feeling he'd married himself an Aunt Emma.

23 Pat O'Brien Movies

THIS ONE TIME, there was no agonizing wait for patrol cars to filter through jammed midtown traffic. And no one in the crowd had cause to remark, "Just try to get a cop when you need one." In fact, there wasn't any crowd. The police got there before one had time to gather, and within seven minutes after the young man had taken his place on the sixteenth-story hotel-room ledge, a patrolman named Goldman with warm eyes and curly hair was out on the ledge with him, just four feet away.

The young man was thin and muscular and his back was curved into a question mark. He wore a flapping T-shirt with one large hole in the center. Beneath the T-shirt a square patch of bandages showed. It was a gray day in March, the first time the wind had blown seriously, and it seemed to be making up for all the other windless days of the month. The patrolman slouched back casually against the building wall, took off his hat and, making a pained face, scratched his head with one finger. Then he lit a cigarette.

"All right," said the young man, "let me tell you right now, I know the whole bit. I mean the casual thing you're pulling with the head-scratching and the we're-just-two-fellows-out-here-having-a-chat routine. I've seen it in a million Pat O'Brien movies. They picked you because you're a family man and you know I have a family and that's the way to work it with me, right? First I get a cigarette to relax me, then I hear about your kids, and we go into a little life-can-be-beautiful, right? If I act real serious, then you say, 'I dare you to jump, show-off. If you really wanted to jump, you'd have done it long ago.' Right? Okay, let me tell *you* something. I'm going. I'm not showing off, I'm not waiting for any crowds. You got an empty house or standing room only, I'm going. Twenty minutes go by on the clock, and I'm off this ledge like a shot. Give me that 'Go ahead and jump' routine and I'm not waiting the twenty."

The patrolman scratched his head again and said, "No, I'm not going to tell you to go ahead and jump because . . ."

"I'm too bright," said the young man. "Because I got too good a head on my shoulders, right? And any guy with such brains shouldn't be getting ready to take a dry dive, right? Oh, you're cute, very cute.

151

How many times have they sent you out on these? You must be the
champ of the whole police department. With the kindness and the
head-scratching. Give me a little life-can-be-beautiful."

"I didn't say it can be beautiful," said the patrolman, loosening his
tie. "You did. Most of the time it stinks."

"Excellent con," said the young man. "Everybody takes the good
with the bad, but the chickens commit suicide, right? You plunge for
the concrete and all you're proving is what a coward you are, right?
You really are the cutest in the business. How many Pat O'Brien movies did you sit through to pick up this jazz, twenty-three? And look how
long you've kept me out here, too. Let me tell you something so you
don't feel too cute. You haven't kept me out here one second more
than I want to be here. I told you. Twenty minutes and I'm flying.
Twenty minutes and I go for that sweet old concrete."

A crowd began to form now, not a giant milling crowd, but a scraggly
one that really didn't seem satisfied with what was going on above.
Officer Goldman spun his cap on one finger and said, "You *are* bright.
I don't care what you say, you're a bright guy. And a lot of what you
say makes sense."

"Do you want to do me a favor?" said the young man, hooked over
in the question mark and leaning toward the patrolman. "Do you want
to do one thing for me, drop the casual routine. The head-scratching,
the yawning, the hat-spinning. It doesn't go. Don't you think I know it's
right out of the old Pat O'Brien manual? Relax him. Yawn it up a little
bit. Act like the one thing in the world you absolutely don't care about
is whether he plunges or not. Try it next time, ace. You care. You got to
care. What have you got, twenty-four straight? I go off this ledge, and
there goes your record. Nobody, not Pee Wee Reese or Ancient Archie
Moore, likes to blow a contest after twenty-four straight."

"Of course I care," said the patrolman, clamping his cap hard on his
head so the wind wouldn't take it. "But I can't help it if I'm casual. I
am casual. If I acted tense and excited, *then* I'd be acting phony."

The police lieutenant who was conducting the operation called Officer Goldman back through the hotel window and, for three minutes,
while the young man hung crooked on the ledge, they conferred, and
then Goldman crept back out again.

" 'Do you think you can handle this one?' " said the young man.
"Isn't that what they asked? 'You don't seem to be getting anywhere
with him. Maybe there's a personality clash.' Isn't that it? Isn't that
what they said? All right, look, after I dive, you tell them you were as
good as anybody they could have sent out. And your record still stands,
because this guy was different and nobody could have grabbed him. If

you want I'll write out a little note saying this is not to count on Officer what?"

"Officer Goldman," said the patrolman.

"On Officer Goldman's record. Because this guy was different. Nobody could have grabbed him."

"I don't think you're so different," said the patrolman, looking up and studying the gray sky.

"Good move, that sky bit," said the young man. "Instead of looking down at the crowd, look up. Get his mind on onward and upward things. Sneak in a little God when he's not looking. Twenty-four straight. You must have two hundred and twenty-four straight. I don't think I'm very different either," said the young man. "I don't say I have more troubles than your last twenty-four guys. The only thing that makes me different is that I'm stepping out into the air. You can pass me kid pictures from now till kingdom come. You can get my guard up or down and you can cigarette me until you're blind, but when that buzzer rings, I'm saying goodbye to you and hello to the pavement."

"What kind of troubles?" asked the patrolman, lighting a cigarette and not looking at the young man.

"Draw him out," said the man. "Very sneakily, get him to talk about himself and then suggest that things are always darkest before the dawn. All right, save your breath. I'll draw myself out. I don't have time to wait for your Pat O'Brien routine. My stomach's the main thing. It's been knotted up since I was ten. Six operations, and last year I started getting tired all the time, no energy—so they took out a coil of it longer than the telephone wire from here to Philadelphia. I went for another year, I'm twenty-nine now, and now I'm tired again. The thing I do is prune trees and I had a good business going, I did big estates, but now I'm too tired and I haven't got the strength to get up on anything. My stomach's the size of an aspirin box now and there isn't much more can come out. I've got four kids and my wife's a bum. You bring her out here to plead with me and I'm off this ledge before you can sneeze. I've always got to go out and bring her back from places. I'm too tired now to keep grabbing her by the neck. So now she can come collect me off the sidewalk with a spoon. All right now, you tell me all the beautiful things I got to look forward to."

The patrolman loosened his collar and bit, speculatively, on a fingernail.

"All right, quit the collar routine. That means we're settling down for a long stay. You know just how long it's going to be. We're clear on that, I hope. But let's say I were to step back through the window now and let's say with my stomach I had another seven years coming to me. I mean you just tell me some beautiful reasons to stay alive the seven.

Television shows? The joy of changing a diaper? I can see my wife a few times? Suppose you just tell me."

"I don't say there are that many joys," said the patrolman, soft blue eyes directly on the young man now. "You're right, I have been out on quite a few of these cases in the past. It wasn't twenty-four, but the last guys I had out here, *believe* me, had as much aggravation as you do, but I was able to convince them of the one thing I believe. Whether you have six months, one year, six years, or thirty, you're better off living. Being dead is no bargain."

"Well, thank you," said the young man, bowing deeper into his question mark. "At least we're not being casual. At least we're getting right down to it. Thank you for that. It doesn't make any difference though. I mean what you're saying is just words. You're helping me pass twenty minutes. You could be reciting the Declaration of Independence. You're helping me pass my last twenty minutes on earth, Officer Goldman, and that's the end of your streak."

The police officer threw his cigarette down on the ledge, ground it out deliberately with his foot, and then kicked it down at the crowd which seemed now to be more respectable in size.

"Now, look, let me tell you something," he said.

"You can tell me anything, Pat, but if that buzzer rings, I'll cut you off in mid-sentence. If you're telling a joke and she sounds, I don't wait for the punch line. You tell that to the sergeant."

"Let me tell you something," said the patrolman, his face more stern than it had been. "I never get sore up here on one of these ledges, because, like you say, it pays off in casualness and I have a record to preserve. But you get me sore, not because you're on any ledge, but because you're so damned smug. You have all the answers. Now listen, I have to whisper some of this, because if anyone hears it I'm off the force."

"Good bit," said the young man. "You worked it right in there. Do you want us to put our heads together maybe, so I can hear you whisper?"

"I'll smack you in the mouth," said the patrolman.

"You'll never get close enough," said the man. "I thought we got that straight."

"All right," said the patrolman, breathing heavily. "Let me get myself together. I'm going to talk low and you can believe this or not because I don't care very much about you any more."

"Good bit," said the man. "You better hurry, though. I'm not waiting for any punch lines."

"I have the kind of heart that if the wind changes direction too quickly, it can stop on a dime and they carry me off in a box. I've been living with that kind of heart for nine years and nobody in the department knows it. This is just the right kind of work for me, isn't it? Climbing out on ledges to grab guys! But I have two years more to retirement, and I'm not *letting* it stop. You have to go out and grab your wife by the neck. I'm divorced fifteen years and I have nobody to go out and grab. Four kids? I have one son and he's with his mother. Do you know what I think of him? It's like a religion and he's the one you're supposed to worship. He stays away from me like the plague. He's supposed to visit me every six months. I haven't seen him in two years. There's just one thing. I happen to think life is worth living. You have a short time to live and one hell of a long time to be dead."

The patrolman lowered his head and the young man began to rub his arms as though the cold bothered him. "So what are you going to do when you retire?" he asked.

"I have a little place paid for in Florida," said the patrolman.

"And what are you going to do down there?" he asked. "Sit in a chair and hold your heart and wait for your son to come?"

"He'll come," said the patrolman.

"No he won't," said the young man.

"He will so," said the patrolman.

"The hell he will," said the young man.

The wind was chilled now and had picked up in speed. The young man hugged himself and shifted from one foot to the other. The patrolman bent over, wiping his eyes, and the two were silent now, as though they were waiting for a bus. They stood that way for several minutes. Then the patrolman said, "The day stinks," not lifting his head.

"It's cloudier than hell," said the young man.

"I really picked the right kind of thing to do," said the patrolman, "pulling guys off ledges."

"Oh, yes," said the young man. "You picked something very cute."

The young man looked across the street and as he studied the clock, the patrolman took off his jacket and put it down on the ledge.

"What's the bit now?" asked the young man.

The patrolman rolled up his sleeves very neatly, and then, with a look at the sky as though checking the weather, threw his cap off the ledge and followed it, executing, except for his legs, a perfect swan dive.

"Hey, I never saw that bit before," said the young man, coming out of his question mark to watch the patrolman as he neared the pavement and then went into it.

"What the hell do I do now?"

The Icing on the Cake

CONVINCED AT ONE TIME he would have to go through life with a slight weight on his heart, Workman had now found what appeared to be peace. He had rented a cabin in his favorite area in the world, a place where thick woods ran suddenly into sand and it was take your pick on whether to call it "the beach" or "the woods." People went there who liked a little of each. Even in the dark days of his first marriage, Workman could feel his spirits start to lift when he rounded an intersection ten miles from this area and made first contact with the summer freshness. One fear of his was that the ghosts of his first marriage would return to haunt him if he spent the summer in the same area; what actually happened is they paid no attention to him and let him go about his business. In fact, to his surprise, the whole complex tangle of his first life had simply slipped off his shoulders like a massive overcoat.

Everything tasted wonderful to him in this summer place. A blueberry muffin or a spoonful of rice. Half a cocktail in the evening made him ferociously hungry, ready to eat tables and chairs. And the sleeping, profound, damp and thorough, was perhaps his favorite activity of all. He had loved this special sleep, even when he had to do it alone, his first wife in another bed, three or four feet away. Now he had someone under the covers with him, Sara, wife number two, with young legs and a furnace of a bosom. Workman could turn any way he liked, twist himself into any sleeping position, and no matter how gymnastic it was, she would twist into it with him, a perfect carbon copy. He had found her at a university in Michigan, prying her away from a young, sorrowfully bearded professor who knew he was going to lose her the second he saw her with Workman.

"You're going to wind up with her," said the young fellow.

"Don't be ridiculous," said Workman. "I'm just passing through, lecturing."

But the young sorrowful fellow was right. And he had known about his loss before Workman knew of his gain.

Now Workman had Sara. He could see her outline through a gauzed screen, light, trim, ecological, her movements midway between walking and dancing. The long straight coppered hair. Workman had once felt that a decade stood, like a high fence, between him and that style of hair. Now all he had to do was reach over and he could slide his fingers into it, any hour of the day or night. It was early September. He was in a separate room, watching a closely matched football game, enjoying it even though he didn't have a favorite team competing. That was another thing he loved about this place—you could rough it and at the same time pick up first-rate television reception. He had his cigars, too, and for the first time in many years could sit back and pour out clouds of smoke with a light and easy heart. His style, in earlier days, would be to take a short thieflike puff and then look for some invisible exhaust so he could get the smoke to disappear before his wife turned a laser-like glare on him. Only on this one issue had he been a little suspicious of Sara. Did she really mean it when she gave him the go-ahead on unlimited cigar smoking? Or would it all change the second they were legally hooked up? Happily, she remained the same, during and after the brief courtship. The only difference was that now, settled in a bit, her fragrance was even more sweet and Midwestern.

To cap it all off, Workman had his father with him, taking a two-week vacation at the cabin. If Workman had to point to one issue that had finally sent his marriage up in smoke, it was his first wife's attitude toward his dad. Silvered at the temples, immaculate and still spry in his seventies, the old man had been widowed for ten years and had very little going for him. He lived alone in a studio apartment on the edge of the city and worked a few hours each day at his old factory job. It was the owner's way of throwing him a bone. The old man traveled about the city on foot; always in the back of Workman's mind was that he would get a phone call one day telling him that his dad, after putting up a struggle, had been pummeled to death by a youth gang. Workman had always felt guilty about allowing his father to live in a studio and not getting him a one-bedroom apartment or one with a terrace so that at least he'd have a second area in which to walk around. Not once did Workman's first wife, acting on her own incentive, ask the old man over for dinner. In truth, he got invited, but only after Workman himself said: "Hey, I'd really like to have my dad over." With a certain resignation and a telltale wiping of her forehead, she would say, "Sure, go ahead and invite him." And it would be Workman who would have to make the call. Once he was invited, she would cook a fine and fairly delicious dinner, one it would be difficult to quibble with. All very decent and correct. But what kind of man was this to be correct to? He played a banjo. He could find fun in almost anything, including the fact that his wife, Workman's mother, because of a graveyard mix-up, had been buried in the wrong part of a cemetery, and for months Workman and son had prayed to the wrong stone.

"What should I have done," said the old man, "sued?"

Once he had been a bank guard, who carried a gun; after months of not getting to use the weapon, he had gone up to the roof of the bank and fired it off a few times to see what it sounded like. He'd won his wife by turning lightning on her in the form of a smile from the balcony during a Jolson performance on the Lower East Side. She'd caught it from an orchestra seat below and met him in the lobby, where he cinched the deal. He could whistle any song in perfect pitch and knew how to produce a sound that was like two separate whistlers in perfect harmony. He could imitate George Raft's intricate tap-dancing style. Do you go around being correct to such a man? Wasn't he the kind of father a daughter-in-law should tease and poke in the belly? Cavort around in front of him and give him a little peck on the cheek? Flirt and call him an old slyboots? The old man had never had a daughter, only Workman. How many years did he have to live anyway?

Summers had been a particularly grim time for Workman. He would rent a house in that favorite magical area of his and immediately feel like a rat for enjoying himself while his aging father lay in a hot studio apartment in the city. Finally, Workman would invite his father out and the old man, sensing he was in for a tense time, would come, not because he was in search of pleasure, but only so that he wouldn't add to his son's grief. He would stay a few days, sunning himself and taking lonely evening strolls on the beach; then he would suddenly appear with his suitcase, packed and ready to go.

"I have work that has to be cleared up," he would say. "And when I have that, I can't relax."

Some work. That factory could have gone on for a hundred years without him. What he wanted was to be away from all that correctness and the sound of his son's heartache, back in his studio where he could trust the stiffness of his bed and be reasonably comfortable, even if he was surrounded by fun-loving singles. Workman asked himself if he was crazy. Did his wife have any case? She and Workman's mother had been fierce enemies from the opening gun, and in that department he could sympathize with her a fraction since his mother had uncompromisingly fought the marriage and never relaxed, even when it was off and running. But to carry this coldness over to his father, a whistler, jokester, tap dancer and innocent bystander—this struck him as being incredible. And it was no small factor when it came to a choice between trying to shore up the marriage or letting it slip down the drain.

When Workman first started hanging out with Sara, he studied her with an eye toward guessing how she would behave with his father. His method was to watch her with other men, at faculty parties. He didn't mind the little room-length separations; how could he when they were welded together with the confident knowledge that they would soon be going home together to eat each other up. Her manner was easy, gay, generous; she actually did poke men in their bellies. She gave them unself-conscious hugs, and her goodbye kisses were more than cordial, too, standing somewhere between friendly and passionate, all of which was terrific because it built up these men and at the same time gave them no reason to think that there might be more fertile territory to explore. A neat trick.

Workman felt little sense of apprehension when he first took Sara to dinner with his dad, and he was on the button in his thinking. She loved men—and hadn't his father been a man for a long time? How could Sara and his father not get on when they both had such fine feelings about Workman. Just as she had nothing up her sleeves in the cigar department, she was the same Sara of faculty parties with the old man. Wearing a long country skirt, her bosom young and generous, she bent over and took his hands immediately, kissed him, and before the dinner had ended, was nuzzling into him like a freshly purchased pup. At the same time, miraculously, she kept a certain dignity, and allowed the old man to keep his. In spite of his occasionally rakish manner, this was important to him. She touched him lightly when she spoke to him and at the same time didn't appear to be fussing over him, something the old man would have resented. Soon he was fussing over *her*, pressing her like a district attorney to make sure she'd had enough to eat. When the waiter said the cream was fresh, and he said, "It better not get fresh with me," Sara scolded him a little and then hugged him to her young bosom as if to say, "You're not that great a comedian, but it's so nice that you're a rascal." They took her to the fights that night, a ritual for the two of them and she sat between them, not asking questions and trying to cram in pugilistic information, but simply delighted to be sitting with them and thrilled they were having such a good time.

To a certain degree, the old man, a slave to routine, had never really enjoyed leaving the city and journeying out to Workman's summer hideaways. The trips seemed like voyages to the end of the earth. Even in the old days, if Workman had simply left him alone, he would not have taken offense. The old man came out to buoy up his son's spirits. So in a sense, once Workman had snapped up his new wife and rented the cabin, he was probably taking unfair advantage when he had Sara call the old man—in early September—and invite him out. Was the old-timer going to refuse her? No way. And Workman was positive, once his father arrived, the old man would have a fine time, easing up on his strict diet and giving dishes like soft-shelled crabs a try. It had worked out fine. After two days in the cabin, predictably, the old man had appeared with his bags packed and said, "I hear I'm wanted in the city." But Sara had simply taken the bags and led him back to his room, unpacking for him while he sat on the bed like a naughty child. And there had been no more talk about quick exits.

Now, comfortably private in his den, Workman could see them together through the screen, Sara shelling peas, poking his father in the belly, the old man getting up on his toes to do Raft at the Palace, Sara, overwhelmed with joy, leaping up to squeeze him and give him a delighted and unashamed kiss on the mouth.

The halftime show was over and Workman had a full two quarters of bruising football to look forward to. He kicked out his legs and felt a satisfying elastic pull in the small of his back, a sensation he experienced only when he was totally relaxed. He had a heavy corona to puff on—the best the Canary Islands had to offer—a cold Gibson that would put a sharp edge on his appetite for the fine shellfish dinner coming up just after the game. Sara knew how important the game was to him and had timed the dinner so that it would be finished in another hour. The old man, grateful to his son for looking after him, would have killed ten men rather than disturb his son's privacy and comfort. By now, Workman knew the routine. Rather than disturb his son while he watched a game or a documentary, the old man, to spin away some time, would take one of his long darkened strolls on the beach. But no longer were they solitary strolls. Now Sara would go along with him, taking his hand, teasing him, then running up ahead till they were beyond Workman's view. He wondered about his father and other women. Surely he had flashed that lightning smile on someone else before he met Workman's mother. How about down at the factory, those short dark seamstresses who had come to Workman's first wedding? It was difficult to envision the old man with anyone other than his mom, but surely, in all those years, with that banjo and that tap-dancing style, there must have been others. And what about now? It was easy enough to picture Sara down at the beach, holding the old man's hand, then running up ahead, and, if she got the urge, suddenly doing one of her wide and unself-conscious cartwheels in the sand, long country skirt flopping about her ears, yellow panties flashing at the moon. But what about the old man? What would he think of those? Did he still *have* those thoughts? And what about his follow-through. Could he still put over the deal? In his seventies? Maybe he'd like to reach into one of those cartwheels the way his son did. Ashamed of himself, Workman pulled a curtain down on these speculations and tried to concentrate on the game. Had he brought his only surviving parent all this distance so that he could brutally invade his privacy? Fling him writhing into the sand with his new wife, Sara? Throw filth at the two of them? The people he loved most in the world.

The cigar and a second Gibson helped straighten out his thinking. So did the damp lazy air. Before long, he was marveling at the thought of all those years he had spent in the wrong gear. He was crazy to get upset. Especially when—after one little adjustment, he now had it all— a gay, generous, delightful, open-spirited new wife—and the icing on the cake—his beloved father, finally easy and content and fully occupied during however many waning precious years God had allotted to him.

Wonderful Golden Rule Days

THE SCHOOL TERM had already begun when the Tapp family moved into Manhattan, so Lawrence Tapp got off to a late start. Furthermore, the school his parents sent him to was a vocational school, and for most of his classes he had neither liking nor aptitude. He led off in Elementary Chemistry by knocking to the floor and breaking a Bunsen burner, which the teacher, Mr. Princer, made him pay for as a lesson in something or other. The term project he elected had to do with sulphuric acid, and that, too, got out of hand, and spilled onto the floor, some of it getting at Mr. Princer's shoes.

Elementary Algebra was a nightmare presided over by a Mr. Allison, who called on people a good deal in class. Lawrence did not fare badly on the written exercises, but he was in mortal fear of being called on. Mr. Allison seemed to sense this fear and at least once a day would recite a problem to the class and then say sadistically, "All right now, there's your problem. Wrap it up for us." And then he would pause before adding, "—Mr. Tapp." Or he might remark, "Show us how simply you can polish it up for us—Mr. Tapp." On occasion, he would say, "Clear it up for us, Mr. Gooding" or "Mr. Lloyd"—two other fourteen-year-old unfortunates who were among the students called on— but Lawrence was the principal target. He never had an easy moment in Mr. Allison's class. He would sit with his head down, looking at his desk blankly and waiting for the voice of doom to summon him to "Handle it for the class" or "Give us a break on this one—Mr. Tapp."

After an hour of Chemistry and an hour of Algebra, Lawrence would walk glumly down the hall to a class in Electric Wiring. It was taught by a Mr. Goldy and might have been Lawrence's most terrifying class had not Mr. Goldy recently lost a favorite aunt under a bus and turned philosopher. Even so, it was bad enough. Attached to the back of each desk was a large, upright board with wires sprouting out of it. The boards were to be used in classroom exercises, and Lawrence, from the first, was bitterly afraid of his. As long as Mr. Goldy talked about friendship and love, which managed to eat up several entire classroom periods, Lawrence felt safe from the board, but he knew it

162

was only a matter of time before he would have to grapple with it. When Mr. Goldy tired of friendship and love, he went into wire splicing. Broken wires were passed around to the members of the class to be given an ordinary splicing. Lawrence felt secure temporarily, because his splicing was certainly as good as the next one's. Regrettably, splicing was only a way of getting into a demonstration of simple circuits on the boards, and the terror came back to him. He could not bring himself to listen to the lecture on simple circuits, which preceded the demonstration, and the thought of going on to parallel circuits made him thoroughly unhappy. There was nothing to do but come in each day, look at his board emptily, and hope for a return of Mr. Goldy's friendship-and-love lectures.

After Electric Wiring came a class called General Work. Lawrence had hoped it would be an hour in which people did nothing special, but it turned out to be a neatly disguised session in metalwork and leatherwork, which wasn't one bit general. You had to make metal brush holders of questionable utility and wallets that never came out right if you didn't cut your leather properly at the beginning. Those who couldn't get the hang of wallets were given an option of doing lanyards to be worn around the neck at summer camps, but it was well known that lanyard-making was for substandard people and Lawrence, although he did poorly with wallets, felt compelled to stay with them. Only one boy, Gerry Kassel, chose lanyards. He had a very bad stutter.

Each day when the five-minute buzzer sounded in General Work, Lawrence felt that a great burden had been lifted from his shoulders. He would have the next hour for lunch, and he would get his lunchbox and eat the sandwiches that his mother had prepared. Guessing what was in them was almost as much fun as eating them. He would then have only two more classes before the day was over—an hour of English, which he did not mind, and an hour of Woodworking, which he actually enjoyed.

There was no apparent reason why Woodworking should not be as fearsome a class for Lawrence as the others. The elements were there: both the tools he was afraid of and the things he had to make, like complicated spinning tie racks and smooth-edged bookends. Some of the best tie racks and bookends made by previous students, who were now in Advanced Woodworking, were mounted, as an inspirational exhibit, on a rack at the front of the class. What distinguished Woodworking from the other classes was Mr. Bradley, the teacher. Lawrence had deep respect for Mr. Bradley, who was a kindly, gray-haired gentleman in his middle fifties, with thick forearms. He felt this way about him even though Mr. Bradley represented a world in which Lawrence was entirely lost. The class was well along in tie racks when Lawrence joined it, and Mr. Bradley, instead of insisting that Lawrence leap in and catch up, asked simply that he get some stock from the shed and sort of play around with it until the others finished their tie racks. Moreover, Mr. Bradley said, his grades would not suffer because he had missed some of the work. Lawrence never forgot that and even rushed to Mr. Bradley's defense when the other kids mimicked his way of starting everything by saying, "Now, you take your piece of stock . . ."

The woodworking class, which came just after lunch, was divided up into teams of two, two being the number of students who shared a tool chest. Lawrence was put with a boy named Ortang, a swarthy lad who at fourteen had to shave. Ortang carried four or five neatly sharpened pencils at all times in his shirt pocket. At first, Lawrence was certain he would not get on with anyone who carried so many pencils. But a look at the hopelessly mangled tie rack Ortang was making provided immediate grounds for friendship. Ortang used every possible excuse to stay away from his tie rack, and each day he would do for Lawrence a comedy monologue in which he played the part of a female about to be seduced. Lawrence thought it was the funniest thing he had ever heard.

When the woodworking class had finished its tie racks, Mr. Bradley announced the next project, one that evoked shouts of joy. Each pair of students was to construct, from stock obtained in the shed, a scale model of an airplane, a Navy Banshee. They would have two weeks to complete the models, after which each pair would draw straws to see which student could keep the model for good. Since Lawrence, unlike the class, had had no baptism in woodwork, he was a little bit disconsolate until Mr. Bradley, walking over to him as he stood in line waiting for his stock, said, "Let's see what you can do, boy."

The remark cheered Lawrence, and he got Ortang aside at once. "I don't know how you feel, but I don't see why we can't make a plane as good as anyone here."

Ortang, who often had trouble being serious, was serious this time. "Darned right. We're starting just the same as everybody. Let's really try to do a job."

Neither of them actually believed they could make as good a model as the others could, but they buoyed each other's spirits and the fact that they were allied with great dedication seemed to make it inevitable that they would build a fine model.

"It might even wind up on the rack down here when we're up in Advanced Woodwork," Ortang suggested.

"Don't see why not," Lawrence agreed.

The teams sat down at their benches for Bradley's opening lecture on the Banshee tail section, which began, "Now, you take your piece of stock," and Lawrence looked around at some of the other teams. He watched a boy named Glazer, who was listening without interest. He was the type of fellow who didn't mind being called on in Mr. Allison's class in Elementary Algebra. He was smart even when he didn't know the answer. He was teamed up with a handsome boy named Reeser, who was president of the freshman class and did very little wrong. Glazer and Reeser would be unbeatable. The Castellani twins were paired up, and they would be hard to beat, as they were a shoemaker's sons and had been raised in his shop. Then Lawrence looked at Ortang, who was doing his female routine in another fellow's ear while Mr. Bradley was talking. He got a sinking feeling.

Nonetheless, the two set to work quite carefully and conscientiously. Each day, when they came from lunch, they would shake hands very solemnly and sincerely, vowing to do a good job, and pitch in. Lawrence found that the fever of working on the Banshee was carrying him through his other classes, which now didn't upset him so much. In two days, he and Ortang had shaped and smoothed the tail section. Mr. Bradley checked it, and cuffed Lawrence on the back good-naturedly, which made him swell enormously. They completed the wings only a day behind Glazer and Reeser, and in the second week started work on the most important part, the fuselage.

Lawrence had been having his lunch with Ortang. The two had decided to come to the classroom early each day to work on the fuselage. Zelda Hofman, the only girl in the class, chided them one day when she found them working before the others arrived, but they turned pompously away from her, and while Lawrence held the fuselage, Ortang sanded it. On the fourth day of the second week, the fuselage was finished. The job was done so nicely that it even prompted one of the Castellani twins to leave his bench and take a look at it—a compliment straight from the heart of a professional.

The final day was for assembly: attaching the tail and wings to the fuselage. Mr. Bradley gave his assembly lecture, and Lawrence and Ortang gingerly lifted the parts of their model from the tool chest. They shook hands for the last time, after looking around at Glazer and Reeser. There were about fifteen minutes to go when Lawrence and Ortang completed their assembly job, almost as soon as Glazer and Reeser finished theirs. Feeling playful, Ortang picked up a steel wrench from the tool chest and began twirling it. It slipped from his fingers and dropped onto the fuselage, breaking it in two and crushing the tail section and one swept-back wing. Ortang picked up both pieces of the fuselage, looked at them, shook his head, and said to no one in particular, "GodDAMMit, GodDAMMit," over and over. Lawrence, who had been watching, stood motionless for an instant, fighting back tears. Then he grabbed the two pieces from Ortang and started toward Mr. Bradley.

It was amazing how quickly he blacked out. He took a few steps, and suddenly his collar and cuffs became too tight. His knees went limp and his head swam, and the next thing he knew he was being held over a water fountain in the girls' lavatory, which was the closest lavatory to the woodworking shop. Mr. Bradley then carried him gently across the room and laid him on a flimsy cot. A cold handkerchief was on his head.

He was coming out of it all right until Mr. Bradley said softly, "Don't worry about the Banshee, Mr. Tapp. We'll give you a couple of weeks to make it up."

Lawrence felt more nauseated than ever. He could never make it up. He told Mr. Bradley he wanted to go home. Mr. Bradley said sure, and he could start making it up tomorrow. There was plenty of time.

Lawrence managed to get home, where he sank into bed miserably and tried not to think of the next day's schedule: Elementary Chemistry, Elementary Algebra, Electric Wiring, General Work, English, and Woodworking, which he now hated more than all the others.

The Humiliation

IT HAD BEEN A MILD financial strain to take his wife and child to Europe and so for the first week Gribitz kept reminding them they were in a special place, much better than Rockaway Beach or Cape Cod. "You're drinking French water," he would tell his son each time the boy took a glassful. And on the way to the seashore, he would lean back and say to his wife, "Fill your lungs with some of that French air." He took periodic checks on their enjoyment, too, asking the boy, "Are you having a good time?" and saying to his wife, "Are you sure it's exactly what you had in mind?" When the boy said, "It's okay, Dad," Gribitz would ask him how many nine-year-olds he thought got chances to go to foreign countries. "Maybe one out of a hundred, tops, and all it is for you is okay."

As for Gribitz, he tried to stuff himself with enjoyment, to look everywhere at once and afraid that by doing so he was seeing nothing. Besides, he could not feel entirely comfortable, because he had not seen a soul he knew. He tried to turn this into an advantage, telling his wife, "Isn't it great that we don't know a soul here, that we can just be by ourselves for a change?" But actually he longed to see just one familiar face, Henry Nester, his insurance man, or even Uncle Hicky, who traveled to exotic places each year and raved about Miami hotels —climbing all over people in Macao and Zagreb with Fontainebleau anecdotes. It was not so much that he was lonely but that he wanted his sense of reality strengthened. How else could he be *sure* he was in Europe? That it was he, Gribitz, not a fellow in a dream. The New York *Times* international edition rolled in and so did a bill from Hipco Dry Cleaners that had trailed him across the Atlantic. But neither really helped. At times, driving along the coastline, he got the feeling that it wasn't really France at all. The plane had actually circled back to America and he had disembarked in the middle of a giant World's Fair exhibit, set up at great expense by crowds of people who were out to get him. At a given signal the natives would drop their accents, whip off their costumes and stand revealed as Philadelphians.

Each night, Gribitz and his wife would take seats at a sidewalk café and stare across the street at people in another sidewalk café. There seemed to be an unusual number of gaily dressed retarded children about, towed along in harnesses by their French moms. Gribitz tried not to notice them but wondered if there were not some summer holiday in which they were all allowed to leave their attics for seaside vacations. One night he picked out a familiar face across the road and said to his wife, "Uh, oh, I see one I think I know, only I hope I don't. If it's him, it's going to start a whole thing, so keep your fingers crossed that it's not. Still, I've got to check it out or I won't be comfortable." He excused himself and crossed the street. A waiter from the café he approached leaped out and began to lure him forward, matador-style, with a tablecloth. Gribitz turned back to his wife, chuckling and said, "These guys are really something." The fellow he went up to was well muscled and had a deep-seamed suntan but also great swoops of hair that might have gone with a concert musician. Beside him sat a petulant wife and two girls in their early teens. "I'll be brief," said Gribitz. "Your name isn't Carroll, is it, and were you once in the Air Force?" The fellow nodded and Gribitz said, "I'll be going back now. Just wanted to nail it down out of curiosity." Gribitz returned to his table and said, "Well, it's him all right, and it's amazing what a whole cascade of things just came tumbling into my head. Well, I've finally seen someone and I know it's me, right here in Europe now, only I wish that fella had been one of at least four thousand other people I could mention."

On the way back to their villa, Gribitz said, "Look I'm not trying to be mysterious. It's the kind of story I just want to slide into when I get comfortable. Hell, I'm not even sure how important it is right now."

As they rolled into the driveway, they heard a harsh, fading scream, as though the screamer had been at it awhile and was doing it reflexively now, having lost interest. They had left their nine-year-old son in the care of a French midwife in the neighborhood. She said she had gone upstairs to close the shutters and seen a blond Swedish type perched in the window with a cooking pot on his head and she had begun to scream, but no one had come to her aid. Gribitz checked the child and then called the police. The man at the other end said he could not come since he was the only one in the station, but if the prowler appeared again, Gribitz was to knock him on the head and hang on to him. They slept that night with the child between them. When Gribitz stirred, his wife said, "I know, I know, it's a horrible experience, I can't sleep either." Gribitz got up on an elbow and said, "Look, I've always been honest, but it's not the screaming thing that's starting to bother me. That cooking pot takes the edge off it. Probably just some nut. What's got me is that fellow I told you about, the one I'd rather not have run into. I thought I'd just think it out and pass it by, but it's not working out that way. I'm just being honest."

"Don't be so honest," said his wife.

The next morning, Gribitz called American Express and then, in the middle of breakfast, suddenly shoved aside a croissant and said, "I don't really love these and I don't see why I have to go through the motions. All right, I'm going after that fellow. Let me rephrase that. I'm going to visit that sunburned guy from the café last night. What it is, is that a long time ago, oh I guess it's fifteen years now, he humiliated me in front of two hundred and fifty guys. Don't ask me how he did it, I was a new officer and he was an enlisted man and it shouldn't have come off that way, but it did. I thought I'd forgotten all about it, hell I don't think I've thought of it once in the last eight years, but I guess it was simmering right there under the surface all along. I guess if this had happened in the States, I would have sailed right on through it but I've got it in my head that it's going to make me uncomfortable if I don't go see him. I've tracked him down to Golfe Saint-Juan, he's out of the service now and with some engineering outfit. Anyway, I'm off to check in on him now, and forget all about talking me out of it. One thing I've got to ask you to do. Hardly any effort involved. Just call me at this number in exactly an hour and a half. In fact I'm not really asking. This is one of those few marriage times when I've got to tell you to just make the call or that's it for us."

"All right," she said, "but there was no real need to frame it exactly that way."

"There was a need, there was a need," said Gribitz, walking toward the car. "Look I've got no time to go into any psychology with you. Just start twirling that dial in *une heure et demie*."

Gribitz drove for half an hour, checked his watch and then stopped off at a roadside café to get twelve cooked snails to go. He was the only customer and two restaurant troubadours asked if they could play and sing for him. "I'm not in that kind of mood," he said, but he finally allowed them to do "Quando, Quando, Quando," a slow cha-cha popular in the States. As they sang to him, he thought about the Air Force and the thing Carroll had done to him. Very simply, what happened was that Gribitz, on his second day as an officer in the Air Force— fresh from college—had been tossed into the thick of an experienced combat Air Force squadron of two hundred and fifty men. One day, the entire squadron had been assembled for a weapons talk, Gribitz sitting at the back of the auditorium, knowing nothing, scared out of his wits that momentarily he would be unmasked as an idiot. In the middle of the lecture, the phone rang, loud and clear, the speaker waiting for it to be answered. Gribitz, a few feet away from the phone, could think of no way in the world in which he could have assisted the caller, since there was nothing in the world he knew about the Air

Force. So while the audience waited, he asked Carroll, who was then a master sergeant, to answer the phone, and Carroll, after thinking it over a second, said "No" with a queer little smile. Gribitz sat up then, and with all two hundred and fifty men looking on, asked Carroll a second time to pick up the phone. "I said no," Carroll replied and Gribitz, his collar suddenly strangling him, had run out of the auditorium on the fourth or fifth ring. The proper procedure, of course, would have been to bring court-martial charges against Carroll for disobeying a direct order and Gribitz, however untutored he'd been at the time, at least knew this much. But he had been just as frightened of his immediate superior and a court-martial procedure as he was of master sergeants and telephones. Doing anything then had been out of the question. Thinking about the incident now, he got a little hitch to his breath, but he had to admit it really didn't seem of Olympian importance. Still, it had stuck in his throat and in many ways spoiled his entire service experience—just as meeting Carroll the previous night now threatened to upset him for weeks to come. The troubadours ended their number, the snails arrived and the check had an extra 20 per cent added on for entertainment. "I wish I had time to argue," he said, paying the cashier. "I'd take you right down to the wire on that entertainment crap. I didn't ask for it and it wasn't entertaining."

He drove another twenty minutes or so and after some muddling about in a cliffside community overhanging the waterfront, he found a house with the name Carroll out front. Mrs. Carroll answered the doorbell and Gribitz said, "Hi, I'm Leroy Gribitz, here to do some business with your husband. Here are some cooked snails. They make them all over the country, practically every roadside inn, but I think you'll find these have a little extra zip to them. At least it's been my experience. Divvy them up with the kids. Is your husband home?"

The woman called inside, then disappeared and when the deep-seamed man came out, Gribitz said, "Howdy, Carroll, I'm the guy who walked across to you last night at the café. To get right down to it I'm A02234907, Grange Air Force Base, 1951–53, the young kid adjutant of Squadron 4507 you did that thing to."

Carroll, who was wearing rimless Ben Franklin glasses, coming into vogue on the Côte D'Azur, took them off his nose, stroked his chin and said, "You know, I think I remember, a young kid come into the squadron, never done a lick of military and comes in as an officer."

"The very kid," said Gribitz. "And while you're unwinding the spool, see if you can remember the little business you pulled on me that I'm here for now fifteen years later. About the telephone."

"I remember that thing," said Carroll, taking a seat at a dinette arrangement of the kind that service families took with them all over the world, even when they were out of service. "You mean when the phone rings and it's clearly the duty of the officer in charge to pick it up and you expected me, a master sergeant with twelve years duty on you, to do your dirty work for you and I wouldn't."

"And when you disobeyed a direct order and made me a laughing-stock on my second day in the service. That's the time all right.

"Now look," said Gribitz, "we're not going to go into service proto-col right now. This vacation is costing me fifty dollars a minute and that's not what I came chasing down here for although I have to admit this is the first time I ever got a look at your side. The thing is, you wiped me out, pure and simple, in front of two hundred and fifty guys I never could look in the face again. You fouled up my whole time in the service—I don't think I got one good night of Air Force sleep. And don't think I didn't think about it plenty after my discharge. The thing is it's fifteen years later, we're both here in this house and we're play-ing that little scene again only with a different ending. In twenty min-utes to the second that phone's going to ring and when it does you're going to be the one to answer it."

"I always answer the phone when it rings," said Carroll, beginning to pick his teeth.

"Now don't be no wise bastard," said Gribitz "or you'll be hearing an entirely different kind of ring. You know damned well what I mean. I've got that phone set up to ring in twenty minutes and it's no ordinary phone call. It's that same one from the squadron fifteen years ago. We both hear it and you're the one that makes a grab for it, not me this time. And before you make any smart-ass comments, let me tell you why you're going to pick it up and not me. We'll start out with what's going on underneath my clothes. I may look the same as I did fifteen years ago, same general body outline and all, but actually I'm like four of what I was. I've been working out like a demon and instead of the fifteen years chopping me down I've now got the kind of power I should have had then. All right, throw that out if you like, because I still don't like to see arguments settled on that score. The point is, I was twenty-three then and I might as well have been two and a half for all of the stuff I had then. I was scared to hear myself cough. Well, that's changed, too, I've worked out a lot of things in my head, chucked out some of the crazy notions that were making me think so little of myself. The point is, I can get things done now, just about anything I want if I concentrate hard enough. How do you think I pulled off this trip. I just set my sails for it and bulled it through with sheer willpower. I can tell that by just listening to me you're convinced and you'd better be, because if you don't pick up that phone, I'll smear you all over the walls, Carroll, both physically and spiritually."

"All right," said Carroll, "when does it ring?"

"I told you when," said Gribitz. "When I said is when. You never should have done that thing to me."

The phone rang and Carroll, after flicking at some rear molars, picked up the phone casually and said, "Carroll speaking. Who's this?" He listened for a while and then said, "Okay, make it chopped steak instead of *côtelette d'agneau.*"

"That was the butcher," said Carroll, laying down the receiver.

"Strike it," said Gribitz, checking his watch. "Ours has another five to go."

"Look, I'll just go beep, beep and pick it up, okay?" said Carroll, "and we got the show packed up and on the road."

"That'll be the day," said Gribitz. "I'll bet you'd love to pull something like that on me."

"You're the boss, Lieutenant."

They sat together in silence and after two minutes, Mrs. Carroll appeared in hip-huggers and said, "The kids said to thank you for the snails."

"Oh, just skip it," said Gribitz. Two minutes after she had disappeared, the phone rang again. On the second ring, Carroll sat back in leisurely style and said, "What if I don't answer it?"

Gribitz got to his feet, stood over him and between clenched teeth said, "You lift up that phone, mother." Carroll stared back at him, then shrugged his shoulders and did as he was told. "Carroll here, answering the phone as ordered," he said. He held the receiver aside and said to Gribitz, "You want me to gab awhile?"

"No," said Gribitz. "Just what you did does it."

"Signing off," said Carroll and laid down the receiver.

Gribitz, who hadn't realized how hard he had been breathing, pulled out a handkerchief and pulled it across his brow. "Well, that's done," he said. "And what's done is done."

"Yup," said Carroll, beginning to pick up some beads his daughter had apparently spilled on the rug.

"You been here long?" asked Gribitz.

"Year," said Carroll.

"That goddamned language barrier is what spoils it. You can learn the lingo but it'd take you ten years to pick up the colloquial stuff. Look, it was just something I had to get out of my system. I know a little bit about myself and if I've got something like that bothering me, it can throw off my whole life. Something like a splinter. It's no bigger than a hair but you know the kind of grief it can give you. Am I getting through to you at all?"

"I guess," said Carroll, waiting with his hand on the door.

"In many ways it's got nothing to do with you. It's me and a thing I have. Hell, you're the first American I've spoken to since I've been in this damned place. Your kids have anyone to play with?"

"They do all right," said Carroll.

"Maybe they can come over and play with mine. That would be a hell of a turn, wouldn't it? Look, when I saw you, I knew I wasn't going to be able to relax until I'd come over here and gotten the damned thing done. Now that it's done, to me it's as if nothing happened. What I'm getting at is that it was nothing personal. Do you see that at all?"

"I don't see much of anything," said Carroll, opening the door for Gribitz to leave.

"All right, then I'll get you for this," said Gribitz, taking his coat. "For just what you're doing right now. I don't care if it takes another fifteen years. You can hide in the goddamned mountains of Tibet and I'll smoke you out and beat your head till you're bloody. YOU'VE GONE AND SPOILED MY WHOLE EUROPEAN VACATION, YOU SON OF A BITCH."

Back to Back
(featuring Harry Towns)

"THE THING I LIKE about Harry Towns is that everything astonishes him."

An Italian writer friend he loved very much had been overheard making that remark and as far as Harry Towns was concerned it was the most attractive thing anyone had ever said about him. He wasn't sure it suited him exactly. Maybe it applied to the old him. But it did tickle him—the idea of a fellow past forty going around being astonished all the time. On occasion, he would use this description in conversation with friends. It did not slide neatly into the flow of talk. He had to shove it in, but he did, because he liked it so much. "Astonished" was probably too strong a word, but in truth, hardly a day passed that some turn of events did not catch him a little off guard. In football terms, it was called getting hit from the blind side. For example, one night, out of the blue, a girl he thought he knew pretty intimately came up with an extra marriage; she was clearly on record as having had one under her belt, but somehow the early union had slipped her mind. And for good measure, there was an eight-year-old kid in the picture, too, one who was stowed away somewhere in Maine with her first husband's parents. On another occasion, a longtime friend of Towns's showed up unannounced at his apartment with a twin brother, thin, pale, with a little less hair than Towns's buddy, and a vague hint of mental institutions around the eyes; but he was a twin brother, no question about it. So out of nowhere, after ten years, there was not one but two Vinnys and Harry Towns was supposed to absorb the extra one and go about his business. Which he did, except that he had to be thrown a little off stride. It was that kind of thing. Little shockers, almost on a daily basis.

Late one night, the slender Eurasian woman who ran his favorite bar turned to the "gypsies," an absolute rock-bottom handful of stalwarts who closed the place regularly at four in the morning (and after eight years of working a "straight" job, nine-to-five, how he loved being one of them) and suddenly, erratically, screamed out, "You're all shits," flinging her cash register through the window. What kind of behavior was that? She was famed for handling difficult situations with subtlety and finesse. Towns tried to grab on to some gross piece of behavior that might have brought on this outburst—the only one of which she had been guilty in anyone's memory. All he could come up with was that one of them had slumped over and fallen asleep with his head on the table. A film dubber had done that, halfway through his dinner. Is that why they were all shits? What's so shitty about that?

If you walked the streets of the city, there was plenty to be astonished about. He supposed that was true if you lived in Taos, New Mexico, but he wasn't convinced of it. One day Towns saw an elderly and distinguished-looking man with homburg and cane hobble off briskly in pursuit of a lovely young girl. She was about twenty feet ahead of him and kept taking terrified looks over her shoulder at him. About that brisk hobbling. It's a tough one to pull off, but that's exactly what he was doing. She was stumbling along, not handling her high heels too well. Even though she was more or less running and he was doing his hobbling motion, the gap between them wasn't getting any wider. It was a crowded sunny lunchtime with plenty of secretaries floating around. Towns seemed to be the only one on the street who was aware of this rope of urgency between the man and the girl; he caught onto it, falling in step with them. The girl twirled through traffic, caught her heel in a manhole cover, and fell, long legs gaping, flowered skirt above her hips, black magnificent cunt screaming at the sky. The man stopped, leaning on his cane, as though he did not want to press his advantage. Towns stopped, too. She seemed to take an awfully long time getting herself together. Not that there was any studied sensuality to her behavior. The confusion appeared to come out of those early terrified looks over her shoulder. The girl was striking and even aristocratic-looking, that movie kind of Via Veneto aristocracy. Dominique Sanda, if you insist. But there was a young-colt brand of clumsiness in the picture, too. She started to run again and the man in the homburg resumed his inevitable pursuit of her. The girl went through the revolving door of a department store and, after a few beats, the man followed her. That's when Towns decided to call it a day. He could not testify to his source of information, but he would have laid four to one they were going to wind up in the lingerie department. They would get there by escalator. What was Towns going to do up there with them? What was he going to see? The manhole tableau was a tough act to follow, so he decided to take it for what it was, a perfect little erotic cameo that might just as well have been staged for his benefit. It was a gift. He owned it and could play it back any time he wanted to.

Now maybe events like that were a dime a dozen in Taos, New Mexico. He doubted it. On the other hand, he had never been there so he couldn't say.

If there were small daily shockers in his life, the broad lines of Harry Towns's life had been clean and predictable. He had a good strong body and a feeling that it was not going to let him down. Thus far, knock wood, it hadn't. He had always sensed that he would have a son and they would have baseball catches in a backyard somewhere. He had the son and they had plenty of catches. About ten years' worth. After a shaky start, he realized he had the knack of making money, not the kind that got you seaside palaces, but enough to keep everyone comfortable. Which he did. Early on in his marriage, he saw a separation coming; he wasn't sure when, but it was coming all right, and it came. He had read somewhere that when it came to the major decisions in life, all you had to do was listen to the deep currents that ran inside yourself, and they would tell you which way to go. He listened to his and they told him to get going. His wife must have been tuned in to some currents of her own. So they split up and there wasn't much commotion to it. He gave them both a slightly above-average grade on the way they had handled it. After all, take a look at the reason they had gotten married. It dated back to a time when, if you slept with a girl, it meant you had somehow "damaged" her and were obligated to snap her up for a lifetime. He had never told that to anyone, including his wife, but under oath, he would have to identify that as the reason he had gone down the aisle with her. (And it was some sleeping. Exactly twice, in a Plymouth, or at least half in and half out of one, with a door open. During the second session, her father had run outside in a bathrobe and caught them at it. His way of handling his daughter's getting laid was to put his hands on his hips, stick out his jaw and say, "I see that position is everything in life.") Towns had to be fair. There was at least one other reason he had gotten married. She was pretty. She'd had a screen test. The first time he spotted her, it almost tore his head off. He wasn't sure *what* he was, and at the time he'd felt it was a little on the miraculous side that he'd been able to get such an attractive girl interested in him. So he felt he had better marry her, because there was no telling what was coming. It might be his last shot at a pretty girl. That had all been a long time ago. He liked cocaine now— let's face it, he had a modest habit going. On occasion, he had slept with two girls at a time and he had gotten to the point where he didn't think it was anything to raise the flag about. The first time, it was really something, but after that, it was just a matter of having an extra girl in there with you. Even if you had twelve to work with, all you could really concentrate on was one.

In any case, there had been some significant detours along the way, but you couldn't say, overall, that there had been any wild outrageous swerves to his life. Only when it came to his father did he get handed a script that was entirely different from the one he had had in mind.

For forty years, Towns's mother and father had lived in a once-pleasant section of the city that, to use the polite phrase, had "gone down." To get impolite about it, it meant that the Spanish and black people had moved in and the aging Jews, their sons and daughters long gone, had slipped off to "safer" sections of the city. Whether any of this was good or bad, and no matter how you sliced it, it was now a place where old people got hit over the head after dark. Young people did, too, but especially old people. Harry Towns's father had plenty of bounce to his walk and had been taking the subway to work for sixty years. Towns was fond of saying that his father was "seventy-five, going on fifty"; yet technically speaking, his parents were in the old department and he didn't want to get a call one day saying they had been hit over the head. Clearly, he wanted to get them out of there. It was just that he was a little slow in getting around to doing something about it. He sent them on a couple of minor-league vacations to Puerto Rico. He took them to at least one terrific restaurant a week and he phoned them all the time, partly to make sure they hadn't gotten killed. The one thing he didn't do was rent an apartment for them, get it furnished, lay out a year's rent or so, take them down to it, and say, "Here. Now you have to move in. And the only possible reason to go back to the old place is to get your clothes. And you don't even have to do that." He was in some heavy tax trouble and he was not exactly setting the world on fire in the money department, but he could have pulled it off. How about the cocaine he bought? A year's worth of it—right there—could have handled six months' rent for a terrific one-bedroom apartment on lower Park Avenue. Which is what his father, in particular, had his eye on. From that location, he would be able to take one of his bouncy walks right over to work and bid a fond farewell to the subway. But Towns didn't do any of this for his folks and it was a failure he was going to have to carry on his back for a long time.

One day, Towns's mother received a death sentence and it all became academic. She wasn't budging and forget about a tour of the Continent before she went under. Maybe Towns would take one when he got *his* verdict; she just wanted to sit in a chair in her own apartment and be left alone. It was going to be one of those slow wasting jobs. She would handle it all by herself and give the signal when it was time to go to the hospital and get it over with. As she got weaker—and with this disease, ironically, you became physically bigger—Towns's father got more snap to him. It wasn't one of those arrangements in which you could say, metaphorically, that her strength was flowing into him. Or that he was stealing it from her. It's just that he had never handled things better. He had probably never handled things at all. It got into areas like holding her hand a lot even in the very late stages when she had turned into some kind of sea monster and the hands had become great dried-out claws. (He had seen something like what she resembled at California's Marineland, an ancient seal that could hardly move. It wasn't even much of an attraction for people; it just sat there, scaled and ancient, and about all you could say about it was that it was alive.) When they took her false teeth out so she wouldn't be able to swallow them, it gave her mouth a broken-fencepost look, with a tooth here and a tooth there, but Towns's father kissed her snaggled lips as though she were a fresh young girl on her way to a dance. He just didn't see any monster lying there. Harry Towns did, but his father didn't. When he was a boy, Towns remembered his father wearing pullovers all the time. He had been a little chilly all his life. The hospital released Towns's mother for a short time. The radiation made her yearn for cold air, so Towns's dad laid there next to her all night with great blasts of bedroom air-conditioning showering out on the two of them. He offered her the soothing cold while his own bones froze. Towns didn't know it at the time, but he was going to remember all of this as being quite beautiful. Real romance, not your movie bullshit. And it hadn't been that kind of marriage. For forty-five years, they had cut each other to ribbons; they had done everything but fight a duel with pistols. Yet he led her gently into death, courtly, loving, never letting go of her hand, in some kind of old-fashioned way that Towns didn't recognize as going on anymore. Maybe it had gone on in the Gay Nineties or some early time like that.

And Towns's father kept getting bouncier. That was the only flaw in the setup. He probably should have been getting wan and gray, but he got all this extra bounce instead. He couldn't help it. That's just the way he got. The only time he ever left Towns's mother was to go down to work. He would bounce off in the morning looking nattier than ever. He was the only fellow in the world Towns thought of as being natty. Maybe George Raft was another one. Towns remembered a time his father had been on an air-raid-warden softball team and gone after a fly ball in center field. He slipped, fell on his back, got to his feet with his ass all covered with mud—but damned if he didn't look as natty as ever. In fact, there was only one unnatty thing Towns could remember his father ever doing. It was when he took his son to swimming pools and they both got undressed in public locker rooms and his father tucked his undershirt between his legs so Towns couldn't see his cock. The maneuver was probably designed to damp down the sexiness of the moment, but actually it worked the other way, the tucked-in undershirt looking weirdly feminine on a hairy-chested guy and probably turning Towns on a little. His father definitely did not look natty during those moments.

It was a shame the old man (an expression that never quite fit) had to leave Towns's sick mother to go down to work. There was a Spanish record shop across the street that played Latin rhythm tunes full blast all day long and into the night. There was no way to get it across to the owners that a woman was dying of cancer about fifty feet away and two stories up and could they please keep the volume down a little. In their view, they were probably livening up the neighborhood a bit, giving it a badly needed shot in the arm. Possibly, on their native island, they kept the music up all the time, even during cancer. On two separate occasions, the apartment was robbed, once when his mother had dozed off. The second time, she sat there and watched them come in through the fire-escape window. They took the television set and a radio. The way Towns got the story, she merely waved a weary sea claw at them as if to say, "Take anything you want. I've got cancer." Oddly enough, they never got to Towns's father's strongbox which was in a bedroom bureau drawer and not that difficult to find if you were in the least bit industrious. All his life, Towns had wondered about the secrets that were in there; and also how much his father made a week. The news of the robberies just rolled off the shoulders of Towns's dad. It didn't take a bit of the bounce out of him. He comforted Towns's mother with a hug and then zipped inside to cook something she could get down.

A cynical interpretation of all this snap and bounciness might have been that Towns's dad was looking ahead. Towns was fond of saying his father had never been sick a day in his life. Actually, it wasn't quite true. He had had to spend a year strapped to a bench for his back and Towns remembered a long period in which his dad was involved with diathermy treatments. They didn't sound too serious, but Towns was delighted when his father could say goodbye to them. That was about the extent of it. He had every one of his teeth and a smile that could mow down entire crowds. Towns's dentist would stick an elbow in his ribs and say, "How come you don't have teeth like your dad's?" Tack on all that nattiness and bounce and you had a pretty attractive guy on your hands. Maybe he was just giving the old lady a handsome sendoff so he could ease his conscience and clear the decks for a terrific second-time-around. Was it possible he had someone picked out already? For years, Towns's mother had been worried about a certain buyer who had been with the firm for years and "worked close" with Towns's dad.

Except that Towns didn't buy any of this. There were certain kinds of
behavior you couldn't fake. You couldn't hold that claw for hours and
kiss that broken mouth if you were looking ahead. You could do other
things, but you couldn't do those two. At least he didn't think so. Besides, Towns was doing a bit of looking ahead on his dad's behalf. He
had put himself in charge of that department. And that's about all he
was in charge, of. He was almost doing a great many things. He almost
went down to the Spanish record shop and told them that they had
better lower the music or he would break every record over their fucking heads. After the second robbery, he called a homicide detective
friend and said he wanted to make a thorough cruise of the neighborhood and take a shot at nailing the guys who'd come up through the
fire escape. He would go through every mug shot in the files to find the
sonsofbitches. Except that he didn't. He came very close to getting his
mother to switch doctors, using some friends to put him in touch with a
great cancer specialist who might give her a wild shot at some extra
life. He was Captain Almost. Over and over, he asked his father if he
needed any money, to which he would reply, "We've got plenty. You
just take care of yourself." One day Towns said the hell with it and
wrote out a check for two thousand dollars; this was money he really
needed, although, in truth, a third of it would have gone over to coke.
Mysteriously, he never got around to mailing it. There was only one
department in which he demonstrated some follow-through. It's true
he hadn't rented an apartment on lower Park Avenue for his parents
and gotten them out of their old neighborhood, but that's a mistake he
wasn't going to make again. He would wait a polite amount of time
after his mother died and then he would make his move, set up the
place, get his father down there to lower Park if he had to use a gun to
get the job done. He sure as hell was getting at least one of them out.
He would give up the coke for that. He would give up two fingers and a
toe if he had to. He was going to put his father right there where he
could bounce over to work and never have to ride a subway again.
About ten blocks away from work would be perfect. Towns's father
didn't want to retire. That business place of his was like a club; his
cronies were down there. And the crisp ten-block walk to work would
keep that snap in his walk. There was more to the script that Towns
had written. His father could take broads up there with him. That
buyer, if he liked, or anyone else he felt like hanging out with. Someone around forty-seven would be just right for him. Towns would scoop
up a certain girl he had in mind and maybe they would all go out
together. He didn't see that this showed any disrespect for his mother.
What did one thing have to do with the other? Once his father was in
the city, they would spend more time together, not every night, but

maybe twice a week and Sundays for breakfast. He had had his father out with some friends and some of them said he fit right in with them. It was nice of them to say that. And even if he did not exactly fit in, at least he didn't put into play any outrageous old-guy things that embarrassed everybody. They would just have to accept him once in a while whether he fit in or not. Otherwise he would get some new friends.

That was the general drift of the script he had written for his father. But the key to it was the apartment. Right after they buried his mother, Towns called a real-estate agent and told her to start hunting around in that general lower Park vicinity. He used the same agent who'd gotten him his own apartment. He read her as being in her late thirties and not bad. Nothing there for him but maybe for his father. Towns's dad and the agent would prowl around, checking out apartments, and maybe get something going. He didn't have the faintest idea if his father's guns were still functional in that area, but he preferred to think they were. Maybe he would ask him. So Towns set the apartment hunt in motion and, after a few weeks, took his father to dinner at a steak house and hit him with it. "Let's face it, fun is fun, but you've got to get out of there, Dad."

"I know, Harry, and I will, believe me, but I just don't feel like it right now. I have to feel like it. Then I will." At that moment, Harry Towns noticed that his father had lost a little weight, perhaps a few more pounds than he had any business losing. He was one of those fellows who had been one weight all his adult life—and now he was a different one.

"I don't have any appetite," he said.

"But look how you're eating now," Towns told him. And, indeed, his father had cleaned up everything in front of him. Then Towns gave his father a small lecture. "Let's face it, Dad, you're a little depressed. You can't live with somebody that long and then lose them and not be. Maybe you ought to see somebody, for just an hour or two. I had that experience myself. Just one or two sessions and I got right back on the track." He didn't want to use the word "psychiatrist." But that's what he had in mind. He knew just the right fellow, too. Easy on the nerves and almost the same age as his father. He had expected to hear some grumbling, but his father surprised him by saying, "Maybe you have a point there." And then Towns's dad looked at him with some kind of wateriness in his eyes. It wasn't tears, or even the start of them, but some kind of deep and ancient watery comprehension. Then he cleaned off his plate and brought up the subject of bank books and insurance. Towns felt he was finally getting in on some of the secrets in the strongbox. He had about fifty grand in all and he wanted his son to know about it, "just in case anything happens."

"There ain't anything gonna happen," said Towns.

"Just in case. I want it split fifty-fifty, half for you and half for your brother."

"Give it all to him," said Towns.

"Never," said his father, with something close to anger. "Half and half, right down the middle. And it's nothing to sneeze at."

"I know that."

"I thought you were making fun of it."

"I wasn't," said Towns. "But will you get the goddamn apartment?"

"I will," he said, mopping up the last of the cheesecake. "But first I have to feel like it."

The appetite thing worried Towns. He was sure it connected to some kind of depression, because he ate so well when he was out with Towns. But he couldn't have breakfast with his father every morning. And no matter how much he loved him, he couldn't eat with him every goddamn night. What about lunches? Was he supposed to run over and have lunch with him, too? He finally teamed the old man up with the real-estate lady, and on a Saturday morning they checked out a few available apartments. On lower Park. That afternoon, the woman called Towns and said his father had gotten dizzy in one of the apartments and hit his head on the radiator. She said she had made him swear he was in good shape before she let him go home. She was all right. Towns got his father to go to the doctor—he admitted to getting dizzy once before on the subway and having to ask someone for a seat —and they ran some tests. They used the same doctor who hadn't performed any particular miracles on his mother's claws. Towns had meant to switch off to another one, but that's something else he had not gotten around to. The tests zeroed in on his prostate and Towns felt better immediately. He had a little condition of his own and he knew it was no toothache, but there was no way it could turn you into a Marineland exhibition. The prostate had to go and the fellow who would take it out was named Dr. Merder. Towns and his dad had a good laugh about that one. If you were a surgeon with a name like that, you had better be good. So they didn't worry a bit about him. The book on the doctor was that he had never lost a prostate case. Towns's dad checked into the hospital. He was concerned about how the business, or "place" as he called it, would run in his absence and he didn't relax until the boss called and told him to take it easy, they would cover for him and everything would be just fine; just relax and get better. The boss was around thirty years younger than he was, but Towns's dad couldn't get over his taking the time to do a thing like that. Once in the hospital, he went from natty to dignified. Maybe he had always been dignified, even though he had blown his one shot at being head of his own business, years before. Using some fancy accounting techniques, his partners had quickly cut him to ribbons and eased him out of his share of the firm. This would have left most men for dead; but Towns's dad had simply gone back to his old factory job as second in command, dignified as ever. In the hospital, the only thing he used the bed for was sleeping. He sat in a flowered New England chair, neat as a pin, reading the books Harry Towns brought him. His favorite kind of book dealt with generals and statesmen, people like Stettinius and Franklin Delano Roosevelt, and the goings-on behind the scenes during World War II. Or at least Towns assumed they were his favorites. Maybe they were his own favorites, and all those years he had been pushing them on his dad. Whenever Towns brought him a book, his father felt obliged to "read it up," as if it would be "wasted" if he didn't. Like food. So whenever Towns showed up at the hospital with another one, he would hold up his hands and say, "Stop, for crissakes. How much can a guy read?"

Along with at least one volume about secret-service shenanigans in World War II, Towns would also bring a fistful of expensive Canary Island cigars. For most of his life, his father had smoked a cheaper brand, Admiration Joys when Towns was a boy, but in recent years Towns had promoted him to these higher-priced jobs. He complained that Towns was spoiling him. Sixty cents was too much to spend for a cigar. And there was no way to go back to the Joys. But he got a lot of pleasure out of the expensive ones. Towns had gotten the cigar habit from his father; he remembered a time when his father would greet a friend by stuffing a cigar in his handkerchief pocket and the friend would do the same for Towns's dad. It seemed like a fine ritual and Towns was sorry to see it go; there was probably a paper around proving it was all very phallic and homosexual. Now, when Towns showed up with the cigars, his father would say, "What the hell am I supposed to do with them?"

"Smoke 'em," said Towns.

"What if I don't feel like it?"

"Then just take a few puffs."

"All right, leave 'em over there."

And he would. He would take a few puffs of each one. So they wouldn't go to waste.

They kept taking more tests on Towns's dad; he didn't leave the room very often, but he did spend a little time with one other patient and he got a tremendous kick out of this fellow. He was trying to impeach the President and Towns's father couldn't get over that. If he had great admiration for people like Cordell Hull and Omar Bradley, his respect for the office of the President was absolutely overpowering. The idea of a guy running around trying to get the top executive impeached tickled the hell out of Towns's dad. It was so outrageous. "You got to see this guy," he told Towns. "He's got a sign this big over his door, some kind of impeachment map. He's trying to get some signatures up. And he's important, too. I don't know what the hell he does, but he gives off an important impression. He says he wants to meet you."

"What's he want to meet me for?"

"I don't know. Maybe he heard you were important, too. Why don't you go over there and give him a tumble?"

Towns wasn't terribly interested in the impeachment man. He was more interested in the tests. But for his father's sake, he met the fellow in the lounge. He was a sparse-haired gentleman, a bit younger than his father, who talked a mile a minute and seemed to be carefully staying off the subject of impeachment. At the same time, he kept checking Towns's eyes as if he were looking for a go-ahead signal. Towns gave him a signal that said nothing doing. "What'd you think of him?" Towns's father asked as they walked back to the room.

"He's all right," said Towns.

"Well, I don't know what *you* think of him, but to me he's really something. Imagine a thing like that. Going around trying to *impeach* the President of the United States. And he's no bum. You can tell that by looking at him. I think he's got some dough." All the way back to his room, Towns's dad kept clucking his tongue about the fellow. He acted as though it was the most amazing thing he had ever come across in all his seventy-five years.

"Would you like to see that map he's got on the outside of his door?"

"I don't think so, Dad."

"I think you ought to take a look at it."

"Maybe I will, on the way out."

They decided to build up Towns's dad by giving him a couple of transfusions before the surgery. While this was going on, Towns ran into a nurse who came an inch short of being one of the prettiest girls he knew in the city. He had always meant to get around to her, but she lived with a friend of his and he claimed that was one rule he would never break. Or at least he'd try not to break it. She had a private patient down the hall and said she knew about his father and that a week before, he had stood outside his door and asked her to come in and have a cookie. Towns wished his father had been much more rascally than that. Why didn't he just reach out and pinch her ass? On the other hand, the cookie invitation wasn't much, but it was something. Towns made her promise to go in and visit him and sort of kid around with him and she said of course she would, he didn't even have to ask. He had the feeling this was the kind of girl his father would love to fool around with in an old-guy way.

The transfusion gave Towns's father some fever, but they went ahead and operated anyway. This puzzled Towns a bit. Except that his father seemed to come out of the surgery all right. He didn't appear to be connected up to that many tubes, which struck Towns as a good sign. Towns kept bringing him books about desert warfare, the defense of Stalingrad, Operation Sea Lion, but he kept them over to the side where his father couldn't see them and have to worry about "reading them up." Before they got spoiled. On the third day after the operation, he brought along a real torpedo of a cigar, long, fragrant, aromatic, the best he could find.

"What'd you bring that for?" asked his father, who was down to one tube.

"Why do you think?"

"I ain't smoking it, Harry."

"The hell you're not."

The next day, his father looked a little weaker, but the doctor said it was more or less normal to take a dip on the way back from surgery. When they were alone, Towns's father asked his son, "What the hell are you doing here?"

"I came to see you, Dad."

He turned his head away, waved his hand in disgust and said, "You ain't gonna do me any good." Then he turned back and chuckled and they started to talk about what was going on outside, but that cruel random slash had been there. Maybe you were allowed to be a little cruel right after surgery. Towns wasn't sure. It was only the second piece of bad behavior Towns could think of since he'd been born. The other had to do with Towns, at around eight or nine, using the word "schmuck" about somebody; he didn't know what the word meant, but his father instantly lashed out and belted him halfway across the city. So that added up to two in more than forty years. "Schmuck" and "You ain't gonna do me any good." Not a bad score. The next morning, the doctor phoned and told Towns he had better come down, because his father's pulse had stopped. "What do you mean, stopped?" Towns asked.

"The nurse stepped out for a second and when she came back he had no pulse. She called a round-the-clock resuscitation team and they were down there like Johnny-on-the-spot. They do quite a job."

"How come the nurse stepped out?"

"They have to go to the bathroom."

"Is he gonna live?"

"It depends on how long his pulse stopped. We'll know that later."

Towns got down there fast. He met the doctor in the intensive-care unit. The doctor asked if he would like to see the team working on his dad and he said he would. He took Towns down the hall and displayed the huge resuscitation units the way a proud Soviet manager would show off his plant for a group of Chrysler execs. His father was hooked up to plenty of tubes now. He was like a part in a huge industrial city. The whole city of Pittsburgh. He was the part that took a jolting spasmodic leap every few seconds. Towns got as close as he could—what the hell, he'd seen everything now. He tried to spot something that wasn't covered up by gadgets. Something that looked like his father. He finally picked off a section from the wrist to the elbow that he recognized as being his father's arm. He was pretty sure of it. "There's no point in your staying around," the doctor said. "I know that," said Towns.

He went up to his father's room and got the cigar. Then he walked to the end of the hall and took a look at the impeachment map. It showed how much strength the fellow had across the country. He didn't have much. A couple of pins in Los Angeles, Wisconsin, New York, and out. On the way down, Towns stopped in at the snack bar and had some peach yogurt. It was the first time in his life he had ever tasted yogurt and it wasn't bad. It went down easy and it didn't taste the way he had imagined it would. He made a note to pick up a few cartons of it. The fruit kind. He went back to his apartment and fell asleep. The call came early in the evening. Towns had promised himself he would fix the exact time in his mind forever, but a week later, he couldn't tell you what time or even what month it had happened.

"That's it, huh?"

"I'm afraid so," said the doctor. "About five minutes ago. I'd like to get your permission to do a medical examination of dad so that maybe we can find out something to help the next guy who comes in with the same condition."

"How come you operated on him with fever?"

"We tried to contact you on that to get your permission."

"You should've tried harder."

"See," said the doctor, "that's just it. We talk to people when they're understandably upset and they say no to medical examinations. In Sweden, it's automatic."

"Work a little harder on what you know already."

"The next one could be your child. Or your children's children."

"Fuck you, doctor."

So that was it. The both of them. And for the moment, all Harry Towns had out of it was a new expression. Back to back. He had lost both his parents, back to back. He leaned on that one for about six months or so; especially if someone asked him why he was "low" or why he was late on a deadline. "Hey," he would say, "I lost both my parents, back to back." And he would be off the hook. He told his brother from Omaha to fly in as fast as possible and take care of everything, clean out his dad's apartment, settle the accounts, the works. He was better at that kind of thing. Maybe Towns would be good at it, too, but he didn't want to be. The only thing he could hardly wait to do was get in touch with the rabbi who had officiated over his mother's funeral. He was a fellow the chapel kept on tap in case you didn't have any particular rabbi of your own in mind. It was like getting an attorney from Legal Aid except that this one turned out to be a real find. He showed up in what Harry Towns liked to recall as a cloud of smoke, with a shiny black suit and a metaphysical tuft of hair sticking up on his head. He turned up two and a half minutes before the ceremony and asked Towns to sum up his mother. "What are you, nuts?" said Towns. "Trust me," said the rabbi, a homely fellow with an amazingly rocklike jaw that was totally out of sync with his otherwise wan Talmudic features. Towns took a shot. He told him they really shouldn't have limos taking his mother out to the grave, they ought to have New York taxis. Whenever she had a problem, she would simply jump inside one and have the driver ride around with the meter going while she talked to him until she felt better. Then she would pay the bill, slap on a big tip, and hop out. That was her kind of psychoanalysis. She couldn't cook and Towns didn't want anyone laying that word "housewife" on her. Not at the funeral. It was very important to get her right. This was almost as important to him as losing her. She was close to cabbies, bellhops, and busboys and she could brighten up a room just by walking into it. And damned if this faded little mysterious house rabbi didn't get her. In two and a half minutes. "Sparkle" was the key word. And it was his own. He kept shooting that word "sparkle" out over the mourners and it was as if he had known her all his life. Towns had never seen a performance quite like that.

After they had buried her in the Jersey Flats, the rabbi asked if anyone could give him a lift back to New York City. Everyone was staying at an aunt's house in Jersey, so no one could. With that, he hopped on the hearse. And then he disappeared; once again, it might just as well have been in a cloud of smoke. And he was only seventy-five bucks. So you can see why Towns was anxious to have him back for a repeat performance. It was enough to get Towns back to religion. Why not, if they had unsung guys like that around? Except that the

minute he showed up at the chapel the second time, something was a
little off. The rabbi looked barbered for one thing. And he was wearing
flowing rabbinical robes. What happened to the black shiny suit that he
had probably brought over from Poland? And he didn't get Towns's
father at all. "Good, honest, hard-working man." "Lived only for his
family." Shit like that. Right out of your basic funeral textbook. The
very thing Towns wanted to head off. His diction was different, fancier.
He could have been talking about anybody. And he seemed to be playing not to the audience but strictly to Towns. It occurred to Harry
Towns that maybe there wasn't any way to get his father. Maybe that
was it—honest, hard-working, et cetera. But for Christ's sake, he could
have found something. "Sparkle" wasn't it—he had used that anyway—
but how about that bounce in his walk. What about nattiness for a
theme. The sharpness of his beard against Harry Towns's face when he
was a kid. Anything. Cigar smoking. Handing them out and getting
some back. His being an air-raid warden. An all-day fist fight he had
with his brother. (When it was over, they didn't talk to each other for
twenty-five years.) Anything at all. Just so they didn't bury a statistic.
Maybe it was as simple as the old second-audition syndrome. A performer would come in and knock you on your ass the first time. He
would get called back and bomb. Show people explained it by saying
there was nothing on the line the first time a performer auditioned. If
you called him back, it meant you were considering him for the part. In
that situation, nine out of ten performers choked. The rabbi didn't
choke. He was as smooth as silk. He probably felt he was really cooking. But he sure did bomb.

Out they went to the Jersey Flats again, and after his father was in
the ground, alongside his mother, the rabbi took Towns aside and said,
"With your mother, I didn't even know who you were." Who in the hell
was he? A screenwriter? So that was it. The rabbi had caught his name
on a picture and felt he had to be classier. "I'm being sponsored on a
little trip to Israel," said the rabbi. "Is there any chance you could meet
me there so we could see it together? It would be meaningful to both
of us."

"I don't give a shit about Israel," said Towns. It wasn't true. He did
give a shit about Israel. When the chips were down, he was still some
kind of Jew. He was just sore as hell at the rabbi for letting him down
and not getting his father right. And for not being that magical fellow
with the tuft of hair who had shown up in a cloud of smoke and almost
got him back to religion. After everyone had climbed back into the
limos, Towns went back to the grave and dropped that big torpedo of a
cigar inside. He was aware of the crummy sentimentality involved—
and he knew he would probably tell it to a friend or two before the

week was over—as an anecdote—but he did it anyway. No one was going to tell him whether to be sentimental or not—not when he had just lost his mother and father. Back to back.

He hung around the city while his brother cleaned things up for him. He said he didn't want anything from the apartment except an old-fashioned vest-pocket watch he remembered. And maybe his dad's ring, with the initials rubbed over with age so you couldn't really make them out. They got the finances straightened out in his brother's hotel room. The money coming to Towns was enough to cover his back tax bill to the government, almost to the penny. He hadn't slept easily for a year, wondering where he was going to get that kind of dough. And there were a handful of salary checks to be divided up. So he finally found out what his father's salary was. It was probably the last secret in the strongbox. He was sorry he found out. They had cut him down to nickels and dimes, probably because he was seventy-five. And here he was, settling his son's tax bill. Towns hugged his brother, saying, "Let's stay in touch. You're all I've got," and then his nephew came dancing out in one of his father's suits. Wearing a funny smile and looking very natty. Towns recalled a fellow he had once worked for who had come to the office wearing his father's best suit, one day after the old man had died. At the time, he wondered, what kind of a guy does that. Now, his brother said, "It fit him like a glove, so why not?" Towns couldn't answer that one. He just felt it shouldn't be going on. About a month later, he changed his mind and was glad the kid took the clothes.

Harry Towns planned on taking a long drive to someplace he hadn't been, so he could be alone and sort things out, but he got whisked off to California on a job he felt he couldn't turn down. He told himself the work would be good for him. Just before he left, he ran into the cookie nurse at a singles place and asked her if she had ever gone in and fooled around with his father. She said she had but her eyes told him she hadn't. Cunt. No wonder he hadn't moved in on her. It wasn't that she was living with his friend. The guy wasn't that close a friend. It was this kind of behavior. She would tell you that she would go in and screw around with your father and then she wouldn't.

He polished off the California work in about a week; whenever it sagged a little, he would say, "Hey, listen, I just lost both my parents, back to back." It burned him up when people advanced the theory that his father died because he couldn't live without his wife. He heard a lot of that and he didn't buy any of it. Towns hadn't been married to anyone for fifty years the way his father had and it didn't look as if there was going to be time to squeeze someone in for half a century. But he just couldn't afford to think that if you loved someone very much and they died, you had to hop right into the grave with them. He

preferred to think that you mourned for them and then went about
your business.

He went on an erratic crying schedule. The first burst came at the
Los Angeles airport, on the way for a quick stopover in Vegas. He was
really smoking with the late-night check-in stewardess at the L.A. airport, a small girl with a huge chest and an angel's face. He almost had
her talked into going to Vegas with him. One extra shove and she
would have been on the seat next to him. He did it right in front of the
Air West pilots, too, and they didn't appreciate it much. On the other
hand, two hookers saw the whole thing and got a big kick out of it.
Then he got on the plane and cried all the way to Caesars Palace. The
hookers saw that one, too, and must have wondered if he were crazy.
He had just finished hustling a stewardess. He might just as well have
been Cary Grant back there at the airport. What was he doing all that
crying for? Back East, he gave himself the job of copying over his
address book. Halfway along, he came to his father's name and business number. He really went that time. For a period there, he didn't
think he was ever going to stop. It was having to make that particular
decision. What do you do, carry your dead father over into the new
address book? Or drop him from the rolls, no more father, no more
phone number, and you pick up that extra space for some new piece of
ass?

He never did get to take that drive. The one in which he was going
to go to a strange place and sort things out. The awful part is that he
never seemed to get any huge lessons out of the things that happened
to him. He was brimming over with small nuggets of information he
had gathered for his work. For example, when frisking a homicide suspect in a stabbing case, the first thing detectives check for is a dry-
cleaning ticket. On the theory that the suspect is going to ship his
bloodstained clothing right off to the cleaner's. When shot at, cops are
taught to jump to their left since most gunmen are right-handed and
will either fire wide of the mark or, at worst, nick your shoulder. He
knew there was no such thing as a second wind in running. If you got
one, it meant you had not been "red-lining it," that is, running full out.
He kept his young son enthralled for hours with this kind of information. But he didn't own any real wisdom and this bothered him. Instead, he borrowed other people's. Never sleep with a woman who has
more problems than you do. Nelson Algren. Don't look over your
shoulder because someone might be gaining on you. Satchel Paige.
People behave well only because they lack the character to behave
poorly. La Rochefoucauld. Take short views, hope for the best, and
trust in God. Some British guy. Stuff like that. Wasn't it time for him to

be coming up with a few of his own? Pressed to the wall, he would probably produce this list:

1. *Be very lucky.*
2. *Watch your ass.*

Because if they could get your father's pulse to stop—considering the way he looked, the way he bounced along, his smile, and the fifteen years, minimum, that Harry Towns had scripted up for him—if they could keep him out of that paid-for apartment on lower Park, and on top of everything, get him to die back to back with Towns's mom, the two of them stowed underground in the Jersey Flats, why then all bets were off and anything was possible. Anything you could dream up. You name it. Any fucking thing in the world.

Mother

Post Time

THOUGH HE KNEW he was the owner of enormous power, he sensed quickly it was important to defer to the wiry little knot of energy who hopped upon his back and guided him on the Important Days. He knew as well that there were others like him, and he was at his most comfortable when he was in their midst, smelling and brushing up against them, feeling their length and sleekness against his own.

His entire life seemed to be a preparation for the Important Days. He had done well on the first of these. He knew this because the great babble that came from a surrounding arc seemed not to be directed at him, but at others like him, and perhaps one in particular. He would circle the large field and stay tied snugly to the other shapes, part of the flow, several in front of him, some alongside, some behind. He enjoyed being part of this communal sea.

The high point of his young existence came during one of the Important Days when he was making his final turn around the arc and slipped back to a kind of tail-like position with all the other shapes charging up ahead. He attached himself to their energy and let them carry him along, feeling free and passive. He knew he had done something wonderful, because the sound from the surrounding arc had a comfortable hissing and booing quality to it, quite unlike the aggressive babble to which he was accustomed. Nonetheless, he was puzzled by the behavior of the controlling knot who rode his back and seemed displeased, twisting his flesh and finally, applying a thwacking instrument to the massive flanks that held his enginelike power. He knew it was important not to invoke the displeasure of this crabbed little force; so he promised himself that on the next of the Important Days, he would forego the darting, dipping freewheeling pleasures of the tail position.

It was a somewhat restricted life but a good one. He was fed amply —great bales of mash. Regularly, he was given chances to defuse the tornado in his flanks by running freely in open greenery. On these occasions, a more relaxed presence sat upon his back. Despite these pleasant interludes, he felt a sense of uneasiness and foreboding though he could not locate its source. In confirmation of these fears, his fortunes took a rude downward turn. On two successive Important

Days, he had been running comfortably, lost in the foam of the other shapes, when the small control knot indicated by various kneading pressures that he was to move in front of them. Though this was well within his power, he resisted gently until the prodding from above became commanding and he was forced to comply. Sick with humiliation, he left the comfortable flow and moved in front, naked, vulnerable, outlawed, exposed to the babble that—on both occasions—grew deafening as he completed the final arc. Throatless, impotent, he wanted to cry out that this was not his decision—that there was no way for him to attach himself once again to the fleshlike stream and be sealed in its midst.

On both occasions, disgraced, his heart hanging low, he had been isolated from the other shapes and paraded before the rising arc, the babble thunderous, outrageous, filling his great body and coating his skin.

His trials were not over. There was yet another Important Day, perhaps the most significant of all. There was more clangor to it; a riot of color; the circling arc was vast. As he was led to the start of the running, the din rose in waves of intensity, as if to remind him that his shameful past deeds had not been forgotten. As if in further reminder of his infamy, a double-winged mask was affixed to him in such a way as to constrict his vision. He had a secret pool of untapped power; he vowed that on this occasion he would turn it in the direction of keeping himself hooked into the flow of shapes on either side.

Through half of the running, he succeeded in doing this, gliding, rocking, a section of the stream, returning to what now seemed his idyllic early days. He could not tell whether the soothing boos and hisses were strictly designed for him, but he declared a part of them for himself and basked in the comfort of them. Then, suddenly, the knotted-up force began to apply the pressures, grinding and pinching at him, urging him forward to that lonely and humiliating position— ahead of the other shapes. Momentarily, he held back. Shoots of anger formed within him, struggling to take root. He channeled a portion of that locomotive power into a single humped and resistant convulsion; but it was a maneuver that was alien to his docile spirit. Pinching, kneading, grinding, the choked little knot forced him forward until he bent to its will. Instead of inching forward, he made the decision, unopposed by the controlling knot, to burst forward and race proudly on toward his humiliation. Unleashing his full bank of energy, he wondered all the while about the irony of his having to apply this great birth-given force to his own disgrace. Almost enjoying the spectacle of his undoing, he plunged even farther ahead of the other shapes until he was running alone, once again, ironically buoyed up by the thunderous babble of the arc that seemed to form an hysterical rainbow above his treachery.

At the end of the running, his disgrace total, he tried to cut short his agony by insinuating himself into the other friendly shapes, to return to that familiar smell and feel so similar to his own. But he was kept isolated and led, once again, in a slow dumb march before the arc. A small particle of the arc ran forward and placed a hot-colored slightly brambled wreath around his neck. Meekly, he dropped his head and accepted the badge of dishonor.

The aggressive babble rose, more thunderous and compelling than before. Powerless, defeated, he kicked at the dirt and tried with all the murky power of his being to fathom why he of all creatures had been singled out to lead a life of such unrelenting shame.

An Ironic
Yetta Montana

THIS IS A STORY ABOUT the one time I outfoxed Hollywood. Open on me arriving at the Pierre Hotel for a script conference with Sandra Moxie, a short, feisty, singer slash actress with a brash, almost harassing style and the uncanny ability to turn around on a dime and become quite touching. Or at least *most* people felt she had that ability. In her recent appearances, I myself had felt that you could see the machinery, that she was telegraphing her touching stuff with the result that it wasn't all that touching. But let that pass. For the moment, let's just say that she was touching enough to get the job done.

As a singer, Moxie had built up a strong following in Key West and Marin County and had received critical plaudits for a film cameo in which she had hit a leering computer programmer over the head with a jar of peanuts and then casually spun around and sung a ballad from a bar stool. The plaudits, for the most part, were foreign plaudits—awards she had to share with Dolly Parton—but there was no question that her alternately harsh and vulnerable style was effective on film. Inevitably, a search began for a property that would take full advantage of the special Moxie capabilities. It was in this context that I was hired by an independent film producer to do the true story of Yetta Montana, the daughter of an East Coast dry-goods salesman, who went west to become a honky-tonk bar owner and the only woman to stake out a fortune in the Klondike Gold Rush of 1897. Amazingly, Montana was still alive, albeit hanging on by her thumbs, and I got to interview her in a condominium in Sarasota. She went in and out on me, memorywise, but for those moments when she was in the game, she was surprisingly lucid. (I should probably add that the celebrated Montana bosom was also—I'm not sure *intact* is the word—very much in the picture.) She wore a replica of her diamond-studded rotary drill around her neck and she had kept some remarkably well-preserved diaries, along with photographs of her hanging out with panhandlers on the Klondike River. She was kind enough to let me borrow these materials and I assured her I would get them back to her in good condition. Admittedly, it was difficult to get a fix on Montana and what her gold-field style might have been like. Nonetheless, I did some fancy extrapolating, took a quick free-form run at the story and sent the result to Sandra Moxie, underlining the fact that it was a *first draft*. Shortly thereafter, I heard she had "a few reservations" (the most ominous phrase in the film biz) but wanted to see me all the same. I had heard she was given to tantrums and violent swings of mood, but I took it as a matter of course that, although some gifted people could be difficult, they tended to meet you on your own terms if you behaved in a firm and professional manner.

In person, Moxie was shorter than she appeared on-screen (where she came across pretty short) but not in the least bit feisty. At least in the early innings. She wore a shapeless garment, a cross between a housedress and a dashiki, and struck me as the kind of person who allowed herself to fall apart for a while and then went on crash programs to get in shape. She didn't appear to be on one of those programs at the moment. She was courteous, speaking in a low, evenly modulated voice; her style, if anything, was on the plaintive and even borderline heartbroken side.

"I heard you weren't entirely pleased with the script," I said, throwing out a signal that I was easy and flexible in the work relationship and certainly not one of those people who fought you tooth and nail for every semicolon.

"That's a fair summation," she said. And then, in a wounded heartbroken rush, she added: "Truthfully, I don't see Yetta Montana. The Yetta I've been expecting is brash, feisty, up one minute, down the next, laughing, crying, wounded, depressed, but no matter what the circumstances, always punching and kicking back at the world—every inch a woman.

"This person," she said, hitting my script, "is a wimp. I wouldn't play her if they gave me an Oscar in advance."

Her outburst put me on the defensive. Fortunately, after long years as a screenwriter I had learned to be at ease in that posture.

"Kicking? Punching? Who told you Yetta was like that?"

"Everyone," she said. "Why do you think I wanted to do the part!"

I let the "wanted" go for the moment.

"Well, I actually met the woman," I said. "And she isn't at all like that. She has some drive—you don't beat out forty thousand rival prospectors if you're a lox—but I didn't see any kicking and punching. Actually, it's the *other* colors that come through. She's soft, whimsical, a little flirtatious . . ."

"How old is she now?" asked Moxie.

"Old," I said, caught. "Pretty damned old. But I assure you people don't change that much. The blueprint is still there."

"When McClintock attacks her girl friend, why doesn't she hit him right over the head?"

"She arranges to have his mule team scattered. That's not exactly Gandhi-like resistance."

"*Arranges,*" she said, with a smirk. "Got a big, strong man to do it for her. That's exactly my point."

She sat down and folded her arms.

"I'm not playing a wimp."

Well, I'd been around the horn a few times with female stars. The-entire-script-is-a-turkey. I-wouldn't-play-the-part-if-you-tripled-the-salary. Poke around a bit and you find out the trouble is: a) she doesn't appear early enough, b) she doesn't want to wear toreador pants and c) the sidekick has a few good one-liners. In other words, Mickey Mouse.

"Why don't we just dig in," I suggested, "scene by scene and see if we can't spot the areas you're objecting to. For example," I said, confident my first few pages were unassailable, "what do you think of the opening?"

"It's a cliché."

"Hold it," I said. "Time out right there. A scene with a *gay* rail-splitter is a cliché? How many scenes have you looked at with gay rail-splitters?"

"Oh, for God's sake," she said, as if I were a hopeless case. "Don't you even go to the movies?"

Well, the truth is, I don't go to the movies that often. I go in streaks, but then, there are long periods when I don't go—and although I have grave doubts about this—maybe there was some kind of trend I had missed. We moved to the second scene, which, in truth, even I wasn't too crazy about so I couldn't blame her for being unenthusiastic. I had dummied up a sentimental farewell confrontation between the teenage Yetta and her father—just before she heads west—in which he warns her not to equate a troy ounce of gold with a troy ounce of happiness. Cast the right actors and you're in business. But if you can't envision a Rod Steiger in the role (with Steiger it flies right off the page), I have to admit it kind of lays there. Unfortunately, her reaction to the scene set the tone for the next twenty minutes or so, in which she halfheartedly conceded I had a usable minute here, another one there. At some point, she maneuvered herself over to the desk and came back holding a stack of papers, clutching them to her chest the way a schoolgirl might carry her first try at romantic poetry. A movie schoolgirl. She blushed a little and for a second she almost had me believing she was pretty.

"Do you mind looking at this?" she asked, handing the material to me. "When I got your script, I became panicky, so I dug into some turn-of-the-century newspapers and did a little work of my own. Bear in mind, I'm not a writer, but see what you think."

What I thought was that the work was not too shabby. Predictably, it got off the ground with a pretitle sequence in which Montana, new to the Klondike, outwardly shy and gullible, suddenly heaves a pan of unsifted gold dust in the face of a crass trail guide. To be fair about it, just because I could predict the resolution of the scene didn't mean that an audience would be able to. After that, the script kind of settled in, except that it *didn't* really settle in and therein lay its effectiveness. She used crazy discordant transitions that worked, just the way she did in her act. Cinematically, the technique was even more effective. *Bam* you're in Helena, *whop* you're in Forty-Mile, *klunk* you're aboard the S.S. *Excelsior* and *voom* you're back in the car, wondering where the movie went. Which wasn't all that bad. There weren't any layers, but so what. It's a goddamned entertainment. Let Fassbinder do layers. The best thing about it was that it was all *there* for me. Tone down the showbiz references, beef up the meeting with the aging Bat Masterson (adding a line or two to explain what the hell he was *doing* there), throw a line or two to Choppy Waters, Moxie's Cree sidekick, and that's it. Sign the script, mail it off and hunker down to audit the profit statements.

As I flipped through the last few pages, she leaned close and the celebrated Moxie bosom brushed against my ear. I pretended I hadn't noticed and she withdrew to a discreet distance, although what the word *discreet* is doing in this tome I'm not sure I can answer.

"You like it?" she asked, pleased in advance. Nobody ever said she didn't have sensitive antennae.

"I do."

"Can I have a credit?"

"Nope."

We both laughed and decided it was as good a time as any to break for lunch. She opened a small refrigerator and took out some berries, melon slices and a few croissants, all of it left over from a breakfast with the Lorimar people. She asked me to bear with her—yes, the studio was tabbing her, but the frugal style was something she couldn't help. It was a carry-over from the years she'd worked in an all-night nail clinic while she was waiting for a break in show business. No doubt this would have been endearing to someone who wasn't crazed with hunger for a hot club sandwich the way I imagined only the Pierre could prepare one. While she warmed up the croissants, I riffled through the books on the shelves and was surprised at the quality of the selections. Normally, in my experience with hotels, it's the Gideon Bible, Taylor Caldwell if you're lucky, and out. But someone had stocked these shelves with Gide, Rilke, *Joseph and His Brothers,* not just Henry James but James's *letters,* for Christ's sake. I picked up a volume by an author I'd never heard of entitled *The Notebooks of Lotte Kastlemeir,* glanced at a few pages and became intrigued. Even allowing for the obvious debt to Mann and Nabokov, the style was instantly winning and unique. I asked Moxie if I could take it along.

"Do you know what this room costs?" she said, setting the food on the table. "Take a dozen."

We sat down to lunch and she asked me if I was married.

"No," I said. "I was, but I'm not."

"You live with someone?"

"Uh-huh."

"Yeah, and I can just see her. Probably a wimp."

To this day I still can't figure out why I was as upset as I was over that remark. Admittedly, it was sudden, unprovoked, major-league rude and anyone would have been upset. But dizzy spells? Strangulated rage? Pass-the-Gristede's-Shopping-Bag-I'm-Hyperventilating? And what happened to my famous above-the-battle posture in which I cluck my tongue and shake my head sadly, the one that really puts people away.

Was I stung because Kai-Yin really *was* a wimp? Actually, I'd never been with a woman who took care of me so totally. From the second I get up in the morning, it's feathery kisses, a bright and cheery smile and a scented cloth for the crust that forms over my eyes whenever we're at our place in Brooklyn Heights. After that, it's back massages, freshly laundered clothing, ingenious flower arrangements—the whole day is a parade of sensual delights. In the food department, all I have to do is *think* exotic, and she's out there with gimchee and a banana flambé. Kai-Yin is solicitous and caring, but does that mean she's a wimp? What happened to the whole Oriental tradition? Are we throwing that out? All right, for argument's sake, let's say she *is* a wimp. I've got a charming little Oriental wimp waiting for me in New Milford. Does that mean that the opposite of a wimp is short, feisty Sandra Moxie who can go from tough to vulnerable?

"Maybe we ought to go back to work?"

"Why don't you go out with Dustin Hoffman's ex-wife?"

Okay, why didn't I leave at *that* point? It's a fair question. I wasn't hired to be Kurt Waldheim. The money jumps to mind, but I'd been well taken care of on the first draft and if the studio said, "All right, bring in Hack Number Two," I'd already established that it was *my* notion, *my* characters and I'll see everybody at the Writer's Guild arbitration. The producer of the film was Norton Kranzler, an ancient "soft lefty" who had shielded blacklisted writers from his villa in Saint Paul de Vence. Was I staying because of my loyalty to Kranzler, a sick man whose voice could barely be heard over the phone and who hadn't had a hit since his brief partnership with Von Stroheim?

She was aware of my struggle—those street instincts left over from the all-night nail clinic. "I don't care if you quit," she said. But it was spoken with a surprising lack of bravado. "I took some development money from the studio. I'll just give it back."

"Anyone can quit," I said, wondering what had happened to the youth whose rapierlike cafeteria thrusts in the Bronx had virtually forced the yearbook editors to name him "The Oscar Wilde of William Howard Taft High School."

"Do you like working with me?" she asked, once again catching me off guard.

"Yes," I said. How could I not like working with her? She'd done the whole damned script for me.

"Do you like me?"

"I don't know how to answer questions like that."

She set the pages aside and kicked her legs up on the table.

"How much did they pay you for this job?"

I told her. It was ten grand more than I'd ever gotten before and I was a little proud of it.

"Jesus Christ," she said. "I know a film *student* in Santa Monica who gets a third of that. DON'T YOU EVER WRITE ME A SCRIPT LIKE THAT AGAIN!"

I didn't quit, didn't correct her grammar, didn't even toss her out the window. What I did do is thank her for the help, tell her I thought I could bring it much closer on the second shot and flip-flop dissolved myself into the lobby. At the moment, I wasn't thinking wounded pride. All I knew was that I had a week's work in front of me and I was home. The second draft paid spit, but we're talking about *seven days*. Not even full-out days. Noon to around 3:30. With sandwiches brought in, I might even be able to knock it off in a weekend. And I'd have my first major credit. Even if they brought in two, three guys, there's no way they can bump me out of first position. And the picture was going to be big. Set aside my personal feelings about the woman—but Sandra Moxie in her first major role, wailing in the gold fields? Forget it, she's got to win something.

Anyway, there was no week and there was certainly no weekend. I had forgotten—there never is. The week turned into ten days which quietly became six weeks and by the time I got it back from the typist and bounced it off Kranzler (who maddeningly wanted some of Yetta's softness restored) I'd lost a season. Moneywise, unless the picture got made, I'd taken a beating.

I flew over to London to see Moxie, who was doing a record promotion there, and checked into the Dorchester, which had certainly changed since the last time I'd been abroad. A guy in a burnoose took me up to my room. When I called Moxie, someone who sounded like a girl friend said she was napping but that she would get back to me. I watched a little rugby on television—the only thing I could pick up—and then I got a call from Moxie's agent saying that she had changed her mind about the picture and didn't want to do it. Just like that. Nothing to do with me, but she'd taken something else. (A Western, I later found out, in which her sidekick is a gay rail-splitter.) Well, could I at least *speak* to her? No, that was out of the question. Contractually, she couldn't talk to me. I pointed out that I had flown a few miles for this meeting and that I'd already seen the Thames. A simple phone call would have saved me a lot of aggravation. He was sorry, but nothing could be done. The funny thing is, he really *was* sorry, in more ways than one. For a year, he had been pitching me as a client; I was there when he told a group at the Dome that he had absolutely no compunctions about mentioning my name in the same breath as Alvin Sargent's.

I was stunned, but I hung around the hotel figuring that as a human *being* she'd at least pick up the phone. No sad stories. I'd been paid for the work. But how do you get compensated for all that time with a tight stomach? For having a blockbuster dangled in front of you and then whisked away? I could have called her, of course, but that would have taken away a chance to feel sorry for myself and to take a look at my wonderful screenwriting career. Twelve years, fourteen scripts, and all I had to show for it was a shared credit on a Cadillac Western and an unreleased rock adaptation of *The Pit and the Pendulum.* I did have a blinking "go" on a horror flick but that was only if the German money held. Maybe it was time to call my own bluff and go up to Vermont and try a novel. I was sure Kai-Yin would give up her acting lessons with Stella Adler. How much could it cost to live up there? Why should I keep killing myself and always winding up with my feelings hurt? I was pretty stubborn about hanging around the hotel, but she never did call and I finally decided to pack it in. The studio was paying for the trip so I did stay in London for a few days. Did they expect me to cheerfully jump on the next plane? After getting my head handed to me? My stay didn't work out too well, and it's probably because my heart wasn't in it. I ate a lousy Chinese dinner, got my ring stolen by a hooker and wound up sitting in the Dorchester lobby with a Czech director who told me that he had just thrown a hundred pages of some guy's script in the fire, but that there were certain writers he'd always wanted to work with and I was one of them. I gambled a little at the 21 Club but even winning a few shekels didn't cheer me up. So I decided the hell with it, I'm gone.

It was on the plane back that the most amazing thing happened. I reached into my briefcase for a last look at the screenplay and came across the book I'd taken from Moxie's suite at the Pierre on our first meeting. I started to flip through it idly. At first, I was so depressed I could barely focus on the print and then all of a sudden I was practically bouncing up and down in my seat with excitement. It was all I could do to contain myself which was important since there were a couple of ICM agents across the aisle who were straining to get a look at what I was reading. But what a find! It's a fictional first-person account of the life of an impoverished young beauty who pulls herself out of the slums of Kitzbühl to become the leading con woman in *fin de siècle* Vienna. Eventually she pulls off a major swindle in which all of Central Europe's *chocolatières* are brought to their knees. But talk about parts for women. From the opening in which she's hauled out of Gmunden Lake (in a failed suicide attempt) to the final moment in which she icily rejects the marriage proposal of the duke of Briganza (she may or may not be bearing his child—you never find out and we may have to fix that), the scenes come pouring out of the pages like a tidal wave. The madcap affair with the great Schnitzler, the fire at the Hairdressers League, the nude boar hunt with Krafft-Ebing in Budapest—if there's anything that woman doesn't do I'd like to know about it. I can just hear someone saying "The kids won't buy it." Well, all I can do is turn their attention to a hilarious little gem of a *schlag* fight with Mrs. Mahler in Saint Stephen's Cathedral. If the kids don't go for that, I'm leaving the business. Obviously, there's enough material for three movies here, and yet, for all the dramatic abundance, it's the tone that really puts it over the top, the sly, deadpan way in which Kastlemeir justifies her outrageous behavior and almost has you believing she had no other choices in life. It's ironic, of course—actually, it's kind of an ironic Yetta Montana—but there's nothing weird about it. It's legit irony—the kind a mass audience can grasp. (There's no reason it won't hold its own in the South.) I don't know *who* you get to do the screenplay. Pinter? Bo Goldman? Maybe Pinter to get you started and come *in* with Goldman. The important thing is it's not going to be me. I'm finished busting my hump on that kind of work. This struck me as a perfect time to take my first shot as a producer. In any case, I didn't take my first comfortable breath until my agent searched out the property and found out it was in the public domain. There'd been a stage version written by a skiing instructor that ran three performances in Gstaad and we put a lock on that just in case.

So I'm sitting around with an extraordinary piece of material that cost me three cents and I can't help chuckling over the way it came into my hands—as a spinoff of my darkest moment in the business.

Casting is no problem. We've got it with Streep's people and of course she'd be marvelous although truthfully, if she passes, I won't be heartbroken. Her price is out of sight and I can't help thinking she's a little severe for the role. Severe is okay, but only if it's combined with playful. I've screened all of her films and so far I don't see the playful. None of which matters since the piece is actorproof. Life's too short to go with Dunaway, but you've got Hawn, Keaton, Fonda, even Shields if you want to wait a few years. Flatten out the rural thing and you might even slip through with Sally Field. Even Moxie, for Christ's sake, although I wouldn't think of it. I can't help wondering, though, about the way she would handle that thin line between severe and playful. But don't worry, I haven't sunk that low. I wouldn't have her in the picture if they gave me a dime on dollar one at the box office, which is ridiculous since not even Lucas gets that. I just pride myself on being able to look at these things with cold eyes.

Mr. Prinzo's Breakthrough

ALTHOUGH MR. PRINZO, a small, hairless man of forty-one, was a highly respected technical director in television and, for a bachelor, earned a fine salary, he was forced to dwell in a tiny, however nicely decorated, apartment on New York's West Side, his only luxury being top cuts of meat for his Airedale. The apartment was not exactly a cold-water flat (hot water did gush through unexpectedly now and then) but, in truth, the best Mr. Prinzo could count on for his midnight showers was tepid. In any case, Mr. Prinzo blamed psychoanalysis for his condition. He had been seeing Dr. Tobes four times a week now for seven years, at a cost to him of $120 a week, and there was no end in sight. The two friends with whom Mr. Prinzo started in analysis both had had their breakthroughs. One, whose problem had been lack of confidence, now was able to shout epithets at bullies, and the second, once unable to relate to intelligent women, was started on an affair with a lady amino acids specialist. Mr. Prinzo, whose basic difficulty was cringing, could hold himself in check now and then, but still felt most comfortable when in a good cringe, and would have been the first to admit he was far from cured. On the anniversary of his seventh year of psychoanalysis, Mr. Prinzo walked through the many doors leading to Dr. Tobes's office and took a seat on the window sill. (There were no couches in the office of Dr. Tobes, who was known for his informality. Sometimes Mr. Prinzo would sprawl out on the floor during sessions and, on other occasions, just lean against walls. Pacing was allowed, too, and once or twice, on muggy days, he and Dr. Tobes had gone out on the fire escape.)

"All my friends are having their breakthroughs," said Mr. Prinzo, "and I don't mind telling you I'd like to have mine. It's high time."

Dr. Tobes was perched owlishly across from Mr. Prinzo, informally chewing up a pencil. It was not only that Dr. Tobes cultivated owlish expressions. He was the dead, spitting image of an owl, a tall owl if such a thing were possible, and he would have passed muster at the most authentic of museum owl exhibitions.

"Can you think of anything that might be blocking the treatment?" asked Dr. Tobes.

"Well, something must be or I wouldn't be cringing after seven years."

"How is that, incidentally?" asked Dr. Tobes.

"A little better. Oh, why lie? I still cringe the minute I roll out of bed and cringe my way right through the day. Look, let's face it, there are still things I can't tell you in here. Oh, I know I've gone into my dandruff fears and there isn't much more I can learn about those dreams in which I'm a stray paramecium. But I'm holding plenty back. I'll give you an example. Where are your diplomas? You think I like coming in here and not seeing a single one? If you ask me, that's being *too* informal. But that's the kind of thing I hold back. It's been bothering me for seven years. Another is your taste in furniture. You just don't go mixing Dutch Colonial and Chinese Chippendale unless you know exactly what you're doing. And why haven't you once, just once, called me by my first name instead of Mr. Prinzo? Oh, I know it's because I'm supposed to be an adult at all times, but you'd think that in seven years you'd slip just one 'Phil' in there. And there are others, too. I might as well get it right out now that I'm a toenail muncher. It *is* a relief just to say these things. In any case, when I get back from the studio I can hardly wait to get my Argyles off before I start right in."

"Any particular foot?" asked Dr. Tobes, writing in a pad.

"I knew I'd get you writing on that one," said Mr. Prinzo. "Both. I seem to do my lefts before my rights, though."

"Why do you feel you can't tell me something like that?" said Dr. Tobes, picking up a badminton racket and studying it owlishly.

"Sometimes I wish you weren't so informal," said Mr. Prinzo. "Maybe if there'd been a couch in here I'd have been out in three instead of beginning my seventh year. *Why* can't I tell you something like that? Because I'm afraid you'll tell, that's why. Oh, I know you won't go blurting it around town, but how do I know there aren't *some* things you won't leak out? I just don't feel I can come in here and tell you anything in the world and not have you make an immediate phone call as soon as I'm out the door."

"Who do you think I'll call?" asked Dr. Tobes.

"I don't like the way you'll casually slip a question in there as though it's unimportant, when we both know it's full of dynamite. *Who* will you call? I don't know. Authorities. Hospitals . . . the police . . ."

"Well, you *are* right about one thing," said Dr. Tobes. "I should have gone into the nature of our compact a long time ago. It was silly of me."

"Silly?" said Mr. Prinzo. "I might have been out of here five years ago. It may have cost me thirty thousand. I'm sorry I said that, I wanted to think it, but it just slipped out."

"That's all right," said Dr. Tobes, with much sweetness. "You may be right. In any case, of *course* we break the compact under certain circumstances. There are a few. For example, if you told me you were going to commit suicide tonight I might call the police and tell them."

"What are the others?" asked Mr. Prinzo. "This is fun to talk about, even though it's very serious. What if I told you I'd committed a murder? You see, that's the kind of thing I could never tell you, and yet if I've got to hold back one thing, I've got to hold back tons. What I need is to be able to tell you everything, without fear, otherwise I'll be in here forty-two more years."

"How foolish of me not to go into this," said Dr. Tobes, slightly abashed, but owlish nonetheless, sort of like an abashed owl. "Mr. Prinzo, you may rest assured that the compact we have is pure and sacred. Dr. Berndo and his boys up at Columbia call it the most inviolable compact known to the civilized world, and I tend to go along. If you confessed a murder to me, I might *urge* you to give yourself up if I felt that was best for you. But I'd certainly never inform the police on my own accord."

"Seventeen?" asked Mr. Prinzo.

"I wouldn't care if you were seventeen or forty-one when you did it."

"I don't mean that," said Mr. Prinzo. "What if I'd committed seventeen murders and gotten away with them all?"

"The thing there," said Dr. Tobes, "is whether I thought you were going to try for another. One that might endanger *your* life. I might call the law then. That's the key to it, don't you see. *Your* life. *Your* welfare. Whatever's best for *you, my* patient. That's the rule Berndo and all of us go right down the line with."

"If I could only believe that," said Mr. Prinzo, not cringing for the moment, his hairless body perspiring now. "If I could only believe that. Oh, the things I might come out with! If I could only believe you wouldn't tell."

By the end of the hour, Mr. Prinzo had gone back over an early apple fight with his older sister (one in which he'd aimed McIntosh cores at her capacious bosoms), and had then cautiously broken new ground by telling Dr. Tobes that on seven separate occasions he'd falsely upped his studio petty cash vouchers and furthermore, felt compelled to do it again. "Now that certainly isn't the kind of thing you'll report. I know that," said Mr. Prinzo, with only the faintest hint of doubt in his voice. To which Dr. Tobes smiled owlishly as if to say, "Well, really now."

"If I could only be sure," said Mr. Prinzo, taking his leave of the doctor.

Hours later, after a long nap at home, Mr. Prinzo slipped out of his apartment building and took a cab to Riverdale in the Bronx.

"I grew up in the same neighborhood as Vincent 'Mad Dog' Coll," said the cabdriver, "and might have ended up the same way had I not mended my ways early in the game."

"I don't want to do any talking on this ride," said Mr. Prinzo. "I just want to get there and take care of something."

In Riverdale, Mr. Prinzo got out of the cab in a neighborhood that screamed of luxury and had little difficulty finding the ground-floor duplex apartment he was looking for. He knocked on the door and when a woman's voice asked who it was, said, "I've got magazines. No I haven't. Look, will you let me in? I've got something crazy to say."

A pretty, busy-looking brunette woman with glasses opened the door. She wore a flowered formal print dress of the type favored by women who serve on committees. It made her seem ten years older than she was and fought to conceal all evidence of the sturdy bosoms that lurked beneath her bodice.

"I don't know you," the woman said, "and I've got invitation lists to get out."

Mr. Prinzo slipped past her into the apartment, sinking deep into the carpeting, and said, "I don't know how long I want to be here. It's a crazy thing. Look, here's why I'm here. When you moved in, the apartment was already two years old. You didn't know the first tenant, but it was my mom and she died here. It's crazy, but I just wanted to be in here for a little while and just walk around the place where my mom spent her last years. I may do some crying."

The woman blinked her eyes beneath the horn-rims, not quite sure what to make of what she had heard, and then said, "It is crazy, but it may be the dearest thing I've ever heard in my whole life." With that, she took Mr. Prinzo's head to her bosom and he made uncontrollable snuffling sounds in there. "How many sons do that for their moms?" she said, stroking his head, her voice catching a bit. "I've got a committee at seven," the woman said. "Our theme for the evening is 'Should We Be Tolerant Toward Intolerance, Too?' but you just stay right here and bury yourself in the atmosphere as much as you like while I'm getting ready. Then maybe you can come back some other time." She left Mr. Prinzo for about ten minutes, and when she came out with her coat on he was standing in the kitchen looking at the sink.

"Mom did her dishes there," said Mr. Prinzo.

"I wish I'd known," said the woman. "I'd never have had it redone in mosaic tile. Look, can I drop you downtown? Then maybe you can come back some other time for a longer session."

"I don't think I'll want to come back," said Mr. Prinzo, snuffling and going to her bosom again. "Not after that sink."

Outside, in the blackness, the woman led Mr. Prinzo to a station wagon and they drove silently for a while. "If more sons would do that for their moms," said the woman, "we'd have less juvenile crime, more understanding, and a better America."

"That's a lot of committee crap," said Mr. Prinzo suddenly. Then he shouted, "I wanted you to be full-blooded, rich and gurgling with life, a liberated woman given to hurling herself into frenzied modern dances. Then I might not have gone ahead. Pull over to that deserted Carvel ice cream stand."

The woman obeyed and as she stopped the car in the deserted lot, asked, "Did your mother work here, too?"

"There was no mom," said Mr. Prinzo, whipping out a small implement used for lifting the lids off junior baby dessert jars. "Goddammit, I meant to bring steak knives," he said. "This isn't going to be any good." With a shrug, he turned out the car lights and, lifting the baby jar opener, fell upon the horrified woman whose last words were: "It's 6:45. I've only got fifteen minutes to make committee."

A little later, Mr. Prinzo lifted her lifeless form behind the counter of the deserted Carvel stand and propped her up against an old sundae machine. He stood erect, flexed his arms and said, "Violence inhabits the meek, too." Then he drove the station wagon back to the duplex and took a cab to his apartment.

The following day, at his regular session with Dr. Tobes, Mr. Prinzo took his place on the window sill and said, "I was going to go into some fresh new traumas I've come up with, but why do it when I've only got one thing on my mind. I've done one."

"One what?" asked Dr. Tobes.

"I've committed one. A murder. Only you're not going to like the one I did. It was the only way I could really test the compact. If you don't tell about this one then I know I can tell you anything. I got your wife."

Dr. Tobes said, "What do you mean you got her? Do you know my wife?"

"I got her. I sort of murdered her. Why am I saying 'sort of'? I really did. I was going to anyway, but then when I saw what she was, I *really* was going to, and I did. What the hell kind of woman was that for you to be married to?"

Dr. Tobes picked up the phone and dialed a number. "Hello, Suze, this is Gar. Did Jean stay over at your place last night, after Intolerance? She didn't *come* to Intolerance? Thanks."

Dr. Tobes put down the phone and said, "Jesus, what did you have to do that for? I'm going to turn around here for a minute." He spun his chair around and put his head in his hands and for several minutes his shoulders trembled and shook. Then he turned back and said, "All right now, look, you've got to go to the police. That's the first thing."

"I knew it," said Mr. Prinzo. "I mean, didn't I just know it. Didn't I know that was the first thing you were going to say. Why should I have been in any doubt? You talked about the sacredness of our compact, sure, but then when the chips are down for one second . . ."

"It's for your own good," said Dr. Tobes. "Here, I'll ring them right up for you."

"Bullshit," said Mr. Prinzo. "Look, I committed that murder for only one reason—to see just how confidential all of this is. I'm not committing any more. And it isn't going to do me any good to go to jail for seventy years. I have a lot of life and good times ahead of me. The only reason you want me to turn myself in is because it was *your* wife. If it was anybody else's, name anyone, and you wouldn't be reaching for the phone."

"You may be right," said Dr. Tobes. "All right, you've got your whole hour left. Do you want to do some dreams? How do you feel?"

"I'll feel a hell of a lot better when you help me get rid of the body."

"I'm not getting rid of any bodies," said Dr. Tobes. "That's not in it."

"It is so and you know it," said Mr. Prinzo. "Anything that'll make me feel better. You said that's the key to it all. It'll make me feel better to get her someplace where she won't be found."

"I've never been in anything like this," said Dr. Tobes. "Jesus, my wife is gone. Hang on a second, I've got to do a little more crying. I'll turn around."

Outside, in the car, Dr. Tobes drove with fury, his eyes a blur of tears. "It isn't doing me any good to see you crying," said Mr. Prinzo beside him. "I don't need to see a doctor doing that."

"All right, I'll try to control myself," said Dr. Tobes. "But Jesus!"

"And take it easy on the driving. That certainly isn't making me feel better."

Dr. Tobes eased up on the accelerator and Mr. Prinzo said, "Each time I had a date, Sis and Mom would crowd me into a corner and make me feel ashamed. Sis once hid the cards under the piano and I found them accidentally, just fumbling around under there. As my hand accidentally touched the card box, I got a definite sexual thrill."

"This is not a session," said Dr. Tobes. "Jesus, you just got my wife. We're not in any session now."

"I didn't get a full hour in your office," said Mr. Prinzo, "and I don't see why I can't finish it up now. You're getting me upset."

"All right, all right," said Dr. Tobes. "Calm down. All right, see if you can pick up the thought again. You'll have to forgive me."

"I want you to be perfect," said Mr. Prinzo. "If you're not, it gets me all rattled."

The sun had gone down when they arrived at the Carvel ice cream stand. "I wonder why I picked an ice cream stand?" asked Mr. Prinzo. "Do you think that's worth analyzing?"

"I can't concentrate on any of that," said Dr. Tobes. "I'm going to see my wife. There'll be quite a bit of crying."

"Do try to be strong," said Mr. Prinzo. "If you get flustered, I'll be all upset, and you're not allowed to let me be that way."

"I'll try and hold back," said Dr. Tobes, "but you're not getting any guarantee."

They put the body in a duffel bag Dr. Tobes kept in his trunk and started back to the car with it. "When I met her she was a *Redbook* reader and do you know that recently I was unable to get my *Virginia Quarterly* away from her? Oh, Jesus, Mr. Prinzo, what have you done?"

"I can't stand it when you're stern with me," said Mr. Prinzo. "Do you realize how hard it'll be for me to tell you things now? YOU MUSTN'T BE STERN."

"I didn't mean to. All right, try to relax."

The pair hefted the duffel bag into the back seat of Dr. Tobes's sedan. "I don't have anything complicated that we're to do now," said Mr. Prinzo. "I just know a very high place near the beach where we can drop 'er down and I'm sure nobody ever goes there, at least on the bottom part. I'm going to go away and this will at least give me time."

The place was on the North Shore of Long Island where Mr. Prinzo had monied relatives. They drove there through the night and Mr. Prinzo said, "You look so different out of doors. How come you don't wear a toupee?"

"Now who is it you *really* want to wear a toupee?"

"Me," said Mr. Prinzo. "Amazing how you get me every time. You're such an amazing possessor of wisdom. That's why I couldn't see you married to, what's her name, I guess we can call her Duffel Bag Dolores now, eh? That was in bad taste. Look, I hope you'll always let me know when I step out of line, when I offend you in any way."

"I'll let you know all right," said Dr. Tobes.

"Now you're putting me on my guard. You mustn't be stern with me."

* * *

They came to a high, barren, cool place where the noise of the surf suddenly beat against the car windows. Mr. Prinzo had Dr. Tobes pull over onto the sand and then, carrying their duffel bag, they climbed a formation of wet rocks until the beach was far below; except for some lights across Long Island Sound, they were completely enveloped by blackness. "I'm not crying," said Dr. Tobes, "but let me give her a last little squeeze." Mr. Prinzo giggled and Dr. Tobes said, "There's not a damned thing wrong in that."

When they had tossed the duffel bag off into the blackness, Mr. Prinzo said, "I'd like to go down below and get my feet wet, as long as we're out here. One thing that has come through in these last seven years is that it's useful for me to grab my pleasures where I may."

Dr. Tobes followed him wordlessly, and below in the sand they removed their shoes and socks. A woman drifted by in a bikini, pensively kicking up sand with her toes, and Mr. Prinzo said, "It's Laurie Prinzo, my sister-in-law."

"I often come here late and wander through the surf," the woman said. "I saw it done in a James Mason movie. Your brother is what makes me so crazy. He really is a big spender. Try to get him to spend a nickel on something that *he* didn't dream up. Oh, he's got it all right. But try to get him to spend a nickel of it. He's really the last of the big spenders."

"This is Gar Tobes," said Mr. Prinzo. "We're just out here doing something. How come you didn't ask me what?"

"I always feel you get to know somebody better when you meet them out in the surf. You see a side of them you never saw before. I've got to get back. I don't know. I may suddenly develop a craving for the Late Show."

She walked off and Mr. Prinzo said, "I hope you weren't offended by my calling you Gar, Dr. Tobes. I felt sort of giddy doing it, the first time in seven years. It was like sex. What did you think of Laurie?"

"She's lovely. I don't feel there's anything wrong in my looking at other women now. It's just that emotionally I'm unable to. It's unrealistic of me, but I can't help it. Oh Jesus, it's starting to hit me now. I'm going to do a little more crying now. I'll try to wrap it up as quickly as I can. And of *course* I realize it isn't good for you to see me doing that. I'm upset, all right, though. I may go back into analysis for a few sessions, myself, now."

In the car, Mr. Prinzo said, "I'm staying at your place tonight."

"I want to be alone and get things straightened out," said Dr. Tobes.

"Now you *are* upsetting me. You probably don't even like me, really. Could you psychoanalyze me if you didn't like me?"

"Yes, I could," said Dr. Tobes. "I'm not saying I dislike you, only that I could treat you if I did."

"How about Joe McCarthy? Wait a minute. Even I can see through that question. I'm trying to find out your political views. Don't even answer. I've got to stay over with you, though. So far, all of this has been okay, but I don't know what's going to happen. What if I get one of my crazy dreams, one in which I'm in a terrible jail feeling so guilty I could just die. Nosirree, I want you right there."

"I'm not sure any of this is analytically sound," said Dr. Tobes, heading the car in the direction of his duplex.

Dr. Tobes sat grave and ashen-faced, all through the night, in a French Provincial parlor chair, while Mr. Prinzo slept in the guest room. In the morning, Mr. Prinzo got up and said, "I feel sort of short-changed. No dream at all. I expected a beaut tonight, after all those things yesterday, and I thought it would have been great having you here so I could dash right in with all the details. I don't like to see you looking tired. Why the hell didn't you go to sleep? Look, there's a boat sailing for Barbados at five this afternoon and I want to be on it, everything arranged. It takes about three days usually to make arrangements, but I want you to hit them over the head with your doctor credentials and get me on there."

"Look, Mr. Prinzo," said Dr. Tobes. "Surely you must realize there are limits to all this. I don't want to do this for you. Surely you must realize I'm a human being with natural feelings of remorse and revenge. I don't *want* to do these things for you."

"There are no limits. You know damned well there aren't. I'm your patient and the only thing in the world that counts is how I feel. You've got to stick to that because if you don't you'll never be able to hold your head up and practice another hour of psychoanalysis. Here's this week's $120 in cash."

"I'm shaky after no sleep," said Dr. Tobes, sipping some coffee and pocketing the money.

"Well, don't be shaky," said Mr. Prinzo. "That isn't going to do me any good."

Mr. Prinzo lounged about the apartment in his pajamas all morning, and when the doctor got back, he said, "I don't like your books. You've got plenty but many of them are just fillers. What are you doing with *Favorite Canada Campsites?* That's the kind of book you shouldn't have in there."

"Why do you feel threatened when you see books you don't approve of? Did you ever ask yourself that? We're not in session now. I got your tickets all right. A patient of mine is a travel agent. They're for five this afternoon, but you'll have to be inoculated in Barbados if you want to come back here. Good-by. I don't feel well at all. It's beginning to sink in about my wife, and I don't care if it's emotional or what, it's a very real feeling of loss that I feel."

"Don't good-by me," said Mr. Prinzo. "You're coming right down to the boat with me. How do you think I would feel if I went off friendless and alone with no one saying good-by? My last impressions of the States would be a place where I was without buddies and people didn't come to say good-by. That wouldn't do me a helluva lot of good."

"I want to sit in a chair now," said Dr. Tobes. "I want to cry. I need a good catharsis and then I'll be better."

"You're coming with me. You know you have to. And I hate seeing you this way. If you think it's helping my treatment, this whole business of the way you're carrying on, you're crazy."

On a last minute impulse, Mr. Prinzo went out to a local clothing shop and bought some clamdigger pants and orange gaucho shirts.

The ride to the boat took roughly three-quarters of an hour, and the two men agreed it would constitute a session, Dr. Tobes taking his notes at red lights. As they pulled into the parking lot at the boat dock, Dr. Tobes said, "We have to close the hour now," and Mr. Prinzo said, "You always nip me off right in the middle of critical things."

Mr. Prinzo had borrowed Dr. Tobes's suitcase, and the doctor helped him carry it toward the boat. Stopping at the foot of the gangplank, Mr. Prinzo said, "Now in one of your letters I want you to tell me if there's a good analyst in Barbados."

"One of my letters?" said Dr. Tobes. "I'm not writing you any letters."

"Oh, yes, you are," said Mr. Prinzo angrily. "Three a week, with picture postal cards interspersed. No one but you knows where I'm going and how do you think I'm going to feel getting no letters from home?"

"I'll send you the letters," said Dr. Tobes. "I don't know about the cards."

Mr. Prinzo went about half the way up the gangplank and then said, "Now start waving."

"I'm not waving," said Dr. Tobes, his voice cracking. "I'm not waving to you."

"Wave," said Mr. Prinzo. "I'll feel good. I've got to be waved off."

Dr. Tobes slowly lifted his arm, and this time an avalanche of tears broke through and flooded his face. "There," he said, choking, "I'm a heartbroken man, but I'm waving."

"Good," said Mr. Prinzo. "That's good. I guess we're going now."

He lifted his head and sucked in the air. "I feel fine," he said. "Say, have you noticed? I'm standing up straight now. I'm not cringing anymore."

"Yes," said Dr. Tobes, and suddenly the tears stopped and his eyes brightened. "You *have* stopped cringing." With that, he whirled around, shouted, "You're cured! You've had your breakthrough," grabbed the sleeve of a dock patrolman and, as the two of them flew up the gangplank to Mr. Prinzo, shouted again, "And you're not my patient any more."

Our Lady of the Lockers

THEY FOUND HER BODY in locker three hundred fifty-seven at Jack La Lanne's Gym and Health Spa on East Fifty-fifth Street. Also in lockers three hundred fifty-eight through three hundred sixty-one. I heard about it on a small island off the South Carolina coast where I was failing to enjoy my first vacation in five years. The highlight of my social activity (not including a little something with the girl at the desk) was a barroom conversation with a stockbroker who spent a great deal of time telling me why he would not go to Elaine's restaurant in New York. He could name me fifteen places that served better pasta. He was not too happy with the way they prepared their drinks. He wanted to know why he should go there and get shoved around by the waiters when the city was bursting with places that treated you with a little courtesy. The celebrities? He knew plenty of them. He was in petrodollars. Kevin McCarthy had once crossed the full length of the Russian Tea Room just to shake his hand. Who in Christ's name, he wanted to know, did Elaine think she was, making him wait an hour and a half for a table? As far as he was concerned, the restaurant was just another overrated hash house that he would not be caught dead in.

I listened to quite a bit of this and then I suggested that maybe he ought to simply put Elaine's out of his mind and go about his business.

He ordered a double something or other, took a long pull on it, and said, "Goddamned good idea."

The story made the island *Bugle.* The body was in an awful lot of lockers, so it was a little tough to work with, but they got a positive I.D. on the girl from her dental markings. A show-biz dentist had done her bite in a distinctive manner. He was very much in vogue a few years back and had done the bites of the entire El Morocco crowd. Also, girls who worked in boutiques. Any girl named Danielle was sure to have had her bite done by this fellow. He did a lot of Nicoles, too. What he did was to sculpt the surfaces of the biter's teeth in a decorative manner that, not incidentally, produced an erotic sensation of screaming intensity in anyone lucky enough to be the bitee. It also enabled the biter to gnaw holes in Gucci belts that needed to be taken in after crash diets, and, in an emergency, to kill small animals. He did the upper right side of my mouth. So I am an expert on this fellow—

since I have been both a bitee and twenty-five percent of a biter. I'll say more about this later—if you're good.

The paper that came in from the mainland was a bit more ambitious and got into blood drops, which, according to one source, pointed almost like an arrow to the Health Spa sauna. This told me that Gumm was the duty detective on the case. Whenever a homicide involved a considerable shedding of blood, he always wanted to know exactly which way the drops pointed. To my knowledge, this has never led to the apprehension of a murderer, or even a suspect, but he stays involved with them. In the old days, when we had humor in the department, we would have referred to this interest of his as Gumm Drops. However, we don't do humor anymore. We have left that to the Adam–12s and the Kojaks. It's probably a good thing, because we were never that funny. Neither are the networks, but they are better than we ever were.

Since my throat got bitten, I've had the phone set up so that no one can get through to me at night. I absolutely have to have eight good hours or I'm a lox. That's the only thing left over from the throat bite. The department understands and has decided to put up with it. If something broke, for example, on my dildo thing (an assault case I'm involved with), the department would send someone over to bang on my door. On the dildo matter, I'm not being cute. If you had seen the damage it had done to a Long Island Rail Road porter's face, you would know what I mean. It was loaded up with something heavy, but it was a dildo and that's how the unknown assaulter wanted to get the job done. Go argue with him. It's one of my unsolved cases, but I don't lose any sleep over it. I'll get it done. It's sort of on the back burner.

As I lay abed on my charming, albeit boring, island off the Carolina coast, Gumm broke through my elaborate protective phone device and buzzed me awake at four in the morning. He was failing to respect the aftermath of my throat injury, which I thought was unfeeling of him, although I did not comment on his rudeness at the time. He told me about the blood drops, of course. He said the emergency unit high-intensity lights had broken down and they didn't have such hot pictures. But they did have a breast with some saliva that would or might give them the blood type of the certain someone with whom they had a bone to pick. And they also had Jack La Lanne's Gym and Health Spa membership list, which included, among the noteworthies, writers of the feminist persuasion, Lubovitcher rabbis and a good many Israelis who quarreled heatedly with the Lubovitcher fellows in the whirlpool bath. I sensed that this was not going to be a factor in the solution of the high crime in question, but I let Gumm go on about it, thinking what the hell, in our industry (as in Charlton Heston's) you never know. Once Gumm had played out his Lubovitcher material, I decided, if not to pounce on him, then at least to take him to task on his rudeness.

"I am on vacation, Gumm," I said, not invoking the issue of whether I was having a good time, since it is not my way to push my sorrows off on other people, as I wish they would not push theirs off on me. "And yet you call me in the darkness of the night and disturb my rest. Why?"

"I am glad you brought that up," said my colleague, the famed blood-drops man. "We searched the young lady's apartment and came across a pile of tape recordings. It was her style to tape her male callers, lovers and otherwise. Some were named Jean Claude, others Jean Pierre. And there was one fellow—let's not beat around the bush—who turned out to be you. My question, therefore . . ."

"I am not now, never have been nor will I ever be a suspect in this case."

"Thank you, Herbert, and I am sorry to have had to be so blunt and pushy."

"That's perfectly all right."

We exchanged goodbyes, and since I had been totally forthright with my friend, I was able to turn over and fade back into the sleep of the just.

The next morning, before setting sail for the Big Apple, I had myself an O.J., two croissants and a cup of coffee, all of it crawling with cholesterol. You could practically see the cholesterol swimming around in it, but what the hell, it was my last day of fun in the sun, so why stand on ceremony.

I positioned myself in the Cafeteria à la Tropicana, so that I would be sitting casually yet not conspicuously next to the fellow with the attraction-repulsion thing about Elaine's. He tried to rope me into some breakfast conversation with an anecdote about how Henri Soulé had opened Pavillon just to spite Harry Cohn, but I didn't go for it. He had material on Clarke's, "21" and even the old Stork Club, all involving guys who would not set foot in them on the ground of honor, but not one nibble did he get from me. My objective was to get another look at him and fix him in my mind. Overnight, he had become a little vague. And after all, he had approached me, uninvited . . . and it was just the two of us in this el weirdo hotel. In my business it is no handicap to walk around with a nice, robust sense of paranoia. It had always been my view that they should have lowered the height requirement years ago and let in guys with what I just said.

In a somewhat different spirit, I paid a farewell visit to the girl behind the desk. There is a certain something that comes over me when I am alone with girls in offices, a kind of clerical horniness. My Air Force commanding officer, a South Carolina man, would have explained it thusly: "Don't you see, Barker, it's the very *absence* of anything hoaney in an office that's makin' you so hoaney." He had been able to prove, in this manner, that the *New Yorker* was the world's most erotic magazine. "No question about it, the *New Yukkeh* tebbly hoaney, the hoaniest publication in all journalism." Whatever the case, the desk girl and I had our farewell congress in the accounting department; when it came time to sign the bill, I saw that the little rascal had completely forgotten to add on the tax, a not inconsiderable saving to your correspondent of sixty-five much-needed little ones.

A word about Our Lady of the Lockers. Her name was Crystal. All but the least discerning of readers will have noted a certain wry, offhanded *je ne sais quoi* tone in the style of these jottings; consult any Central Park West shrink worth his—what is it now?—sixty dollars a pop and he will tell you that this is a defense against the tenderness of the subject. And he will be on target. My feelings for Crystal were strong. I loved Crystal. As to her name, I do not wish to do battle on behalf of it. It was as Crystal that she appeared to me. As Crystal, I accepted her. I looked at it this way. She might have been named Misty.

Later, of course, there would be the Jean Claudes and Jean Pierres, but when I first met her there were gynecologists and stockbrokers. She appeared at the precinct with a complaint that a gynecologist was threatening her and would not give back her couch. At first, I thought this was a reference to some freaky new birth-control device. But she meant couch, as in Bloomingdale's furniture department. Normally, I would have had a question or two to ask her, since obviously there were holes in this story. But Crystal had spent several of her formative years in Calcutta; as a result, her story, in its delivery, took on a Higher Logic. Of *course* a mean gynecologist was threatening her and refused to part with her couch. So I agreed to pay the gyno a visit. Understand quickly that a visit from one of us fellows is not one of your basic social calls. And it is not the gun that adds sauce to these visits of ours. (Except for the butt, I myself am extremely reluctant to bring my gun into play. Had my attitude been otherwise, I would not have incurred my throat bite.) Whatever the case, we have refined the "little visit" to a high art. The gyno, sweating profusely, relinquished the couch and promised to be good. (Despite an incipient case of emphysema, he had been doing a little telephone breathing, too, which I didn't know about. He promised to stop that, too.) Whereupon Crystal, drawing once again upon her Eastern background, made me see with perfect clarity why I should use a police emergency truck to deliver said couch to her East Side digs. From the time Peter Stuyvesant first strolled the mud paths of Gotham, this has been a violation of departmental regulations.

I did not move in with Crystal. She did not move in with me. We cut it down the middle, her living with me a little, me living with her a little, no one firmly living with anyone, which finally got Crystal, of all people, irritated. This struck me as being ironic, since the young wench, as the astute reader no doubt has gathered, was not one of your standard cop-type girlfriends. Or perhaps the astute reader has not no doubt gathered it. Crystal came to our Americas courtesy of the Swedish embassy, Thailand, Guam, Rio, a cooking school in Brest—and other points too numerous to mention in all but a Dickensian effort. As a child, she had been hidden on trains, smuggled through border checkpoints, kidnapped by right-wing uncles. Her face was vintage Continental Heart-Stopper. Her body was tall and still growing. She was the only woman I have ever met who was past twenty-one and getting taller. "Do you like eroticism, Herbert?" she asked, after the couch was in.

"Oh, I guess I could get into a little of that."

Whereupon I made my basic reflexive headlong dive for her bones. She told me to relax and went to work with fruit, feathers, a needle and thread, and some moves taught to her by a Bangladesh Sufi who was known as "the Picasso of the Pelvis."

She had made a detailed study of nerves, pressure points, veins, and whatever else it is one studies when one has determination, a lot of time on one's hands and wants to find out everything there is to know about whatever it is one calls the male member. One hopes one comprehends. "Look, look," she would say, excitedly. "Look how he stands up. Look how curious he is."

And I would look.

Why then, the reader with normal curiosity will have a need to ponder, would this lustrous creature take more than a casual interest in a New York City detective? A personable enough young fellow, but—examined with cold eyes—not one of overpowering appeal. Crystal, though no stranger to Dresden, Port Said, the Tour d'Argent and little jade shops in Bangkok, was new in town. Remember, this was before the Jean Claudes and Jean Pierres. She had put into the city after a period in La Jolla, some months in upstate New York and a mysterious trip to the famed Iowa State Writer's Conference. Whatever the nature of her transaction with the gyno, she had dispatched it quickly. And then there was me. I can only speculate that I fit into some weirdo New York-romantic-detectivey-Singing-in-the-Rain fantasy of hers. (She was a bubble-gum-chewin' popcorn-swallowin' eyeball-poppin' cinema freak.) Or who knows, maybe the kid really liked me. I am often complimented on my "dead eyes."

We filled up four and a half months like nobody's business. (It is generally the ladies who keep track of such things, i.e., "I went with Sven for ninety-two days." Observe that, in this case, it was your faithful correspondent.) It meant a lot to me even if it did begin to screw up my investigative rhythm—once *l'affaire* grew bumpy. And can you imagine why the crazy wench wanted to break up? Because she wanted me to move in with her. Permanently. Or her to move in with me. Consider that for a moment. *Her* move in with *me.* And here comes the clincher. *And take care of her.* On detective's pay yet. (Admittedly, she was multilingual, and did offer to work with the Gabon delegation at the U.N.)

In any case, she was proposing a crazy mismatch. Harry and Ben's Delicatessen taking care of the Four Seasons. Some kid from Dalton going one-on-one with Earl the Pearl, then facing Catfish Hunter. I mean, come off it. I was over my head the first minute she came into the station and offered me a Godiva mint. (How I yearned for a second one.) So I said no and she took it poorly. She stood me up a lot. She stranded me in the lobby with two tickets to the Ukrainian National Folk Dance Festival, which you can imagine how desperately I wanted to see. Or how about my solo act at Pearl's with Eugenia Sheppard's entire Saturday column, in the flesh, staring at me. (I waited two hours and finally told Pearl to proceed with the lemon chicken.) And then Crystal apparently grew bored and became what I probably interrupted her from becoming—the number-one Big-Time Delicious-Terrific Super Bowl of a girl of which there is only one a year (they come in around soft-shell crab time). Halston-to-Dali-to-Gernreich-to-Warhol, over to Evans-to-Stark-to-Ransohoff, shift one, two, three and so on to the Jean Claudes and Jean Pierres, which is where I lost track. And would you believe, right in the middle of this merry-go-round of coke and class, the little rascal (growing in ballsiness as well as height, I might add) would have the temerity to excuse herself from, say, a Stones concert and call Old Faithful here for "a little pin money." And I would come up with it, too, on one occasion sacrificing a new holster I had my eye on. Because I still loved her. She had taught me to take my shoes off in my apartment. She once bought me the most fantastic set of trains a man ever dreamed of, the kind I'd stop and look at in windows and figure only Getty nephews ever got to have. (It wasn't even my birthday—and you can be sure I didn't ask where she got the money.) She whispered erotic tidbits in my ear, rendering them in a perfect Liv Ullmann delivery that would have fooled the great Bergman himself. She never once broke rhythm or sequence in bed, even when I had taken an outrageously wrong turn, obvious to the two of us; she made love to my feet, ignoring a GI injury incurred on Pork Chop Hill during that boring Korean fracas; except for the one time she almost O.D.'d on Chicken Pakora at Gaylord's, she always smelled Tahitian; she greeted each day with a smile. She got my bite fixed (just the upper right, as it turned out, due to a falling-out with Dr. Wen over my Detective's Dental Plan). Not so deep in the recesses of my thinking, I figured that after all the Jean Claudes and Jean Pierres, who knows, maybe she just might . . . but now she was in all those lockers, and I was on my way back to New York City, scene of the crime, although, frankly, I was not going directly to either La Lanne's or the Bureau. First I had to get out my dry cleaning and check my plants. I figured I would sort of ease into it.

My senses sharpened as I crossed Sixth Avenue. "I guess you can always tell a New Yorker," I said to the driver of my Checker, "by the way he refuses to call Sixth the Avenue of the Americas." By rough count it was the four hundredth time I had made that observation. Once in the city, I could not stop beginning to work. Why was that white-sneakered citizen of Spanish descent reading *Forbes* in front of the Art Students League? Wrong tune. A moving van parked alongside Bendel's in broad daylight? Surefire hanky-panky. There in front of À La Vieille Russie was Arthur "too Faut" Walker, whom I had the honor of busting for pimping too conspicuously in the lobby of the Pierre. Oh, the book I had on that dude. His love for middle-aged Jewish women (eventually his undoing). His brief stint as one of the Low-Balls in downtown Philly. (He did the falsetto parts.) But why go on? We turned up Madison. Could that possibly be a zee of "girl" going down in the window table of the Carlton Delicatessen? A certified class collar for your correspondent (not to speak of the publicity splash for proprietors David and Aaron). I pushed on. Had it been a key, I might have asked Purification Riviero to jam on the brakes. But for a trifling zee? *C'était sans importance.* We moved further east, locus point of the cinephiles, me making a mental note to see the latest by Paul Mazursky, that Flaubert of the Polo Lounge.

I scooped up my mail (mostly Carte Blanche brochures, tempting me with Founding Father coin collections), noted that Upper Class Productions was still in business on the floor above me (four hard-working light hooks, masquerading as P.R. consultants—and they had better hurry up and send the redheaded NYU sophomore down for tea and whatever or that would be the end of their neighbor-detective's live-and-let-live policy).

I took down my BEWARE, SCARLET FEVER VICTIM door sign (with Spanish translation) and went straight to the plants, which I was happy to see were hanging on gamely. I turned off WRVR and thought for a moment of all the wasted Paul Desmond and John Coltrane (designed to fake out pillagers and looters) that had poured out into an empty room. What happened to all that music, where did it go and what a nifty riddle to pose to my Civilization and Philosophy Seminar at Hunter on Thursday night (paid for by Mayor Beame and all you nice taxpayers out there).

Everything was as I had left it; my framed Police Academy diploma, machete collection, indirectly lighted train set, freezerful of Frankie and Johnnie steaks, which the boys were kind enough to send over as a door prize for the Homicide Cruise (canceled due to budget-cutting). Gently cursing myself for forgetting to pick up fresh garlic at Gristede's, I commenced to whip up a Caesar salad. And then I noticed that my Clue Box was missing.

That made three. The demise of Crystal; her taping of my voice (and it better not be the conversation I thought it was); and now my vanished Clue Box. Admittedly, there was little of value in the leather portmanteau, a gift from a Lindsay aide for successfully guarding his body aboard an El Al airliner en route to a fact-finding tour of Haifa (his goal: to find out how that wicked city kept its fleshpots under control). As I recall, there was a finger (in alcohol) for study in relation to my dildo beef; a swatch of a Chilean diplomat's sports jacket, to be boiled down into what might or might not turn out to be liquid coke; a can opener with an almost microscopic speck of either blood or Tabasco sauce, related to an unclosed squawk in Harlem; a copy of *The Sayings of Marcus Aurelius,* signed "To Herb Barker, My Favorite Crime Buster" by Mario Puzo at Patsy's. (He did not have a spare copy of *The Fortunate Pilgrim.)*

You get the idea. Couple of fortune cookies, an old address book with RAQUEL WELCH'S PHONE NUMBER in it from when I once almost got eleven weeks' Technical Adviser work on one of her pictures except that (story of my life) the budget couldn't sweat it. So there was nothing, really, that I could not get through the day without. It wasn't as if Urban Renewal or the future of Southeast Asia was at stake. I just wanted my Clue Box back. And it meant somebody had been lurking in my apartment, which gave me, allegedly hard-boiled soul that I am, a queasy feeling. Sudden unexplained noises give me the willies, too. I have to see what I am dealing with, and even then, I am not always such a complete bargain—as evidenced by my throat bite.

I summoned Conchita, who worked six days a week for the light hooks upstairs and one afternoon a week for me. Conchita had the only living duplicate of my key and was as honest as the day is long, which fact was helped along by my knowing about her husband, Carmen, and the three-to-seven he had staring him in the face if anyone ever looked into the hot-car complaint that was out on him in Rhode Island. Which I would never consider doing. Using signs and giggles, Conchita indicated that a man, "very nice," had appeared in the hallway and helped her rewire the vacuum cleaner so she could make my carpeting "very nice." I now had two very nices to work with, so with a light *droit du seigneur* tap on her charming Latin *tochis,* I dismissed Conchita, since I did not want to find myself drowning in a sea of evidence.

What happens with one of these Gucci-style slayings is that a couple of hundred East Side sleuths are turned loose and get to trip over each other's toes for forty-eight hours. If no suspect is popped within the appointed time, the team quickly gets trimmed back to two or three sluggish, heavy-lidded types and anyone in the Bureau with some kind of an erection to see justice served, which in this case, of course, was me. I dropped around the Bureau a day early to get congratulated on my suntan. In the lobby, dealers of a small-fry variety rushed forward to show me how clean their arms were, a salute to my two exciting years as a rookie junk dick. This display of clean arms was a sure sign that my old friends would be back at the Maritime Union before the morrow, making quick buys from Norwegian seamen, a few of whom would turn out to be (heh, heh) members of our team. Twenty-four hours had passed and all Gumm had so far was an Israeli who claimed he was a highly feared Secret Service operative and a Tel Aviv literary agent. He was a Jack La Lanne's regular, had no alibi and was on record as once having picked up Crystal at J.F.K. in the rain and taken her for drinks at the University Club. Gumm thought he had something and I thought he didn't. "When you take this Jewish guy and put him together with the fact that the blood drops point right to the sauna . . ." *Avec le minimum de politesse,* I told Gumm I would catch his act some other time.

I went to the Property Clerk's office and listened to the tape and of course, it was exactly the one I was hoping it wouldn't be: A six-in-the-morning call I had made to Crystal on the occasion of my fortieth birthday which was supposed to go by smoothly and didn't. I'll just hum a few bars. It had the word *vulnerable* in there six times; followed closely by three or four "afraids." Knowing my six-in-the-morning style, it's a safe guess I used the phrase "inability to form a close relationship" a few times—I didn't listen to the whole thing. This is what she had to go and tape. I am seriously not allowed to drink and I had excused myself on my birthday, operating on the thesis that who tapes such things? Crystal does, or did, anyway. Under the circumstances, it was going to be difficult to ask her why. I just hoped she hadn't made a deal with Carly Simon to bring out a whole album of the stuff.

What I had to do was tap dance around for another twenty-four hours; there was no rule that said it couldn't be creative tap dancing. These are some of the things I did:

1) Went to the police equipment store and got a little more lead stuck in my slapjack (basically a time-killer).
2) Visited New Jersey. The girl, not the state. New Jersey Ryan. Friend of Crystal's until they had a falling-out over some insoluble issue. A disputed tube of eyeliner. Something along those lines. New Jersey is an M.A.W. (model-actress-whatever, with an emphasis on the whatever); strong evidence exists that it was her name that kept her from making That Extra Step. Georgia, fine; Carolina, no problem; Mexico, why not? Even Israel gets an outside chance. New Jersey? No way. But she stubbornly clung to it—need I say that there are people like that?—and now she is a soft thirty-eight or so and it's a bit academic. Dates South Americans, wearily turns up at discotheque openings, and will act in porno films if someone uses the word *art* with some regularity, pays her slightly above Equity minimum, and lets her wear a thin mask (the last is negotiable). Total earthly possessions if she were knocked off à la Crystal: a trunkload of junk jewelry, second-time-around Givenchy gowns and (surprise!) an authentic Klee, which she hides in her makeup table. She told me I never quite realized how hard Crystal took it when we split up. I said I understood and she said, "No, you don't understand. She really, really took it hard." I said I *knew* she took it hard and she shrugged and said, "You don't understand." Then, finally, I understood.
3) Got a haircut from the Turk, who told me there was a new kind of wise guy in town, blond-macho-gay, stalked the new discos, got off on sudden, unprovoked openings of people's heads in men's rooms. The Turk gave you very little, including the work he did on your sideburns, but what he gave you was choice.

4) Visited New Jersey, the state this time, not the girl. Went to see Ronnie Steamroom (I don't know his real name—Lieberson, I think), who runs half a dozen health clubs in that state after having been encouraged to leave Manhattan by some serious gentlemen he had rudely misled in a bat-guano commodities deal. And if he ever came back across the George Washington Bridge, even to get his dry cleaning, he was a strong favorite to show up as a McDonaldburger. He told me that it was not uncustomary for parties to go on in health clubs, late at night, when the last ad exec had left and the sauna was cold. This was not much, but it was something.

5) Dropped by to see Katrina, my streamlined mid-seventies securities analyst grown-up Danish girlfriend. Had our basic dispute over who had picked up whom that first time. I let her win that one. Had our usual debate over who it was that was horny on this particular occasion. I gave her that one, too. Disrobed and went into a brief squabble, in mime this time, over who it was that was going to put it to whom and who was going to do the putting. I handed that one over, giving her three for three. Anyone who knocks this new woman's thing has been hanging around with the wrong people.

These are some of the colorful results of my activities: New Jersey's Klee got slashed, hateful thing to see and don't even bother asking if it was insured; as he got off the E train at Sutphin Boulevard, someone threw hair dye in the Turk's eyes (he's all right); an unknown party got into Katrina's apartment—we fixed the time at 4:15 in the A.M.—and broke one of her kneecaps with a standard Philadelphia-style crowd-control hickory nightstick—left at the foot of the bed. Nothing appeared to have happened to Ronnie Steamroom. Thunderously obvious conclusion: Whatever it was I was doing, a person or persons unknown had found it unattractive.

For my part, I hated the kneecap thing. There just wasn't any way to be wry or ironical about it. Because of the nervousness of some of her securities deals, I had gotten Katrina a permit for a thirty-eight which she kept in her night table—but there had not been any way for her to get at it. The party had made his or her entrance and exit via some jalousied windows, which was no mean feat, since Katrina's apartment was kind of a rooftop eyrie in an old leftover super-tall brownstone in the East Seventies. An agile person, to put it mildly, had pulled this thing off. Whoever tore up the Klee had had to do some fancy footwork, too, come to think of it, since New Jersey, at the moment, had been living in a woman's residence with a dead elevator. More intricate rooftop action here. I stayed with Katrina for twenty-four hours at Flower Hospital and for twenty-four hours I was in love with her. It takes something along those lines to get me to go that way—a busted kneecap.

The following day, I asked Gumm to assign me officially to the Crystal case. He said I ought to finish up the dildo item first and I maintained that I could handle them both at the same time. He said I knew perfectly well I could not handle two things at once and I said I know, I know, but that I had thought it through and was convinced I could do the two of them. "With this Crystal girl," he said ". . . you weren't by any chance . . . uh . . . ?"

"Wiggling it in there? Is that what you were going to ask?"

"Well, actually . . ."

"Because if that's what you were going to ask, I suggest you don't ask it."

"Why don't you just go to work?"

"Why don't I?"

And I did. But we had measured each other for a beat or two and it was Gumm who had decided to break it off and I have a sneaking suspicion it was because of my throat bite.

It had been a humiliating experience. I owed one to someone. You would be amazed at all the times that tension causes us fellows in crime to go at each other, with serious consequences. It certainly would be a source of great embarrassment to all parties concerned if I were to take my feelings out on old Gumm, my immediate superior.

I realized it wasn't *Swann's Way,* but somehow had the feeling I would be able to read the Medical Examiner's report on Crystal with objectivity. So I curled up with a copy in the Property Office and whipped right through "Liver Weight and Condition" and "Contents of Intestine." "Quality of Urine" gave me no trouble at all; indeed, I read it with mounting fascination. It was not until I came to "Quantity of Semen, and Location of Tears in Vaginal Membrane" that I felt a need to set the manuscript aside. The prose rhythms were sound, the imagery vivid, but it just wasn't for me. Latent Prints had come up with a few smudges on the parallel bars that were traced to an agent in the William Morris office (on the day of the slaying he was in Massachusetts catching Dick Shawn in *Richard III).* Gumm's Israeli suspect had knocked over the polygraph test as if it were a Syrian lemonade stand. I could not quite pinpoint the quarter we were in, but I had the feeling it was late and we were down three touchdowns.

With no particular song in my heart, I went over to check out the Health Spa. I told the receptionist—Italian, mischievous—she oughta be in pictures and she told me if I didn't take a special two-month tummy-trim program, I might not make it through the summer. I told her she had it all wrong, that the roll above my belt was a deliberate attempt to cultivate a kind of soft, casual, diplomatic Kissinger Look. Then I showed her my tin and the romance came to an abrupt ending. I looked over Crystal's lockers and I got very glum. A sign had been pasted across them: NOT IN USE. What was it, some kind of mourning period? For the lockers? I didn't see much exercise being perpetrated, but there was a lot of arguing going on. Maybe that's the way they reduced. They argued it off. A fellow said he heard the Ali-Foreman fight was fixed and now he could not enjoy it anymore.

"But you *did* enjoy it," said the guy next to him.

"I *did*," said the first fellow, "but I don't anymore."

"You can't suddenly not enjoy something you once enjoyed," his friend argued (with some logic, I thought).

"The hell I can't!"

I had some figures jiggling around in my head . . . arrival of duty detective, probable time of death, onset of rigor . . . but they were not going to do me much good. I am bad on time and terrific on shoe imprints. No one else in the Bureau puts much stock in them, and as a result I am looked upon as kind of a lacrosse player. On President Street. It was an off-hour. On hand were a couple of self-employed decorators and a few Depression Victim execs working out to make sure they looked under forty. I covered the gym carpeting; the only one to give me any grief was an actor I recognized as playing cop parts in all the movies shot in New York. He wanted to know what I was doing on the gym floor, fully dressed. It was enough to make a fellow go for his weapon.

In fifteen minutes I established firmly what I sort of knew before. That someone incredibly agile was in the picture.

I went over to Melon's and ordered three bacon cheeseburgers, each one a classic. Jack O'Neill wanted to know if I had come off a fast.

"No, I been looking at a lot of exercise machines."

Then I headed for the Donnell division of the Public Library, where I do my thinking. Much thinking transpires there, and the sound of all that thinking helps my thinking. I checked out *Jewish American Literature: An Anthology* and spread it in front of me to make me look honest. The first thing I thought was that it's true what they say about homicide. But then, I could not remember what it was that they said. That third cheeseburger had cost me a step. Then I remembered: With a homicide, you had to be there. That is, there was no way to compensate for the fact that I was not on the set when the body was discovered. You could look at M.E. reports until the cows came home, but there was no way to duplicate the feel and tone and impact of that moment when the lockers got opened. It's like trying to describe to someone how good *The Sorrow and the Pity* is.

So I had to take another tack; forgive the clumsy syntax, but if I didn't know about Crystal, who in the goddamned hell else did? (Hardly realizing it, I had read a little Wallace Markfield and enjoyed the hell out of him. I made a note to pick up *Teitlebaum's Window.)* Then I forced myself to focus on my affair with Crystal and for some reason I could not get off the Cranky Period. *You don't really love me. You don't understand me. You don't understand how a woman feels. You're selfish.* Hardly Simone de Beauvoir–level insights, but she certainly did have a good fix on me. *Michael was the only one. He understood me. Only Michael.* And that's the name, of course, that I was searching for. Crystal had made more than a few stops en route to my particular hot-dog stand (as she was to make others after she checked out). But she had tarried for quite some time at Michael's place. Her other lovers had been cruel, each affair ending, if memory served, with Crystal being shoved down a flight of stairs. Michael was different, however. He had never shoved her down a flight of stairs. And once she had decided to push on, he had never recovered. He tried other women, Crystal look-alikes, but that didn't work out. He lived alone, modestly, upstate, where they had lived together. According to Crystal, he kept candles in the window. A rich kid, he had had to keep a low profile because of something involving an inheritance. I was never jealous of Michael. Crystal had shown me his photograph, lots of hair, Grand Prix-type face. No problem. I liked the fact that he had once been good to her and thought that was very middle-aged Continental of me.

The department had interviewed everyone in the city of New York, including the fast-growing Dominican population, but I had a feeling they had missed Michael. It meant I would have to give up a Kurosawa Festival, but now I knew what I was doing the next morning.

I headed back to my place; more nonsense of a particularly odious type. Someone had been poking around a second time. The lock was good—I used something that had been sold as "Beyond Even Medeco" —but the windows had been fiddled with. My vertical-screen Sony (which, frankly, had come off a truck) was intact. Same for my harman/ kardon stereo (also off a truck, except I pitched in and bought the speakers). But someone had been fooling around in my bed. There was much blanket-and-sheet turmoil and in the middle of this petit whirlwind of bacchanalia lay the missing finger from my Clue Box. Sans alcohol. I took it all like a soldier until I realized some son of a bitch had grabbed my train set.

* * *

Up I went, one flight, to the hookers, High Class Unlimited, or whatever the hell they called themselves. I talked to the woman in charge of the equipment box, whips, leg shackles, etc., and asked if she had heard anything funny transpiring in my apartment. I also pointed out that I wanted the redheaded NYU sophomore right that second or a moving van there Monday, since I was tired of hearing bond salesmen being whipped at five in the morning. She said she hadn't heard anything funny in my apartment and that the redhead only did "quickies." I said get her out of there fast and she could string together a number of "quickies" and it would do nicely. The redhead was a gentle girl and seemed to feel a heavy sense of responsibility about her assignment, that is, the keeping open of High Class Unlimited. "I think I've forgotten something," she kept saying, as we went about our nefarious work. "Are there some things I'm leaving out?" I told her she was doing fine. Later (as they used to say before the Erotic Revolution) we sat around and discussed art history, which she was studying at NYU before embarking on a marital venture. She was a nice person. She just wasn't my train set.

It is said around the Police Academy and such that cops of all races, religions, creeds and geographies speak with a single tongue and are united in a tight coppish brotherhood. That is probably true, the sole exception being the New York City detective, who is viewed in the outlying districts as some kind of Armenian type. Such was the nature of my reception when I made a courtesy stop at the Piedmont Police Station and inquired as to the whereabouts of Michael Jeffrey, Crystal's former lover that everybody forgot about, including me. Coolness and briskness were the order of the day. Prodding about for their soft underbelly, I complimented them on their Emergency Service and Ballistics Unit, which I had heard was the equal of any in the country, including Chicago and especially New York.

A breakthrough occurred and I even got a couple of fat beaming smiles. Michael Jeffrey had died in a fire about a year back. The fire was a little "funny"—enough so to justify a coroner's inquest, which had come up empty. He had lived with a woman of international extraction who had hauled ass about twenty minutes after the inquest report. This meant that all the time Crystal was telling me about Michael pining away, there was no Michael. Indeed, Michael, long ago, had gone up in smoke. Which meant that maybe Crystal had never seen Guam, Rio and that cooking school in Brest, either. Was it going to turn out that she was a girl from Bayside? Or that I had imagined her, the way I'm still not absolutely sure I once took a sudden impulsive trip to Trondheim? Very Transcendental Meditative and very unsettling. Michael's parents still lived in Piedmont, and it was to their house that I hied.

My guess was that they were Jewish folks who had gone over to the other team of which there is no one in the world more bland and Apple Pie than such ex-Semites. Mr. Jeffrey (né Jefkowitz?) showed me football trophies, and the like, involving his son, Michael. Such people do not cry or show grief after a loss. They show trophies. There was also a sister, Dolly Jeffrey, who was evidently made of more ethnic stuff and had never bought the inquest report on her brother for a second. Several weeks back, she had headed for New York City, who knows, maybe to nose around and do something about it.

They say a man's job is where he lands; a fellow gets into the shingle business, not because he has always dreamed of shingles, but because he happens to fall into it. There's him, there's shingles and he goes and does them. I don't happen to subscribe to this theory. My feeling is that he and shingles have always had a rendezvous with destiny. Something drew him to shingles. And thus it is with homicide. It is no accident that I am a homicider, and the way I know this is when I hear something like Dolly Jeffrey's heading, two weeks ago, for New York to check further into her brother's death. My heart begins to thump like a son of a bitch. There is no difference from when it pounded the first time on the one I cracked in the Holland Tunnel (see *Daily News,* April 9, 1955, page 5, my first collar). My heart behaved that way on my premiere collar, and it will on my last. I'm not talking about the collar so much as when I can smell the collar.

Shift now to Dr. Wen, the Taiwan Tooth Fairy, Cavity Man to the Stars, whose I.D. on Crystal's mouth I hadn't been too pleased with, right from the gitgo. In one sense, it was better than fingerprints, which have been known to wear off in some cases (age, disease); no two mouths are ever alike. On the other hand, who in the hell was there to challenge him? He had done some work on my bite (I was a Crystal referral), quitting in midmouth, as it were, when he spotted a flaw in my Detective's Dental Insurance Plan. Then and there, he had lost my vote as Mr. Integrity. I recalled he had done some work for the navy in World War II. I had a marker out with Naval Intelligence which I decided to call in; within six hours I learned that his tie with the navy had been canceled when they discovered he had been making deals with naval pilots to falsify their dental reports—and thereby get them grounded. How the evil spool did unwind on our Oriental friend. With two of my colleagues, I lit out for Versailles, or its equivalent thereof, which Dr. Wen had built for himself in Great Neck Estates. A male servant, of prunelike disposition, informed us that Dr. Wen could not be disturbed at the moment, as he was occupied discussing root-canal work with one of Alan King's nephews. Though my pulse quickened at the mention of the famed Great Neck comedian, I insisted that my business could not hold, and proceeded, along with my fellows, to the main hall.

Maps spread out before him, Dr. Wen appeared to be planning bike trips through Vancouver. No nephew of the celebrated Great Neck jester was in evidence. After first tossing up a great cloud of Eastern civility, Dr. Wen managed to get across his point that we were motherfouquers for invading his home. I told him I knew about his naval caper. Nothing. I introduced Karl Polski of Immigration and Customs, who produced documents indicating that Dr. Wen was an illegal alien, even though the fix had been put in several years back, the point being that a new administration was in that didn't know or care about the fix. We got him a little on that one. For my concluding act, I brought on, to a tidy round of applause, Arnie Dix, who had taken over for me in Junk and had chapter and verse on Dr. Wen's Xylocaine gig and how part of his allotment found its way to inmates at Attica at a net gain to the doctor of some fifteen large a year. What I am saying is that we had the middle clogged, the wide lanes blocked, and Dr. Wen had no outside shot. He told me he had falsified the dental I.D.

Meaning the girl in the lockers was not Crystal. Meaning nine chances out of ten that the girl was Dolly Jeffrey, who had investigated her brother's death only too well. Meaning ten chances out of ten that it was Crystal, alive, well, bright-eyed and bushy-tailed, who had gotten Dr. Wen to falsify the I.D.

All of the above suggestions checked out.

"How in the hell did she get you to do a thing like that?" I asked this question of the not so good Dr. Wen, after I had made a quick call to Gumm and brought the fellow up to date. And no sooner had I asked than I knew *la réponse*. The same way she had gotten me to shake a gynecologist down for her couch. Or that, for no apparent reason, a leading Wasp financier had handed her a 10 percent interest in a chain of Greek luncheonettes. And that an East Sixty-seventh Street landlord had rented her the reception hall of a former emerging-nation embassy for one hundred and sixty dollars a month, utilities thrown in. It was all tied in to the trouble I used to have when people asked me, "Exactly what does she do?" I always sort of knew what she did, but I could never catch her doing it and I was smart enough not to try too hard. It just wasn't any fun knowing, finally, once and for all, that she did do it.

Now, apparently, she had a new hobby, depositing parts of young girls in lockers of health clubs. By no stretch of the imagination could I imagine Crystal actually taking apart such girls, but now I had to wonder about that, too. When I first began to half live with her, I remember the subject coming up of what she would do if she ever caught me in an extracurricular activity on her. "Twist your neck, break your bones, crack your feet, make them all into powder and throw them in the toilet." All of this accompanied by graceful, almost Noh Theater gestures. Charming, I had thought to myself. Absolutely charming. Real storybook stuff, throwing witches into fires, slicing off the dragon's head. "You got to hear this," I told a group of my friends. "It's the most goddamned charming thing you ever heard." And I would have her say it for a couple of friends, who agreed it was charming, too, maybe not as charming as I thought it was, but, no question, heavy in the charm department.

Now I had to wonder. I thought of New Jersey's words (probably the only time anyone had ever thought of her words): *"You'll never quite understand how hard she took it when you two split up."* And then I made myself stop wondering. There was no way Crystal herself could have actually performed the taking apart of another pretty human being. Maybe the packing and loading, but never the other. And that was that.

But she was on *some* kind of campaign.

Taking back my trains, for example, unmistakably had her touch. Stealing my Clue Box? A Crystal special. Klee-slashing, a definite maybe and using my bed for mad venereous bouts, right on the beam, although I am not so sure where the finger fit in (and would prefer not to think about it). The dye in the Turk's eyes?—I don't think so; smashing Katrina's kneecap, not her style. Proceeding along these lines, how would she be able to swing into people's windows at nosebleed altitudes, given as she was to walking into buildings and falling off ladders due to false pride and an unwillingness to get involved with contact lenses, even though I told her how good the soft ones were?

Let me avail myself of an opportunity to set things down the way my Hunter College professor of rhetoric would like it. (The reader will be kind enough to sprinkle in ibid.s and *loc. cit.*s, since we have not gotten to them and won't until the stretch drive of the fall semester.)

1) Crystal was mad at me.
2) She did not want anyone getting close to the fire, the fire that Michael Jeffrey was suspiciously caught in, that is.
3) Crystal was very mad at me.
4) She had acquired a new and reckless partner on her ride along Life's Highway.

It was this last item that had me stuck on a dime when I received one of those lovely bonuses that occasionally accrue to us lonely souls who toil in the homicidal vineyard. My bench came to the rescue, pouring in a badly needed bucket. Gumm called. At God-alone-knows-what punishing cost to the taxpayer, his men had established that Crystal had taken up with a limo driver. (In her heyday, Crystal would hire limos to pick up *Women's Wear Daily.*) He had been a stunt man for Linguini Westerns (budgeted slightly higher than Spaghetti Westerns). His nickname was "Loose." There was a sheet on him, peppered with assault and battery notations. He was no stranger to the slam. His style was to open the heads—suddenly and unprovoked—of the following types in discotheque men's rooms:

a) Anyone who ignored him.
b) Anyone who paid attention to him.
c) Anyone who did none of the above.

This petty quirk had made it difficult for him to secure employment in his chosen occupation and driven him into the limo-driving game. A note on his sheet used the phrase "Blond; macho-gay." A further notation indicated that—by way of introducing himself—he was known to tumble down three or four flights of stairs. The Turk, of course, had alerted me to the presence of such a person in the neighborhood watering spots. And had gotten dye in his eyes for his trouble.

From all evidence, Crystal and her new partner (how it pains me to use that godforsaken nickname—all right, here goes), "Loose," were still in the area, seemingly unaware that I knew she wasn't the locker girl. As attested to by the fact that Ronnie Steamroom was pistol-whipped on Mulberry Street while making a surreptitious trip to the city for some special Italian salad oils.

Though points would be awarded for speed at this juncture, I had now to contend with yet another phenomenon that will be recognizable to those who at one time or another have engaged in police activities. It is called Fear of the Collar. What happens is that just when you are on the edge of wrapping up a case, there comes about a sudden and obviously self-defeating urge to see a Clint Eastwood film, study macramé, attend the Stuttgart Ballet, fix defective wall switches and perhaps enter into heated debates on whether a Ducati can stay with and even burn a Kawasaki at one hundred and twenty miles an hour (entering Hartford). The phenomenon was once explained to me by a departmental psychologist (yet another budget victim, long gone, forced to go into film criticism) as having to do with not wanting to outdistance your dad. In the oedipal race for your mom. Or something like that. (I once had it down cold.) If one's dad was a cop, F.O.T.C. became all the more fierce. So I had to fight it like a sumbitch. And fight it I did, walking out on Eastwood's *Eiger Sanction* when he was halfway up the mountain. (Forgive me, Clint, although frankly, the second I saw you show up as an art history professor in the first frame I sensed you were in big trouble.)

My throat bite began to ache. Was there such a thing as arthritis of the throat, responsive to tension and seasonal changes?

In our heyday, or hey-season, Crystal, though almost fully grown, had been a great hide-and-seek player. Few people had time to conceal themselves in closets, under beds, behind hatracks and then leap out on a person's shoulders, but Crystal did. The problem was where in the city of New York to look for a once-charming but increasingly violent hide-and-seek player and her limo-driving stuntman friend? I had two thoughts: We had once vowed to further cement our romance with the acquisition of a Rhodesian Ridgeback, a new breed of dog known not so much for its white-supremacist attitudes as its willingness to learn a trick a day. There was a kennel in Brooklyn. Crystal and her companion were holed up in it, the stuntman keeping his artillery focused on the street, Crystal playing with the Ridgeback puppies. Dreadful idea, right? *D'accord.* Another Brooklyn idea was the trailer-court man who was an expert in hallucinogenic mushrooms—grew them, ate them, shared them with interested friends. Crystal had been fascinated by the fellow, had popped a few and stared at the moonlight over Sheepshead Bay while I waited in the squad. That's another place I might have a peek at.

Except that while I was having these thoughts, I was also feeling my way along some rope of instinct that led me to the IRT, en route to the South Bronx. Where I had grown up and been raised by Helen Reilly, who for all practical purposes was my mother, my own folks having gone off a cliff when I was a babe—a whole separate story. How did Helen's death affect me? Let's just say that I couldn't even look at the South Bronx on a map. Any case that took me there got transferred over to some close colleague. With a gun to my head, I could not think of Helen Reilly's old phone number (and mine), much less dial it. When she died I told Heavy Eddie, the handyman, just to get rid of everything in the apartment, and not tell me what he'd done with it. I buried her and then I blanked out the whole thing. And now I was taking a casual subway ride to the South Bronx. They sure had a lot of blind ads in the subway. Appeals for blind vets, blind moms, blind dogs. Anything blind went right up there in the Bronx subway ads. To give you an idea of my feelings about going up to the South Bronx— looking at all that blind material was comic relief. A sneak preview of Tati's latest.

I had told Crystal all about Helen Reilly. "I wish you could've known her," I'd say.

"I do know her," she would say back to me.

Some vegetable guy would try to sell us defective tomatoes and Crystal would say, "Helen Reilly would have told him to shove those tomatoes up his ass." And she was always right. Not on the precise language —Helen Reilly was a lot softer than Crystal imagined her—but on the sense of her; she really knew what Helen Reilly would have thought or said. Very eerie stuff. If the faithful reader will permit one last saccharine note, Crystal was probably the only one in the world who knew what Helen Reilly meant to me. Which is why I was taking this jaunt to the South Bronx. Which is not exactly Saint-Tropez. To add to the merriment, I was soaking wet in a madras shirt and slacks. Which came from Barney's and not off a truck this time.

Getting off at Jerome Avenue and One Hundred Sixty-first Street was easy. Strolling over to the old apartment on Morris Avenue would be the hard part. Climbing the stairs and ringing the doorbell? Like being told you have a touch of the Big C. I found some childhood rocks I used to jump down from in Joyce Kilmer Park, and as a charming diversion, totally fruitless, as it turned out, jumped down from them again. I looked at Yankee Stadium and thought of Charley Keller showing up for a game, dark face, brooding shoulders. That helped me about as much as a children's aspirin. I crossed the Grand Concourse, thinking of the safety slogan with which I'd won a carton of Thanx candy bars: "Follow the red and green; you'll wind up in the pink." (So how come I'm not writing for Carson?) I was on Morris Avenue, a division of San Juan now, staring at the building, a sudden middle-aged vomiter. Heavy Eddie, big, black, the handyman from the birth of the building, around one hundred and five now, came out and by way of greeting me, hit me with his belly. Lot of haw haws, welcome back to the plantation, Massah Herbie, and you'll never guess who took over your mommy's apartment. Amazing. Took the furniture that I had stashed, the whole thing.

"I know, I know, I know," I said. "I know."

"Prettiest little girl, and she said she knew your mommy. Up there with a gentleman she says is her brother or something."

"I know, I know, I know."

Up to date, trendy as ever, Heavy Eddie wanted to swap Robin Yount ancedotes with me; I figured I might as well get right at it. You're scheduled for surgery, don't put it off. In the great tradition, I laid a dime on Eddie, got the key from him, took the deepest breath of my career, and walked up the stairs to 3N. Then I took the second deepest breath of my career and committed breaking and entering on my old apartment in the South Bronx.

The piano was in the wrong part of the living room, the beige rug was poorly placed, the imitation fireplace had real logs in front of it—but apart from a few blunders along these lines, everything was much the way I remembered it. This was a bit boring, since I had sensed I would find it this way. Nonboring came when I took a little stroll into the bedroom. I'm telling you, if ever there comes a time when there is no David Merrick, someone ought to get in touch with this girl. In my mother's bed, yet. With her friend. And in my mother's nightgown. Beat that, Mr. Krafft-Ebing.

"Hi, Herbie," said Crystal. "What do you think of what I did? This is Loose. Loose, Herbie."

Are you ready for the fact that I said, "How do you do?" And that we shook hands. We did.

Quickly, however, the temperature rose. Forget about the air conditioner. Forget the South Bronx. Think Gobi Desert. Loose was in a crouch, a mannerism left over from one of his Italian Westerns.

"I'm not gonna pull a knife on you," he said, his voice strangely high-pitched, Irish choirboy. True to his word, he did not. What he pulled was a broken bottle (Châteauneuf-du-Pape, I later learned) and with a deft and rather graceful underhanded movement (that showed a certain familiarity with Borges's early classic, *The South*) made contact with my shoulder, producing five small fountains of blood. I would like to be able to say that the dreamlike quality of the moment was numbing. It was not. It hurt like a son of a bitch.

"Oh, Loose," said Crystal, sitting up petulantly, my dead mother's nightgown drawn, with feigned casualness, to just the right level above her knees. She scolded him as if he had dropped ashes on the rug.

The time had come for me to unsheath my weapon, which I did, although—due to the highly personal nature of our trinella—there was little chance I would immediately go boom boom. Alert to my physical and psychoschmycho discomfiture, Loose seized the opportunity to make tracks. I made them, too, following him through the door past the incinerator (what a proud day it was when we said hello to that class innovation and farewell to the hellish dumbwaiter) and to the end of the hallway. It was at this point that I got to see firsthand his famous calling card, falling down three flights of stairs . . . and not hurting himself. After a quick sniff of what I took to be ancient traces of delicious Bronx cooking smells, I followed him to the building lobby, across to the second, or "D," wing. Here, Loose treated me to a new wrinkle, what appeared to be his tumbling back *up* the stairs—a variation he may very well have introduced for my benefit. And then we were on the roof, but not before I had paused—amazingly—for a split second at 6F, home of Dick Schreiber, a plodder who had gone on to fame in Boston cardiology. If Schreiber, a grind, believe me (I'm not talking about Levinson of 4F, who really had some stuff), attained those heights, you mean to tell me I couldn't have made it in medicine, at least in anesthesiology?

To the roof. What followed would most likely have been your traditional cops-and-robbers chase across the rooftops of the Bronx, with the possible result that Loose would have leaped and stumbled and twirled his way to freedom—since the only moving target I've ever hit was a skeet or two on the deck of an Oslo "party boat," another one of my great vacation ideas. And also, I get nauseated on rooftops. So Loose would probably be free and padding about in Venezuela today if he had not made the mistake of killing Heavy Eddie, the one-hundred-and-five-year-old handyman who had once rushed me to Morrisania Hospital when a collie bit my six-year-old *tochis*. He killed him with another of those goddamned broken bottles. I could not figure out where he was getting them until I realized he had one of those Gucci shoulder bags filled with them. He had some style. I don't know how Heavy Eddie got up there so fast. They had probably repaired the elevator, the first time it was running smoothly in twenty-two years. And he was up on the rooftop and when I passed him I knew he was dead because of his smile. I know that dead smile. There is a dead frown and a dead smile, but they are both dead. One thing I know is dead. So I forgot the fact that we were running along Bronx rooftops (well sort of, anyway) and I took off after Loose and held my own. That is, I kept the gap between us down to around half a rooftop. To give him his due, it was because he was stopping to do tricks along the way. What was he doing, auditioning? I would probably still be running after him out in Gila Bend somewhere if it hadn't been for the fact that he stopped for a minute and did some leg extensions. I don't know.

Maybe he had a legitimate cramp. I could have let one fly right then and there and put an end to the shabby episode in that manner, except that I guess I had something else in mind all along. When we were at close quarters, he unsnapped the Gucci bag and pulled out another bottle which he broke on the base of a combination clothesline/TV antenna. I assumed this bottle had my name on it. I waited a couple of beats, faked once to my right—thought of Heavy Eddie, my mother, Crystal in my mother's goddamned nightgown, the two of them in my mother's bed, all this to kind of get myself morally covered—and then I bit his throat out.

As I've probably indicated, I had wanted to make that move for some time and had been looking for the right opportunity. What had happened is that when I incurred my own throat bite (on Broadway, right across from Zabar's) I had double-pumped, in the classic Walt Frazier style, and the wino I was trying to belt out had not gone for it. He had not, of course, bitten my throat entirely out, but he had gotten his teeth in there pretty good, enough to make me sleepy every morning of my life. And after a good sleep. So I guess it had been simmering away, subliminally, for some time. And, of course, I also had Dr. Wen's bite to work with, so I suppose, unconsciously, I had wanted to get my money's worth, too. So I had done it back to Loose. Not double-pumping, and with only a single head fake. Which he had gone for. Like so many of these things, once you get it done it really isn't all that much. Let me share with you something that I have learned. The fantasy of biting out an entire throat is much more stimulating than the actual deed.

It did not look as if much of a crowd was going to collect on the rooftop. It did not look as if anyone had been up there since F.D.R. died. So I figured I had time for a cigarillo or two.

I went back down to my old apartment and used the phone.

"Who are you calling, Herbie?" asked Crystal.

"My answering service."

She was tidying up, as if she were expecting six for dinner. I sat down on my mother's old flowered living-room couch.

"How do you like the way I fixed it up?" Crystal asked.

"Great."

And it *was* great. Apart from a handbook on backgammon hustling, a little out of sync, I could not see one goddamned item that was different from when I was growing up and going to Cardinal Hayes. Just for fun, I checked inside an Oriental vase on the bookshelves, and there were the ten silver dollars Ned Reilly, my uncle, had given me out of his Firemen's Pension Plan.

"What other girl would have done this for you?" she asked.

"I sure as hell can't think of any."

The outrageous part is that if you stripped away a few considerations —murder, throat-biting, masterpiece-slashing, etc.—it *was* an extraordinary thing to do for a fellow.

"Now, Herbie," she said. "What would you like to eat?"

"Anything," I said. "I'm not really that hungry."

"You say that all the time." She was an extraordinary cook, and it was true, I did say it all the time and whatever she came up with, I got rid of it like it was going out of style and just about fainted with delight.

She brought out some cold tortellini, kind of half Italian, half Jewish, and don't ask me how she pulled it off, but it smelled a little Irish, too. I didn't actually get to taste it. I think she was genuinely hurt and surprised when Gumm and company showed up; I've never seen anyone look so disdainful and aristocratic when they were getting the cuffs put on them. Maybe Jackie O. would do it that way, but she's the only one I can think of. I wasn't sure what I wanted to do with the second chapter of my life, but two things I definitely wanted to avoid were 1) watching Crystal get hauled away in the paddy wagon and 2) meeting her eyes.

I stayed around for half an hour or so, and actually considered moving back to the old apartment. And then I quickly unconsidered it. I locked it up; that night, I called my brother in Laramie and told him to get rid of the place and its contents once and for all, take care of the whole thing. He's good at that stuff, even from Laramie.

No more surprises. (Just one, actually.) All that swinging in through windows had been Loose's work. The Piedmont crime-busters reopened the Michael Jeffrey arson case and it's pending. Crystal is in the women's slam, which I don't want to know about. Loose did the kneecap number. And they had dispatched Dolly Jeffrey as a team. (Loose had been dating a La Lanne's instructor, male gender—and had thusly gained access to the gym for the after-hours session.)

What continued to plague me was who it was that had actually done the Thanksgiving turkey slicing on Dolly Jeffrey. I had just about given Crystal a full pardon on that score when the tortellini I'd wisely refrained from eating came back from Microanalysis with a lab report setting forth a complete list of its unhappy ingredients . . . flour, sugar, cornstarch, etc., that stuff, but also (for a quick death) potassium cyanide; (for a slow one) arsenic; and (presumably for a fascinating "fun" send-off) a certain species of Canarsie Trailer-Court Mushroom. All I could think of was: *That little rascal.*

And she *was* from Bayside.

Business Is Business

For TWENTY-FIVE YEARS, my father worked for a man named Schreever who was the president of Schreever Laces. He was a boyhood friend of my father's and they started the business together. My father was not good at business manipulations. After a few years, he decided to devote himself exclusively to the factory and work on salary. It would be better that way since he would have fewer headaches. But as the business prospered, the factory expanded. My father had a dozen production assistants under him and about seventy-five women. He enjoyed being in charge of so many people. Even in his executive position, he was the first one down to the factory and the last one to leave in the evening. Everyone else on the street was certain my father owned half the business and he didn't really deny it. It was a flourishing business. But privately, to us, he said he had less headaches not having anything to do with the business end of it and he was tickled to death he didn't have to worry about those things. He invited me down to the factory once on a Saturday. I was in for the weekend from military school and it was a big thing for me because he'd never invited me down before.

The factory was deserted and my father switched on the lights. He took me around, showing me the piles of laces, rayons, silks, the sewing machines, patterns, and the cutting machines. "You really want to see something, kid?" he asked. He took a pile of rayon material in his hand and switched on the cutting machine. He slid the materials alongside the blade of the cutting machine and it sliced through the pile like a knife through soft butter. "What do you think of that?" he asked. I said it was pretty good. Actually, I didn't see what he was knocking himself out about. If he hadn't been my father, and if this hadn't been the first time he'd paid any attention to me I'd have told him it was lousy and showed me nothing. My father went inside to the latrine for a second. I wandered out of the factory into the showroom where the finished laces were on display for buyers. They were under glass and I went up to the showcases and stared at them. My father ran up behind me and slapped me across the mouth. I thought I was too old to be slapped and for that reason I started to cry as he tugged me back into the factory. "You don't ever go where you're not supposed to go," he said. "I brought you down here to see the factory. The showroom is someone else's territory," he said. Then he told me how many girls he had under him, where they worked and how they were always goofing off near the Coke machine and how he had to be strict with them so they would learn not to loaf. He told me how big the factory was, the exact dimensions. He told me the value of the factory in case Schreever ever had to liquidate, which was highly improbable. A number of years later I saw a car lot attendant go berserk in Cleveland. He leaped up on a Buick and beat his chest telling the whole world that the sea of cars in the lot belonged to him and no other man. The first thing I thought of then was my father and his factory.

The first time I met Schreever was at my military school graduation. I had always heard him mentioned in exalted terms and I was scared when they brought him over to me. Later, Cubby, a football player whom I idolized, told me I was shaking like a leaf when I talked to him. I had seen a picture of him with my father. They were at the beach and they were both young. At that time it seemed they were the same height. When I saw Schreever he was actually much taller than my father. He asked me what I was going to do later on. I told him I wanted to go to college but I wasn't sure I knew what I wanted to take up. "Going to college is a very expensive proposition," he told my father. "The boy ought to know exactly what he wants before he enters. I think he ought to consider something like accounting very seriously. Be a big help to him." My father agreed. He acted funny around Schreever, did a great deal of laughing. When Schreever asked where my mother was, my father hollered out "EDNA" across the parade grounds. My mother left three women and came running over. Schreever gave her a $25 defense bond for me.

When Schreever had his heart attack, I was living at home and going to school in the city. My mother had been after my father to ask for a share of the business and not go on all his life working for a salary. My father kept saying he didn't want the headaches. My mother said that Schreever had three homes and an apartment and we couldn't even have a place in the country every summer. My father said he'd see about it, but would she please leave it to him. "Besides," my father would say, "I'm sure Mrs. Schreever doesn't have an ermine stole like you do." That would always quiet my mother down and then my father would say he'd see about it anyway just to satisfy her although it would probably mean all kinds of headaches. Just at the time Schreever had the attack, two salesmen in the firm approached my father saying they were going to form their own outfit and would my father like to come along and be their "inside" man. He would be considered a full partner. My father was considering it when he went to see Schreever in the hospital. Schreever said it would all be over without my father. The business couldn't last a day without him and if he stayed on he could have a substantial raise in salary. Seeing Schreever dying in the hospital changed my father's mind. He turned down the two salesmen who decided not to go through with it without my father. Schreever got better and left the hospital.

My mother asked my father why he didn't ask for a share in the business instead of settling for a raise. "You can't do business with a dying man. You can't bargain with a man who's had a heart attack. It's not ethical," my father said. But this time he was plainly shaken. He seemed to realize that he'd made a big, obvious mistake and he said to my mother that when Schreever recuperated fully he would "really talk to him this time."

Whether Schreever had made enough money and wanted to take it easy the rest of his life or whether he'd been given an ultimatum by the two salesmen was not plain. But suddenly my father announced at dinnertime one night that after twenty-five years in the lace business, Amos Schreever was retiring. The new owners of Schreever Laces, Inc. would be two of the firm's salesmen and himself. They would all have to invest a considerable sum of money to buy out Schreever. But the best part was yet to come. My father had spoken to Schreever and out of gratitude for twenty-five years of devoted service, Schreever was going to put up my father's share of the investment.

Meanwhile, my father took his last cent out of the bank as half of the investment and borrowed the other half from my uncle, who was a gynecologist. Schreever would come up with the money when it wasn't conspicuous so the other partners, the two salesmen, would not be irritated and take offense. "This is something that has to be kept very quiet," my father told us. "It's not good business ethics for Schreever to be doing this for me. It's simply a gesture of friendship and if the two salesmen found out it would be horrible."

Still, an air of tension hung over our house as my father started out in his new business venture. We had a dinner during which we toasted his success, but everyone laughed a little too easily and forced a good time. My mother was told she would have to pull in on the household budget at the beginning until things got straightened out. The lace business had its first bad season in twenty years. The buyers came in, took a great many numbers down, but really didn't buy too much. It was thought that Schreever had been a much stronger figure in the business than anyone realized and his absence was really hurting them. My mother, after a few months, asked my father at dinner if Schreever had been around recently and if Schreever had said anything to him. My father said Schreever was at his Florida home recuperating.

"What's wrong with you, Edna?" he said. "A man in the condition he's in and you expect him to worry about business. You really don't understand anything." We got a letter from the Schreevers in Florida saying the weather was wonderful and then another from them in New Orleans. My father laughed nervously and said it was good they were getting around. He hoped it was doing the old boy's health some good.

Living at home, the way I was, it was easy for me to see the change that had come over my father. He was obviously upset constantly, but it came out in a very strange way. He began to bring his factory home with him. Everything in the house had to be done in a precise, exacting way. He went around piling and lining things up. At the dinner table, he would scrape the crumbs off the tablecloth with a knife after dinner, getting every single one even if it took half an hour. Once I took some butter from a side of the dish that hadn't been started and he knocked the knife out of my hand. He went around cleaning and dusting and making things neat. He made his bed over at night in distinct motions as if he were doing it by the numbers. He grew farther apart from my mother. She asked him whether Schreever had gotten in touch with him, and he said, "Shut your goddamned mouth." Another time she asked him in another way and he said, "You know it *is* possible I misunderstood him. That's been known to happen in the history of men, too. Maybe I took something for granted that really wasn't the case." But it didn't sound as though he meant it. As business got worse, we continued to hope that Schreever would come through.

When my father had an attack of sciatica and had to sleep on a board, we took a place in the country near a lake. The rental was pretty high and my sister and nephew came to live with us. There was the talk, of course, that my father's illness was mainly psychological, but at any rate, it was painful. He was stationed in the parlor and we had to tiptoe past him. The slightest creak would start him groaning. We tried to make everything pleasant for him and keep his mind off business, but he was on the phone every day speaking to his place.

I lied about my age and took a job as a policeman across the lake. I was to carry a gun and keep unauthorized people off the private beach. The gun scared me out of my wits. But at night I would swim the lake to our side. That always refreshed me and I would not think about the gun until the next day. I always had the feeling it would go off in the holster and take my leg off.

One night I swam the lake and came home. I changed my clothes and went into the back room for a game of GRIPs with my nephew, Harry, who was five years old. We made up the game and it used to drive him crazy. I would get him in a grip, making up a name for it, saying it was an Elementary Alligator Grab or an Advanced Boa hold, and no man had ever gotten out of it. He would start to laugh and then I would get him in the grip and after a while ease up, letting him slip out. When he got out he would squeal with delight, begging me to get him in an Intermediate Japanese Panther Lock. I had him in one of the grips when my mother came over to the side of my father's board and said she had a card from the Schreevers. My father didn't say anything. She said she would read it. It was from Naples and it said, "Dear Henry and Edna, Are enjoying sunny Italy and will go on from here to Switzerland. Europe is truly wonderful, everything we ever dreamed of. Will see England if there is time and we don't get too overtired. Hope you and family are enjoying best of health, we remain, the Schreevers." My mother showed my father the card which showed the Schreevers standing in front of some ruins. I saw it later and Mr. Schreever looked tall and suntanned, better than at my graduation. My father turned away and said, "You're always digging me, Edna. All my life you've been digging me. And now that I'm sick you're digging me worse than ever."

We drove home in a gloom at summer's end, stopping every couple of miles because the radiator got overheated. My father had his tonsils taken out, which seemed to cure his back ailment. There was no talk of Schreever or business on the way home or in the house for the next month. We were certain it was all over and my father *had* really misunderstood him.

One Monday night, after working overtime, my father flung open the door, whisked my mother off her feet and blurted out, "The Schreevers are back. They called me at work. They want us to come up to their Connecticut place on Sunday."

My mother was more excited than she'd been in a long time. She made him calm down and tell the story slowly at the dinner table. Mr. Schreever, it seems, had called my father while he was in the factory, telling him he was having a little cocktail party on Sunday and would he like to come and bring along the wife and boy. There would be no one else there and they could have a nice little talk during the afternoon.

We had a victory drink and my father chided my mother for being so silly all these last months. "You don't understand business ethics, Edna," he said. "Number one, the man was a sick man, and number two, it just would've been lousy if he'd done something for me and those partners of mine found out about it."

My mother spent the rest of the week selecting a new outfit. A new suit was bought for me. The car was Simonized and my father had his nails manicured. He took a sunlamp treatment at the barbershop and came back with a fairly good tan. My mother had her stole cleaned and brushed and her hair done at the beauty parlor. Just before we started out, my mother suggested that maybe we oughtn't take the car. "After all, they're smart people. When they see a convertible they may think we're doing very well. You never know, Henry, they might think we have property investments."

"That just shows you how much you know about business," my father said. "Get in, Edna, and stop your nonsense. If you've been in business just two days you know that it's always best to look your very nicest. No one wants to have anything to do with a slob."

We drove up with the top down and the air nice and cool. My father got some good music on the radio. A sign on one of the turnoffs said SUNNY ROADS ESTATE—THE SCHREEVERS—and we turned in. The driveway seemed about a mile long. There were many little houses along the way to the main house. In front of it stood the Schreevers, both dressed very simply but graciously. Mrs. Schreever had a boxer heeling at her side. They greeted us and the first thing they commented on was the car and how well we all looked. "A con—*ver*—tible," Mrs. Schreever said. "Isn't it beautiful. And look how wonderful she looks. And that suntan on Henry. And look at that lovely stole on Edna. My, you look *won-der-ful,* my dears."

I was given the boxer to play with and my parents went into the bar to drink. They talked for about an hour, all about the Schreevers' European trip and how they had found all sorts of perfumes and gifts over there to take back. Then Schreever brought up the old days and how they had both started out together and how far they had come over the years. Everyone got a little tipsy except my mother. My father did a great deal of laughing and smiling whenever Schreever opened his mouth. The hours went by. My mother started to poke my father. He looked at her like she was insane. She kept poking him, casually so no one would see, but he kept smiling and laughing at Mr. Schreever. They talked about Abel Starr, a boyhood friend of theirs who had gone to prison and how they had both visited him; they kidded about how they had discussed slipping a file to him in a cake. It got dark on the porch and then we were up and saying goodbye, my mother still prodding my father, and my father still smiling and laughing with Mr. Schreever. Then we were in the car driving home, my father a little tipsy and my mother silent. After a while, he seemed to realize what had happened. My mother didn't say a word. "I guess it was just meant to be a little social gathering after all, Edna. It's really not good business to talk about money at someone's house. It'd be a sorry mess if I was to go and ask for money when someone had invited me over for cocktails." My mother asked him to stop the car. He pulled over and she threw up at the side of the road. She came back crying in a loud, snuffling way. My father put his arm around her as he drove, saying he really would ask him in the city. No more fooling around. All of us knew that moment that he would never ask him. It was the first time I had ever seen my mother cry. But it was also the first time I had ever seen my father put his arm around her.

Living Together

SHOT DOWN TWICE IN MARRIAGE, loser after a multitude of affairs, Pellegrino, in his forties, was about to pack it in romantically, when a fresh and delightful young woman suddenly bobbed up before him at a party like an apple in a barrel. Her eyes were wide, her movements graceful. She spoke with an ingratiating chuckle. Pellegrino's date was a good-natured blonde who had been raised in trailer courts and with whom he had come, characteristically, to a dead end. She could not have cared less—but the new woman was courteous and discreet, telling him only that she worked as an executive on the eighth floor of a well-known department store. When she wandered off to stand at the edge of the party, Pellegrino was far from smitten but full of questions. She wore a tweed jacket, tailored slacks, was somewhat older than the women he was used to. Was she too "responsible" for him? He had a charge card at her department store and enjoyed wandering through the men's clothing section. What if he simply showed up on the eighth floor? Would she dismiss him with a cynical laugh? He caught another glimpse of her and grappled with the most important question of all— did she have enough tush? A harsh, nonhumanistic concern for some, perhaps, but not for Pellegrino.

To be on the safe side, he made no effort to see her, shopping at a department store he wasn't that crazy about. Still, the idea of her nagged at him, that chuckle, the question of her body. Once in a while, he summoned her forth for a brief, slim-hipped fantasy in the night.

A year later, fate poked him in the ribs—he met her again at a reunion for people with strong sixties concerns. He failed to recognize her; her hair was swept back, her great eyes tipsy over the rim of a cocktail glass. Was she a little faded around the edges? The hostess introduced them with great expectations. Pellegrino was correct, then swiftly went about his business—yet another blonde, a little overweight but at least a folk singer.

But she stubbornly kept after him—he remembered virtually swatting her away—until she yanked at his lapels and said, "Don't you even remember me? Katherine? The wedding reception?" The instant she identified herself, he realized he had been in love with her for a year, although he was, of course, careful not to tell her this. After a quick, forlorn look at the folk singer, he said he had thought about her a lot. What an amazing stroke of luck to run into her again. She said she had gone to Scotland to read books in solitude and had thought about him often, too. What a waste, they both agreed. He apologized for not recognizing her. But was it really his fault? "You've rearranged your hair," he said. Instantly, she reached back and let it fall, if not tumble —moving closer to the woman he remembered, though far from on the nose. He wanted to leave with her. Suddenly he realized that they had been talking across a wounded veteran in a wheelchair, her friend. He knew what that chuckle of hers was—compassion. To his everlasting shame, he made only reflexive small talk with the veteran, then yanked her away. In his defense, he could only tell himself 1) he was afraid of people in wheelchairs and 2) such was his love.

They tumbled through the streets to a restaurant he knew. Beneath the marquee she raised a horrified hand to her mouth and said, "Here!" Never in all the time he was to know her did she explain her resistance to the innocuous eating place. They took a table in the rear. For an hour or so he reveled in that sweet chuckle, his only possible disappointment in her being perhaps one reference too many to cartoons she had enjoyed in *The New Yorker*. As far as he knew, they were alone, bathed in a private light. Later, he found out the owner had observed them and told a cherished waiter: "Pellegrino is with a woman."

At midnight, on their way to an undecided destination, they kissed in the street, or rather, tried out each other's mouths with a happy result.

"It's probably not a good idea to go home together, is it?" she pleaded. Though he had arguments on hand to buttress both sides of the question, he more or less agreed.

"But half an hour after I see you again . . ." she trailed off. He tucked the promise away, as if in a wallet. They kissed again; this time he reached around through silk and was amazed he had ever questioned the excellence of her tush.

He could not honestly testify that he was counting the days until their next date, but when he saw her, he fell in love again, this time with her apartment, a floor-through in Murray Hill with sallow light and luxuriously worn furniture, the pieces confidently spaced apart—a serious person's home. (*Monastic* was the word that lingered.) Amazingly, they both owned copies of a bestselling poster. His was framed. In a masterstroke of carelessness, she had affixed hers to the wall with a thumbtack.

Breathlessly, she sparkled on. She came from a family of nurses. Twin brothers lived in China. Her favorite books? Ones written by retired members of the diplomatic corps. He sat in silence. From time to time, he glanced at his watch. Then he said: "Time's up."

"Oh, my God, I didn't," she said.

"You did."

Dutifully, responsibly, she marched off to her loft bed, Pellegrino behind her, almost in step. The bed had no guardrail. One bad dream meant curtains for the sleeper. They made love, failing by some margin to enter paradise. But when he saw her dressing in the sallow light beneath the staircase, his knees became weak; he flew at her silhouette.

And so they began to not quite live together. Three days on, four days off. She raced to get him concert tickets, artfully arranged his chair so that he was suddenly and painlessly watching BBC productions. They slept together at his place while her cats starved. Other nights, he packed her off, clinging to his need to see strangers whom he no longer enjoyed.

"Oh, please," she said to him one day, "let's live together."

"I'd do it," he said, "but I want it to come from me, spontaneously." The next night it did. Finally, seamlessly, after ten years of profitless fencing, Pellegrino shared his life with another person. He waited for a heavy beam to fall across his shoulders. Slowly, cautiously, he stood erect.

She took up perhaps a bit too much drawer space. But she charmed his friends and cooked healthy, weightless concoctions, making subtle use of garlic. Tirelessly she made beds. She helped him with his work. Pellegrino, a writer of movie trailers, was stuck one day, unable to break through on a low-budget film—the theme, adolescent turmoil in Eastern Europe. He mentioned it in bed. The next morning he found her huddled in a chair; she'd stayed up all night, thinking he wanted her to come up with an entire trailer on her own. He hugged her, told her that wasn't it at all. Within minutes, she gave him a fresh angle of vision. By tacit agreement, they called it encouragement, though she did much more.

To a friend, he said, "She's made every moment of my life a delight."

They traveled. He took her to his favorite hotels. She approached them cautiously; then, to his slight irritation, she seized them up as if they were her own discoveries. To duck room service, they bought their own groceries. He sent her on ahead with bundles so that his entrance to the lobby could be formal. She made up songs with Pellegrino as the central character, spinning wild lyrics in the air; miraculously, when all seemed lost, she reined them in, got them to rhyme. She told him he was beautiful, that women took secret looks at him. "That's ridiculous," he said. But how could he help loving it when she said these things?

At night, with his nose pressed against the wool of her freshly laundered nightgown, he forgot for the moment about death.

But then things took a turn. The trailer business dried up, a casualty in a complex strike. At first Pellegrino felt unaffected, even amused. He had never been on strike before. Here was a chance to try out the sensation. He had planned to write a play on just such an occasion. He pounced on his typewriter. No play came. On a whim, they changed apartments, having been charmed by high ceilings and a rococo detail or two. They quickly saw it was a mistake—too long, too thin, a sliver of a space held out over raging midtown traffic as if by a hand. Pellegrino's daughter came to visit, fresh from art school, carrying prize-winning sketches and disapproval. Trying to please the child, she wound up serving undercooked hams. The three of them sat in silence at neighborhood restaurants, then returned to the small flat. Seeking privacy, they circled one another in cold geometric patterns. When the daughter left, Pellegrino pawed at the dirt while the strike took its grim toll.

To break up his afternoons, he took to watching foreign films at local art houses. One day, he gashed his wrist in the men's room of a culture complex. He thought of suing but lacked the energy. Holding a paper towel to the wound, he went upstairs to the movie house. There, while his blood pumped, he watched two hours of French irony.

He went back to the apartment to stare at his love. Oblivious to the screaming traffic, she sat beneath the louvered windows, sampling lightweight British mysteries. A tumbler of cognac, meant to be concealed, peeped out from behind a lamp base. She'd left her job to help Pellegrino, nursing him when he had no illness. Recently there had been talk of an advanced degree in international relations. It remained talk. She had taken on weight. He'd squinted his eyes to block out an extra chin. No longer could it be finessed. In the refrigerator, tins of gourmet macaroni came and went. Was it time to bring in the word *fat?*

He walked into the bedroom, actually a space created by a room divider, and wondered how he had reached this state, a serious fellow, age forty-five in view, with no booklined study. He looked at her side of the bed. When they first began to live together, she'd hollered out defiant antiwar cries in her sleep, left over from old sixties rallies. He'd found this charming. Now she did great, silent, heaving rolls, an ocean liner during a stormy crossing. His choice was to lie on the floor or roll with her.

He walked back to the living room. She looked at him, as she always did, happy, expectant. In truth, she'd stayed away from stronger books for just such occasions; the mysteries could be interrupted at no great price. He told her he didn't have this in mind at all. The two of them crammed together in a skinny apartment. And he certainly hadn't known about the drinking. Did she think he wanted to team up with a juicer? (How he'd longed to use that word.) And it was high time they talked about the fat stuff. He wasn't talking about a few pounds, which he had to concede he had put on himself. He was talking full-out fat. Did the phrase El Grosserino mean anything to her? Was that part of their arrangement, that she would pork up for him? And what about the fabled women he was supposed to be allowed to see but somehow didn't? It's true, it's true, she'd said go right ahead, just don't fall in love. Well, that was some condition. They had talked about a child. Forget that, please. That's all he needed, a new family in a shitty apartment with a porked-up juicer.

She listened to all of this with a quizzical smile, as if somehow she had wandered into the wrong theater to see a bad play but was too generous or polite to leave. It was only when he said that he hated every single second of his life that the color ran out of her face. "All right then, go," she said. "Or *I'll* go." With lightning speed, as if sprung from a trap, she flashed across the room and lunged for a battered suitcase.

"No, no," he said, panicked, blocking her path, "never." With all his might, he hugged her to him, arms encircling her thick waist, which he was now convinced could be trimmed down after two or three weeks of intensive exercise.

"I wouldn't blow this for anything in the world."

The Trip

WHEN THE TIME CAME for me to go to college, my mother decided she would go with me. Since the college was fifteen hundred miles away, in the Midwest, and since I was very young to be going to college, it seemed to her the proper thing to do.

My mother pretended there was nothing strange about her taking me to college. She told me that I should wait and I would see that every fellow who showed up at the college would have his mother with him. While I was packing, I tried to argue with her. "It's ridiculous for you to go," I pleaded. "You can't stay there, and you'll have to go right back."

"I just want you to get straightened out, Ronald darling," she said.

I couldn't argue too strongly, because I was afraid she would change her mind at the last second and not let me go. And besides, she changed the subject. To T-shirts. She said that even if I wasn't going to be the richest boy in college, I'd have more T-shirts than anyone. It was true. I had plenty of T-shirts, but that had nothing to do with her coming with me.

My father took us to the station. I waited downstairs with my luggage, while he went to the garage. My mother came down wearing a full-length fur coat and a veil over her face and dyed blonde hair.

"When they see me in this outfit, they'll think we're so rich they won't even let you into college," she said. I thought she was overdressed. When my father pulled up in the car, we got in. My mother said, "Ronald thinks I don't look enough like a mother. He was always that way. What did you always say when I came to school on Parent's Day in public school?"

"I don't remember," I said.

"Yes you do, darling," she said. "He always used to ask me 'Why can't you look like the other mothers?'—didn't you, Ronald?"

"I suppose so."

"He was afraid I wasn't motherly looking enough," she said. "You should have been proud of me."

My father wasn't listening. His whole life now was his car. It was a new one and the first he'd ever owned. He had bought it with the money he had earned in the past two or three years, the same money he was using to send me to college. He had given my mother a little bundle of it, all rolled up and marked with a white wrapper, COLLEGE

MONEY. But, as I said, his car was everything now. As he drove, he kept up a running commentary on his maneuvers. Each time he shifted a gear or turned a corner, he would explain elaborately, saying, "My thoughts on that one were why take a chance in a three-way intersection," or "I handled it that way because there was a Pontiac pressing me from behind."

A porter took our bags at the station and my father first kissed my mother and then me good-by. He told us both to write from college, and he told me not to get too smart and too high-class to suit him. Before he left, he asked the porter if he could make a U-turn in the station. The porter said he couldn't and they got into a brief discussion of driving.

The train was on time. There were bunches of young girls in cashmere sweaters and tight skirts and I began to feel embarrassed about having my mother with me. She still had on the veil. I think if she had taken off the veil, it wouldn't have been so bad. The porter took my mother and me to our seats, which seemed to be pretty far back in the train. "Where's he going?" my mother asked me. "I'll bet he thinks we're lovers or something." She yelled to the porter. "Say, you don't think we're lovers or something, do you?" The porter laughed and said, "Could be, ma'am. You're a mighty young woman." My mother nudged me and winked. "Well, for your information," she said, "this is my son. I'm a fast thirty years older than he is."

"Cut it out, Mother," I said. I'd been through this routine thousands of times, every time I went somewhere with my mother. We sat down. "Well, it could be, you know," she said. "You don't think someone could take us for lovers?"

"No," I said. "And will you cut it out."

Some of the young girls began to drift into our car. It really hurt me to be there with my mother. She caught me looking at them. "Look," she said, "you don't have to worry about me being here. You want one of those girls, you just go right over there."

"Just like that," I said. "Just go over there."

Actually, I don't know what I would have done if I had been alone. Probably sat there just the same. But this way, I was marked as a fellow with a mother and there wasn't a chance.

"You get yourself a girl," my mother said. "And I'll get myself a fellow. Inside of two seconds, I bet I could get one."

"I know," I said, "I know you could."

In a little while, my mother asked the porter if the club car was open. When he said yes, she asked me to come back and have a drink with her. I said I'd rather wait and she said, "I never had to worry about *one* drink. If you have to worry about *one* drink, you're through. I brought up my children that way, and it's what I believe."

We went back to the club car, and my mother ordered whiskey sours for both of us. There were some college girls in tweed skirts sitting at the back of the car. One of them had a guitar and was strumming chords on it. I had the feeling they were staring at us when we came in. I drank my whiskey sour, and my mother caught me looking at the girls. "I know your taste," she said. "I know it like a book. Show me a crowd of girls, and I'll pick out your father's taste and your taste."

"I don't have any taste," I said.

The girl with the guitar began strumming the "Whiffenpoof Song," and the other girls sang the words. My mother ordered a second drink. "You'll be hearing that from now on," she said to me. Then she said she felt like dancing and got up and walked toward the girls. I was going to remain seated, but then I got up and followed her. My mother asked the girl with the guitar if she knew a rhumba. The girl looked at the other girls, giggled a little, and began to play something with a Cuban beat. My mother began to clap her hands and shake her head as if listening for the beat. "You've got it, you've got it," she said. She tapped her feet and then broke out in a dance as if she had an imaginary partner throwing her out. "Wherever I go, I get rhumba," my mother said, a little out of breath. "You've got to give me credit for that." The train took a curve and threw her off the beat, and then a porter came out and said that dancing in the club car was against the rules. "Dancing is," my mother said loudly, "but not what I'm doing. I haven't moved my feet. That's not dancing." She got into an argument with the porter.

One of the girls asked if she was my mother.

"Yes," I said.

"We were trying to figure out whether you were mother and son. Darlene guessed you were a theatrical act."

"No," I said. "We're mother and son."

My mother told the porter to go get the head conductor and they'd see about whether you were dancing if your feet weren't moving. I took my mother by the arm and asked her to come back with me to our car. "Will you *please* cut it out, Mother," I begged. "I'm swaying," she said, "and he tells me I'm dancing. I like that."

I got her back to the car, and we sat down in our seats. "Well," she said, "I got a little rhumba out of it at least. What other mother that you know would do something like that?"

"What was so important about doing a rhumba on the train?" I asked.

She didn't hear me. "If I really wanted to, I could've gotten that porter in trouble," she said. "That's really a new one. I'm swaying back and forth and he tells me I'm dancing."

"He probably thought you were dancing," I said.

"I never heard of that. Even if I *was* dancing, he shouldn't have opened up his mouth to me."

A little later, the lights went out in the car and I went to sleep.

In the morning, we had to switch over to another train, one that led right into the college town. We got a seat next to a shriveled-up little lady who carried a cane. My mother asked where she was from and the lady said "Boonville," which was the town around which the college was built. "Watch this," my mother said. "I can make friends with the devil himself."

Housing for me was one of the things that had been a problem. I didn't know where I was going to live when I got to college. We had reservations at the hotel, but school was beginning in two days, and I had to have another place to live.

My mother asked the woman about Boonville, and the woman said it was an awfully nice town, but that all of the out-of-town college people had a tendency to spoil it. My mother whispered to me, "She doesn't like out-of-towners. Watch how I handle her." That was one of my mother's habits. Whispering almost out loud right in front of the person she was whispering about. My mother asked the woman where she herself lived, and the woman said she lived alone with her unmarried daughter who worked for an insurance company. My mother asked if she had any room in her house, and the woman said it was a big house, but they never liked to take in boarders. "She doesn't take in boarders," my mother whispered to me. "I'll have her eating out of my hand."

A man came around with sandwiches, and my mother bought some for us and also one for the woman whose name was Mrs. Sloan. My mother told her some funny stories, and in a little while the old woman was laughing and slapping her knee. "Your mother is certainly a wire," she said to me. When the train stopped, she said to my mother, "You stop around tonight at our house with your boy, and we'll get him fixed up with a room." My mother thanked her and we parted at the station.

"You see how I handle them," my mother said. "She never had a laugh like that in her life."

We checked into the Star Hotel, which we had been told was the best hotel in the college town. The receptionist was a pretty woman with one arm. She looked up our reservation and told us our room number. Then she asked whether we wanted single beds or a double. "Don't tell me you think this is my boyfriend," my mother said. "Oh, this is too good. This is something I have to tell everybody. I can't get over this. Tell the truth. You *did* think Ronald was my boyfriend, didn't you?"

"Oh," the woman said, smiling. "I guess I knew he was your son all right."

"This is something I can't get over. How old do you think I *am?* If I told you how old I was, you'd probably faint."

"Oh, you're not as old as all that," the woman said. The other women clerks came over and soon my mother had them all laughing hysterically. I sat down because I knew it would take a while for her to get finished. The lobby was full of men who seemed to be there on business. All they talked about was the weather and highways. "Now you go on out there to 31 where it crosses 12 and you see a fork opposite the ham house. Get on 85 . . ." I felt very shaky and unsettled, and it seemed as though I would never actually get around to something like studying. My mother finally promised all the desk clerks bras, which are what my father manufactures, and then we went upstairs in the elevator. "How do you like the way I make friends everywhere I go?" she asked. "Two seconds longer and they would have given me the whole hotel."

"I'd like to get unpacked so I can go over and register," I said.

The bellhop took us to our room. "How did you like the way she asked us if we wanted a double bed? Don't you think she thought we were lovers? In all seriousness, she thought we *were.*"

I unpacked quickly, showered, got dressed, and told my mother I was going to the school to register. Outside, I still had the shaky feeling. I couldn't relax, and I felt smothered. As I filled out some forms, an older student invited me over to his house for a fraternity dance that evening. I told him I'd try to make it, and then I went back to the hotel. My mother had changed into a new dress. "Do I have too much perfume on?" she asked.

"It's pretty thick," I said.

"This particular brand seems thick, but it settles quickly, and in a little while you don't smell anything."

It was getting on toward evening, and it was dark outside. We had dinner in the hotel, and then my mother suggested we call on Mrs. Sloan so I could get settled with a place to live. We got a taxicab and gave the driver Mrs. Sloan's address. As he drove through the small town, my mother said, "It's funny, isn't it, how the very person you don't think will be able to help you helps you. That's why I say it's better not to leave a stone unturned. I'll talk to the devil himself if he'll help me out." The driver went out past the town and into the suburbs and past a miniature golf course. "You wouldn't think that woman could ever laugh and in two minutes I had her laughing." We came to a dark street with one house at the end of it. The lights were on and the driver said, "This is it." We got out of the cab, and the lights in the house went out. My mother and I went up to the entrance and rang the bell. No one answered. "The son of a bitch," she said.

"Let's get out of here," I said. The cab hadn't left, and we took it back to the hotel. "It wasn't her," my mother said. "I'll bet you a thousand dollars it wasn't her and it was her daughter."

"A lot of good it does me," I said.

"I could have had her eating out of my hand," my mother said. "I didn't meet her daughter so I couldn't cope with her."

At the hotel, my mother asked me to come in and have a drink. "It'll make you feel better," she said.

I told her I didn't want a drink. I wanted to go up and read. She said all right, and she'd be up in a little while. I went upstairs and sat on the bed. Then I read for a while. After about an hour, I came down and went into the bar where my mother was. There was a jukebox on, and she was swaying to the music with her head held back as if she were carried away. "Look at my feet," she said to the bartender. "What am I doing, swaying or dancing?"

"I can't really say," the bartender said. "Swaying. Dancing. Anything you say."

"We had a louse on the train who couldn't stand dancing. The world could come to an end and he still wouldn't want you to dance. The ridiculous part of it was I wasn't dancing. I was swaying. Just like I am now. Right, Ronald?"

"I always sway," my mother said to the bartender. "My son will bear me out. Even here where you don't care about dancing, what am I doing? Swaying."

I told my mother I thought I'd like to go over to the clubhouse dance to which the older student had invited me.

"All right," she said. "You can go later. I want you to meet my fella." She put her arm around the bartender. "I'll bet you'd never believe he was my fella," my mother said. The bartender eased away, laughing. "Now he doesn't want to be my fella. Two seconds ago, what were you crooning into my ear?"

The bartender laughed and looked at me.

" 'Those Little White Lies'," she said. "You should hear him sing.

He doesn't know the words, but he loves to sing. He was singing in my ear."

My mother asked me if I wanted a drink, and I said I didn't, but that I'd really like to go to that clubhouse.

"If they like you, you can live there," I said. "You don't have to stay with a Mrs. Sloan."

"Okay," my mother said. "Good-by," she said to the bartender. We went upstairs in the elevator.

"He's cute, isn't he?" my mother asked.

"He's just a guy. I didn't see anything special about him," I said.

Inside the room, my mother opened her closet and asked me what I thought she should wear.

"Maybe you shouldn't go with me," I said.

"You generally like me in something tailored, don't you?" she asked.

"I don't care what you wear," I said. "I really mean it, though. I don't think you should go."

"When you talk stupidly, I can't talk to you. There'll be a thousand mothers there."

"There won't be," I said. "If I come in with my mother, they're liable to think I'm a jerk. They don't want to meet *you*. They *invited* me."

"I'll go there for two seconds altogether. If you're afraid I'm going to stay there and cramp your style, you're wrong. I'll stay there for two seconds."

She went into the bathroom to change. When she came out, I said, "I don't want you to go, Mother," and we had an argument. I told her I knew why she was sending me to college. That it was to make up for the way she'd treated me as a child. I told her I remembered the Negro girl she'd hired to take care of me when she went off with her girlfriend for weeks and months at a time. I told her that once my friend Gordon had come to the house and she'd been lying there in a slip and ordering me to bring her things and Gordon had asked me later, "What is she to you anyway, a stepmother?"

She said that there'd never been the closeness between us that there had been between her and my sister. "You've always had an ugly streak in you your sister never had," she said.

I told her about the country and how she'd sent me down each evening to steal a red rose for her hair and how I hated it and how much it embarrassed me. And as I shouted at her, all the shakiness went out of me and I felt much better. Soon I was arguing all alone, feeling very good, bringing up things I thought I'd forgotten all about. How she'd embarrassed me by making me sing on the stage; how she'd tormented me by waking me up to entertain for company in the middle of the night; how she and my sister would get together and embarrass me about girlfriends. Some of the things I brought up were almost a little nostalgic and my mother was sitting back now, not angry, but a little amazed at how I could remember all these things. And then I told, with a little smile, about the time she had brought a bandleader into our hotel room in Wisconsin one summer and turned on the sink water and thought I was sleeping.

"I was awake," I said, smiling a little. "I wasn't sleeping."

My mother's nose got very fat all of a sudden and her face became contorted. She started to cry, and I said to her, "I didn't mean that one."

She cried for a long time, and then she opened her purse and took out the bills that had been lying on the frigidaire at home the night before, marked COLLEGE MONEY. She counted out a number of them and put them on the dresser. She said it was to pay for college and that she was leaving the next morning. Then she went downstairs to the bar. I stuck around in the room and fell asleep, and the next morning, just as she promised, she kissed me good-by, got into a taxicab in front of the hotel, and left me to begin my first year of college.

Marching Through Delaware

ONE NIGHT, driving from Washington to New York, Valurian, for the first time in his life, passed through the state of Delaware, and felt a sweet and weakening sensation in his stomach when he realized that Carla Wilson lived nearby. All he would have to do is sweep off one of the highway exits; at most she would be half an hour away. Twenty-two years before, at a college in the West, he had loved her for a month; then, in what appeared to be a young and thoughtless way, she had shut the door abruptly in his face. Much later, he became fond of saying it was a valuable thing to have happen and that he was grateful to her for providing him with that lovely ache of rejection. But in truth, and particularly at the time, it was no picnic. He remembered her now as being thin-lipped and modest of bosom, but having long, playful legs and an agonizingly sexual way of getting down on floors in a perfect Indian squat. She had no control over her laugh; it was musical, slightly embarrassed and seemed to operate on machinery entirely separate from her. She had an extraordinary Eastern finishing-school accent, although to his knowledge she had attended no Eastern finishing school. She was an actress; he reviewed her plays for the local newspaper. Members of the drama group, some of whom had been in Pittsburgh repertory, referred to him as the "village idiot." Although she often did starring roles, the most he ever awarded her was a single line of faint praise. On one occasion, he said she handled the role of Desdemona "adequately." He was quietly insane about her; in his mind, the paltry mentions were a way of guarding against any nepotistic inclinations. It was a preposterous length to go to; she never complained or appeared to take notice of it.

Although he remembered quite sharply the night he got his walking papers, he had only disconnected, bedraggled recollections of time actually spent with her. She wore black ordinarily, had a marvelous dampness to her and trembled without control the first time they danced together. "Are you all right?" he kept asking. "Have you perhaps caught a chill?" There were some walks through town, one during which a truck backfired, causing Valurian to clutch at her arm as though it were a guardrail. "Oh, my God," she said, surprised, delighted and not at all to demean him, "I thought I was being protected." Her mother swooped down upon them one day, a great ship of a woman, catching Valurian in terrible clothes, needing a shave. In a restaurant, lit by ice-white fixtures, she spoke in an international accent and told them of her cattle investments and of killings at racetracks around the world; Valurian, still embarrassed about his shadowy face, prayed for the dinner to end. Later, he took them back to his rooming house and lit a fire; turning toward them, he saw that Carla had hopped into her mother's lap and gone to sleep in it like a little girl. He had never slept with her, although she gave him massive hints that it would be perfectly all right, indeed, highly preferred. "Oh, I'd love to be in a hotel somewhere," she would say as they danced. Or she would begin her trembling and say, rather hopelessly, "When I feel this way, whatever you do, don't take me out to some dark section of the woods." Ignoring the bait, he gave her aristocratic looks, as though he were an impeccable tennis star and she was insulting him by the inferior quality of her play. In truth, her dampness, the black skirts, the Indian squats, all were furnacelike and frightening to him. A boy named Harbinger had no such problems. She alerted him to Harbinger, saying she had run into the cutest fellow who lived in town and always hung his argyle socks out on the line where the girls could see them. It was as though she were giving him a last chance to get her into hotels or to sweep her out to cordoned-off sections of the woods. But he had always seen his affair with Carla—could he dignify it with that phrase?—as a losing battle, with perhaps a few brief successful forays before the final rout. One night, for example, he surprised her by batting out a few show tunes on the piano, singing along, too, through a megaphone, a talent he had kept up his sleeve. She almost tore his head off with her kisses, although, in retrospect, they were on the sisterly side. Toward the very end, he showed up on her dormitory steps with an alligator handbag, a Christmas gift she didn't quite know what to make of. Inevitably, she summoned him one day to talk over an ominous "little something"; polishing up his white buck shoes, he walked the length of the campus to her dormitory where she told him she had stayed out all night with the argyles boy and that she would not be seeing Valurian anymore. He called her a shithead and for weeks afterward regretted being so clumsy and uncharming. There began for him a period of splendid agony. The first night, he was unable to eat and told a German exchange student—who had suffered many a rejection of his own—that any time he couldn't get fried chicken down he was really in trouble. A week later, he strolled by to see Carla as though nothing had happened; she told him that Harbinger was more in the picture than ever. She started off to rehearsals and he tailed her; she broke into a run, and he jogged right after her, as though it were perfectly normal to have conversations at the trot. On another occasion, he lay in wait for her outside the theater, grabbed her roughly and said, "Off to the woods we go. I have something to show you, something I'd been unwilling to show you before."

"What's that?" she asked, teasing him.

"You'll see," he said. But she wrenched herself away, an indication that Harbinger had already shown her plenty. He stayed away then for several months, taking up with a green-eyed Irish girl who had great torpedoing breasts, thought all Easterners were authentic gangsters and with no nonsense about it simply whisked *him* off to the woods. One night, before graduation, he went to a dance, feeling fine about being with the Irish girl, until Carla showed up with the argyles man. He continued to dance, but it was as though his entire back were frozen stiff. He saw her only one more time, paying her a good-bye visit and asking if he might have a picture. "No," she said. "I don't understand it," he said, "a lousy picture." But she held fast—and that was that.

He left school, went through the army as a second lieutenant in grain supply and then, for ten years or so, led a muted, unspectacular life, gathering in a living wage by doing many scattered fragments of jobs. He was fond of saying he "hit bottom" at age thirty, but, in truth, all that happened was that he developed asthma, got very frightened about it, saw a psychiatrist and, in the swiftest treatment on record, came upon a great springing trampoline of confidence that was to propel him, asthma and all, into seven years crowded with triumphs in the entertainment world—a part in a play that worked out well, a directing job that turned out even more attractively, films, more plays, television work and ultimately a great blizzard of activity that took a staff to keep track of.

From time to time, he had heard a little about her, not much—that she had gotten married quickly (not to the argyles man), had a child, gotten divorced. That she had settled in Delaware and never left. Although from time to time the thought of her flew into his mind, it was never a question of his wallowing in this particular memory. Valurian had little cause to feel slighted by love. Along with the chain of professional triumphs had come a series of romantic ones, a series of women, each attractive in her own way, ones that Carla no doubt had seen in films and read about in columns. He had as much confidence with women as he did with his work. He *owned* women. When he thought of Carla at all, it was never to wonder what she was up to, but to speculate on whether she read his reviews, the interviews with him, the column mentions. What indeed could she really have been up to all those years? In Delaware. Bridge? Scrabble? The Johnny Carson show? Getting a taste of the sweet life via the *Times* theater section? The marriage, no doubt, had been to an accountant. Or was it a stockbroker? Saturday nights, spell that nites, with three or four other young marrieds, Delaware young marrieds, young married Delaware swingers at Delaware's top nite spot. He could imagine those couples, too. The jokes. The talk about switching. And salves. Bedroom salves. They all used bedroom salves. She had been divorced. After that, she had probably tried to land another second-rater. She loved the theater; no doubt she'd go after a local theater notable this time, one who whipped together Chekhov plays and was terribly temperamental. Wore heavy Shetland sweaters. Get rid of the taste of that routine stockbrokering first marriage. What *really* could she have been doing with her time? Did she have any idea that Valurian had been to the White House? That, indeed, he was driving back from the White House now. And that it wasn't his first trip. He'd met De Gaulle. Did she know that he had slept with actresses whose names would make her gasp? That he *turned down* dinner invitations from Leonard Bernstein. Lennie Bernstein. How could he explain to her that the only sadness in his life was that the circle of important people he had yet to meet was an ever-shrinking one and soon to be nonexistent? Oh, she had read about him, all right. How could she have escaped knowing about him, following his career? Everyone knew about him. And when you consider her special interest in Valurian . . . she probably kept a scrapbook. Far from a preposterous notion. How many lonely, divorced nights had she spent kicking herself for not having spotted the seeds of it in him, his possibilities? How close she had come to an extraordinary life and never, at the time, realized it for a moment. What did that say about her judgment? She probably wondered about that every day of her life. Hadn't she loved the theater? He owned the theater. He was the theater. And whom had she passed him up for: An argyles man. Every time she thought of that little stunt, she probably chewed at her wrists in agony. And she had *summoned* him to give him the news. And then refused to give him a picture. *She,* get this, hadn't wanted to give *Andrew Valurian* a picture. It was almost too much for the mind to comprehend. It would take a computer to handle that one. Well, she was probably in a constant sweat about it, night after night in Delaware. In Delaware, mind you. How she must have punished herself all those years. And here he was, Valurian, coming back from the White House on his way to a party at Sardi's that was probably going to bore him to death. How many years of her life would she trade to show up at that party? On his arm. Two, five, a decade? To top it all off, he was only half an hour's drive away from her at most. God, if she knew that . . . If he ever drove by and called on her, stopped at her dreary, divorced

Delaware house, at the very least she'd go right into shock. Faint dead away on the spot. More likely, she'd tear off her clothes and fly at his groin. Would she in a million years be able to find her voice? Never. So she would probably just kneel at his feet and pray and let it go at that. The poor lost miserable wretch.

Oh well, he thought, screw her, and drove off for the big city.

Sex

The Gent

(featuring Harry Towns)

SHE WAS A PRETTY, dark-haired thing with big black eyes, the daughter of his friend Gus, and he had watched her grow up on the beaches of East Islip. From the porch of the cottage he rented each summer, Harry could see her fly along the water's edge, doing cartwheels, leaping over dunes, practicing ballet steps from *The Nutcracker*. She giggled and fought with her friends and tried on makeup, and when she got older, she worked at the farm stand. Then she went off to one of the good schools. But she came back for the summers. And when she had matured into a young woman, Harry got the feeling she was interested in him. Grace was nineteen—well built, with long legs, sizable breasts and a playful-looking rump—when this notion of his took hold. She had the good schools in her voice, too, which was a weakness of Harry's and, as far as he was concerned, put her over the top.

Her parents owned a summer house right down the beach from Harry's cottage. Whenever they gave a barbecue, they would invite Harry over, and at some point in the evening, Grace would corner him and with her black eyes shining ask him about the communications field and how to break into it. Or sometimes she wouldn't ask him about the communications field but would poke him and tickle him and tell him to loosen up. One day he drove her into town to get some lighter fluid for the barbecue. With her skirt drawn back, her hands in her lap and her tanned legs kicked up on the dashboard, the pressure was so intense he almost had to stop the Jeep. At the checkout counter, she said she had gotten her own flat in the city and why didn't he come by and say hello. When he said he'd think about it, she let out a frustrated growl and pinched his ass in front of three customers. So it wasn't his imagination. She was there for him. Yet he kept his distance. He was a good deal more than twice her age, which explained it somewhat but not entirely, since he was no stranger to young women. Also, he lived alone and was divorced, so he was covered in that department. And it certainly wasn't fear of her mother, Nora, who had actually encouraged him. Nora was a cool and complex woman with a million

271

thoughts colliding behind her troubled forehead. Whenever she saw Harry and Grace together, she looked on with interest. One day she took Harry aside and said, "I don't see why she can't have a mentor."

So Nora was on board, but the main reason he stayed away from Grace was that he did not want to hurt Gus. Gus and Harry had been friends since high school and had played on the same football team. Gus was a great big curly-haired bear of a man who smoked a dozen cigars a day, ate anything he wanted—despite a dangerously expanding waistline—and generally enjoyed life tremendously. He was Harry's hanging-out buddy, and they got together in Manhattan at least once a month. As a union official, Gus was entitled to a chauffeur, but he insisted on doing his own driving in the city, even though he was terrible at it. He would pick up Harry in his Lincoln Town Car, and with his cigar waving to make points and sometimes taking a little blow to make things worse, he would somehow weave them safely up to Sylvia's in Harlem, or Wally and Joseph's across town, or all the way down to Little Italy for a feast on Mulberry Street. He fancied himself an expert on food, and Harry, who thought he knew something about it, too, was content to sit back and let Gus do the ordering and be generally seignorial. On the nights they got together, Harry got to mingle with Gus's friends—busted-out jazz musicians, ward politicians from Harlem and medium-level wise guys from President Street in Brooklyn— the kinds of people Harry would never meet in the normal course of things. There were hookers in the mix as well.

Gus's best quality was his loyalty: A friend could do no wrong. Harry had produced his share of stiffs in the movie business, but as far as Gus was concerned, each one was a gem and should have been nominated for an Academy Award. And Harry repaid this loyalty in kind. On one occasion, Gus was accused of mishandling union funds and was forced to take a sabbatical and lie low in Providence for a couple of years. Harry, without being asked, had sent him five hundred here, five hundred there, and Gus had never forgotten it. As it happened, when the heat was off and Gus got his old job back, Harry was busy with a TV series and rarely got to see his friend.

"Now that I'm doing good, you never call me," Gus complained over the phone. "I guess you're one of those foul-weather friends."

As much as he might have wanted to, there was no way Harry was going to sleep with Gus's daughter.

So he bit the bullet and hunkered down and it wasn't that awful. He lived alone in a duplex on Manhattan's East Side that belonged to a wealthy cousin of his who owned an advertising agency and had homes all over the world. Harry paid the cousin a nominal fee each month, a fraction of what the place would have cost had it been rented legitimately. The only catch was that he had to show up to entertain his cousin's clients at lunch once in a while. Additionally, a crew would arrive every couple of months or so and use the apartment as a backdrop for an advertisement, which really set Harry's teeth on edge. That, and the fact that he couldn't have his name on the tenants' directory. There were times Harry felt like a kept woman. But if this was so, he was being kept in a grand manner. The top floor of the duplex was covered by a glass canopy, and Harry slept each night beneath a shower of stars.

At this time of his life, Harry wasn't happy and he wasn't unhappy. He was treading water in the romance department. There was a National Hockey League executive in the building across the street who came over and rolled around with him a couple of nights a week and then went back to her own apartment, an arrangement that suited her as much as it did Harry. Yet Grace was always out there on the edge of his thoughts. More than once he had wondered what it would be like to be in bed with her.

Harry ran into her once on the street and she was only medium friendly. After saying hi and introducing him to a couple of good-looking yups, she went off arm in arm with them. Harry guessed she had a new agenda going and he could close the chapter on her, which left him both disappointed and relieved. Gus told him she had gotten a job as a researcher at NBC.

One day Harry got a call from Gus's accountant saying that his friend had drowned off the coast of Providence. Evidently, he had jumped off a fishing boat to take a swim, got caught in the tide, lost his breath and turned blue. By the time the fishing-boat captain and the Coast Guard got to him, he was dead. There was some question as to whether he actually drowned or had a heart attack, and this never got resolved.

"All I know," said the accountant, "is that he leaves a great gaping hole in our lives that can never be filled."

Harry could have done without the gaping-hole reference. What was he doing, trying out material for a eulogy?

It took a while for the news to sink in. Gus had been such a force. It wasn't so much that he loved life, he *was* life, and it was hard to imagine him gone.

There was a ceremony at Campbell Brothers Funeral Home on Madison Avenue. A large group of Gus's nighttime friends were there, most of them looking gray and haggard in the daylight. A contingent of hard-looking men came up from Miami Beach. Grace was prettier than ever in her black dress and seemed properly subdued. Nora had a fixed and quizzical look on her face. She'd been aware of some philandering on Gus's part, and the funeral seemed to be just another day at the office for her. After the rabbi had spoken, the accountant followed with a eulogy, and sure enough, he came in with the gaping-hole material. Harry had jotted down some notes of his own on the theme of size —the size of Gus's appetite, the size of his heart, the size of his hopes and dreams—but he was not called upon to speak, which really pissed him off.

After the ceremony, Grace invited a small group of friends back to her apartment, and Harry decided to go along. She lived in a basic one-bedroom flat on the top floor of a downtown high-rise. Harry knocked back a couple of Stolis, ate some crabmeat hors d'oeuvres and exchanged reminiscences about Gus with a press agent. Then he thought he might as well go home. He'd worn a suede safari hat to the apartment and had tossed it on a bureau in the bedroom, but when he looked around, he couldn't find it. Grace followed him into the bedroom, bumped her hip against his and told him not to worry, she was sure it would turn up. All he had to do was drop by the next day and she would have it for him. So she was up to her old tricks again.

He decided to write off the hat, but she was on his mind more than ever. He'd noticed, at the apartment, that she had developed a careless, fidgety quality that made her even more desirable. He lost all interest in the National Hockey League executive.

One night, over drinks at Clarke's, he described his confusion to a small-time hustler named Bobby, who had been a friend of Gus's and who made his living selling hot brooches he got from a jeweler in Vegas. Bobby had been out of town and missed the funeral. Harry told him how attracted he was to Grace and that she'd made it clear to him that she was his for the asking, but that he had stayed away from her because of his friendship with Gus. Bobby, who'd spent six years in prison as a young man, looked at him as if he were crazy.

"Fuckin' guy's dead now," he said. "What the hell are you worried about?"

Well, maybe that's the way they thought in prison, but it had nothing to do with Harry. Gus's death made it all the more impossible for him to go after Grace. What was he supposed to do, step over Gus's body and fuck his daughter? If he'd had any kind of balls, he would have fucked her when his friend was alive and taken the consequences. What kind of swine would do it now?

So he held his ground, and Grace did not make it easy for him. She called him a couple of times to invite him to screenings and sent him a note that read: "You were spotted on Christopher Street by one of my spies, Harry. Why didn't you come over and say hello?"

He ran into her one night at a Christmas party given for network executives. She was standing at the bar, talking to a blonde woman who looked familiar. After studying her for a while, Harry recognized her as being one of the kids Grace had grown up with in East Islip. Her name was Trish, and as a kid she'd been a gawky thing; she still was, except now the gawkiness was under control.

Grace dragged her over to see Harry, and after squeezing him and telling him he wasn't going to get away this time, she disappeared in a swirl of network executives, leaving him alone with Trish.

Straightaway, Harry told her about the trouble he'd been having with Grace and his dilemma.

"She can be aggressive," said Trish in what Gus would have called a whiskey voice. "But I'm sure you'll be kind."

She had silky hair, and Harry loved the way she attacked her cigarette.

They chatted for a while. She said she was a copywriter at an ad agency. Harry remembered her father. Harry didn't like her father very much.

Grace came back and grabbed Harry's arm, tucking it between her breasts, and said that she and her friends were going downtown to check out a new club on Jones Street.

"And you're coming with us," she said to Harry.

She was falling out of her dress and she was painfully beautiful, but her eyes and the shape of her face reminded him of Gus. So he said he'd love to go along but he had to finish a pilot the next morning and would have to take a rain check. She insisted, yanking at his arm, and there was the possibility of a scene, but somehow he managed to get out of there.

He hung around on the street enjoying the fresh air and let a few cabs go by. Then he saw Trish leave the building. She said she was in the same boat as Harry and had to get some copy ready first thing in the morning.

"Can I give you a lift?" he asked.

"Why not, why not," she said with a theatricality that killed him. "Why not, indeed."

He kissed her in the cab and the kiss lasted around seven stoplights, and suddenly he didn't know what part of town he was in. He asked her what she would think about coming upstairs for a drink.

"Why, Mr. Towns," she said, fluttering her eyelashes. "Whatever did you have in mind?"

That killed him all over again.

He paid the cabdriver and unlocked the door of his building. As they waited for the elevator, she glanced at the tenants' directory and wondered why he wasn't listed. He said it was a long story and then told it to her anyway.

"But someday," he said as he unlocked the door of the duplex, "some way, I'm gonna get this apartment for myself."

He poured some drinks and led her up to the bedroom beneath the glass canopy, and then out to the terrace, where you could see the Fifty-ninth Street bridge and listen to the hacking cough of the internist in the next apartment. They talked some more about the spot that Grace had put him in and about East Islip, and he kissed her again and her body went limp as a rag doll's. He'd been prepared for a long, patient seduction and was a little disappointed that it hadn't worked out that way. But the National Hockey League executive had gone off to join the Edmonton Oilers and he had nothing going at the moment, and in Harry's uncertain existence, you took what was offered to you and forgot about tomorrow. So he held her hand and led her to the simple white bed beneath the stars with the mirror alongside that was shaped like a caballero. After undressing her and making love to her face and her hair, he entered her, for his own pleasure, for the love of his friend Gus—and to strengthen his perception of himself as a man of honor.

The Holiday Celebrators

THE MAN NAMED MOSS was sitting in a hotel room on a Labor Day morning with his ears up close to a rented radio. The room was filled with flowers, and Moss, a short man with heavily Brylcreemed hair, was inhaling a tea rose, when a second man entered, his arms full of mountain laurel leaves, throwing winks at Moss.

"I brought you these," said the second man, winking in all directions. "How's it going? Great, I'll bet."

"Put them in that vase over there, Beamer," said Moss, his ears practically inside the radio now. "I don't like the way it's going at all. Why'd you bring me laurel when you know they don't smell?"

"Don't scold me," said Beamer. "The woman said they'd start to smell after the first day. I don't know flowers." He began to wink uncontrollably now, tossing them off at machine-gun speed, hurt and angry ones. When some of the fire had gone out of them, he said, "What do you mean it isn't going well? You're always saying that. You said it last Christmas and you said it the Fourth of July."

"And I said it last Thanksgiving and I was right," said Moss, turning the radio up a trifle and sucking in the tea rose fragrance.

"Oh, you're just trying to scare me," said Beamer. "I'll bet we're in. I'll bet we can call up Trefler and collect right now. What are you going to do with your five thousand?"

"I'm not doing anything with it until I have it," said Moss, twirling the radio dials with fury now. "There's nothing on now but Marlboro commercials. Look, you and Count are going to have to do a bit tonight."

"Don't scold me," said Beamer. "It isn't necessary."

Wearing a 1940s fingertip coat, the man who was called Count entered now, his arms, too, filled with flowers. "Petunias," he said. "Sorry I'm late. Rehearsals. I'm either going to have to give up theater or at least get out of Ibsen revivals. When he bogs down, he really bogs down. Are we in? Can we collect?"

"We're not in," said Moss, flipping off the radio now and thrusting his head into a bouquet of marigolds. "I told Beamer I wanted the two of you to do a bit tonight."

"A bit," said Count. "We're doing the show Off Broadway in a reconverted gymnasium. Did you ever rehearse Ibsen twelve hours straight on a basketball court? Are you sure? All right, I'll do it."

"It's important, this bit," said Moss, his head buried in marigolds. "I keep thinking of last Thanksgiving."

Beamer and Count left the room now and, in the street below, got into Beamer's Volkswagen. "How can you mix in acting with this thing we do?" said Beamer, starting up the car and winking at the gas gauge.

"You wouldn't understand," said Count. "You're not in showbiz."

They drove through city traffic and then out to a suburban area, finally pulling their car to a halt on a small street adjacent to a busy six-lane thruway. A pedestrian trestle arched over the highway, and the two men took their places on this trestle, directly above the cars flying toward the city. Beamer rested a giant flashlight beam on the trestle ledge and Count said, "I'll tell you when."

"Was that a scolding?" said Beamer.

"Don't aggravate me," said Count, with a theatrical flounce, and stared at the highway. The traffic, which had been thick, almost bumper-to-bumper, was petering out, and the cars scurried along now in isolated threes and fours. When one such group was several hundred yards off, Count said, "All right, now," and Beamer, winking in a businesslike manner, flicked on his powerful beam, catching the lead car, a Fiat, square across the dashboard. The small car began to wobble giddily, then finally to swerve, and in doing so, placed itself in the path of an oncoming year-old Cadillac, which caught it solidly, flipped the foreign car up into the air, and then itself swung off the highway and into a red maple tree. Violently twisting about, but unable to avert the melée, came a Lincoln which went into a series of savage rolls and then finally tumbled to a sulking halt, its radio turned up loud to fifteen minutes of Sarah Vaughan. Beamer and Count raced down to the highway, and when they got there, a few tired screams were coming from the wreckage. Beamer sat down on the grass beside the highway, winking languorously, while Count went from car to car peering into each one, fumbling about, and then making checkmarks in a small notebook. A young girl with a lithe figure and gaping wounds emerged from the Lincoln and said, dementedly, "Band-aids. Get band-aids and you can have me."

"I'm counting now," said Count. "I never help any of you."

"Your friend is winking," said the girl with a wild stare.

"He has a condition," said Count.

Other cars began straggling to a halt now and after checking the Fiat, Count snapped his notebook shut, signaled to Beamer, and the two walked briskly to their Volkswagen and fled the scene.

"Christ, where are we going to find a florist open at this time of night?" said Count, as they sped back to the city, violating all speed limits.

"What are those along the highway?" said Beamer. "I don't know flowers."

"Pull up," said Count. "How can I tell from here?"

Count gathered some of the roadside flowers into a bouquet and the pair flew back to the hotel room, their car a rocketing blur in the night.

"Coxcomb," said Count, as he arranged the flowers in a bowl.

"Get them right over to me," said Moss, nostrils quivering. "How'd it go?"

"Fine," said Count.

"We'll get the news at 11:45," said Moss, his head concealed in the coxcomb. Several minutes later, he said, "Beamer, flip on the radio. I'm involved with these flowers."

Beamer flipped on the radio now, and after several flashes concerning Wall Street, the announcer said, "With only fifteen minutes to go before the official end of the Labor Day holiday, the traffic fatality total stands at 395, still five deaths shy of last year's all-time record of 400. With the holiday about to end, there is a fair chance that last year's gruesome record may fail to be broken."

"How many did you say you got?" asked Moss.

"Eight definite," said Count. "One more possible."

"We're in," said Moss. "Call Trefler and tell him we'll be over to collect."

The Operator

LOTITO, WHO HAD FLOWN SOUTH to pry himself away from an engagement gone stale, did not at first break them down into individual girls. He stood in the airport, eyes still sour with sleep, let them wash against him in perfumed waves. He saw them finally in small chattering clusters, then filtered out one at a time, noticing there were more redheads than usual. Cubans, he thought, and it pleased him that he knew this.

The rent-a-car receptionist surprised him with a British accent. Her desk was in an open corridor, battered from all sides by raging trade winds. "Don't you catch cold here?" he asked, setting down his baggage.

"It's everyone's opening line," she said. "But I do begin to shiver a little about now. You're from New York. What struck me about that city was the top-to-bottom phoniness. As a matter of fact, only in Spain do you seem to escape it."

Lotito rented a budget car and told her he was an artist of satirical drawings. Her legs went on and on; he was afraid to think how tall she might be. When she stood up, he noticed her figure fell a fraction below minimum requirements. Still, the British accent and those freewheeling months in Spain put her over the line. No telling what he would run into this trip. He might need loneliness insurance. "How about dinner?" he asked.

"There are plenty of escorts," she said. "But you don't seem as phony as the other New Yorkers. Your work is of high interest, too. Call me."

He drove to a small hotel at the center of the island, the sun, already strong, cutting at his forehead through the windshield. Three years before, on his first trip, he had strolled past the beachfront of this hotel and seen a young girl reach into her bikini bottom for a second to scratch her behind. Lotito had filed the hotel away in his mind for a future visit.

The Spanish desk clerk told Lotito to please report anything improper in the hotel, anything that needed expediting. He was very neatly dressed, in business suit and white shirt, and Lotito wondered if it would be possible to sneak girls past him into the rooms. "What are you an executive of?" he called after Lotito.

"Nothing. I do satirical sketches."

"Have a good time anyway," said the neat clerk.

The bellhop told Lotito he had just missed a young girl who looked just like Joan Collins, wore sunglasses, and each night went charging into the rooms of all single men at the hotel. "Wait a minute," he said, setting Lotito's bags down, "is she still here? Nope, you missed her all right." He cackled and slapped Lotito's shoulder.

"Cut it out," said Lotito. "You're a bellhop."

The boy roared, smacked Lotito again. "She had some pineapples, too," he said. "Out to here. And you missed her."

When the bellhop left, Lotito saw a cronelike Spanish chambermaid peeking at him from the linen closet. Toothless and leathery, her legs, nevertheless, were strong, and Lotito wondered whether he ought to whisk her into his room and offer her five dollars. Then be able to boast that he had had Spanish sex before he was even unpacked. In his stories, he would substitute the twenty-two-year-old Collins type for the crone. He saw himself making the offer only to have the chambermaid dash off, report him to the neat exec below.

Suffocation-conscious since early childhood, Lotito pried at the air-conditioning slats to let in blasts of chilled air. A female voice next door shouted, "It sounds like you're trying to break in here, and I wish you'd stop it."

"Well I'm not," answered Lotito.

"Quit or I'll tell the manager."

Annoyed, Lotito became imperious. "Madam, you've been sadly misled." He tried to imagine her, a hefty New York blonde, stealing a week between the sheets with a Spanish lover. Perhaps she would get her fill of Latins and find the pink-skinned Lotito a novelty. "I guess I was a little noisy," he hollered through the wall.

In bermudas, Lotito ran to the beach, suddenly afraid he would get no sun in three days, have to return, fair and mottled, without his money's worth. The beach mat he grabbed smelled urine-splashed, but he fell upon it, hurrying to get a suntan. He remembered his grandmother's beach advice: "Move closer to the sun where it's hotter." A hotel guest passed by and said, "You've had it, feller. You ought to see yourself."

"What do you mean?" asked Lotito.

"You're blazing red," the man said. "I figure a burn like that will cost you three nights of agony."

"I just got here," said Lotito. "You must be mistaken."

"Your funeral, feller," said the man, moving on.

Three Spanish children and a tattered Spanish-looking dog chased a ball, trotting over Lotito's stomach. "With the whole beach," he shouted, gesturing toward the endless expanse of sand.

A sharp-nosed woman, heavily cold-creamed and sharp-boned, joined Lotito. "I don't know where to put myself," she said, "so I thought I'd come over and socialize. You look like a man of taste and whimsy, my two favorite qualities. Sometimes you meet someone and know you can talk to them. Am I upset! The girl I'm with came down here to meet her fiancé, Charlie. So far they've included me in on none of their plans. They haven't socialized with me once. But do you know why they won't get away with it?"

"Why's that?" asked Lotito, wondering if her behind were sharp-boned, too.

"Because, no matter what any of us believe, we all agree there *is* a Lord."

"I have to giddyap," said Lotito, getting to his feet. "Someone said I was done to a crisp."

"Nice socializing with you," the woman called after him. "I'm the one who thought you were breaking in. I can see I was wrong.

"When I'm taken out to dinner, it's Dutch," she cried.

His skin smarting, Lotito ordered a fruit drink on the hotel terrace, sucked in the salt air, and said to himself, "This is it, what I came for, a swell time." A pretty girl, dramatically tanned, of indeterminate age, sat beside him. He thought it might be the lovely behind-scratcher of three years before, flowered now into womanhood. Shy in the city, Lotito bravely took a breath and said, "Hi there."

"Don't look behind you," she whispered, "but my fiancé is over on the side. He hasn't seen you yet."

A Spanish policeman trotted by on a horse, the animal taking polite, mincing, well-trained steps in the sand. As he reached the terrace, the Spaniard thwacked his riding crop on the railing, testing its strength. "All I said was hello," Lotito whispered back. "I just thought I'd tell you," said the girl, "before Jorgé saw us together."

Lotito moved to another chair and wondered if he hadn't been too abrupt with the cold-creamed woman. Maybe her sharp-nosed religious intensity would lead to frenzied, fanatical, bedroom payoffs.

An elderly man, clear-eyed, waist spilling out of tight Alpine shorts, introduced himself as a Swiss businessman. "But I know your society," he said to Lotito. "Fantabulous country, America. With its hidden persuaders, disappearing lines between the sexes.

"I'll tell you what to do," he said, drawing close, poking Lotito's knee. "Instead of going back, you take a trip through Central Europe. Then write an international thriller, liberally spotting it with lush descriptions of European locales. I love to read that stuff, long descriptive sections on places unknown to me. America wants that and the idea is yours, okay?"

"I can't really spare the time," said Lotito. "And it's not really my line. I'm in illustrating."

The Swiss's face reddened. "I give him an idea . . ." he said, neck bloating, beginning to take short, angered breaths.

"Why get angry?" said Lotito. "You can't expect someone to just drop everything and take up a new occupation."

"Son of a pitch American," said the Swiss.

The sun suddenly hopped beneath a cloud as though yanked by a stagehand, and Lotito returned to his room; two extra beds had been moved in, giving him four, erasing all walking space. He fell upon one and grew panicky that all might go unused, that he would have to spend the entire vacation in the room with four empties. He saw himself messing up three each night to at least let the chambermaid know there had been mischief.

Craving sensuality, Lotito walked toward the great luxury hotel nearby, breaking into a trot when he spotted its marquee. A network of female activity buzzed about the pool. Two tanned blondes with yachting caps and thin-slivered swimsuits dipped their toes in the water, exchanging French phrases. Lotito saw himself being invited into their circle, taken along on *nouvelle vague* Riviera cruises, being thrust into the center of subtle tangled relationships, all involving bored, casual, pointless Seberg-type lovemaking. When one broke free to get hot dogs from the grill, Lotito rushed forward, pointed to the dogs, asked, "They as hot as they look?"

"Crude approach," said the girl, who rejoined her friend. Clasping hands, they giggled, gave each other swooping kisses in the neck, and then walked toward the lobby, each with a hot dog, young golden buttocks trembling in the sun. So what, Lotito told himself, remembering entire passages from a popular sex guidebook: There'll be some who won't respond, others who will.

A thick-featured brunette with spaced teeth sat beside Lotito. Her body, tapered and willowy, was out of joint with her face, as though she had borrowed it for the trip. "Both of us seem to be new," she said. "I'm a designer of smart clothes angled for the junior missy trade. You might wonder how one so young can occupy a position of such responsibility.

"Well," she said, hanging her head with a blush, "the truth is I got myself a lucky break." Bad breath whistled through her teeth, carried by the wind, attacking Lotito. The long plane trip, he thought, forgiving her. But what if it were permanent, the result of nerves drawn taut in the tough, competitive, clothing game. Too risky, he thought, getting to his feet.

"Restless," he said. "Can't sit still. Maybe I'll see you around." The breath would probably keep her dateless, chained to the lobby. If all else failed, he would come by late, casually offer her dinner mints. A middle-aged man with bloodshot eyes and biblical hair stood beside Lotito and asked, "Pick up any quail?"

"I'm down here for a rest," said Lotito.

"I once knocked off a peace marcher, both of us standing, in the living room of her pad. I'll never forget it."

"How come you tell that to someone right off the bat, when you've just met them?"

The man cocked his head at the sky, as though looking for an answer in the clouds. "Proving my masculinity," he said.

"You're a frank guy," said Lotito. He thought of throwing in the towel, relaxing, asking the man to take a drive, the two of them exploring the island, checking out grotto ruins, watching the peasants gather up the harvest, perhaps getting invited to native huts for educational good times. Later, they would do masculine things: eat a steak dinner and watch the fights, debate the Commie menace.

Far off, beyond the hotel, Lotito spotted an airline hostess walking barefoot along the beach, hips metronome-like, shoes in hand, legs muscled from contemplative toe digs in the sand. "Got to keep bouncing," he told his new friend and followed the girl to some black seasplashed rocks retained by the hotel for their scenic wonders. She turned her face to the sun and sat on one; Lotito worried it would soak her bottom.

Whirling when he approached, she said, "My dress fool the boys. I really Sponnish, down here for the cosmetics convention." Her skin was caked-up, raw. Exploited by rouge barons, thought Lotito. She seemed more nervous than Lotito, whipping out a walletful of pictures, old boyfriends and cousins in the Navy. Communion stuff, too. He told her his name was Luther Lotito and she said she had just been ditched by an American gas executive after seven months. "Why he no love me any more, Lootz?" she asked, breaking into a tattered, caked-up cry.

"Crazy guy, I guess," he said. The tears failed to touch him, instead gave him confidence. "I'm in a small hotel nearby," he said, taking her slippery hand. "Why don't we have a drink there." She said she had to catch the public bus in two hours, but why not. In the luxury hotel lobby they could not, for a few moments, find the exit to the street, and Lotito found himself breaking into a panicky run, hauling the girl behind him. On the street finally, the girl said, "Have you ever been with a virge, untouched, like her mama made her?"

"There have been all kinds," he answered.

Lotito sat her in his room and went to the terrace for heavily spiked fruit-punch concoctions. The bar girl mixed them, then began to arrange leaves into delicate tropical latticeworks, one to adorn each drink. "Skip the fancy stuff," said Lotito, gathering them up incomplete.

He found her perched on one of his four beds, barefoot, hugging her legs. "I don't tell you the truth," she said. "I'm no virge. I sleep with him for seven months, and when we are finished, he keep me away from his 'merican friends. And now, a Sponnish boy in my town won't even look me in the eyes."

"Then the Spanish people are nuts," said Lotito, feeling he had said his first good thing in years.

They finished their drinks and Lotito flung her back on the bed. Stiffening, she said, "Switt kisses, Lootz. I only like the switt ones." Worried about her skin, he kissed her gently, and she whispered, "Don't get me pregint, Lootz." He made love to her imperfectly then, stopping in midflight, after which she said, "You very nice, Lootz. Otherwise you send me back pregint."

On the way to the bus station, she invited him to a festival in her mountain town, giving him elaborate traveling instructions. She would dance with Lotito, proudly flaunting him at the gas exec. He said he would be there and then excused himself with a headache, leaving her to wait an hour and a half for the bus. What's wrong with me, he thought. She's a human being, a person. Yet she might as well be a valise. Why can't I hear her. Why can't I give a shit about her.

And I'm not fulfilled either, he thought, returning to his hotel. In the room, she had remained tented beneath the sheets; he had seen more of her on the hotel rocks. He walked into a small shop, hunting curios for two hospitalized aunts. The clerk, a young blonde girl with straggled hair, said, "Well, of course, honey chile, bless yoah dear old heart." She switched then to a Viennese accent, did a little cockney imitation, returned to the Mississippi routine. Charmed out of his boots, Lotito told her he did cartoons for a big American syndicate.

"You do," she said, leaning forward. "I'm not as wicked as I sound. Maybe next year I will be. I'm age nineteen. I've had one affair, one and a half, really. The half just broke up, wham bam thank you Sam. Goddam. I'm just going to party, party, then off to Italy for some real giggles."

A bell rang; the girl began to close the shop, carrying giant medieval planks and sliding them against the doors. She wore a flowered shift, close to underwear. Suddenly she leaped up and began to chin herself on one of the planks. "Used to be able to do twenty of these," she said, legs tucked up behind her. Lotito, with dry throat, thought he was in love with her. "Perhaps we could have dinner," he said.

"Can't manage it, honey chile," she said. "Daddy no let. He's right inside. Got to just party, party with old friends. Want to buy something?"

"How could I concentrate?" he said. She lit a cigarette, let it dangle from her mouth and with hand on hip, said, "Ave ze steef uppair lip, bébé," and gently shoved him outside. The French routine was her weakest, but he loved her anyway.

Back in his room, he stared at the Lootz bed, finally covered it with a blanket and lay down on a second one. The air conditioner spread a film of chilled air over his body; he hugged himself in terrible loneliness. Sleeping awhile, he awoke in blackness, the night making him tremble; yet somehow he was cheered, nervous, expectant. He shaved, body still chilled, skin stinging with first day suntan. Almost dressed, head reeling with adventure, he leaped in socks from bed to bed. On the terrace, the air was perfumed, dangerous, smelled of fruit. He asked the bellhop where to eat. "Our penthouse, sir, delicious veal."

"But you're only two stories high."

"There's one up there," said the boy.

There was one, too, small, wicked, candlelit, much guitar music. Lotito swilled two Gibsons, asked the waiter about steaks. "We are a veal house, sir," he said with an insulted heel click. Lotito ate lightly, then spotted two young girls a table away, talking intimately, both with deep bangs. The Gibsons still alive in him, Lotito decided to take them on as a team, something he had never done before.

"I'll be frank," he said, standing at their table, some old movie dialogue returning to him. "I'm all alone, quite lonely. I wonder if you would allow me to show you my favorite city." Heads together, they conferred, said why not, they'd be delighted. "And I'll just take care of this," said Lotito, spearing the check.

In the cab, he slipped an arm around each, felt rims of foundation garments; he horselaughed to himself, exultant that he had landed a team. The girls said they were nurses; Lotito permitted himself a fantasy in which both were in his room, using many beds, the girls antiseptically clean, unshockable, perhaps wearing uniforms for extra thrills.

They began to speak of Sweeney, an orderly from psycho. "Some of the things he pulls can make you split a gut," said one. Her friend said you really had to know him to appreciate his wackiness. Lotito joined their laughter, gave them benevolent squeezes, an indulgent uncle, charmed by two capricious nieces. He suggested an old Spanish mansion, converted to a night spot, full of trellises, romantic balconies, blackened secret nooks. You had to ring a buzzer for admission. Lotito lifted one so she could reach it, found her leaden, massive-thighed beneath her peasant skirt. He felt a blink of electricity in his crotch, wondered if he had awakened a sleeping hernia. "That's cute," she said as the doors slid open.

"A table for my two friends and I," said Lotito and was led to a darkened many-sofaed room where he spotted the hot-dog blondes of early afternoon. Spanish lovers caressed their bare feet. "What goes on here?" asked one nurse, when they had finished drinks. "A great piano player in the next room," said Lotito. "Yeah," she said, "but what goes *on?*"

Anxious to please, Lotito swept them from club to club: an old steamer turned into an atmosphere-rich jazz den, a bongo palace concealed behind a raging waterfall. In the munitions room of a fabled island fortress, now a kosher snack bar, one nurse spoke again of Sweeney's capers, the night he hid the psycho ward bedpans.

"I don't think I'll ever come down here again," said her friend. "I think it stinks down here."

"You have to adjust to it," said Lotito. They spurned his offer of a nightcap at his place ("We couldn't, don't have our flats on"). Gracious, he let them off at their hotel. A little bow and a flourish. "That's *la vie,*" he said, waving them off.

Beneath a lamppost, his loneliness checked, Lotito looked at his watch, grew quickly restless. What if Sweeney had gotten a sabbatical, sat in their room this very moment awaiting orgies. Perhaps he should have tried to split them. Pure as a team, divided they might be ribald, devil-may-care.

Vacant, rudderless, Lotito wandered into a nearby gambling casino, pictured himself ironically winning fortunes, the least of his worries, having to return to his hotel in monied loneliness. A bespectacled tourist made pretentious dice-throws. "A little under-the-armpit action," he said, hurling them out on one roll. "The behind-the-ear double-twist," he hollered on another. Disgusted, Lotito bet against him, won two out of three times, began to pile up hundreds.

Ashes from Lotito's cigar dropped on the table; a head croupier ran out, scooped them up with a tiny silver dustpan while the action froze. "You were supposed to tip him, sport," said the man of self-conscious dice throws. "Up yours," mumbled Lotito. The croupier thought he said "pair of fours," slid Lotito a pile of chips when eight the hard way showed. What do I need it for, Lotito told himself, cashing in.

Outside the casino, a blonde in tightly braided coiffure lit a cigarette. Her evening gown fit sleekly, ice-white, her behind high, tight, self-assured. Lotito pictured her sliding in and out of affairs, unmarked, always poised. An Ava Gardner unheralded. Sixty per cent beyond his reach. Yet the gambling sounds made him reckless. "The action's good," he said, avoiding her eyes.

"Oh, is it," she said, strangely girlish, touching his wrist. "Look, this is going to sound odd. I was supposed to meet my boss down here, but then he wired he couldn't come. Whatever you're thinking, forget it. He's ninety-five and a half and couldn't even if he wanted to. Anyway, I'm dying to go into the casino. I've never been in one and I wouldn't dream of stepping in there alone. Would you take me in. I promise not a peep out of me. I have ten dollars of my own I want to bet on something."

"My pleasure," said Lotito, extending his arm. *"Entrez."* At the crap table, she reached for her ten. "Fool around with this," said Lotito, handing her fifty. She lost it on a roll. "Happens," he said, chuckling, handing her fifty more. She bet in the same style he did, against people's faces, personalities. Hundreds disappeared. "Are you sure this is okay?" she said, squeezing his arm. "You win, you lose," he said. Sickened, he went to cash a check, five minutes later cashed another.

Envisioning two sixes, a thirty-to-one shot, he reached for a chip and she stayed his arm. Double six showed. "I've got to be allowed to play my hunches," he said. "I was being economical," she whispered. A third check perished; enfeebled aunts would have to be wired for the hotel bill.

"Maybe women bring you bad luck," the blonde said as they left. "I don't believe those fairy tales," he said, hailing a cab. Whisking her to the trellised night spot, he hustled her into the blackened, many-sofaed room, began to kiss her arms and neck, rushing to recover his hundreds. "You're going too fast," she said. "What about romance?"

"Maybe you're right," he said, drawing back. "All right, tell me about yourself."

"Not much doing," she said. "City apartment, two roomies, both of them nuts on men, real sleepers. Personally, I can't see it. I have this dream, about once a week, in which someone is chasing me, some kind of monster. I run ahead screaming; always wake up in a sweat. I can't figure it out. I went out with a psychiatrist once. He said it had something to do with sex. But you know how crazy they are. I just don't care about sex, so how could I be dreaming about it. I can live without it beautifully."

"Perhaps there's never been the right one," said Lotito. They danced now, barefoot, swaying gently in one place. She tolerated his hands on her rear, unaware of its treasured status. "Must you breathe so hard," she whispered, following a dip. Slashed, he saw a picture of his chips going up in smoke. "If you just hadn't stopped me on that double six call."

"Are you still making a fuss?" she said. "You lost around thirty dollars."

"Is that all you counted?" he said, enraged. "Do you know how much I blew, the hundreds? For that I'm taking you home."

"Perhaps if you'd slow down," she said, the cab skidding into her hotel driveway, "our relationship might grow."

"I have no time for relationships," he said, paying the driver. "Not in three days."

In the empty street, he wanted to reel the evening back, start all over. He thought of running back for the blonde, blowing all three days on her, hacking his way through to shy exploratory kisses by vacation's end. He would calm her fears, polish her off in the city. At the very least, there would be introductions to her roommates, both certified sleepers.

Elite Spanish couples came pouring out of a thickly hedged estate, the girls debutantes, thin-waisted, hips overspilling, bosoms heavily poured, trained from birth to honor men. Hidden by day, they lived after dark when the streets were bare, rich laughter for their dates, defiant looks for straggling Yanks.

He thought of returning to the casino, gambling with fury till his crumpled remaining fives turned back to hundreds, that way winning back the night. He wondered if the sour-breath designer of early afternoon were still in the lobby, her mouth possibly sweetened by double cuba libres. Would she snap him up if he sauntered by? He saw himself calling the long-legged rent-a-car wench, suggesting a predawn ocean skinny-dip; if she hesitated, he would feign surprise, call her chicken. Surely the desperate, sharp-boned hotel socializer had remained dateless to the last. Perhaps at night, she would shed her cold cream, talk less, crave romance, blind to its source.

Lotito stumbled along, reached a ruined street, its hotels gone to seed. A girl ran out of one, breathless, handsome legs foaming in a white pleated skirt. Her hair was auburn, bristle-thick; she seemed to be holding her clothes on. "Can I walk along with you?" she asked, taking Lotito's arm. "Let's hustle, there's a maniac in there. We had a date. I was a couple of hours late, you know, fooling around. He's in there and I swear he tried to kill me. Spanish guy. They're all like that."

She said she was a French-Canadian girl, lived in a small town near Montreal, which was fine until the Italians moved in and spoiled it. "They're greedy, you know, and not very clean. Not like the Swedes we have, although they tend to be a little on the sneaky side. Of course, you've got your hands full with your Negroes and Jews." Her musty thick-bristled hair smelled of Canadian barns.

Oddly, Lotito found her prejudiced views erotically stimulating. They walked arm-in-arm, the girl peering back over her shoulder now and then, Lotito moving evenly, lest a false move send her up in smoke. You try and you try, he thought, and nothing happens. Then you sit back and presto, this! He felt he had learned a lesson. From now on, no forcing, just sitting back.

"I don't think he's following us," she said, with a final backward glance. "Look, I wouldn't go back to my hotel if you gave me the whole vacation free. Do you mind if I bunk in with you, just for the night? Tomorrow I'll get right out of your hair."

"What the hell," said Lotito. "I've got a few extra beds."

In his hotel, the clerk was asleep; Lotito slipped over the counter and got his keys, slipped back, and led her to his room. Inside, with one swift motion, she yanked free her dress, stretched high in bra and expensive panties, then said, "Ooops, too many drinkies," and vomited on the pillow. Lotito went into the bathroom, stood there in darkness as though waiting for an all-clear siren, then returned. "Sorry, darling," she said, snuggled into a second bed. "Snooze time. Tomorrow, after I've used your sweet paste, I'll give you a big kiss."

"You couldn't help it," he said, flicking off the light. He stayed awake, in half an hour, with held breath, slid in beside her. "No touching," she mumbled, "or more whoopsie." He returned to his bed, stayed there awhile, then dressed and tiptoed outside. The night sky was breaking up, like puzzle pieces. For some reason, the gambled-away money bothered him more than ever now. He figured it out to six weeks' salary. There was a little left.

An all-night store was open, several blocks from his hotel. He walked inside, spent half his remaining money on a transistor radio, Japanese. He took it unwrapped, the sound unsampled. In the empty streets, he kept it on low to far-off Latin music. A car passed him, slowed down, followed him awhile, then ejected a girl in elaborate bouffant hairdo. It went with much taller women. She lit a cigarette, trailed him a few steps, then said, "You lookin' for good time. I do you, you do me, the works."

"My hotel's out," he said. "No women allowed."

"Follow," said the girl.

She led him to a dump along the ocean bay. Shells of crippled cars, piled up sinks, a cracked bidet. Staring, blank-socketed TV sets. "You have present for Sheena?" she asked. He gave her fourteen dollars, all he had. The radio was picking up police calls. She bared her bodice, propped him against a fence, did half a dozen measured-off things to his body. Once, with the bay whispering, he touched her hair. "No mess," she said, tapping his hand.

Bracing himself against the fence, he decided it was simply not working out and there was no sense forcing it. But in the morning, he would get up bright and early, do things right and this time *really* have himself a ball.

The Investor

SINCE THERE WERE NO open beds at the hospital when he arrived, the man had been put temporarily in a room used for storing defective bottle caps. Seven days after his admission, he lay there among the caps, his eyes bulging sightlessly at the ceiling. A bowl of Spanish shawl fish stood on the table beside him with a note against it that said, "Your favorites, from Mumsy." Four doctors conferred in low voices around him and when the specialist from Rochester arrived, they broke their circle to help him off with his coat. The specialist was a neat man with little feet, given to clasping his hands behind his back, rocking on his heels, making smacking sounds with his lips and staring off over people's shoulders. No sooner did he have his coat off than he was rocking and smacking away, his glance shooting out of the room into the midday sun.

"I'll tell you frankly," the resident doctor said to him, "I didn't want to go out of the house." He was a nervous middle-aged man, not technically bald but with patches of hair scattered carelessly about his head. "We've done a pile of work on him and I say if you don't have a specialist in the house, you're not a hospital. But it *is* a baffling and everyone kept saying bring in Rochester and I do agree you get freshness when you go outside. Keep going outside though and you're not a hospital. In any case, the house has done it all, Doctor. Blood, intestines, heart, neurological. We don't get a sign of anything. Come over and have a look at the bugger. He hasn't moved a muscle in a week."

"Not just yet," said the specialist, rocking and smacking, his eyes high, glancing off tops of heads now so that the resident doctor found himself looking into the specialist's neck.

"I've heard that you don't look at patients immediately in Rochester," said the resident doctor. "We go right over to them here. Oh well, I guess that's why one goes out of the house."

"Nourishment?" asked the specialist between smacks.

"Yes, I know you're big on that in Rochester," said the resident. "A few nibbles of an American-cheese sandwich now and then. That's all he's taken. We thought we'd go intravenous tomorrow."

"Pulse?"

"Fairly normal," said the resident. "I like your reasoning. I have to confess there was a time I wanted very much to practice in Rochester."

"The patient's temperature?" asked the specialist, looking directly overhead now as though annoyed by a helicopter.

"Irregular. It's one hundred one and seven-eighths just now. We're using the new electronic thermometers. They're awfully good, get you all the way from twenty-five to a hundred and fifty degrees, and they work in eighths. We're fussy about temperature, and record every fluctuation. It's a program the house is developing—Snub Pulse, Study Fever. It's our pet around here, and we thought we might even interest Rochester in converting."

"What was it yesterday?"

"Let me see—" said the resident, studying a chart. "It was one hundred three and five-eighths, down around two points today."

"And the day before?"

"One hundred even," said the resident.

"Tell me," said the specialist, lowering his eyes slightly for the first time since his arrival, "was it by any chance in the nineties the day previous?"

"Ninety-nine and three-eighths," said the resident.

The specialist stopped rocking and his eyes met the resident's full this time. "It held steady at that figure three days before that, didn't it?"

"Why, yes," said the resident. "Right on the button four straight days. You're good. Funny, you think you've got something down pat, temperatures, for example, and far away in another house, there's someone running circles around you. Excellent show, Doctor."

"Plimpton Rocket Fuels," said the specialist, his eyes wide now, his mouth open.

"Fuels?" said the resident. "Is that a hive? I didn't see any sense to skin work, since the whole thing's so up in the air. I just skipped right over it. Our house dermatologist checked him though and found his skin clear."

"Electronics," said the specialist.

"I'm surprised you buy that theory up in Rochester," said the resident. "Why, the radiation level is so low here in Queens, it would take . . ."

"You don't understand," said the specialist. "Electronics. Electronics stock. I'm in it. For seven days your patient's fever chart has followed the exact pattern of Plimpton Rocket Fuels, which closed at one hundred one and seven-eighths today. I know because I called my broker and asked him whether I should stay in."

"I don't know what to do about a thing like that," said the resident. "You think it's mental, eh? We're not equipped to do head work."

"It's a glamour issue, too," said the specialist, peering at the sun. "That means wide swings. Christ, if only he'd been on a good, solid blue chip. All right, I'll have a look at him."

The patient was a neutral-looking man who might have played hotel clerk parts in movies. The specialist took his wrist and rocked back and forth with it a few times as though trying to lead him from the bed into a tango.

"Of course, you see more of these in Rochester than we do," said the resident, "but it seems to me all he has to do is liquidate his holdings. Such a man has no business in the market."

The specialist kneeled now and whispered to the patient. "Are you in Plimpton?"

The patient was silent.

"How many shares of Plimpton do you own?" the specialist whispered.

The patient continued to stare goldfish-like at the ceiling, but then his hands fluttered.

"Pencil and paper," said the specialist.

"We've got everything," said the resident, diving into the bedside table. The patient's hands took the equipment and in a weak scrawl wrote:

Stock Market not for our kind. Drummed into me from childhood. Work too hard for our money. Had a thousand, wanted to put it into Idaho Chips. Remembered Mom's words. Not for our kind. Would have been rich. Once lost a hundred on cotton futures. But no stocks. Thanks for your interest, Jerry.

"But why Plimpton?" the specialist said to the window, crumpling the note. "Of all issues to get on. Gorch Gas, and we'd have a chance. All right, it won't affect anything, but try to get some liquids into him. There won't be any till the board opens tomorrow, but keep me informed as to any changes in temperature."

"We check temps every twelve minutes around the clock," said the resident doctor. "We're very careful about that. You'll have to twist our arms to get a pulse reading from us, but we're champs at temps."

The specialist visited the patient at four in the afternoon the following day. "I know, I know," he said to the resident, "she jumped two and three-eighths today. That stock will give you fits. If you think that's a swing, watch it for a while. You've got to be out of your mind to stay with Plimpton. Still, it's exciting, a crap game every day. Tell me, did he go with it?"

"Right to the fraction. You remember, the stock opened a little soft and he was up taking applesauce. But that wave of late-afternoon buying finished him right off. I've got him in ice packs now. I was up all night with our temps and the Dow Jones index. I thought there might be some more of this. The house is terribly sensitive about epidemics. I came up with an ulcer patient in the ward who was on Atlas Paper Products for three days, but I checked the market today. Atlas went off four even and our ulcer man closed at one hundred three and a half. So I guess the Plimpton fellow is all we've got. You must see much more of this in Rochester than we do."

"I don't want to talk about Rochester," said the specialist. "We've got a sick man and if I know Plimpton, there isn't going to be much time. If I was on one, I wouldn't want it to be Plimpton. Get his wife down here. Maybe she can tell us how this started."

The patient's wife had a vapid but pretty face and a voluptuous figure. "I guess you know your husband's hooked up to the market," said the specialist, his eyes wandering off down the hallway. "So we thought we'd get you down here. Do you know of anything he had to do with the stock market that might have gotten his fever tied on to Plimpton Rocket Fuels?"

"Jerry doesn't like anything white collar," said the woman, flouncing and rearranging her figure on the chair. "I'll give you our whole marriage. He got me on the phone once by accident and we got to talking and he asked me what I looked like and I told him red hair, green eyes and big boobs. So he come right over and we got married. I don't know if he goes to the stock market. He goes to the burly a lot. He says he likes the comedians but I suspect he's looking at boobs."

"You don't feel he's ever diddled around on the big board then?" said the specialist, making soft, speculative smacking sounds with his lips.

"Well, I don't know," said the woman. "Jerry delivers yogurt. He's not in the union so he has to do his deliveries on the sly. He doesn't like anything white collar. Is any of that what you mean?"

"You haven't helped us," said the specialist. "We've got a sick man."

When the woman had flounced off into the elevator, the resident said, "We're only human. What can any house do against opposition like that?"

"She can go to beans," said the specialist. "What's Plimpton doing now, one hundred four and a half? That means it's all up to the President. He's coming over at eleven tonight. You'd better tune in on him."

In his address, the President called for an end to spiteful silences in our relations with the Russians and Plimpton took it on the chin to the tune of a five-and-a-quarter-point plunge.

"I know, I know," said the specialist, getting out of his coat and making for the patient's bed. "His fever's broken and he feels better. Look, I've had this baby since it came on the boards at two dollars a share and if you think Plimpton is going to sit at ninety-nine you're all wet. Did he close with it?"

"Of course," said the resident. "But something's going on in him. We've never seen anything quite like it. Get your ear down on his epiglottis."

The specialist did so and said, "It's a clicking sound."

"Not unlike that of a stock market ticker tape, wouldn't you say?"

The specialist got down again and said, "It goes tick-a-tack-tick-tick, tick-a-tack-tick-tick. Is that the way you get it?"

"More or less," said the resident.

The patient's hand fluttered and the resident dove forward with a pad.

He wrote, in bolder, somewhat less feverish strokes this time:

No connection. Joke. Also do police sirens, foghorns, and Chester Morris. Do you like to kid around, too? Jerry.

"I'd get plenty sore," said the specialist, "but I'm gentle to patients, cruel only to relatives and visitors."

Plimpton picked up only an eighth of a point the following day, but the specialist was grave and irritable. "The worst," he said. "I know it's holding firm in the nineties, but I heard something nasty from a gynecologist friend of mine. He claims Plimpton may buy Tompkin Rocket Fuels. You get a Plimpton-Tompkin merger and our friend will go up like a torch. All right, there's something bothering me and I'm doing my bit now." The specialist picked up the phone and said, "Hello, Connie, look I want to unload Plimpton. No, I'm not crazy. I've got a patient whose temperature is on it and I've got to try to get it down. Maybe I'll get back in when this thing is resolved. All right, Conrad."

"I never thought I'd see the day when I'd let Plimpton soar and not soar with it," said the specialist, his eyes wandering off into a broom closet. "But you're either in the medical profession or you're not."

"I just want to say that I've never seen anything quite like that in medicine," said the resident. "And I want to shake your hand and tell you that it comes not just from me but from all of us."

"There'll be none of that," said the specialist. "Let me see now. Put a call through to the company. I say do anything if you've got a patient who's liable to go up like a torch!"

"This is a new sound in doctoring," said the resident, putting through a call to Wyoming. The specialist grabbed it away from him, smacked his lips a few times and said, "I don't want any board of directors. Get me the company physician. That you? Look, I want to stop that Tompkin merger if I can. I've got a patient, nice lad, whose fever is hooked up to Plimpton and this merger is going to kick him way upstairs and out of business. Yes, it's my first. Heard of a clergyman whose pulse was tied up to the '51 Cardinal fielding averages, but I think that worked differently. I'm vague on it. You won't do a thing? I didn't think so, but I thought I'd give it a try."

The specialist hung up and said, "He says if he as much as opens his mouth, it's socialized medicine. I'm not sure if he's right but I haven't got time to go figuring it out. I'd better take a look at our man."

The specialist took the patient's pulse and said, "I hope he and his wife don't have any little dividends. All right. I know. That's not funny."

A note in the patient's handwriting was affixed to his pajama lapel. It said:

What kind of a soak are you putting on me for this treatment? I forgot to ask about the soak. If it's steep, somebody's going to get it in the craw. Yours, Jerry.

"In our confusion, we forgot to submit a partial bill," said the resident.

"I don't want to talk dollars," said the specialist. "Practice medicine. Did you see me sell my Plimpton?"

"I've seen things I've never seen before."

"I just don't want him going off like a torch," said the specialist.

Plimpton vaulted four points early the next day on the strength of the Tompkin merger speculation, but the rumor was quashed before noon and the stock settled back with a two-point gain. Trading then became brisk, and the net result was fine for the market but unfortunate, of course, for the patient. Rails, utilities, industrials, all had nice gains by closing time. Specifically, Plimpton raced up to 105 3/4 and then the worst happened. At five in the afternoon, the specialist appeared in the hospital and did not remove his coat. "I don't feel up to examining him right now," he said to the resident.

"I want to say something on behalf of all of us," the resident replied.

"I know, I know," he said to the resident. "You're very kind. But perhaps if I'd sold just a day earlier. Or spread a rumor about bad management in the company. You don't think as clearly as you should when you're in the middle of one of these."

"We feel we've been privileged to see at work one of the finest . . ."

"You're very kind," said the specialist. "All right, I suppose we ought to call his kin, the wife, and get her down here."

"Once in a man's life," said the resident, "he's got to break some new ground, to do something out of his deepest heartfelt yearnings. I'm going back to Rochester with you, if I may."

But the specialist's eyes were off somewhere in the isotope ward. In twenty minutes, the wife was there.

"He went at three this afternoon," said the specialist. "We did everything we could, but you can't tamper with the economy. It's too powerful. It was something we couldn't anticipate. The stock got up to one hundred five and three-quarters and then split two for one. He didn't have a chance. When he dropped to the new price, fifty-two and seven-eighths, we hot-toweled him and he did rally a point or two, but when the board closed for the day, it was all over. Look, I know I should hold back awhile, but I'm all keyed up and I'm blurting this right out anyway. You're quite lovely. Have you ever been to Rochester?"

"My mother said all doctors were bastardos, and we paid them in crops, the main one being asparagus spears. Are you sure you're not saying all of this because of m'boobs?"

"I'm a doctor," said the specialist, staring off over her pompadour.

"I ought to collect up Jerry, but I'm not collecting anyone who's always hung out at the burly," said the woman, taking the specialist's arm. "I hope you're a decent type."

"Taking a bride is in the finest medical tradition," said the resident. "I'm backing you both to the hilt and will see to it that the house takes care of Jerry."

With that, the specialist flew out of the hospital with the woman, pouncing upon her once in the railroad sleeper that whisked them northward and once again the same evening, minutes after they arrived at his bachelor duplex in the Rochester suburbs. He held his pounces to two daily through their one-week honeymoon, but on the eighth day of their marriage, the specialist found himself tearing home in mid-afternoon to institute a third, between hospital research and afternoon clinic. The couple then went to five, the doctor giving up afternoon clinic completely. It was only then he realized, at first in panic and then with mounting satisfaction, that they were on a new issue, something called Electronic Lunch, which had come on the big board almost unnoticed but seemed to be climbing swiftly thanks to recommendations from two old-line investment services.

Death

For Your Entertainment

AT FIRST, MR. ORDZ noticed only that the master of ceremonies or star of the television show wore a bad toupee, one that swept up suddenly and pointedly like an Elks' convention cap. It seemed to be a late-hour "talk" arrangement, leading off with a singer named Connie who did carefully ticked-off rhythm gestures: one to connote passion, another, unabashed frivolity, and a third naïveté and first love. The show was one Mr. Ordz did not recognize, although this was beside the point since his main concern was to avoid going upstairs to Mrs. Ordz, a plump woman who had discovered sex in her early forties. In curlers, she waited each night for Mr. Ordz to come unravel her mysteries so that she might, in her own words, "fly out of control and yield forth the real me." Mr. Ordz had had several exposures to the real her and now scrupulously ducked opportunities for others.

Four male dancers came out now and surrounded the singer, flicking their fingers out toward her, and keeping up a chant that went "Isn't she a doll?" then hoisting her up on their shoulders for the finale.

"Doesn't she just hit you over the head?" asked the m.c., pulling up a chair. The setting was spare, a simple wall with a chair or two lined up against it, much in the style of the "intellectual" conversation show. "I'd like to hit you over the head, too," said the m.c., "but I can't and I've got to get you some other way." Mr. Ordz snickered, sending the snicker out through his nose. It was a laugh he used both for registering amusement and also slight shock, and it served the side function of clearing his nasal passages. "All right, now," the m.c. said, "I used Connie to hook you, although I've no doubt I can keep you once you're watching awhile. Hear me now and hear me good. I've got exactly one week to kill you or I don't get my sponsor. Funny how you fall into these master-of-ceremony jokes just being up here in front of a camera and with all this television paraphernalia. Let me nail down that last remark a little better. I don't mean kill you with laughter or entertainment. I mean really stop your heart, Ordz, for Christ's sake, make you die. I've done work on you and I know I can do it."

Mr. Ordz thought the man had said "hard orbs" but then the m.c. said, "Heart, Ordz, stop your heart, Ordz. All right, then, *Mr.* Ordz. For Christ's sake, listen, because I just told you I've only got a week."

Mr. Ordz turned the dial and watched test patterns, which is all he could get at two in the morning. He looked at a two-week-old *TV Guide* and saw there was no listing for a panel show that hour on Tuesday morning and then he called the police. "I'm getting a crazy channel," he said, "and wonder if you can come over and look at it."

"Wait till tomorrow morning and see if it goes away," said the police officer. "We can't just run out for you people."

"All right," said Mr. Ordz, "but I never call the police, and I'm really getting something crazy."

He went to bed then, tapping his wife gently on the shoulder and whispering, "I got something crazy on TV," but when she heaved convulsively Mr. Ordz sneaked into the corner of the bed and pretended he wasn't there.

The following evening, Mr. Ordz buried his head in a book on Scottish grottoes and read on late into the night, but when two in the morning came, he put aside the book and flipped on the television set. "It'll be better if you put me on earlier," said the m.c., wearing a loud checkered jacket and smiling without sincerity. "You'll fiddle around and put me on anyway, so why don't you just put a man on. All right, here's your production number, Ordz. I don't see any point to doing them. It's sort of like fattening up the calf, but I'm supposed to give you one a night for some reason."

The singer of the previous evening came out in a Latin American festival costume, clicking her fingers furiously and doing a rhythm number with lyrics that went "Vadoo, vadoo, vadoo vey. Hey, hey, hey, hey, vadoo vey." She finished up with the word "Yeah" and did a deep, humble bow, and the m.c. said, "It'll go hard if you turn me off. I don't mean I can reach out and strike you down. That's the thing I want to explain. I can't shoot you from in here or give you a swift, punishing rabbit punch. It isn't that kind of arrangement. In ours, I've got six days to kill you, but I'm not actually allowed to do it directly. Now, what I'm going to do is try to shake you up as best I can, Ordz, and get you to, say, go up to your room and have a heart attack. I don't know whether you have heart trouble and another thing is I'm not allowed to ask you questions over this thing. But I *have* researched you, incidentally. It doesn't matter whether I like you or not—the main thing is getting myself a sponsor—but I might as well tell you I don't really care for you at all. You're such a damned small person and your life is such a drag. Now I'm saying this half because I mean it, and, to be honest, half because I want to shake you up and see if I can bring on that heart attack. And now the news. The arrangement is I'm to bring you only flashes on airplane wrecks and major disasters. It was a compromise and I think I did well. At first I was supposed to give you politics, too."

Mr. Ordz watched the first news item, some coverage of a DC-7 explosion in Paraguay, and then switched off the show and called the police again. He got a different officer and said, "I called about the crazy television show last night."

"I don't know who you got," said the officer. "We get a lot of calls about television and can't just come out."

"All right," said Mr. Ordz, "but even though I called last night, I don't go around calling the police all the time."

The only one Mr. Ordz knew in television was his cousin, Raphael, who was an assistant technical director in videotape. He went to see Raphael during lunch hour the next day. It was a short interview.

"I don't think that's any way to get a man," said Mr. Ordz. "I can see a practical joke but I don't think you should draw them out over a week. What if I *did* get a heart attack?"

"What do you mean?" said Raphael, eating a banana. He was on a banana diet and took several along for his lunch hour.

"The television set," said Mr. Ordz. "What's going on with it is what I mean."

"I'll fix it, I'll fix it," said Raphael. "What are you so ashamed of? If you were a cloak and suiter, as a relative I'd come to you for clothes. You won't owe me a thing. Buy me a peck of bananas and we'll call it even. This is a lousy diet if you can't kid yourself a little. And I can kid myself."

"You don't understand what's going on," said Mr. Ordz, helplessly, "and I don't have the energy to tell you."

He went back to his job and late that night, instead of making an effort to stay away, he flicked on the set promptly at two. The m.c. was wearing a Halloween costume. "All right, it's Wednesday," he said, "and the old . . ."

Mr. Ordz cut the m.c. off in midsentence by turning the dial to another channel. He waited four or five minutes, feeling his heart beating and then getting nervous about it and squeezing his breast as though to slow it down. He turned back the dial and the m.c. continued the sentence, ". . . heart is still beating, but what you've got to remember is that . . ." Mr. Ordz flipped the dial again and waited roughly ten minutes this time, squeezing down his heart in the same manner, then flipped back and picked up the same sentence once more: ". . . this thing is cumulative. It looks better for me, it's more artistic, if I bring it off at the tail end of the week. Sort of build tension and then finish up the deal, finish you up that is, right under the wire. What's that?"

The m.c. cupped his hand to his ear and peered off into the wings, then said, "All right, Ordz, they tell me you've been fooling around with the dial and it shocks you that you can't really miss a thing even if you switch off awhile. I don't care if you're shocked or not, and the more shocks the better."

Mr. Ordz stood up in front of the television set then and said, "I haven't talked to you yet, but you're getting me mad. It doesn't mean a damned thing when I get mad unless I hit a certain plateau and then I don't feel any pain. I'm not afraid of heart attacks then or doctors or punches in the mouth, and I can spit in death's eye, too. It has no relation to my size or my weak wrists and abdomen. I'm just saying I'm mad now, and when I am I'm suddenly articulate, fear no one and can get people. I don't care where you are. You've just come in here and done this to me and I swear I'll get you and I know I can do it because there are no obstacles when I feel this way."

"Calm down," said the m.c., lighting a cigarette. "Just sit down. All right, I admit I'm a little rattled now but it doesn't affect anything. I'm in a studio all right, but it's cleverly disguised and no one would guess where we're set up. So all the anger in the world isn't going to change anything. Just calm down awhile and you'll see what I mean. Sing, Connie."

The hard-faced singer came out as a college coed in sweater and skirt. She pawed naïvely at the ground, waiting for the lift music, and Mr. Ordz shouted, "And I don't want to hear her, either!"

"Who told you?" said the m.c., rising in a panic. "That's more work for me. You can't keep a damned secret in television. All right, I suppose you know you can have three alternates. The Elbaya flamenco dancers, Orson's Juggling Giants or Alonzo's Acrobatorama."

"I'll take the Acrobatorama," said Mr. Ordz, shaking his fist at the set again. "But it doesn't mean I'm going along with any of this or that I don't want to get you just as bad as ever. I just like acrobats, that's all, and never miss a chance to see them. Then I'm going to watch your damned news and I'm going to bed." Mr. Ordz settled back to watch the acrobats, who did several encores.

The m.c. came on again. He had changed his Halloween costume to a dinner jacket and he was puffing away at a cigarette. "All right, I'm going to go right into the news tonight. I *am* a little rattled and there's no point denying it. Do you think that this is what I wanted to be doing this week? I just want to get my damned sponsor and get out of here. That's all for tonight and here is your disaster coverage. I like you more than I thought I would and I got them to allow some sports. It's about a carload of pro football players that overturned in New Mexico, but it's sports in a way."

The following day, Mr. Ordz went to see his doctor about a pain in his belly. "It's either real or imagined," he said to the doctor.

"Can you describe it?" asked the doctor.

"It's sort of red with gray edges and is constant."

"It'll probably go away," said the doctor. "If it turns blue, let me know and we'll take it from there."

Mr. Ordz stayed in town that night to see a foreign film about a tempestuous goat farm. When it was over, he went down to the hotel. He was all alone and the TV set was on. His m.c. was dressed like the *La Strada* carnival man.

"I expected this," said the m.c. "The research showed you have to peek under bandages. If a doctor said, 'Your life depends on it,' you'd have to sneak a peek anyway. So I knew you'd stay away from your set tonight, but I also knew you'd have to peek at *some* set. Whoever knocked research is crazy. Now look, forget last night when I said I was rattled. I know one thing. I've got to have a sponsor or I go nowhere. If I could reach out there and personally slit your gizzard I'd do it without batting an eyelash. As it is, I'll just have to torment your ass until you go by yourself. Incidentally, I can tell you the details. Research said you'd be here tonight, so by some finagling around I was able to get on much earlier, almost prime time. You can pick up the disaster flashes when you get home at two. Here's your Acrobatorama and if anyone comes in while we're on, we turn into a trusted, familiar network giveaway show."

When Alonzo's men had taken their third encore, Mr. Ordz took the train home and rode between the cars. At one point, he giddily dipped his foot way down outside the car, but then retrieved it and rode home for the two o'clock disasters.

The following night, Friday, Mrs. Ordz joined Mr. Ordz on the television chaise and showered him with love bites on the nose.

"Hold off," said Mr. Ordz. "I don't tell you things, but I've got to tell you this." He filled her in on the secret channel and the m.c.'s threats, but her lids were closed and she whispered, "You're speaking words, but I hear only hoarse animal sounds."

"I can't get through to anyone because I'm too nervous to say what I mean," said Mr. Ordz. "If I get angry enough, if only I can get angry enough, everyone will hear me loud and clear."

"Wild," she said through clenched teeth. "You're wild as the wind."

"I wish you would hold off," said Mr. Ordz, but his wife would not be shunted aside, and he finally carried her stocky body upstairs, getting back downstairs at 2:30 A.M. The hard-faced female singer said, "He told me to tell you that he had a cold but that he'd be back tomorrow night if it killed him. I don't know his name either. He said he didn't have time to line up a replacement and that you should just go to bed, unless you want to hear me sing."

"No," said Mr. Ordz. "I don't care what you do. I'm not going along with this. I just want to see how far the whole thing carries."

"Oh, that's right, you're the one who wanted acrobats. Do you think I'd do this crummy show if I had something else? But I figure one exposure is better than none and you might have some connections. I also do figure modeling. We're skipping the news tonight. Since you don't want me to sing, I have a modeling session I can still grab. I only do work for legit photogs."

In the morning, Mr. Ordz called in his secretary and said, "It's in defense bonds, savings stamps and cash, but it works out to six thousand dollars and I want my wife to get it."

"So just give it to her then," said the girl. "I don't know what you mean."

"I want you to know that it's for her if something happens to me."

"Don't you feel well, Mr. Ordz?" asked the girl. "You're supposed to put that in a will and it doesn't mean anything if you just tell it to me."

"I'm not bothering around with any wills. I told it to you and you know it and that's all."

"But I can't enforce anything," said the girl.

"Don't argue with me. You just know."

The m.c. was wearing an intern's costume when the show came on much later, and was blowing his nose. "It was a pip all right. I used to get one cold a winter and I guess I still get them. All right, now that it's come down to the wire I'd be teasing if I didn't admit it has crossed my mind that your heart might *not* stop and here I'd be without a sponsor. Research did tell me about the pain in the belly, though, and of course that relaxed me. You're on your way. I get your life tonight, Ordz. Now look, this is the equivalent of your smoking a last cigarette. You're sick of me, I'm sick of you. If you go upstairs right this second and drink a bottle of iodine, the deal is you don't have to sit through the whole damned show. Fair enough?"

Mr. Ordz dropped his cheesettes and said, "So help me God I'm getting mad."

"And believe me," said the m.c., "the show stinks tonight. I do a whole series of morbid parodies of songs, real bad ones like 'Ghoul That I am,' and we've got a full hour of on-the-spot coverage of a combination fire and explosion on a children's school bus. Go upstairs, get yourself a necktie or two . . ."

"I'm getting to the crazy point where I can spit in death's eye," said Mr. Ordz, rising from his chaise.

". . . Rig them up noose-style to the shower nozzle, slip your head in there snugly, and we'll all go home early."

"I'll get you," shouted Mr. Ordz. And with that, he smashed his hand through the television screen, obliterating the picture and opening something stringy in his wrist. Blood spurted out across Mr. Ordz's six volumes of Churchill's war memoirs, sprinkling *The Gathering Storm* and completely drenching *Their Finest Hour*. Mr. Ordz studied his wrist and, until he began to feel faint, poked at it, watching it pour forth with renewed frenzy at each of the pokes. On hands and knees then, he went up to his sleeping wife and clutched at her nightgown. "I erupt, I erupt," she said, in a stupor, and then opened her eyes. "Jeez," she said, "are they open at the hospital?" She got on a robe, and by this time Mr. Ordz had lost consciousness. Blood soaked Mrs. Ordz's nightgown as she gathered her husband up in her stocky arms and said, "God forgive me, but even this is sexy."

At the hospital, the doctor got a tourniquet and bandage on Mr. Ordz, who miraculously regained consciousness for a brief moment and peeked quickly under the bandage. "There are still people I have to get," he said. But then a final jet of blood whooshed forward onto the hospital linoleum and Mr. Ordz closed his eyes and said no more.

When he began to see again, people were patting lotions on his face. "You're getting me ready for a pine box," he said, but there was no reply. More solutions were patted on his face. He was helped into a tuxedo and then lugged somewhere.

Out of the corner of one eye, he saw his m.c. and two distinguished executive-type gentlemen soar out of the top of the building or enclosure he was in. The executives were holding the m.c. by the elbows and all three had sprouted wings. Then Mr. Ordz was shoved forward. Hot lights were brought down close to his face and cameras began to whir. A giant card with large words on it was lowered before his eyes, and one of the lotion people said, "Smile at all times. All right, begin reading."

"I don't want to," said Mr. Ordz, "and I'm getting angry enough to spit in all your eyes, even if I *am* dead." But no sound came from his mouth. The lights got hotter. Then he looked at the card, felt his mouth form an insincere smile, and heard himself saying to a strange man who sat opposite him in a kind of living room, munching on some slices of protein bread, "All right now, Simons, I've got exactly one week to kill you. And I'm not using entertainment talk or anything. I really mean take your life, stop you from breathing. There's nothing personal about all this. It's just that I've got to get a sponsor. But before we go any further, for your viewing entertainment, the Tatzo Trapeze Twins."

The Canning of Mother Dean

It wasn't exactly a question of tossing a little old lady out into the cold. It was more a matter of tossing a *tall* little old lady out into the cold. Aside from her height, Mother Dean was a perfect little old lady. She had lovely gray hair. She wore glasses. She always kept a shawl around her shoulders. She crocheted endlessly. (Since none of the crocheting jobs ever seemed to get finished, it was difficult to tell what she was working on.)

For twenty-five years, Mother Dean had held forth as housemother of the Rho Delta fraternity at Southern State University in Illinois. It was an important spot, since Rho Delta, being a small organization and unable to compete with other fraternities in athletics, went in heavily for tradition. And most of the tradition centered around Mother Dean. At six each evening, for example, the members of the fraternity would gather round the door of Mother Dean's room and sing a song, beckoning her to come to dinner. Mother Dean was always the first to enter the dining room, the first to be served and the first to leave. The chair alongside her at meals was for Dr. Dean, who along with Mother Dean had founded the fraternity twenty-five years back. No matter how overcrowded the dining room became, the chair was kept vacant, and every Sunday, at the noontime meal, the chair was served a chicken dinner.

Mother Dean was not terribly articulate and witty, but she had several winning routines to fall back upon. Whenever a member was without a date on a critical evening, Mother Dean would go over to him, put her arm through his and say, "Don't fret, child. Don't you remember? *I'm* your date." She was wonderful, too, with alumni. On Homecoming Day, she would stand in front of the Rho Delta House and greet each old grad with a glass of apple cider. Many an alumnus who had not been too demonstrative toward her during his undergraduate days would come tearing up the street, scoop her up in his arms and say, "You look younger than ever, Mother Dean. Are you still my girl?"

And each year, after the Homecoming football game and the alumni dinner, after she had unwrapped her gift from the Rho Delta Alumni Association, Mother Dean would be called upon to make a speech. "M'boys, m'boys," she would say. "I want you to know that you're *still,"* and here she would pause for emphasis, "that you're still m'boys." Then she would sit down and begin to cry, and the alumni would give her a thunderous, standing ovation.

Mother Dean, then, enjoyed strong alumni backing, and occupied a comfortable niche in the web of Rho Delta tradition. It seemed amazing, therefore, how swiftly and casually the Rho Delta fraternity made its decision to release her after twenty-five years of service. Actually, it was not the exclusive idea of the Rho Delta fraternity, but more the doing of two brilliant transfer students from the University of Vermont named Line and Campbell. There was no discussing them separately. You couldn't just talk about Line. It was Line and Campbell. They were a team. Line came into rooms first, but that was the only difference between them.

Three months after arriving at Southern State University, Line and Campbell wrote and published a book which filled students in on all possible answers to examination questions that might be asked during a hated course on land taxation.

The book was only the first of the Line and Campbell projects. They would disappear in their room for a week and then emerge, Line first, followed by Campbell, with a new scheme. One involved a local disc jockey program featuring classical records in which male students who sent in fifty cents could dedicate sonatas to their girl friends. Another was a pizza stand on the very fringe of the campus. Line and Campbell were able to get an Italian in from St. Louis to work the counter.

The expulsion of Mother Dean, too, was a Line and Campbell project. After a typical hibernation, they emerged one day with a series of giant charts which they brought to the weekly fraternity meeting. A hint of the urgency of their project came when someone arose early in the meeting to make a motion on mascots, and Line moved to table it. Previous to the arrival of Line and Campbell, parliamentary procedure had been restricted to an occasional argument over "who had the floor." In the recollection of the Rho Delta fraternity members, no one had ever moved to *table* something. And when Campbell rose, grandly, to second the tabling motion, the effect was thrilling.

The team made their case against Mother Dean. It was a sound one, based exclusively on dollars and cents. One of their charts was a Veal Cutlet table. Mother Dean bought hers in a local butcher store owned by a boyhood friend of the late Dr. Dean. The chart showed how a yearly saving of $1750 could be effected by having cutlets trucked in from nearby Madison City. Another was a salary analysis showing how a reasonable reduction of the housemother's salary over the next five years would amount to a saving of $6600. Few had even realized Mother Dean was *given* a salary.

Significantly, Mother Dean was referred to by Line and Campbell in their argument as *Mrs.* Dean. Before uncovering the final chart, Line pointed out that, "It's perfectly obvious to us you can't sort of limp along and make any progress if you're bogged down by all of this sort of meaningless tradition."

"Mrs. Dean," said Campbell, "is a sweet old person, and if you favor that sort of thing, why fine."

"But when it's costing you dollars," put in Line, "and it's perfectly obvious to all that this sort of thing can lead to bankruptcy, it's another story."

With that, the team unfurled the final chart, one which indicated that over the past twenty years, $1600 had been invested by the fraternity in serving Dr. Dean's vacant chair.

"Now, *really*," said Campbell.

"It's this very sort of thing that got us started," said Line. "This kind of pointless ceremony. In our opinion, it's Mrs. Dean who stands in the very center of it."

"God knows," said Campbell, "we're not denying she *is* a sweet old person."

"But if you'll permit us to say so," said Line, "sweet old people finish last. And this is hardly the sort of way to go about running a sound organization. For this reason, we'd like to move that Mrs. Dean be given two weeks' notice and that the fraternity set about locating a younger woman of sound financial judgment to fill the position of housemother."

"And I'll, of course, second the motion," said Campbell.

There was opposition, but it was voiceless and uncertain. For one thing, the fraternity had never been called upon to decide a question of such moment. It was like being asked to vote on motherhood or God. You couldn't just get up and defend either. There was too much to defend. Where would you begin? Also, there was a feeling in the air that those who rose to oppose the measure might be forced to sit down by some mysterious tabling motion introduced by Line and Campbell. Finally, Kittels got up. He was a Wyoming boy who frowned upon "book knowledge," boosted common sense, and spent long hours shining his shoes to a furiously high gloss. It was said he could lighten tense situations with folksy remarks.

"We may," Kittels began, "be tearing up the alfalfa patch over nothing. Now since when do we measure old Mother Dean's worth in cash dollars? Sheeeeet. We all know she costs us a couple of bucks . . ."

"About $17,000 a year," said Line.

"Well, o'course, *I* don't carry charts in *my* jeans," said Kittels, sitting down. Ordinarily, the final Kittels remark would have drawn a titter or two, but now there was only silence. Folksiness was not the answer to the Line and Campbell brand of sophistication. Goodley arose. He was a small boy who scared students enrolled in the same classes with him because of the tremendous size of his head. Whenever he walked into a new class carrying a briefcase, took a seat in the first row and brought out a notebook, immediately students would rush to get transfers. He was bright, but certainly not as brilliant as the size of his head would seem to indicate. Once he had had a coronary in the middle of a gin rummy game and had gone hurtling into a bathtub clutching his chest. There was tension, thereafter, whenever he rose to speak. He was obviously shaken now, as he began.

"I think," he said, in a trembling voice, "we're making a grave and serious mistake. I think that we will all live in ignominy if we pass this motion." He hesitated, thinking of his next remarks, and Line and Campbell set up a chorus of "Hear, Hear. Hear, Hear, Hear, Hear." No one was certain what the Hear Hears signified, but they sounded so parliamentary and British that everyone was respectful of them, and a few members joined in the shouting. Goodley was so disturbed at this point, he said, "I can only say that I'm going to sit down."

The opposition thereafter became totally ineffectual. Sanders, who told a great many war stories, arose and said, "You all know I had m'face shot off during the war. Well, I just want you to know I didn't have it shot off to come back to something like this." No one saw the connection between his face and the Mother Dean situation. Then Rooney got to his feet. He defended people. Girls complained of him that he was very protective, but dull. He defended girls, and he defended Mother Dean. Sometimes in the evenings he would stand alongside her, his arms folded, his head erect, defending away. "One of m'favorite boys," Mother Dean said about him. "If Mother Dean gets the axe," Rooney said at the meeting, "I'm packing my bags."

Before the vote, Line cautioned members not to forget the charts, and Campbell came in with a single dramatic phrase—"$17,000." The motion carried by a small margin. It was decided that the fraternity should tell Mother Dean of its decision at a meeting to be held after the Sunday initiation of new members.

There was no way of telling whether Mother Dean sensed her coming misfortune. She continued to rock her chair, to crochet, and every once in a while to talk to herself. Only once did she deviate from her normal routine. It was at dinner one night when she rang the table bell and asked the fraternity if she could call her sister long distance. To a man, the fraternity agreed to the call. In fact, it was not until the preparations for the Sunday initiation that Mother Dean revealed she knew something was afoot.

As part of the ceremony, there were always eight freshly cut logs, each of them standing for some quality such as Envy or Truth which initiates were either to embrace or reject.

Senior Rho Deltas, or "Log Men," were each assigned to a log, and when initiates approached, they would stand up on the log and read a poem which went with the log. Mother Dean had for twenty-five years been assigned to Virtue. Each time her turn came, two members would help her up on the log, and she would say, "I am Virtue. You must learn to recognize me and enjoy me. For I am a dear and faithful companion." Seconds before this particular initiation, Mother Dean asked if she might switch with Perfidy, and since there was no time for debate, Goodley took over Virtue, and Mother Dean stood opposite the log she had asked for. A minute later, the initiation began with Sanders leading the three members-to-be to the door of the ceremonial room, knocking and announcing, "I have three lonely travelers from a distant land who wish to be admitted."

"Admit them," came a voice from the room.

The blindfolded initiates were led into the room under an arch of wet sauna leaves, where key portions of Omar Khayyam were read to them. After that, they were brought opposite the logs. Patience, Valor and Trustworthiness sounded off, and then Mother Dean was helped up onto Perfidy, fumbling at her pocket for a little piece of paper. "I am Perfidy," she read. "You must guard against me, for just when you do not expect me, I will creep into your bosom and cause you to do evil things against your brethren, such as taking away his livelihood." No one could remember a livelihood reference having ever been included in the Perfidy verse before, and Goodley hung his large head as he stood up on Virtue and asked the initiates to recognize him and enjoy him. When the initiation was over, the three new members were slapped with the wet sauna leaves as they removed their blindfolds, and the entire group sang the Rho Delta Hymn.

When the three new members left the room to dry themselves, a meeting was called, and it was decided that Line and Campbell, as sponsors of the expulsion motion, should be the ones to tell Mother Dean of the fraternity's decision. The sergeant at arms brought her down and she stood before the group, pulling her shawl around her, saying, "It's chilly down here. I don't understand how you boys don't catch your deaths."

"The heat comes up most of the time, Mother Dean," said one of the members.

Line arose, followed by Campbell, and said, "You may have had hints about this, Mrs. Dean, and it's sort of difficult to put it properly, but quite simply, the fraternity has sort of asked me to tell you that it's going to have to get on without your services."

"You'll be given two weeks' separation salary," said Campbell, "and, of course, all the cooperation we can offer."

Mother Dean pulled the shawl tighter around her shoulders. "I *have* known about this for some time," she said. "And I just want to interject one comment."

For a moment, there was a stir of hope in the room. As if it was about time someone had interjected something. As if perhaps Mother Dean would say something to dispel the Alice in Wonderland atmosphere. The charts were gone. Line and Campbell were silent. Had a vote been taken at that very second, there wasn't a doubt that the Mother Dean decision would be overturned. "I just want to interject," said Mother Dean, beginning to cry. "Oh, I don't know what I want to interject. I guess I just want to interject that you're still," she said, pausing, "that you're *still . . . all . . .* m'boys."

"We didn't *all* vote to do this, Mother," said a member.

"I know you didn't," said Mother Dean, "and I'd just like the permission of m'boys to make a call to my sister."

To a man, once again, the group granted permission for the call, whereupon Rooney rose and defended Mother Dean to the top of the stairs. Late that afternoon, Mother Dean packed her bags, accepted a two-week salary check from Line and Campbell, hailed a cab and left the Rho Delta fraternity.

For some weeks thereafter, occasional mumblings of discontent were heard in the house, but it took time before a full-scale feeling of guilt erupted and swept the fraternity. The Line and Campbell book kept up its sale, and the pair continued to exert considerable influence in the fraternity. Until one day, Line was seen—without Campbell—strolling on the campus at the side of a large, motherly type girl. She was known to be the president of a college science fiction club and rumored to be a specialist in offtrail lovemaking. Line spent more and more time with her, and Campbell, as a result, spent more and more time alone. Without Line, Campbell seemed naked and uncertain. One day, someone caught him in a phoney Gletkin reference. Campbell had been carrying *Darkness at Noon* with him for some time (he always kept at least one book under his arm), and at lunch made reference to the hero, Gletkin. A literature major at the table pointed out that Gletkin was not the hero. He thereupon questioned Campbell closely on the book and soon revealed to everyone at the table that Campbell had read no more than the book jacket. And when Campbell had left the room in embarrassment, someone else pointed out that, come to think of it, Campbell had never really said anything of consequence since he'd been there, that it was always Line who spoke brilliantly and Campbell who backed him up with a "We can't emphasize that too strongly" or an "And these are no empty words." The team appeared to have crumbled. It was no longer Line and Campbell. It was Line, and by the way, Campbell.

Actually, however, it was not until the incident of Aunt Hortie's arm that the fraternity began to regret its decision and yearn for the days of Mother Dean. Aunt Hortie was the new housemother Line and Campbell had flown in from Kansas City. She was in her early forties and, although she bore a rather sharp resemblance to Line, especially from profile, the likeness was not so great that anyone cared to make accusations. Aunt Hortie performed fairly well. She immediately began trucking veal cutlets in from Madison City, and although they had a slightly wooden, frozen taste, everyone remembered the $1750 savings and agreed it was worth the money. She did away with the Dr. Dean chair servings. She insisted only that there be a little brandy served at each meal; when certain members abstained, Aunt Hortie collected theirs in a bottle she kept in her room, so that the brandy would never be wasted.

And then one evening, after she had been with the fraternity for several weeks, Aunt Hortie put her arm on the table. It was a large, fat arm, rather bluish, that took up quite a good deal of room, and when she propped it up on the table, several members asked to be excused. The next night, Aunt Hortie wore an elbow-length glove to dinner, but it was too late. The damage was done, and members were soon crying for her head.

"Why didn't you tell us about Aunt Hortie's arm?" Line and Campbell were asked at meetings. "So she saves on veal cutlets. What good is it if we have to look at her arm?"

And then the subject would switch violently to Mother Dean.

"I don't care what you say," said one member, who spoke in dramatic, measured tones. "You-took-a-dear-sweet-wonderful-little-old-lady-and-you-threw-her-out-on-her-ass."

So grieved were the members of the Rho Delta fraternity over their treatment of Mother Dean that few paid any attention when Line and Campbell announced they planned to return to the University of Vermont for the fall semester.

"Oh, yeah," Kittels said to the group in their most miserable state, his shoes glistening in the damp meeting room. "You sent her packing like a beagle on a deerhunt. But have you got an address? Do you know where she is now?"

"I stood here in this room," said Goodley, with a mournful shake of his tremendous head, "and I told you as God's my judge you were making a grave mistake."

"You-took-her," said the dramatic fellow, "and-you-threw-that-beautiful-little-old-lady-out-into-the-cold."

At no time was the guilt and grief of the group any thicker than one Sunday afternoon in early summer when half a dozen members, driven from the dining room by Aunt Hortie's arm, gloves and all, sat on the stoop of the house watching a Summer Queen parade. The group was entirely joyless. They had no entry in the parade. Asked to leave, Aunt Hortie had produced a contract, which assured her of at least a two-year stay in the house. It had been negotiated with Line and Campbell who were now in Vermont. When the alumni had learned of Mother Dean's dismissal, most of them had stormed away from the house and sat in nonfraternity stadium seats during the Homecoming football game.

There was perfume in the air, but it had little meaning for the six members who sat out on the stoop watching the tail end of the parade. The floats had just about disappeared, and a few straggling cars were bringing up the rear followed by several police motorcycles. It was one of these last cars that bore special interest for the six members of the fraternity who sat on the stoop with their heads in their hands. For in the back seat of the car, driven by a middle-aged woman in a large, Easter-type hat, stood a tall, erect woman with purple-tinted hair, waving a parade banner. The woman was almost certainly Mother Dean, but if this was so, it was a different Mother Dean than the six members had ever before seen. It was an erect, splendid Mother Dean with no shawl around her shoulders and an almost indecently high angle to her bosom. And at her side, with a camel's hair topcoat in his lap, sat a dark-haired middle-aged man with a ring on his finger that glinted in the sun. And as the car pulled slowly up in front of the fraternity house, this man drew the woman (who was now recognized almost unmistakably as Mother Dean) down beside him and dropped his arm around her shoulder in much the same position as the alpaca shawl had lain so many times. And when the car, a late-model convertible, disappeared finally in the distance, it might have occurred to the six members, who now blinked their eyes in wonderment, that they had definitely not kicked a little old lady out into the cold. They had kicked a tall, slender, erect little old lady out into the cold, which is an entirely different matter.

Show Biz Connections

ONE DAY MR. KREEVY, a shambling, Lincolnesque man of thirty, took a thorn out of a distinguished stranger's foot and got himself a wonderful deal involving girls. Until the thorn extraction, Mr. Kreevy had never done well with women. His only satisfactory memory in that direction was a masseuse in Tokyo who worked with her feet and had given him a few extra minutes of seductive toe digs about the lower back. A dance critic by profession, he exercised little finesse in his handling of the ladies; at lunch once, an aging member of a touring Yemenite folk troupe suggested she found his shambling, Lincolnesque qualities attractive, but he had frightened her off with a loud, whinnying horse-laugh.

One night, after dashing off a cynical critique of the pachonga, Mr. Kreevy left his cramped dance critic's office atop a Manhattan skyscraper and headed for his favorite place of all—the elevator. Somber when entering elevators, Mr. Kreevy, once he saw he was to be alone in one, would strike mid-floor ballet poses, straightening up as he approached possible stops and then falling into others when he was in the clear. He would then emerge on the ground floor wearing a guardedly funereal expression. On this particular evening, Mr. Kreevy, anxious to test a grand jeté, rang the down button with a certain giddiness; when the doors opened, he was disappointed to see seated on the floor a distinguished-looking old gentleman with Edwardian whiskers stroking one bare foot.

"Get that button on 'hold,' will you," said the man. "I've got a thorn in here and I've been going up and down with it. It isn't my first. I've had others, but this one is deep. I think they come in through my spats."

Mr. Kreevy, self-conscious when meeting new people, let fly his bellowing, toothy horselaugh and the old gentleman said, "What in hell do we need that for. Look, do you think you can get 'er out of there. Just poke around and she'll slide out. I never can do them myself."

"I never went for feet," said Mr. Kreevy, falling into a suspicious, defensive crouch, and the old gentleman said, "They're sweet-smelling if that's what you're on guard about. Get moving, will you. I have an inkling this one's a deepie and they can be murder."

316

Suspiciously, Mr. Kreevy knelt down, and in several seconds his craggy, Lincolnesque fingers had plucked out the thorn.

"Done with style," said the old gentleman. "Now look, I don't stand around pumping your hand in gratitude if that's what you're after. I *really* pay off. For an ordinary extraction I generally pass along your pick of any American compact car, whitewalls, service and parts for a year. But this one really *was* deep and wait till you hear what you're getting."

"I'll settle for the car right now," said Mr. Kreevy, throwing up a defensive smoke screen of surliness.

"You'll take what I give you," said the old gentleman. "Be at my office at six tomorrow afternoon." He shook Mr. Kreevy's long, hairy, Lincolnesque fingers, gave him his card, and when the elevator reached the lobby, disappeared into a midnight crowd.

The next afternoon, Mr. Kreevy, in shaggy, Lincolnesque clothes, appeared at the old gentleman's exquisitely paneled, secretary-less office and threw his bony legs up on the man's huge, bare desk in a manner that had always offended girls. The sign on the door had said, IRVING'S SUITE, and Mr. Kreevy, in what he considered earthy, log cabin directness, asked, "What's the Irving bit?"

"My wife wants me to change it to Brad for class," said the old gentleman, "but I'm hanging on to it. I figure you need one show biz touch to make your classiness all the more authentic. You're going to be glad you passed up the car. What I've got for you involves women, and from what I've seen of those ways of yours, and those socks you wear, you need this like life itself."

Mr. Kreevy felt for his socks and pulled them out of his shoes. They were a strange swamplike color with beige stripes. He had several dozen pairs of them, having bought them in job lots, and they were the only kind he wore.

"I'll still take the car," said Mr. Kreevy, his great teeth horsy and sly.

"What I do," said the old gentleman, "is throw you in among women who are finished. They're in disasters of various kinds and they have, say, twenty minutes to live. You appear to them and suddenly they don't mind that style of yours the way they would if they met you under different circumstances. You're the last man they'll ever have a shot at. Are you getting the picture? You show up, they know it's all over and *bam*, you're all set. As soon as you finish up I whisk you out of there. *You* don't die, just them."

Mr. Kreevy threw his head back in what was to be a contemptuous horselaugh, but no sound came forth, and in spite of himself, he began to perspire. He tugged nervously at his anklets, and, embarrassed over his own words, croaked, "How do I get started on one of these?"

"I'll start you off right from this office. When you come in here, maybe I'll be present, maybe I won't. Anyway, just lie down on that couch over there, holler out . . . Oh, I don't know . . . holler out, 'What are Shelley Winters?' and close your eyes. I'll set it up that way. Let's do one now to get you rolling."

"I'm not so sure I go for this whole thing," said Mr. Kreevy, but as he said it he was backing his way to the couch. He settled back, loafers smudging up the fabric, whispered the Winters line and found himself on the deck of a flaming yacht, its bow beneath the surface.

"Am I visible to everyone or just the girl?" he tried to shout back, but by the time he got it out, a tall, high-cheekboned young woman with dirt-begrimed face was making her way toward him. "We're going down, but I'll be damned if I'll panic," she said. "Who are you, you vile man?"

"I show up on these," said Mr. Kreevy, not really sure what manner to assume.

"You're certainly a dreadful-looking person. I didn't notice you before. Keep your distance and don't get any vile ideas just because we're on our way down. Did I ever meet you at the Garretts' in Southhampton?"

"I don't know any Garretts," said Mr. Kreevy, wondering how much time he had.

"Isn't this a chore," said the woman, dragging deep on a cigarette as the flames came nearer and more of the yacht went under. "I suppose you're supposed to become demented or something, but I'll be damned if I'm giving in to any of that. Look at those asses over there, shouting and carrying on as if it made any difference. If you can't wind it all up with a little reserve, what good is the whole business. God, you're a frightening-looking creature."

"Yes," said Mr. Kreevy, uncertainly, "but I'm the last man you'll ever see."

"Yes, and quite a specimen you are, too. At least if you weren't so wretched-looking. You keep your distance or you're getting one right in your gizzard. Whoever thought you up must have had some joke in mind."

The water came up to both their waists then; they were the only ones who seemed not to have been washed overboard.

"Well, I suppose this is it," the girl said. "God, you're a beast. At least if you were *int*eresting-looking . . . Oh, heaven help me," she said with a little shiver and at the same time she shut her eyes, reached over and tweaked Mr. Kreevy's buttocks, then went under, Mr. Kreevy at that very instant being whisked back to the couch.

"The answer's no, no one but the girl can see you," said the old gentleman. "I'm sorry I couldn't get through to you. How'd you do? I stood by to find out how the first one went."

"It was no bargain," said Mr. Kreevy, running two fingers over his great, horselike teeth. "I'm not so sure it worked out at all. I got a little feel out of the whole deal."

"I'm not going along to hold your hand if that's what you're after," said the bewhiskered gentleman. "I think the others ought to go smoother. You're no Paul Newman, you know, and that style of yours doesn't help. All right, out you go. You can do as many of these as you want, but I've found that one a day works out best. Besides, I've got another man coming in and need the office."

Affecting a scowl that had no real conviction behind it, Mr. Kreevy shambled out of the office and later, upon returning home, found parked in front of his building a new red compact car with this note under the windshield wiper:

I'm tossing in the car. You either run a class operation or you don't.

Irving

That night, in his bleakly furnished room, Mr. Kreevy had trouble sleeping and writhed about in his simple Lincolnesque bed till dawn. At his office the following day, he was unable to concentrate on a tango diatribe and finally laid it aside, setting out for the old gentleman's office. There had been no whitewalls on the compact and Mr. Kreevy was all prepared to needle the distinguished duffer about the omission. But the office was empty. On the old gentleman's desk was a note which said:

If it's you, Kreevy, I forgot one thing. I wouldn't use Shelley Winters again. Try another name, anyone as long as it's show biz.

Irving here

Grumbling with hollow irritation, Mr. Kreevy settled back on the couch, hollered, "What are Joannie Sommers?" and appeared instantly in a small cabin that had a Japanese smell to it. The floor was tilted at a violent angle, and the furniture was all poured together at one end as though a giant had seized the cabin and was holding it up for inspection. Thrown in among the furniture was a plump woman in gaping negligee, a yellow-haired fairy princess who'd been married several years and failed to mind her calories.

"The earth just opened up and down I went into it," she said. "They'd been talking earthquake around here awhile, but we never thought we'd really be *in* one, not when you're a tourist. I didn't know

you were in here, too. You're not Japanese, are you, although I suppose your teeth could be. You're sort of a Japanese Great Emancipator
type. God, how I'm babbling. We're all washed up, you know. We're
about a thousand feet down and as soon as whatever we're in closes
together, that's it. God, you're probably the last man I'll ever see. Not
that I'd ever betray Milt."

Unable to suppress a great, gloating whinny, Mr. Kreevy shoved
aside a bamboo breakfront and hauled her out of the furniture, her
legs plump and princesslike as she emerged. "The last thing I'm going
to do is betray Milt," she said, "not while he's innocently putting over a
transistor deal in Tokyo. But hold me close, will you. Didn't anyone
ever tell you about those beauty salons for men they have back in
Newark. I'm sorry I said that. It wouldn't make any difference if you
were gorgeous. I don't sell out husbands."

The cabin tilted once again as though the inspection were continuing. "What have I got, maybe three or four minutes to live," she said,
pressing her fragrant head against Mr. Kreevy's hollow chest. "I'm selling out Milt. Here's a suggestion as long as we're on a limited time
schedule. Bite my earlobe as softly as you can. It puts me right in the
mood."

With a great cynical whinny of triumph, Mr. Kreevy put his molars to
work, and as great shock waves of sound split the air above them, the
princess gasped, "You have your transistors, darling," and the two fell
among some Japanese room dividers, mutually selling out the man in
Tokyo. Minutes later, the roof split apart, admitting tons of Oriental
soil, Mr. Kreevy slipping back to the couch as the first dirt clump entered the cabin.

"I was out grabbing a coffee and danish," said the bewhiskered gentleman. "Sorry I missed you. How'd it go? Better this trip, eh?"

"It was okay," said Mr. Kreevy, cautiously, certain there were some
grains of fertilizer in his socks, but feeling around and finding none.

"Cagey rascal, aren't you," said the Edwardian oldster. "Look, I'm
not stopping these if that's what you're worked up about. They just go
on and on. And it isn't one of those deals in which you have tons and
tons of pleasure and find out that too much pleasure is a bore. This
just stays good. Now tell me, how was it? Sometimes I really wish I
could get out in the field."

"It was all right," said Mr. Kreevy, still wary, hunched over on the
couch like Neanderthal man guarding a triceratops cutlet.

On subsequent days, without missing a single session, Mr. Kreevy
appeared to a celebrated fashion model on a doomed El-Al airliner, a
robust Kiev tractor girl about to hang for black marketeering, and a
weekending French governess caught aloft in a defective cable car.

Each of these and dozens of others followed the same pattern. The fashion model dubbed him "King of the Uglies" but then slipped out of her jumper when a wing fell away; the tractor girl grunted with displeasure, then peeked at the scaffold outside her cell and fell earthily at his knees; the governess screamed *cochon* but eagerly capitulated when the cable began to snap.

One afternoon, a month after the extraction, Mr. Kreevy, his confidence at a peak, no longer shambling along in Lincolnesque humility, walked briskly in for a session and took his place on the couch in a businesslike manner.

"How are they going?" asked the elderly gentleman, not looking up from his work.

"Very well, thank you," said Mr. Kreevy, all wariness gone.

"I told you," said the dapper Edwardian. "Remember how suspicious you were. I told you it was a class operation. Oh, well, see you sometime."

Mr. Kreevy showed up this trip in a thickly humid thatched hut, the tropical air so foul and thick he was barely able to breathe. Animal skins covered the dirt floor and outside there was a pound of drums, the beat uneven and somewhat amateurish. Huddled in a corner, her hand shaking as she sipped a cocktail, was a woman of about thirty-five, with blinding red hair and theatrical makeup on her face. She had on khaki shorts and her hips flowered out so brazenly from her spare waist that Mr. Kreevy had to look down at the skins.

"Do you mind if I tell you something," she said, walking toward Mr. Kreevy. "You're terribly attractive."

"I am not," he said, afraid to check her hips again.

"Don't even *ask* what I'm doing here," she said, emptying her glass with a crimson hair toss that made Mr. Kreevy's backwoods knees go soft. "No one'd believe it in a thousand years. I'm part of a goddamned movie company. We could've shot the damned thing in Hollywood but Nudelman wanted authenticity. A Grade Z film and he's after authenticity. We're getting it all right. We got here on a goddamned religious holiday and they've killed all the leads and the whole production crew. They'll be in here any second now. I'm just a lousy extra on the thing."

She seemed to notice Mr. Kreevy for the first time all over again and said, *"Oh, my God."*

"What?" he asked.

"Nothing," she said, hanging her head. "It's just when you smiled, I got a funny feeling inside. Hasn't happened since high school. I'm crazy about your kind of smile."

There was no triumphant gloating in the barely perceptible whinny that came from Mr. Kreevy's throat. It was a sweet, modest, grateful sound and no sooner had it issued forth than the girl clutched his wrist and said, "Please don't do that. It's not fair. You're terribly appealing, you must know it, and I have enough to worry about now without becoming involved."

"Look," said Mr. Kreevy. "There are a few minutes. Just try to hold out if you can. I can't explain but I think I can get us out of here. Are they coming?"

The girl peered outside the shack and Mr. Kreevy dared this time to look at her hips, surprised he did not turn to stone. "They just got Fowler in the neck with a spear," she reported. "He was our diction instructor. They're about seven huts down. I really needed authenticity."

"Maybe I can pull this off," said Mr. Kreevy. "I love you."

"I think I love you, too, you crazy beautiful nut, even though I didn't want to get involved."

Mr. Kreevy stood in the center of the shack and concentrated with all his might, getting into a crouch and squeezing hard until he trembled. When he opened his eyes, he found himself trembling on the couch. The mysterious gentleman was seated behind his desk, his great plumed pen flying across a sheet of paper.

"Something's come up," said Mr. Kreevy. "I want to get a girl out of one of them. I love her, and she's got to come out."

"Well, you can just stop right there and forget it, because there's no getting them out. The idea is to go in there, watch them panic a little, enjoy them and that's that."

"Well, I'm springing her," said Mr. Kreevy, "no matter what you say." He yanked the giant plumed pen out of the old gentleman's hand and held it against his distinguished throat. "Now you just come along with me and get us out. I'm a desperate man."

"You've just canceled out the thorn extraction," said the man softly. "All right, on the couch alongside me."

Mr. Kreevy took his place beside the old gentleman, continuing to hold the plumed pen in a threatening manner. They held hands, the senior citizen muttered something and the pair reappeared inside the crude Congo hut. "You brought along your friend, lovie," said the girl. "Is he going to talk to them out there?"

"Thank God you're safe," said Mr. Kreevy, flying to her side. The cocktails had made her unsteady on her feet.

"All right, get us back," said Mr. Kreevy.

"Nothing doing," said the old gentleman. "I can't do it and even if I could, I don't like you any more and wouldn't."

Mr. Kreevy took the redhead's hand and led her to the center of the hut. "This worked before," he told her. "Let's do it together. Close your eyes, squat down a little and concentrate real hard."

"Fun," the redhead said. "We did things like this at the studio."

They held hands, mutually sealed their eyes, shook and trembled together, but to no avail.

"You're lying," said Mr. Kreevy, seizing the old gentleman by the throat. "You *can* get a girl out of one of these."

"All right, you've got me," said the older man. "They do come out in certain situations."

Gratefully, Mr. Kreevy released his grip, only to hear the Edwardian add, "But somebody's got to stay behind." With that, the oldster shrieked, "What are Gracie Fields?" and soared aloft, the redhead at his side as though she'd been yanked upward on a string. Mr. Kreevy remained rooted to the dirt floor. The pair hesitated just a moment at the roof of the thatched hut, long enough for the old gentleman to issue his own triumphant old man's whinny.

"Help me," Mr. Kreevy pleaded to the redhead, her hips dazzling him at this new angle.

"He seems to know celebs," she said, stroking the Edwardian's be-whiskered chin. "And I'll do anything to get a break in show biz."

Then, as the first natives broke in, walking uncertainly to the beat of their amateurish drum, Mr. Kreevy watched the couple twinkle off into the sun.

The Night Boxing Ended

I WAS THERE THE NIGHT BOXING ENDED.

It had certainly been in the doldrums and then, mysteriously, a month before, there had been a sudden geyser of interest, thousands jamming the auditorium for a routine heavyweight fight. Perhaps they sensed the end and had come to pay their respects. In any case, it had been an old-time fight night and it was not so much a question of people behaving as though it was the good old days. It really *was* the good old days, turned into good new days. As though nothing had happened in between. The fighters had gone at each other for twelve rounds in thrilling fashion, and there was much rich enjoyment in the house, much talk about future bouts, especially in the heavyweight division, and how delicious they might be.

I missed the next card, two weeks later, just as well since it turned out to be a dog; the night I am talking about came two weeks afterward, another sold-out affair and you had your hands full rounding up a ticket. I flushed out a single down front and went alone.

I am really not so sure exactly how interested I am in boxing. I know I like the action outside the ring, the smell of it all, and it has something to do with my Uncle Roger. My father was laid up for several years with something complicated involving his shoulders and Uncle Roger did a lot of filling in for him, taking me to the fights each Friday night at the St. Nicholas Arena. I don't think he looked at the ring once. He stood up in his seat, with his back to the fighters, and said hello to people he knew. And at the end of every match, when the fighters touched gloves and embraced, he would say, "You see, they really love each other." He looked a little like Edward Arnold, the old movie actor, and there were times I wondered how he would be as a full-time father. Probably not so great as a steady diet, but he was bluff and vigorous in short stretches and I liked the idea of his being wounded in the Meuse-Argonne campaign. An incipient hernia had kept my own father out of the war. Enough on Uncle Roger. Except for one thing. When he died, he completely faked me out. There had been a stretch of ten or fifteen years when I hadn't seen him at all and then, out of nowhere, we became close again, right up to his death. What he did was go into a hospital and then call me about twice a week at my office to ask how I was. About half an hour before he checked out, he called to say "How are you doing?" "Fine," I said, "only I can't talk right this minute." "Okay, kid," he said, "stay well," and then, according to some calculations I made later, he died in less than an hour. Never gave anyone a chance to say goodbye. This really worried me. A year or so later I started going to the fights after a long layoff and maybe it has something to do with not saying goodbye to Uncle Roger. And maybe it doesn't.

In any case, on this historic night I am trying to describe, I put two Gibsons under my belt and got there in time to watch the first two prelims, four-rounders which went the distance and both of which I picked wrong. The next fight (as it turned out, the last one in history) was a heavyweight affair, scheduled for eight rounds, which it almost went. I often wonder, thinking back to that night, whether there was some way you could tell, something in the air, a different kind of buzz in the crowd, an expectation. I can't in fairness say there was a trace of any of this. The house had begun to pack in fairly well, and you knew that by main-event time the few extra ringside seats would be filled. The beer tasted right on target. There were some Stop-That-Bloody-Battles and May-I-Have-The-Next-Dances and I guess you might have called the crowd medium lively. One of the heavyweights was a Latino, young, good-looking, muscled-up kid with a Rolling Stones haircut. The other boy—and this was perhaps the only unusual note—was an Irish kid from some apple-pie town in the Midwest where you never expected them to have Irishmen. He was the right weight, but he seemed to have the arms of an accountant, not a ripple on him, and plenty of slack stuff around the midsection to boot. You'd have a hard time even calling him supple. He had a pounded-in dock-walloper's face, however, that went with an entirely different kind of body. I wasn't too worried about him. Often, fighters with this type build would come on with a tough, nasty style and cut you to ribbons. The first two rounds were kind of routine. You found out the Latin boy was a wild swinger and the Irish kid could box and got pinked up easily when he was hit. He threw only lefts and might just as well have kept his right hand in the locker room. Midway through the third round, the crowd began to stir and you got your first look at the fellow who finally caused it all. He was located around seven seats off to the right of me, one row ahead and he had been slouched all the way down, so much so I thought the seat was unoccupied. He was a fairly clean-cut young fellow, sleeves rolled back, the good solid neck of a Marine drill instructor. Gradually, he sat erect in his seat and began to get on the Irish boy. It had been a ragged night for catcalls, and, in any event, there is usually one heckler who takes over his section. If his material

is good, there is an unwritten code that no one in the area will challenge him until he runs out. Well, his voice was loud, and his material
was strong although you could not really say it was turned with any
great wit. He got on the Irish kid first, saying, "For Christ's sakes,
throw the right" and "What are you waiting for, St. Paddy's Day."
There were some modest laughs around him, but they were encouraging rather than hearty; the way you coax along a comedian until he
warms up. Through the next round, he stayed after the Irish fighter and
threw in some wordy comments about his own experience as an amateur. "For Christ's sakes, I done better than that in the Gloves" and
"At least I was no One-Handed Harry." Once again, not really inspired
stuff, but he really did have a point. You had the feeling that all the
slack-armed Irish kid had to do was use his other hand and he would
have the fight. This kind of thing can be most annoying. Next round, a
Puerto Rican heckler tried to take over. "You miss him again, you give
me a cold," but the first fellow's material picked up in power and you
had to go with him. He got on the Latin fighter now, and it was strong
stuff, although you had the feeling every remark went 20 per cent too
far. "Hey, he's just off the banana boat, you know," he cried. He had a
beer in his hand now and waved it in orchestration. "Look at his hair.
He's just a goddamned Beatle. He's just a goddamned Greek Beatle.
Hey, bananas, get back on the boat. Hey you goddamned Greek geek.
Hey banana-head. Hey you junkie Greek bastard." Nothing really that
unusual. Certainly nothing that altered the fight, which was a particular
kind of frustrating stinker. Looking back though, I suppose you might
say there were two clues that something was up. The word "bastard"
was somehow fishy in a catcall. You'd hear some strong talk but it was
always of another stripe. And it was the first time I'd heard the word
"junkie" invoked by a heckler. He picked it right up at the start of the
next round, staying right after the Latin, only now he was on his feet
and somehow you sensed that the fighters heard him. He still held the
beer, his face was wet and if there was a trace of good-natured needling in his style, you'd have had to look awfully close to find it. "You
goddamned Greek," he screamed. "You dago Beatle. You wop son of a
bitch. You ginzo mother. GET BACK TO JERUSALEM, YOU
JUNKIE KIKE GEEK."

"Hey, watch that kike stuff," said an elderly politician-type in the
row behind, "shame on you." But the heckler was beyond control. He
switched now to the Irish fighter, face pinked up, right hand still a
virgin, and the two men, heckler and pug, across twenty yards or so,
seemed to be wired together. "Kill the bastard," he yelled. "For
Christ's sakes, use the other hand. Take it the hell out of storage.
What's it there for. KILL THE BASTARD. KILL THE SON OF A

BITCH. KICK HIS BALLS, PUNCH HIS EYES OUT. KNOCK HIS HEAD OFF. KNOCK HIS HEAD OFF. KNOCK HIS HEAD OFF."

And the Irish fighter responding finally, followed instructions to a T. The writers present tended, generally, to say the head "floated" out into the sixth row ringside, where it was caught by a gentleman in the haberdashery business, not, as a matter of fact, a regular fight fan. I don't really think it "floated" at all. It was probably the Rolling Stones hairdo that gave it this appearance. Actually, it sailed out rather swiftly, in the style of a baseball hit off the end of a cracked bat, not with blinding speed either, but with a certain amount of zip to it.

The heckler slumped back in his seat, saying something like "at-taboy," and of course, for me, it was no big deal. I was just saying good-bye, officially, to Uncle Roger.

The Interview

"Name, please?" asked Mr. Dworkin. "I didn't get to study your résumé."

"Rachele," said the young woman. "With an 'e' on the end. Rachele Flanders."

Lovely name, thought Dworkin. Would look good on our personnel chart. Help us sound like *Time*. Balance off Saul Feinschreiber and Fred Spalanzanni. Dworkin, too, why kid around? Wouldn't be much without that final "e" though. Wonder why she put it on there. Doesn't like things standard. Probably likes unusual kinds of kisses with little tricks to them. Underwear with strange ribbons. Got to have a twist to it. Come at her in a straightforward way and you're dead. Likes to be taken unawares in coal bins and on stairways. Everything she does has to have a final "e" on it.

"And your age, Miss Flanders?"

"Twenty-three."

Means she's been out of college two years. Worked fourteen months at *Gasoline Topix*. Leaves ten months unaccounted for. Probably had an affair with an executive, married man, finally had to leave *Topix*. Became too much. Lunches with him, few stolen hours after work, everything quick, nervous, never comfortable. Never get him to stay over, not even one night. Play the lute for him, nude dances, nothing worked. Midnight comes, he's out like a shot. Said he'd leave his wife, but no sign of it. Went into analysis instead. She finally just drifted away from the company. The other ten months? Waitress probably. Wash away big industry. Good, earthy job. Get to sweat. Black armpit semicircles on blue-denim blouses. Terribly sensuous. Late hours. Meet all types. Affair with a sculptor no doubt, erase the neat exec. Spanish sculptor. Worked in iron. Massive, complicated things, new wave, unappreciated. Impotent, but long, nude hours tracing her anatomical lines. Great pelvis, one of a kind. Still friends, but could never work out fully, completely.

"I see you were born in Illinois . . ."

"Yes, sir."

Like the "sir." Little deferential. Probably needs a father. Call her "Miss Flanders," always a little stern, keep her slightly flustered, quietly, slowly exert power and then one night, whammo. You're taking advantage of your position, Mr. Dworkin. Damn right I am. And what about Mrs. Dworkin? Nothing at all to do with it. Then take me. I need your strength. I need you to command me to do things. Anything, as long as you're very grave and stern about it.

". . . and then moved to the state of Washington. When Daddy died."

Right about needing a father. Old man probably drank himself to death. I look a little rumpled, troubled, that's probably what does it to her. Can't resist dissipation, self-pity. Probably boarding schools when the old man died. Nightgowned sex talks till all hours with a roommate named Prissy. What's it like? What's it really feel like? Smuggled-in pornography. Whisked out of boarding school when mom landed an industrialist. European villas. Mom with cigarette holders and gold pants, having endless love affairs. She finally has her first. A French tutor, lots of hair and sensitivity. In a woodshed. Awls and lathes and sawdust. Not very satisfactory and through it all, someone watched. The gardener's son. Caused some sort of wonderful hang-up. Only a stern fatherly type can cut through it, grant satisfaction.

"You're now living in the Village . . ."

"It's been one year. I love it."

Village chick now. At least four cats, two pregnant, all with hysterical names out of the classics. Try anything. Seminude parts in shoestring-budget 8-mm. films. All featuring out-of-focus chases through Village alleys and symbolic throat-cutting in pizza-joint rest rooms. Anything goes. Drugs, of course, and three men in a bed, all night long, with no sex, just friendship and intimacy. Pottery course at the New School, little water-coloring on Sundays. Affair with one Negro jazz musician; on a dare, take your breasts out in a Forty-second Street film house. Great pad, roaches, little fireplace and lovemaking to *Tristan and Isolde.*

"Have you looked through some of our books, Miss Flanders?"

"Yes, I have."

Didn't flinch when she said that. Looked right at me. I gave her some strong ones, too. Means she saw *Female Sex Aggression.* Couldn't have missed it. Signed by an authentic psychiatrist, but plenty hot. Had to see the illustration on *Gulf Coast Hoyden,* too. Can read about female sex aggression without batting an eyelash. Probably had some analysis. Talk about everything. No holding back if you're going to get anywhere. Nothing's dirty. Everything's all right. Just don't hurt anybody. God only knows what she went into with the doctor. Any sex urge, any wild thought and out on the table it had to go. Otherwise, would have been money down the drain. Can't shock the doctor. He's heard them all. Got a little affair in mind? Doctor will tell you to go right ahead and have it. Good for you. Healthy. Hungry? You've got to eat. Have the affair. Do the crazy thing. Could probably lunge across the desk, grab her tail. Wouldn't fluster her. Mild stuff. Discuss indecent exposure. Big yawn. Cut out the small-time stuff. Four years of deep Freudian analysis and you expect her to worry about Gulf Coast Hoydens . . .

"Would you have any compunctions about working on a strong line of paperbound books?"

"None whatsoever."

Beautifully handled. Didn't blurt it right out. Little pause before she said yes. Probably has to be seduced a little and that's not so bad. Doesn't just whip her clothes off. Have to coax her a little. Like being back at the Sigma Phi Gamma house. First few times, you undress her. Lovely. No compunctions whatsoever. Plenty of virility on paperbound books. Never mind that *Transatlantic Review* stuff. Back to basics. Gulf Coast Hoydens, Hitler Spy Nymphs. Gang Broads of Spanish Harlem. Probably saw pictures of my two sons on the desk. Virile-looking rascals, even if they're four and eight. Virile-looking dad.

"The salary is seventy-five dollars. Is that satisfactory?"

"I thought perhaps eighty dollars."

Wonderful. A fighter. Not a big, ugly twenty-dollar fight, but a good little one, just for fighting's sake. A little struggle, tough little hands, a little teeth, wonderful little maddening bites. An angry little fist. Should I or shouldn't I? she asks herself. What the hell, she answers. Then come furious and savage little embraces.

"We might be able to work something out. You get along reasonably well with people?"

"Yes, I do."

Crossed her legs when she answered. No control over that. Involuntary. No control over her body. Nervous legs. Nervous little fingers. What can she do? Can she help it if her body loves to make love? Is she to be punished, stoned? Gets along well with people. I'll bet she does. Through one period, sleeping with four at one time. Philosophy student, writer, the Spanish sculptor, and a man who put shellac on the floor once a month. With the shellac man, it "just happened." Am I really so terrible? she asked. Am I doing anything so hateful? Did I really damage myself? When it was all over, I still felt like a virgin.

"You know the hours . . . nine to five each day and three weeks of vacation every year.

"It sounds just fine."

Regular hours. She's done the Village scene. Had it up to here. Had her fill of orgies, blew enough cocaine. Keep your one-sonnet-a-year poets. Wants to wash her hair more than once a month. Ready for something strong and honest and virile and fulfilling. Had enough forty-year-old children. Ready for a man. Married? Makes no difference. Make her feel like a woman. Fulfillment. Clean and open. No nonsense. Orgasms for a change. Regular hours. Stern, grave, virile. Dworkin.

"Well, thank you for coming by, Miss Flanders. I'll be making my decision over the weekend and will get in touch with you either way."

"Thank you, Mr. Dworkin, for taking the time to see me."

"I'm afraid I've misplaced the résumés," Mr. Dworkin said to the next applicant. "What is your name again?"

"Scott," said the young lady. "Joan Scott."

Nothing much for the personnel chart there. Pretty bland. Bet the Europeans would flip over her, though. Probably spent six months touring France and Italy. Drove them wild. Loved her naïveté, the way she screwed up their language. But, oh, that clean American smell. That clean American underwear. Spent hours getting drunk in that forest of clean, blonde Iowa hair . . .

The Death Table

In europe, Gorsline got wind of a small printed card that told each man exactly how he would die. The concierge at his hotel in Paris was the first to refer to it, in tattered English, but then the man had segued into anecdotes of a favorite cousin's treatment at the hands of the Nazis and there had been no getting him back on the subject. At a furious, drunken Soho party, Gorsline thought he heard a British jazz critic mention a certain "death table," but the man had gone off to do discothèque dances with two girls from Jackson Heights and Gorsline had had to let him slip away. One printed reference to the card existed, a letter to an English-language newspaper in Rome, asking about it and whether it was possible to see one. The newspaper said that it had heard of the card, too, but had never been able to get hold of a copy. It touted the letter writer, M. L. of Sussex, on to *The Prophet* by Kahlil Gibran.

Gorsline had always wondered how long he would live, where he would die, whether there would be loved ones; but more than anything, he was starved with curiosity to know exactly what the deal would be, a long-drawn-out thing, one of those blessed swift affairs, something in between. He was really out of his mind to know and thought it was unfair that there was no way to get an advance tip, which surely would not hurt anyone or upset the large order of things in the slightest. It seemed to Gorsline that if you found out, you would simply take a deep breath and go about your business, but at least the goddamned suspense would be ended. Why all the secrecy?

One night, Gorsline took his wife gambling at Beaulieu, where he gave her some money for *boule* and then went deeper into the casino to play *trente et quarante.* He could not stand to gamble with anyone he knew around, feeling corseted and awkward. Driving home later, his wife seemed unusually silent, her face pursed and grim. Gorsline asked her if she was feeling all right and she said, "I was waiting to get away from there. It's nothing except that it got me all upset. I was standing and watching the roulette table and this man, I don't know whether you noticed him, he had white lips, he kept moving from one end of the table to the other and every time he moved he'd brush up against me, against my breasts. I thought I was imagining things, and I'd move back and give him plenty of room, but then he'd do it again, my breasts and lower, too. I was going to call you or tell someone, but then you came along and it was over and what was the point."

"Except that it's not over," said Gorsline. "I'll drop you off at the house and then go get him. You know I don't let things like that slide. What would I do for sleep? White lips, eh? The son of a bitch."

At the casino, Gorsline checked lips from table to table and then spotted him, arms around a beefed-up low-cut number many years his junior. Look at what he's got on his arm, Gorsline thought, and the mother has to go get himself a little extra. The couple seemed to be winning consistently. Gorsline waited until they knocked off a *zero-deux cheval,* then elbowed in to grab the man's fragile arm and whisper, "It's all over, sweetie, I want to see you in the john on a little matter pertaining to my wife and make it quick. Don't tell me you don't understand English, because I'll switch into anything you got."

"I understand, I understand," said the man sadly. "Swedish, but I'm fluent in your tongue." He excused himself and then walked along at Gorsline's side, following him into the empty men's room. Gorsline backed him against the washstand and said, "You goddamned mother, what the hell's the idea. You thought you'd go grab yourself a little something and get away with it. What'd you think she was, some hooker? I ought to smear you all over the mirror." Gorsline raised his fist but somehow could not feel any rage. Why hadn't his wife just walked away after the first one? He thought of the time in public school he had hit Edward Fliegel over and over in the body, saying, "Fight, coward."

"Who's the coward?" Fliegel had asked, arms at his sides.

"Please," the man said now, "I confess all. But you are not a savage. I know that already. You'd be hitting a doomed old man. Besides, I will give you something that you may have heard of and that will please you."

"All right, get it out fast while your luck's still running," said Gorsline, but there was not a chance in a thousand he would hit the man. With that, the white-lipped Swede reached into a vest pocket and produced the very card that had burned in Gorsline's dreams.

"I'll explain briefly," said the Swede, "and then I really must return to my, er, daughter. It's tied to roulette and quite simple. You wait for the spin of the roulette wheel at midnight of the night you receive the card. That's this evening, of course. The table is divided into six parts. If the number that comes up is one of the first six numbers, then you go by cancer. The second six, I believe, is heart and any one of the third six numbers are highway things. And so on. I believe you also have stroke and suicide as major categories, and of course, the last six numbers are simply 'other,' which can be anything from nephritis to kuru or laughing sickness, the oddball ones. Zero is oven explosion, although it never comes up and you needn't worry about it. It's all written out for you on the card and I really must go. I'm sorry about the other thing."

"All right," said Gorsline, fingering his new acquisition, "just watch your step next time I show up with my wife. You're going to get into real trouble if you keep that up. Listen, you must have played. What'd you get?"

"Leukemia," said the man, turning on the faucet. "It's started already. The white lips."

Half an hour remained before midnight, and Gorsline checked his watch twice against the radio to make sure he would be right on the button and get the exact midnight spin. The Swede had gone back to the table and begun to lose heavily. Gorsline played blackjack and won, but the chips were meaningless, like cornflakes. He studied the card, gray and stained like an Olympia novel, wondering how many others had used it. The categories were as the man had described them and Gorsline wondered what to root for. He hoped only that it would stay off cancer and also miss "other," which would leave him up in the air. He was not sure about stroke and felt he could do without that one, too. A few minutes to midnight Gorsline walked close to the high-stakes roulette table and wedged in beside a British manufacturer who took deep breaths each time a player made a big bet. At precisely twelve o'clock, Gorsline heard the words, *"Faites vos jeux, messieurs,"* and wondered whether he was to make a bet as part of the deal. The card was no help at all on this score and he decided to bet the limit on black for extra spice. *"Rien ne va plus,"* said the attendant and spun the wheel, Gorsline shutting his eyes and then opening them to watch the little ball. *"Onze,"* shouted the attendant and Gorsline quickly checked his chart, smacking his fist with delight when he saw he'd gotten "heart." Just great, he thought, and almost forgot to pick up his winnings. A quick bingo in the center of the chest and you were right out of there. Even when it went a little slower, he did not associate it with any real pain. No question, he had gotten the best deal and he walked with a little bounce as he left the table.

"How'd you do?" asked the Swede, who met him in the center of the casino.

"None of your business," said Gorsline. "Since when have we become buddies? Listen, what do I do with this card now?"

"Pass it on," said the downcast Swede.

*   *   *

The next day or two were fine ones for Gorsline, but his feelings soon turned a corner and he became depressed. For a while he speculated about strokes, wondering whether they were not a better deal after all, and there were some moments when he even chewed on the exploding-oven arrangement that came with zero. But all in all, he felt he had come off rather well, except that he could not stop brooding. He had come to Europe for a month's vacation with his wife and they lived in a small boardinghouse overlooking a thunderously beautiful cove in the South of France. Each day now he would sit in a beach chair and stare at the water, not even bothering to undress and keep up his suntan. Though there were only a few days left before his return to the States, he could not stop thinking about death and about one time in his life in particular. A time when his father had failed a medical examination for life insurance, the policy doctor telling him he was an "uninsurable." His father had not been able to go to work and had sat around the apartment in a cloud of despair, unshaven, without appetite. Several weeks later, another doctor had given him a clean bill of health, but Gorsline now could not stop thinking of his father's face through those uninsurable days and how frightened he had been about having an uninsurable dad. He had been married long enough so that he and his wife were keyed to fractional changes in each other's moods. Inevitably, one night after dinner, his wife asked him what was wrong and Gorsline, who for some reason had not mentioned the card, now told her the complete story of the white-lipped man and the roulette wheel and how he had come up with heart on the midnight spin.

"So," she said. "Great. I'd take it myself, any day. What are you so glum about. You got exactly what you wanted. I'd grab it and run."

"No," said Gorsline, pushing away his dessert. "You don't understand. Oh, it's okay and everything, but what if the damned thing fouls up. I mean, let's say I put in thirty years thinking I've got a heart attack in the bag and then all of a sudden I get wiped out by a dose of Parkinson's. Or some meatball with a broken bottle gets me in a bar some night. Let's say I get really down one day—the way only I can get —and decide to do a little number on my wrists. Or I walk out on a highway and some skunk in a VW comes along and creams me all over the pavement. Don't you see the hitch? Where the hell am I then?"

The Little Ball

WHEN THEY BROUGHT Mr. Lester in and put him on the bed, his stomach seemed lined with a large hand. Each time an egg boiled or a nurse walked or a fresh sheet crackled, the hand closed on all the tender parts inside him and made him grab the sides of the bed or someone passing by. Sometimes he held himself, trying to get smaller, so that there would be less of him that hurt. He was hoping there would be some special regimen that would make him well, and Dr. Rich said there was one, but that the important thing was not to get excited.

"I don't want to hear that," Mr. Lester said, lying on his stomach and crying. "I can follow anything you tell me, if it means eating lemon peels for eleven years, but how can I not get excited?"

"You're getting excited now," said Dr. Rich. "You've got to learn to control yourself."

When Dr. Rich left, Mr. Lester stopped crying and walked very slowly to the telephone. He told his wife he didn't want any visitors because everyone he knew would probably get him excited. He said it was okay for her to visit every other night. And then he walked back to bed and began to do things slowly and without excitement. He ate some pills very softly, and then smoothed the sheets with a minimum of effort. He prayed that everything would be nice, and when the hand closed inside him, he found himself hugging his stomach gently instead of vigorously. At night, he decided not to get out of bed and wash, but to turn off the light switch and slip quietly off to sleep. He had asked Dr. Rich for a private room in which he would be able to control the sheet crackles, but Dr. Rich said semiprivates were better in these cases, and after he had slept about an hour, the lights went on and an attendant brought in a man's clothing. "Your room's here, sweetie," the attendant said, and then wheeled in a large man, sliding him with much effort onto the bed. A woman was with the man and Mr. Lester said, "Is there anything I can do to help you?" and the woman said, "I don't think so."

The big man had a cowlick and sad eyes. She held his hand and looked into his eyes and Mr. Lester said, "I'll give you some privacy." He pulled the curtain between the two beds and tried to go back to sleep, but the light shone in his eyes and he lay there, keeping himself calm and waiting for the woman to leave. The couple did not talk, and after twenty minutes or so, the woman said, "Good night, Beans" and left. The big man then pulled open the curtain, and leaning on his side with much effort, said to Mr. Lester, "They gave me an enema by accident downstairs. It was for a guy who was going in to get operated on. I was lying in the admitting room and someone says, 'I got a wee present for you, Laddie' and slips it to me. The guy it was for is probably still waiting for it."

"It's such a big place they make mistakes," Mr. Lester said. "But overall they're very good, I think."

"I'm in for a bad back. I work for the gas company and I got it lifting a pipe. You can lift your end fine, but if the guy you're lifting with doesn't lift with you, you're dead. I was lifting with an old guy today and he can't lift his ass, so my back goes out. I wasn't really thinking. I was really teed off at the young kid burner they give me. Some of our work is pretty rough and today I had some pipe with a sharp edge so I called for the burner. He's a kid and you should have seen the job he did. I said to him, 'You call that burning, I ought to burn your ass off.' And he gives me an argument. He thinks he's a great burner. I been with the company eleven years, this is the first time I come close to leaving a man underground. I was going to leave him in a hole. He got me so upset, I lifted that pipe bad. I can't blame the old guy, even though I'll never lift with an old guy again. What are you in for?"

"I have an ulcer," said Mr. Lester.

"Oh, I know about those," the man said, leaning closer to Mr. Lester. "We got a guy on the job with one. You can't needle him. He just smiles and walks away. We do a lot of needling on the job. In fact, that's what most of it is. We'll get on a guy until he's ready to swing a pick at you. But you can't needle this guy. He just drinks himself some milk and smiles. You stick it into him and he just smiles. You have to drink tea all the time, don't you?"

"Milk," said Mr. Lester.

"I know," said the big man, his eyes sad and like a dog's. "But we call it tea to this guy when we want to stick it in."

"It isn't bad," said Mr. Lester. "You get more than milk."

"Well, I guess I'll get some sleep," said the big man, yawning. "I can sleep anywhere. I go right out. You better get some sleep, too. You got to get ready for your tea."

Mr. Lester slept about four hours, and in the middle of the night, his calm gone, got up to go to the bathroom. It was about four in the morning, and he could not get back to sleep. When the light came, the big man yawned and stretched. "I caught you going to the bathroom," the man said. "What are you, nervous or something? You got to cut down on the aggravation for what you have."

"I didn't go because I was nervous," Mr. Lester said. "I just went."

"I get aggravated doing my kind of work, too," said the man. "When someone aggravates me I go home and do my mosaics in the bedroom. My wife sees me and says, 'What's aggravating you?' and I plow right by her into the bedroom and do them. I'm not supposed to get off my back, but I'm going to hit the john now."

There was one latrine for the room. "Okay," said Mr. Lester. "I'm going to just lie here."

"You better," said the man. "You don't have any breakfast coming."

Mr. Lester held the sides of the bed and waited for the hand to close. An attendant brought a full breakfast for the man and an egg for Mr. Lester. He peeled off the shells and the man came out and said, "I've got to get a full breakfast into me. What have we here? Toast, eggs, cereal, juice, milk. I see you got your tea."

"I got an egg," said Mr. Lester, putting salt on it.

"You don't mind if I stick it in a little bit, do you?"

"Not at all," said Mr. Lester. "You can't bother me. If a man can't take a little ribbing, nothing is any good." He finished the egg and picked up a book.

"I see you've got a book," the man said. "My brother, his name is Beans, too, went up to play basketball at Holy Cross, but he didn't like it there. He said they were a bunch of stuffed shirts. He's about as big as I am. What do you do when you get out of here?"

"Go back home," said Mr. Lester.

"Back to the aggravation, eh?"

"I'm not going back to any aggravation," said Mr. Lester.

"Oh yes you are," said the man. "I can see the way you get upset. You'll go back to the same thing. I have an apartment at fifty-five dollars a month, gas and electric thrown in, five rooms, and I'm not moving for the world. There's no aggravation. I'm not paying those big rents. They'll give me scribbling to do the first week I'm back and then back to pipes. If I had to do scribbling all the time I'd get what you got. That'd be murder."

Mr. Lester kept his eyes on his book, reading the same sentence over and over.

The man turned his sad eyes away from Mr. Lester and said, "I hope my wife remembers to bring my radio. What we do is turn it up loud at home, as loud as you can get it, and crack jokes along with the guy on the radio. If he says something, we crack a joke right back at him."

Some time passed and Mr. Lester sipped a small glass of the cream he was to take each hour.

"Tea time, eh?" said the man.

"I'm going to go out and sit on the porch," said Mr. Lester, gathering his bathrobe around him.

"Don't forget to come back for tea," said the man.

Mr. Lester walked out on the porch. There was no sun and a man with a machine attached to him was sitting on the only bench. Mr. Lester walked over to the railing, chewing some skin from his fingernails, and when a nurse walked by he grabbed her arm and said, "Can I talk to you? Are you allowed to talk? I'm very upset. I can feel myself going and I'd better talk to someone."

"I'm allowed to," she said. She was blonde and not pretty until she smiled, when her mouth became surprisingly white and delicious.

"I have a man in the room who's driving me crazy. I could handle him under ordinary circumstances, but I can't now. He's kind of like a Stanley Kowalski. Does it sound snobbish of me? I don't really care if it does. I've got to get away from him. Under ordinary circumstances, I *prefer* a Kowalski. I get along better with someone earthy. But I can't take him now. He's probably just a good-natured slob, but I can't take him now. I feel it in my stomach and I know if I don't get out of there something bad is going to happen to me. Does all of this sound awful?"

"Not at all," said the nurse. "You get it all the time. In fact most of the patients switch rooms one and a half times. The thing is, there has to be one open. And if you switch and get another loser you're kind of stuck."

"That's okay," said Mr. Lester. "Look, I feel better just talking to you. You're damned sweet to listen to me. I think I'll be all right now. I don't think I have to switch. It isn't cowardice or anything. It's just that I can't be upset now. I need manners and good taste. But I don't have to switch now."

"Then you try it again. And if you want to change, just tell your doctor and he can arrange it in a minute."

"I don't have to change now. I can't get over how nice you are. You'd better go now."

"That's all right," said the nurse, her smile getting better. "I can stay here if I'm helping you."

"I'm okay now," said Mr. Lester. The nurse said good-by and the sun came up. The man with the machine attached to him had gone away now, and Mr. Lester took off his pajama top and got some sun on his body. He skipped the next milk-sipping and then came back to his room where there seemed to be a great commotion.

An old, gray-haired man, the color gone out of his face, had been wheeled into the room on a stretcher. Apparently, he had been brought in by mistake. The attendant had gone to straighten out the records, leaving the old man in the room.

Mr. Lester's roommate had been sitting up, talking to the old man. Now he said to Mr. Lester, "He's had seven operations, and he's in for the eighth. He's nervous. You ever hear anything like that? I keep telling him, for Christ's sake, you got nothing left. What the hell are you nervous about?"

The old man's face was blank, as though he heard nothing.

"I said to him, for Christ's sake, you been through it before. I can't see what the hell he's so nervous about. He's gone down there seven times already. He's all cleaned out."

Mr. Lester took some milk. The old man was wearing peculiar pajamas and the roommate pointed to them and said, "How do you like those? They're World War I combat pants. He's going into combat." The roommate poked the old man and said, "What the hell are you so nervous about? You think they got some new surprises down there for you? You been through it all before, for Christ's sake."

"I'm going back outside," said Mr. Lester. He eased past the stretcher and went outside to the phone booth, to call Dr. Rich. "Look," he said, "this is going to sound silly, but I've got to get out of that room you put me in. I'm there with a Stanley Kowalski-type guy and I've got to get away from him. I can't describe what he does and it's not that I'm running away from him, but it's getting me all worked up in my stomach. I can see the danger signals and I thought I'd better call you. Look, I'll probably change my mind, but I feel that way now and I've got to get out. Another thing is I don't want him to know I'm moving on account of him. I don't want to hurt the guy because really what he is is just a good-natured slob. I want it to seem that it's your decision. You want me closer to some office or something. You see?"

Dr. Rich said he thought he could arrange it. "Can you hold out until tomorrow morning?" he asked.

"I don't think so," said Mr. Lester. "It sounds crazy but I don't think I can get through the night with him without something awful happening."

Dr. Rich said all right then, he'd be over in the evening, and Mr. Lester went outside to the bench again. The sun had disappeared. A man in a very ornate bathrobe came over and said he was a professor of organic chemistry. "I'm concerned about the lowering of the intellectual level in this country," he said. "Before I came in here I used the word 'anomalous' to my class and a boy in the front row—this was a sophomore class—thought I was talking about an omelette. If they don't know what anomalous means in the sophomore year of college, how the hell are we going to get through to them?"

"I don't know," said Mr. Lester. "I can't worry about that. I'm all upset, and I have pains in my stomach."

The professor went away and Mr. Lester stayed out on the porch for two more hours. He saw the nurse and said he'd decided to switch after all. "Is there a bed open?" he asked. "I've told the doctor and he's coming over."

She said one was open, but to go in and look it over first and make sure he liked it. "It's a smaller room and there isn't a bathroom. The man in there is very serious. He was just brought in with a coronary and might go either way. He's a radio announcer."

"Sounds good," said Mr. Lester. He followed the nurse into the new room. The radio announcer was propped against some pillows, and plasma jars were strung up about the bed. Three nurses stood around him while a doctor wrote in a notebook. The man was bald and frightened and he was crying. One of the nurses held his hand.

Mr. Lester's nurse took Mr. Lester over to the man and introduced him. "This is Mr. Lester, who's going to be your new roommate." The radio announcer extended a limp, wet hand and said, "Fine. I just want to know which way the little ball is going to come out." Mr. Lester shook his hand and said, "You'll be all right."

Then he went out of the room with the nurse and said, "Now look, I want this to seem as though it's coming from my doctor. I don't really care about Kowalski but I don't see any point in offending him."

"All right," said the nurse. "The room is okay?"

"Swell," said Mr. Lester.

Mr. Lester went back to his room. The old man was gone now and there was fresh linen on his bed. The big man was listening to a radio. He turned it down a little and said, "My wife brought the radio. I don't really enjoy it unless we have a whole crowd around it cracking jokes. We get the beer and then we all sit around and let the announcer have it. I'm getting hungry. Somebody been sticking it into you outside?"

"I went out to get some sun," said Mr. Lester. "I feel better with a little tan on my body."

"You don't get any dinner, that's for sure," said the big man.

"That isn't true," said Mr. Lester. "I think I get cereal."

"You know what would happen to me if they just gave me cereal?" said the big man. "When I'm hungry I got to have my meal. Couple of the guys are coming up to see me tonight. I told them to just bring the beer. We'll give you some beer. You know what that would do to you with what you got? I wouldn't want to be around. You better just take your tea."

The man turned the radio up and Mr. Lester kept his head in a book during a long commercial. Dr. Rich arrived after a few minutes and pulled the curtain around Mr. Lester. "Has the situation altered?" asked Dr. Rich.

"It's deteriorated," said Mr. Lester.

"Then we go ahead with the new arrangement." Dr. Rich leaned forward and whispered, "By the way who is Stanley Kowalski? You had me hung up on that all morning."

"He's a character in a Williams play, *Streetcar Named Desire.* Rough, animal-like, but heart of gold. Brando played him."

"Oh," said Dr. Rich. "We saw *Glass Menagerie,* but we missed *Streetcar.* I couldn't figure that Kowalski thing out. In any case, it's all taken care of. Have you had any pain?"

"I don't know," said Mr. Lester. "I've been so upset I can't really tell."

Dr. Rich drew the curtain then and left.

"I'm going to be leaving you," said Mr. Lester to the big man. "The doctor wants me down the hall closer to the Isotope Ward."

"That right?" said the big man.

In a little while the blonde nurse came in and said, "The room you requested is ready for you now, Mr. Lester."

Mr. Lester smiled thinly and said, "You mean the room the doctor wanted for me, don't you, nurse?"

"Oh yes," said the nurse. Mr. Lester followed the nurse outside and said, "For Christ's sake, what did you say it that way for? Now he's going to think I'm chickening out. Oh, what the hell. Thanks, though, for everything."

He went back into the room to get his things and when he had them, he said, "I'll put my head in to see you again, Beans. Take it easy."

"No, *you* take it easy," said the big man. "You got to with what you got."

"We'll both take it easy," said Mr. Lester.

"Uh-uh," said the big man. "You. Just you. *You* take it easy."

"Okay," said Mr. Lester.

The big man turned up the radio while Mr. Lester, the hand really closing hard now, dug his fingers into the nurse's arm and retreated down the hall. The new room was dimly lit. Mr. Lester thanked the nurse and she left after she had straightened the bedsheets. Some of the tubes were still strung up around the radio announcer, but the nurses had gone. Mr. Lester sank back on his bed and waited a long while until the hand inside him stopped closing. He took a sip of cream then and a deep breath. The room was very quiet and the sheets felt cool and clean. "Is there anything I can do for you?" Mr. Lester asked the bald radio announcer. "Prop up your bed or get you something? I can get around."

"No," said the announcer, crying softly. "I'm waiting to find out which way the little ball is going to come out. Not for me so much but for my family and all I've been working for all my life."

"You'll be all right," said Mr. Lester, sinking back deeper into the cool sheets and relaxing for the first time since he'd been in the hospital. "Of course you've got to take it easy and rest an awful lot. You have to carry those pills and take a lot of naps, and you have to watch the stairs. You can't do much of anything. Not with what you got."

Yes, We Have No Ritchard

SINCE MR. DALTON had seen many films and plays and read a good deal on the subject, he expected, after he died, to find himself before a Cyril Ritchard-type clerk, wearing white and seated at a desk. Wings were optional. Droll remarks would follow, in British accent, such as, "We've got your records right here; what took you so long?" There would be a file cabinet and much shuffling of papers and talk about "bringing your records up to date." The "front office" would be mentioned and sooner or later the "boss," in such remarks as, "The boss is sure going to be riled up when he sees these typing errors." Plenty of white figured in Mr. Dalton's thoughts, too, cloaks and clouds and harps and floating things and subordinate people, too, all with such amusing comments as, "I've got to get my wings fixed."

What actually happened is that Mr. Dalton didn't get Ritchard, or, for that matter, anyone whose personality he could really nail down. The man did not wear a white robe, and Mr. Dalton, later on, could not recall what he wore. Something kind of vague and watery, if he wore anything at all. He certainly didn't have flip, or even impatient things to say, and he sat at something that wasn't a desk, and maybe he wasn't even sitting. He seemed to be a little lower than Mr. Dalton, and may have been sitting on a rock, although Mr. Dalton could not even be sure of that. Mr. Dalton himself could not remember whether he felt light and airy or whether there were clouds around, and none of the Hollywood things had happened at all. Except perhaps one. He seemed to be wearing a pair of sandals he had once purchased at Vic Tanny's Gym and Health Club so as not to get athlete's foot when working out in the gym. What else he was wearing, he couldn't say—or even if he *was* wearing something.

What was most disconcerting to Mr. Dalton was that he could not remember any elevator ride. It was the one thing he counted on most of all and he was *certain* there would be one in there somewhere, a ride upward, and then, when they were finished with him, the decision as to whether to send him up or down. Mr. Dalton did not know whether to speak or wait to be spoken to, but he was so upset, he said to the man with the nebulous face and no distinctive personality, "Look, I don't remember any elevator ride. Oh, you know what I mean. I don't really

344

mean an elevator ride. Maybe you use a Volkswagen or a coal car, but I've got to know whether you've got a good side and a bad side here. Just tell me that and anything you say from here on in is all right with me."

"We have a good side and a bad side," the man said, and this relaxed Mr. Dalton and he felt at least there was a little something to the movie ideas he'd gotten.

"But I'll bet you don't even have it the Hollywood way," Mr. Dalton said. "Up and down is the way they do it. I'll bet you have it left side and right."

The nebulous man, if he was a man, said, "That's correct."

The reason Mr. Dalton was glad about this was that, however unsophisticated it may have sounded, he was quite certain that he had been a nice man during his life. He knew many people probably felt that way about themselves, but he was certain, at the very heart of himself, that he really *had* been nice and wasn't just feeling this way to buoy his spirits. If you stacked up his good deeds against his bad ones, the good ones wouldn't just outweigh the bad ones, they would win ridiculously and overwhelmingly, no contest. And it wasn't that there was one sneaky thing he'd been trying to cover up and atone for by piling up millions of good deeds. There was nothing sneaky at all, and even if there *had* been (there hadn't), well, by God, he was still nice. He'd say that to anyone, whether he was dead or alive or whatever the hell condition he was in now.

"Did you know I've been nice?" he asked the man."

"I know," the man said.

"You probably have records and you're going to pull out a sheet on me. You have everybody's file, don't you? You have a file cabinet somewhere."

"No," the man said.

"It's not at all the way I'd imagined it," Mr. Dalton said, or thought he said. "When do we get started?"

The man said, "We could have started a little while ago, before you started talking. Or now, later, any time."

"Do I get a say in where we get started?" Mr. Dalton asked.

The man looked through him and Mr. Dalton thought, "He isn't saying anything because a little personality was beginning to come through. He clammed up just in time. A little more and I could have pinned him down."

And then Mr. Dalton wondered whether you were allowed to think things to yourself when you were dead. He turned off his mind for a while, just to be on the safe side. He thought of water, which was like not thinking at all to him. Maybe when you were dead, if you began thinking things they counted against you.

"We'll go now," the man said.

"Say some more, so I can get the hang of you," Mr. Dalton said. Mr. Dalton felt he was good at pinning personalities down, packaging people. If the man said just a little more, Mr. Dalton would have him, and perhaps be able to do a routine on him, one as good as his George Burns imitation. Mr. Dalton could not remember whether he himself had been in advertising or not. The only thing he could remember was that somehow, somewhere, at some time, he had been at Vic Tanny's.

They seemed to walk somewhere and, try as he might, Mr. Dalton, although he'd promised to check the man's outfit, what he looked like, his walk and mannerisms, forgot to do these things. He remembered only that the man had seemed to be a little lower than him. Mr. Dalton brought up *Green Pastures* as something he'd liked and then said, "I'll bet you think I'm just trying to butter you up, to say I like your racket, know about it and some of my best friends are heavenly clerks or whatever you are."

They passed a Danish modern sofa with shiny wood and Mr. Dalton thought, "Now there are two things I know. The Tanny slippers and the sofa. I wonder if there'll be any more. Maybe there are only two things you recognize in this whole trip or maybe twelve. I wonder how many?" He said to the man, "I know I'm wearing Tanny slippers and I recognized a Danish modern sofa. That's all that's tangible. Will there be anything else? Anything else I can recognize or touch or sort of make reference to?"

"One more," the man said. "Air conditioning."

"I've got him now," Mr. Dalton thought. "Now I can tell what kind of person he is. From that last line of dialogue." And yet for the life of him, Mr. Dalton could not pinpoint what kind of man he was, although Mr. Dalton himself seemed to recall once being in advertising or at least being good at packaging people.

They stopped walking, if they had been walking. Mr. Dalton knew only that they sure as hell weren't standing still.

"Are we here?" Mr. Dalton asked. "I mean, where I'm going to be?" Then he added, "Forever, that is," feeling a little silly, as though he were in one of those heaven movies again.

The man nodded.

"I can't remember," Mr. Dalton asked, "whether you took me to the left or to the right. Let me get one thing straight. I hate to be a bore, but you do know I'm nice, don't you?"

The man nodded.

"And left is your nice side and right is your bad side?"

"Yes," said the man.

"Then you took me to the left, right?" said Mr. Dalton, not without apprehension.

"No," said the nebulous man. "To the right."

Mr. Dalton, rattled, and feeling he had every right to be rattled, said, "But why? You're probably not convinced that I'm nice, correct?"

"No," said the man.

"I know then," said Mr. Dalton, quite convinced he had the answer. "You have a reverse sort of logic up here. You put the nice guys on the bad side and the bad guys on the nice side. There's a perverse someone at work up here. Isn't that it? It's foolish, you know, because all us nice ones will know, even while we're on the bad side, that we're still nice. You're just being perverse for its own sake. Why do you do that? Just to be different? Listen, do I get to punch you if I don't like something here?"

Mr. Dalton took a look at the man and for a brief second thought he could actually see him and size him up. He guessed he had forty pounds on the man.

"Look, I mean no disrespect," said Mr. Dalton. "A week from now, if I see you again, and I suppose I do (Hollywood again), I'll probably feel stupid. But you must take an awful lot of abuse."

The man said, "I've got to go now."

"Don't go," said Mr. Dalton. "I've got to get organized? Why did you put me on the bad side?"

Mr. Dalton tried to grab the man and hold on to him, looking around furiously, thinking, "Christ, I'm backed against the wall. If only I could get one of those breaks you're supposed to get when you're at an all-time low." He looked up and down the right side, where he was to be and got the break. He spotted a print he had seen once before at Bloomingdale's department store and a man he knew as Mr. Sydel. Mr. Sydel was engaged in doing something to the ground or whatever it was beneath him. "Look," said Mr. Dalton, "I know him. I don't care what in the hell he told you, and maybe this is the first un-nice thing I've ever done, but he is not a nice man. He stole paper from some kind of crazy company I used to work for with him and even if he was never caught he really was a crook. He's still a crook. And it wasn't the only bad thing he did. I can't document any others, but believe me there were others. How in the hell can we be put on the same side? You know he's bad, don't you?"

"So I understand," the man said. "That is, I don't really know, but one of my colleagues so informs me."

"He's slipping," Mr. Dalton thought. "By that statement he told me something that will enable me to package him, pin down his personality. He has 'colleagues,' which means he's classy, has studied . . . But, still, I'll have to know more."

"If you both know he's bad, how come he's down here? Don't tell me. You've got the bad side divided up into sections. On one side you put bad guys, like Mr. Sydel, on the other, people like me? Correct?"

"No," the man said.

The air conditioning went on, and Mr. Dalton felt himself relax, in spite of himself.

"Look, for Christ's sake, what's the deal? You have a good side and a bad side, right?"

The man nodded, but looked impatient. "I really have to go."

"Two more minutes won't kill you," said Mr. Dalton. "Who the hell do you put over on the good side? People who are nicer than me? You have some sort of score and I didn't score high enough, is that it? The place is crowded up with people who got higher scores, right?"

The man began edging away, and Mr. Dalton said, "You stay right here. I never punched people as much as I should, but by God, I'll punch you if I have to." But then Mr. Dalton felt demolished and said, "Stay with me another minute, will you? Maybe I'll never see you again and there won't be anyone to tell me what to do. How to get along here. What the hell the rules are. I mean if it's forever, I have to know, don't I?"

"I do have a schedule, Mr. Dalton," the man said kindly.

"Can you call me Philip?" Mr. Dalton asked. For a second he felt a joke coming on, like, "If I get friendly with you, can you fix traffic tickets?" but decided not to ask it. When the joke went out of his mind, the panic started again.

"What I started to ask is how in the hell I get over on the good side? Can you name me one person who's over there so I can get an idea of what you've got to have, where I missed out?"

"I can't do that," the man said.

"Why, for Christ's sake? I'm a dying man. I'm dead and I'm dying all over again. I need some help."

"All right then, I'd rather not go into this, but we don't have anyone over there. There is no one on our good side."

"It's for the staff?"

"No, even the staff doesn't use it. For a while we had women with enormous bosoms over there, for a very short while, but everyone saw the fallacy in that and so now no one gets in."

"There's no one on the good side," Mr. Dalton said. "That means we're all over here, right?"

"Yes," the man said.

"What's it like on the good side? Can anyone see it?"

"There's no point," the man said. "In an extreme case, if it will make someone feel good, we take him or her over, but it isn't such a hot idea."

"I don't have to see it," Mr. Dalton said. "Maybe I'm a little curious, but that's all. Naturally, what bugs me—I'm talking calmly but I'm really stirred up about this—is that Mr. Sydel and all the Mr. Sydels have to be on the same side as me. I mean you say you know I was nice and you say you know he was a creep. How do you square it? Does he do another kind of thing up here? Does he do harder work?"

"No," said the man. "Now I really have to go. I'm getting, frankly, very irritated."

"I don't care about that," Mr. Dalton said. The man looked at him sternly and Mr. Dalton said, "Of course, I care, but you've got to tell me. Do I get better food? That's ridiculous," he added quickly. "I'm dead and I don't eat. I don't, do I?"

"If it's necessary," the man said, "we bring food in."

"Would you bring food in for Mr. Sydel if it was necessary? For all the Mr. Sydels? That's it, isn't it. You'd bring it in for me and you wouldn't for him . . . ?"

"No," the man said.

"What then? There has to be something. I get to go out and have sex once a million years and he doesn't, right? That's how you get him."

"No," the man said. "You both do. The figure is wrong. It's once a fortnight."

"I get prettier girls?"

"Sometimes. And sometimes he does."

"Then what—what? I've been good. *He's been a bastard! What? What? What?*"

The man seemed to make a note on a piece of paper or something. "I'll see that you get some medication," the man said.

"I don't want any. You'd give it to Sydel, too, wouldn't you? Keep your medicine," said Mr. Dalton, weeping, demolished.

Then he stopped crying and blocked what seemed to be the man's way. "The air conditioning. That's it, isn't it? I get to feel it and he doesn't. I should have known. For an eternity, Sydel sits here knowing there's air conditioning and he can't feel it and I can. That's his punishment. That's my reward."

"He feels it, too," said the man, employing a snotty tone.

"I beg you," said Mr. Dalton on his knees. "Look, I have no shame. I cry in front of you. I cry, I scream, I beg, I have no pride. Tell me, please tell me. Please."

And then Mr. Dalton glanced down at his own sandals. "Tanny's," he said. "That's it. I have these slippers and he doesn't. He walks barefoot for an eternity, a million eternities, and you give me, us, slippers from Tanny's and we feel nothing in our feet and he feels every bump, every splinter, every whatever the hell you've got here. I have you now, you stubborn sonofabitch. I do, you know. I defy you to tell me Sydel has Tanny slippers on, too."

"Al Roon's Athletic Club on Eighth Avenue in New York City," said the man, and he seemed to have lost his composure the slightest bit. Mr. Dalton waited now, waited for *him* to speak.

"We, uh, couldn't get Tanny's so we got Roon's. There really isn't any difference. It's purely administrative. If we'd gotten Tanny's, we certainly wouldn't have used Roon's. You're really making a big thing out of nothing. Tanny's, Roon's, the spirit is the same, I assure you."

"But by God, *we've* got the Tanny's and the Sydels have the Roon's and never mind the administrative stuff. That's it and you know in your black heart that's it and don't you sit there and tell me it isn't."

"No, no, no," said the man. "You've got it all wrong, Mr. Dalton."

"Philip," said Mr. Dalton, sitting on something, possibly a chair, and folding his arms. "And you can go now."

The Neighbors

LANG HAD ALWAYS FELT that the way to solve the neighbor problem was simply to thrust yourself into the day's activities, to go about your business and ignore the new fellow and his unpleasantness. But Gionfriddo was no ordinary neighbor. Lang could sense his presence. Although he could not look out and see him, he was aware of his movements, could almost smell him. Lang actually made a physical effort to shut the other man out of his consciousness, biting down on his gums and clamping shut his eyes; but it was as though the other man had a way of sending a sentrylike finger through Lang's defenses, to steal beneath his T-shirt, to press upon his chest.

The morning Gionfriddo moved in, Lang had felt a thrumming begin around his neck and for the first time was stifled and wanted to move. He knew that was impossible, that it would not solve the problem anyway. What if he moved next to someone worse than Gionfriddo, worse than ten Gionfriddos. The trouble was all inside his own head and had to be worked out there.

At first, Gionfriddo had many visitors and Lang thought that might be the key to it. They actually *did* set up a commotion and, at least during the daytime, it was difficult to be unaware of the clatter. But then the flow of visitors slowed to a trickle and Lang remained uncomfortable. He began listening for his neighbor's guests, coiled and tense, as though daring people to come and make a commotion so that he might justifiably flail out at them.

Then there were no visitors at all except for an occasional weekend one, and Lang was able to settle down and be annoyed by Gionfriddo alone. By his square wooden grin. The tall bad teeth. By his ascots. His nauseating sales records. By all the times he used the word "periphery." Actually, Lang had spent only one evening with Gionfriddo and his wife, six months previous, and, at the time, it seemed the world's most unlikely prospect they would ever wind up neighbors.

As a matter of fact, Gionfriddo had kicked off the evening (it was a dinner party) by insulting Lang's neighborhood, calling it "pseudo." It was one of those dividing-line insults, half good-natured, half malicious, and it had caught Lang off guard, spearing him in the stomach and making him tense for twenty minutes. Lang's wife had looked hopefully toward her husband *(her* neighborhood had been insulted, too), and it had taken Lang two martinis and the better part of an hour to make a limp comeback. "You know that neighborhood of *yours* doesn't sound too jolly either, old boy." But by that time everyone had forgotten what Lang was coming back at.

It was then, right before dinner, that Gionfriddo had begun to throw "periphery" around. He did not like people who were out there at the periphery. "Either you get right in there at the center of issues or you keep your damned mouth shut," he said.

Although the net of his accusation took in Lang, as well as everyone in the room, he seemed to have his heavy guns sighted in on one guest in particular, a well-known judge who had just been eased out of the hospital after a coronary. Yellowed and slow-moving, the once great jurist told benign nonstimulating anecdotes of his early career, holding on to end tables when he began to feel worked up.

"That's an example of what I mean," Gionfriddo would say at the end of a story. His face was lean, the skin drawn tight over the cheek-bones as though he were pulling G's in an experimental jet. "Someone who stands out there at the periphery and tries to lecture other people on what to do. Nothing personal, you understand, this is all for the sake of argument, but you people who stand out there get me sick."

There was never anything personal, he wanted everyone to know. And he never really meant anything he said. It was all for the sake of argument. The dinner was seafood, plump oysters and succulent shrimp, larger than any Lang had ever eaten.

"I don't like you," Gionfriddo said, thrusting a long finger across the table at Lang, who was reaching for the chili sauce. "I don't care whether you live or die. I want to get everything I can out of life and if you go up in smoke, it won't bother me in the slightest. I won't push you in front of a car. I won't cut your ribs with a knife. But if anything like that happens to you, it's no skin off my nose. Now this is just for the sake of argument, you understand. I don't necessarily feel this way. I'm just taking this philosophical position for a moment. But go ahead and knock it down. Tell me why I should care about one soul other than Mr. Me. I splashed a firebomb on the heads of four hundred Gooks in Namsam in the Korean War and I haven't lost a wink of sleep over it. Anyway, go ahead, tear all this down. Take potshots at it."

"To not care about your fellow man is to say that life is worthless." It was all that Lang could muster. There was silence at the table. Lang was a lecturer in sociology and it was apparent that more had been expected of him. "I happen to believe that man has worth," he contin-ued. "To ignore or hurt someone is to reduce the stature of all men."

The enfeebled jurist came to his rescue with a weak and folksy yarn about the first couple who had ever come before him for a divorce.

"Periphery stuff," said Gionfriddo, shoving his plate away in disgust. "Nothing personal, we're just debating, but you people are out there on your tangents expecting the world to skip to your tunes." Gionfriddo's wife was a rangy attractive woman who walked in a straight-legged way as though she were on stilts. Earlier in the evening she had said she thought psychiatrists were fake and that all people who went to them were just feeling sorry for themselves. At the dinner's end, she dug her fingers into Gionfriddo's hair and said, "The fireworks. The adorable fireworks in his head."

Later in the evening, over cordials, Gionfriddo put his head next to the retired judge's and said, "If I thought you were really serious, I'd like to give you a philosophical punch in the nose."

The elderly judge rose, his jowls quivering, what little color he had fast spilling out of his face. "Now look here, young man," he said. "Darling," said his wife, taking his elbow and easing him back into the chair. The evening passed quietly then, tapering off with mild talk of Fellini films and the worth of the Peace Corps. "With all due respect to your stature and your field of endeavor," Gionfriddo had said to Lang as they made for their respective cars, "I was a little disappointed in your staying up there at the conversational surface all the time."

That was the style of Gionfriddo the one evening Lang had been in his company. In other words, he was not that bad. There were the ascots, of course. The fake boyishness. The foot-tapping while he waited for you to get finished talking. His comedy style was awful, too, just fast and lively enough to fake some people into thinking he was funny. All Lang got out of it was the hysteria.

Now, irony of all ironies, they were neighbors. Gionfriddo was far from unbearable. You might even be able to take him in small doses. An accidental meeting on the street, a drink perhaps, maybe even another dinner party. He did have a little bite to him which is more than you could say for most people. But this was different. This had no cutoff point.

There had been the accidents, one after the other, like wild dice hurled from a cup. First Lang's, a sightseeing bus taking a tight, lumbering, main street turn; Gionfriddo's next, a bee sting, at first benign, suddenly grim, poisons galloping through his veins, uncheckable, life-snuffing. And now they were just to lie there in disintegrating silence, plot to plot, stone to stone, tomb to tomb, eternal neighbors for God knows how many thousands, how many millions of years.

The Family Man

Let's Hear It for a
Beautiful Guy

*Sammy Davis is trying to get a few months off for a
complete rest.*

—Earl Wilson,
February 7, 1974.

I HAVE BEEN TRYING to get a few months off for a complete rest, too, but
I think it's more important that Sammy Davis get one. I feel that I can
scrape along and manage somehow, but Sammy Davis always looks so
strained and tired. The pressure on the guy must be enormous. It must
have been a terrific blow to him when he switched his allegiance to
Agnew and Nixon, only to have the whole thing blow up in his face. I
was angry at him, incidentally, along with a lot of other fans of his, all
of us feeling he had sold us down the river. But after I had thought it
over and let my temper cool a bit, I changed my mind and actually
found myself standing up for him, saying I would bet anything that
Agnew and Nixon had made some secret promises to Sammy about
easing the situation of blacks—ones that the public still doesn't know
about. Otherwise, there was no way he would have thrown in his lot
with that crowd. In any case, I would forgive the guy just about anything. How can I feel any other way when I think of the pleasure he's
given me over the years, dancing and clowning around and wrenching
those songs out of that wiry little body? Always giving his all, no matter
what the composition of the audience. Those years of struggle with the
Will Mastin Trio, and then finally making it, only to find marital strife
staring him in the face. None of us will ever be able to calculate what it
took out of him each time he had a falling-out with Frank. Is there any
doubt who Dean and Joey sided with on those occasions? You can be
sure Peter Lawford didn't run over to offer Sammy any solace. And
does anyone ever stop to consider the spiritual torment he must have
suffered when he made the switch to Judaism? I don't even want to
talk about the eye. So, if anyone in the world does, he certainly deserves a few months off for a complete rest.

Somehow, I have the feeling that if I met Sammy, I could break through his agents and that entourage of his and convince him he ought to take off with me and get the complete rest he deserves. I don't want any 10 percent, I don't want any glory; I just feel I owe it to him. Sure he's got commitments, but once and for all he's got to stop and consider that it's one time around, and no one can keep up that pace of his forever.

The first thing I would do is get him out of Vegas. There is absolutely no way he can get a few months' rest in that sanatorium. I would get him away from Vegas, and I would certainly steer clear of Palm Springs. Imagine him riding down Bob Hope Drive and checking into a hotel in the Springs! For a rest? The second he walked into the lobby, it would all start. The chambermaids would ask him to do a chorus of "What Kind of Fool Am I," right in the lobby, and, knowing Sammy and his big heart, he would probably oblige. I think I would take him to my place in New York, a studio. We would have to eat in, because if I ever showed up with Sammy Davis at the Carlton Delicatessen, where I have my breakfast, the roof would fall in. The owner would ask him for an autographed picture to hang up next to Dustin Hoffman's, and those rich young East Side girls would go to town on him. If they ever saw me walk in with Sammy Davis, that would be the end of his complete rest. They would attack him like vultures, and Sammy would be hard put to turn his back on them, because they're not broads.

We would probably wind up ordering some delicatessen from the Stage, although I'm not so sure that's a good idea; the delivery boy would recognize him, and the next thing you know, Sammy would give him a C note, and word would get back to Alan King that Sammy had ducked into town. How would it look if he didn't drop over to the Stage and show himself? Next thing you know, the news would reach Jilly's, and if Frank was in town—well, you can imagine how much rest Sammy would get. I don't know if they're feuding these days, but you know perfectly well that, at minimum, Frank would send over a pure-bred Afghan. Even if they were feuding.

I think what we would probably do is lay low and order a lot of Chinese food. I have a hunch that Sammy can eat Chinese takeout food every night of the week. I know I can, and the Chinese takeout delivery guys are very discreet. So we would stay at my place. I'd give him the sleeping loft, and I'd throw some sheets on the couch downstairs for me. I would do that for Sammy to pay him back for all the joy he's given me down through the years. And I would resist the temptation to ask him to sing, even though I would flip out if he so much as started humming. Can you imagine him humming "The Candy Man"? *In my apartment?* Let's not even discuss it.

Another reason I would give him the sleeping loft is that there is no phone up there. I would try like the devil to keep him away from the phone, because I know the second he saw one he would start thinking about his commitments, and it would be impossible for the guy not to make at least one call to the Coast. So I'd just try to keep him comfortable for as long as possible, although pretty soon my friends would begin wondering what ever happened to me, and it would take all the willpower in the world not to let on that I had Sammy Davis in my loft and was giving him a complete rest.

I don't kid myself that I could keep Sammy Davis happy in my loft for a full couple of months. He would be lying on the bed, his frail muscular body looking lost in a pair of boxer shorts, and before long I would hear those fingers snapping, and I would know that the wiry little great entertainer was feeling penned up and it would be inhuman to expect him to stay there any longer. I think that when I sensed that Sammy was straining at the leash, I would rent a car—a Ford LTD (that would be a switch for him, riding in a Middle American car)— and we would ride out to my sister and brother-in-law's place in Jersey. He would probably huddle down in the seat, but somehow I have the feeling that people in passing cars would spot him. We'd be lucky if they didn't crash into telephone poles. And if I know Sammy, whenever someone recognized him he wouldn't be able to resist taking off his shades and graciously blowing them a kiss.

The reason I would take Sammy to my sister and brother-in-law's house is because they're simple people and would not hassle him— especially my brother-in-law. My sister would stand there with her hands on her hips, and when she saw me get out of the Ford with Sammy, she would cluck her tongue and say, "There goes my crazy brother again," but she would appear calm on the surface, even though she would be fainting dead away on the inside. She would say something like "Oh, my God, I didn't even clean the floors," but then Sammy would give her a big hug and a kiss, and I'm sure that he would make a call, and a few weeks later she would have a complete new dining-room set, the baby grand she always wanted and a puppy.

She would put Sammy up in her son's room (he's away at graduate school), saying she wished she had something better, but he would say, "Honey, this is just perfect." And he would mean it, too, in a way, my nephew's bedroom being an interesting change from those one-thousand-dollar-a-day suites at the Tropicana. My brother-in-law has a nice easygoing style and would be relaxing company for Sammy, except that Al does work in television and there would be a temptation on his part to talk about the time he did the *Don Rickles Show* and how different and sweet a guy Don is when you get him offstage. If I know Sammy, he would place a call to CBS—with no urging from any of us—and see to it that Al got to work on his next special. If the network couldn't do a little thing like that for him, the hell with them, he would get himself another network. Sammy's that kind of guy.

One danger is that my sister, by this time, would be going out of her mind and wouldn't be able to resist asking Sammy if she could have a few neighbors over on a Saturday night. Let's face it, it would be the thrill of a lifetime for her. I would intercede right there, because it wouldn't be fair to the guy, but if I know Sammy he would tell her, "Honey, you go right ahead." She would have a mixed group over— Italians, an Irish couple, some Jews, about twelve people tops—and she would wind up having the evening catered, which of course would lead to a commotion when she tried to pay for the stuff. No way Sammy would let her do that. He would buy out the whole delicatessen, give the delivery guy a C note and probably throw in an autographed glossy without being asked.

Everyone at the party would pretend to be casual, as if Sammy Davis weren't there, but before long the Irish space salesman's wife (my sister's crazy friend, and what a flirt *she* is) would somehow manage to ask him to sing, and imagine Sammy saying no in a situation like that. Everyone would say just one song, but that bighearted son of a gun would wind up doing his entire repertoire, probably putting out every bit as much as he does when he opens at the Sands. He would do it all —"The Candy Man," "What Kind of Fool Am I," tap dance, play the drums with chopsticks on an end table, do some riffs on my nephew's old trumpet and work himself into exhaustion. The sweat would be pouring out of him, and he would top the whole thing off with "This Is My Life" ("and I don't give a damn"). Of course, his agents on the Coast would pass out cold if they ever got wind of the way he was putting out for twelve nobodies in Jersey. But as for Sammy, he never did know anything about halfway measures. He either works or he doesn't, and he would use every ounce of energy in that courageous little show-biz body of his to see to it that my sister's friends—that mixed group of Italians, Irish and Jews—had a night they'd never forget as long as they lived.

Of course, that would blow the two months of complete rest, and I would have to get him out of Jersey fast. By that time, frankly, I would be running out of options. Once in a while, I pop down to Puerto Rico for a three- or four-day holiday, but, let's face it, if I showed up in San Juan with Sammy, first thing you know, we would be hounded by broads, catching the show at the Flamboyan, and Dick Shawn would be asking Sammy to hop up onstage and do a medley from *Mr. Wonderful.*

(He was really something in that show, battling Jack Carter tooth and nail, but too gracious to use his bigger name to advantage.)

Another possibility would be to take Sammy out to see a professor friend of mine who teaches modern lit at San Francisco State and would be only too happy to take us in. That would represent a complete change for Sammy, a college campus, but as soon as the school got wind he was around, I'll bet you ten to one they would ask him to speak either to a film class or the drama department or even a political-science group. And he would wind up shocking them with his expertise on the Founding Fathers and the philosophy behind the Bill of Rights. The guy reads, and I'm not talking about *The Bette Davis Story*. Anyone who sells Sammy Davis short as an intellectual is taking his life in his hands.

In the end, Sammy and I would probably end up in Vermont, where a financial-consultant friend of mine has a cabin that he never uses. He always says to me, "It's there, for God's sake—use it." So I would take Sammy up there, away from it all, but I wouldn't tell the financial consultant who I was taking, because the second he heard it was Sammy Davis he would want to come along. Sammy and I would start out by going into town for a week's worth of supplies at the general store, and then we would hole up in the cabin. I'm not too good at mechanical things, but we would be sort of roughing it, and there wouldn't be much to do except chop some firewood, which I would take care of while Sammy was getting his complete rest.

I don't know how long we would last in Vermont. Frankly, I would worry after a while about being able to keep him entertained, even though he would be there for a complete rest. We could talk a little about Judaism, but, frankly, I would be skating on thin ice in that area, since I don't have the formal training he has or any real knowledge of theology. The Vermont woods would probably start us batting around theories about the mystery of existence, but to tell the truth, I'd be a little bit out of my depth in that department, too. He's had so much experience on panel shows, and I would just as soon not go one-on-one with him on that topic.

Let's not kid around, I would get tense after a while, and Sammy would feel it. He would be too good a guy to let on that he was bored, but pretty soon he would start snapping those fingers and batting out tunes on the back of an old *Saturday Evening Post* or something, and I think I would crack after a while and say, "Sammy, I tried my best to supply you with a couple of months of complete rest, but I'm running out of gas." He would tap me on the shoulder and say, "Don't worry about it, babe," and then, so as not to hurt my feelings, he would say he wanted to go into town to get some toothpaste. So he would drive in, with the eye and all, and I know damned well the first thing he would do is call his agents on the Coast and ask them to read him the "N.Y. to L.A." column of a few *Variety*s. Next thing you know, I would be driving him to the airport, knowing in my heart that I hadn't really succeeded. He would tell me that any time I got to the Coast or Vegas or the Springs, and I wanted anything, *anything,* just make sure to give him a ring. And the following week, I would receive a freezer and a videotape machine and a puppy.

So I think I'm just not the man to get Sammy Davis the complete rest he needs so desperately. However, I certainly think someone should. How long can he keep driving that tortured little frame of his, pouring every ounce of his strength into the entertainment of Americans? I know, I know—there's Cambodia and Watergate, and, believe me, I haven't forgotten our own disadvantaged citizens. I know all that. But when you think of all the joy that man has spread through his night-club appearances, his albums, his autobiography, his video specials and even his movies, which did not gross too well but were a lot better than people realized, and the things he's done not only for his friends but for a lot of causes the public doesn't know about—when you think of all that courageous little entertainer has given to this land of ours, and then you read that he's trying, repeat *trying,* to get a few months off for a complete rest and he can't, well, then, all I can say is that there's something basically rotten in the system.

The Scientist

HAD THE CEREMONY been scheduled for Warsaw or New Delhi, he would have flown to either city immediately and without question; the very distance, the exotic setting, would have given a certain weight to the award. But many of the delegates were Europeans, anxious themselves to make a trip abroad, and there had been a decision to take the proceedings, almost literally, to Granville's doorstep; he was happy it had worked out that way. He would be able to continue his routine, which he now prized above all else in life.

Upon taking his stool at the luncheonette, he was given his tea almost immediately; there was no need to place an order. Granville was familiar with most of the town's residents, at least those who milled about at the noon hour, yet the woman who eased her way past his stool was new to him. Granville looked at her, not quite with alarm, but as though she were an animal he had caught intruding upon a small, carefully tended garden. As she worked her way past Granville, she clutched at his arm with what seemed to be an iron tentacle and it occurred to him that she was probably older than any person he had ever seen in the town. Her skin was dark and folded like an old, forgotten memo, and her eyes had a wild, chickenlike pop to them. It did not surprise him that she began to speak to him and it surprised him even less that the talk centered on the importance of staying spry and alert; also, her feeling that it was wrong to put old people to death, no matter what the circumstances. He listened with some interest, yet there was a curtain between them; he could get no more involved than if he were a journalist doing an interview. At most, she was twenty-five years his senior; yet this talk about "alertness" had nothing to do with Granville. Old Age, Death, Alertness—he had not yet gotten around to thinking about them. He would take care of them "later." Once, as a much younger man, he had gotten an unguarded look at his reflection in the mirror of a tennis-club locker room and seen a new and somewhat slack conformation around his buttocks—the first significant change he had noticed in his body. It had bothered him at the time and then he had simply put it out of his mind. The old woman beside him said that her grandchildren were quite proud of her and that when anyone asked how she was feeling she would sing "Glory, Glory, Hallelujah" to them. Granville enjoyed talking to her. But he did not really hear her. She was a prop, a background sound, a decoration for his daily routine.

It was flattering to think that men from as far away as the Soviet Union not only knew of his work but had traveled all this distance to honor him. His achievement had been legitimate, and yet Granville knew that in a sense he had been "playing over his head." As a young athlete many years before, he had had a similar experience; an average shooter, he had begun, during one basketball game, to score points from all over the court, almost involuntarily, each of his shots mysteriously guided through the hoop the instant he released the ball. Many years later, he had had one such day in his laboratory, a sudden breakthrough, for a few hours his mind yawning untypically, gaping wide; like an insane man he had clutched at the chance, working with demented fury, time counting for nothing, grabbing at the bait, catching enough of it, holding on and then settling back in exhaustion with his prize. The award had been earned and yet Granville knew that he had been responsible for "helping things along" ever so slightly. He was outwardly bumbling, absentminded, somewhat dissociated—yet it was a practiced style, and there was very clearly another side to Granville, one that saw to it he was taken care of. A key man on the committee was Krulski, a Pole. He had been on the East Coast several years before, an almost painfully dour, monotonous-looking man. Granville had invited the Pole to spend the weekend at his country home. Even as he performed this "simple act of kindness" to a lonely man, Granville was aware of its potential use to him. Then, too, Granville's very appearance—easy, comfortable, reassuring—must have helped him enormously. For so many years, he had been the complete opposite of these qualities; he'd been unstable, suspicious, somewhat paranoid. And yet, in a curious way, he had gradually changed and come closer to being what he appeared to be—as though he'd been forced to catch up with his physical image.

Granville paid the check, tipped his hat to the old woman and thought suddenly of his mother who had called early that morning just in case he'd gotten his dates mixed up and forgotten about the award luncheon. She had had a lingering cough, cold, slatelike, and he wondered if she was ever going to lose it. Through the many years of his married life, he had gotten almost completely away from her, but his wife's death had marked the end of his Liberation. Though he vowed it would never happen, in an almost sly manner he had gotten closer to his mother than ever before. He told himself they were on an entirely new basis, however.

He took the steps of the Town Hall briskly, very much aware of how vigorous he must have seemed to anyone watching. There were times, after sucking at his pipe for many hours, that he could not really get to the top of an honest breath, but he could not imagine reaching a stage in which he would be unable to dash up the Town Hall steps. His picture had been posted in the alcove and he was pleased to see that an open-shirted one had been chosen—one that made him seem both rugged and distinguished. He smiled at the receptionist and then thought of his mother's cough and wondered whether he should not schedule dinner with her for the following evening. It occurred to him that there might not be that many opportunities left. And then, still looking at his picture in the alcove, he imagined himself getting the news of his mother's death and putting his "plan" into action; he would drive immediately to an old resort in the Pennsylvania mountains where she had taken him so often as a boy—and sit at a bar and order a whiskey and think about her in the flush of her youth, and talk to the bartender and cry a little—and in that way honor her memory. He was not sure the resort still existed, but even if it had been turned into a dance hall or a skating rink, it would serve. He had been over the "plan" many times in his mind and was fairly certain he would follow it when the time came.

The Pole was the first to greet him at the Reception Hall. Their handshake was warm, yet broken off quickly, as though each of them feared that too much warmth might be observed and interpreted incorrectly. Granville said hello to many of the others and then took a short stroll with Krulski, both men walking with heads bowed slightly, arms locked behind their backs; it was a manner Granville had quickly adopted after his first international conference, one that came so naturally to him now he would never have considered it an affectation. They spoke English, coming back again and again—as they had that weekend—to such words as "humanity" and "mankind." It was politely fraudulent talk; Granville might have been uttering alien sounds in a Buddhist temple. Yet without the nuances of a common language, it was as close to communication as they were going to get. For a moment, as they stood on the terrace, Granville noticed that the Pole bore an almost nervous resemblance to his late uncle George. When Granville's mother was young and fatherless, according to her stories, it was always her brother George who had protected her, made sure she was warm at night, stole to get her dresses. Perhaps Granville had been kind to the Pole for more complicated reasons than he suspected.

There had been a time when meetings and luncheons did not bore him so much as frighten him, when he was happy to get them over with as soon as possible. He wanted this one to stretch on indefinitely and was a little sorry when the delegates were finally beckoned to the table.

It felt comfortable sitting down with these people, some of them men of considerable achievement, all of them there to honor him. During the morning call, his mother, when she had been able to still her cough, had made the award seem even more important than it was. Even when he had broken off from her, through all the years of his marriage, he had defended her enormous gift of enthusiasm. He could not comprehend what it would be like to accomplish something in life and not have her there to exult, to be bowled over in her special way.

Considering the importance of the talk, he had thought of reading from a prepared text, but then realized there was little need for that. He thought briefly of his graduation, when he had gotten no further than the opening line of a memorized speech and had been gripped by a sudden rush of terror and forced to sit down in humiliation. It was terribly remote. It might have happened to another person, in another life. He was in command now. He owned his thoughts. They were as much a part of him as the brisk little trot he used for the Town Hall steps.

Once introduced, he took his time getting to his feet and for a moment stood at the dais without speaking a word. He listened to the delegates applaud with genuine fervor; their affection for him was warming—a cloak might have been placed about his shoulders.

"How remarkable," he began, finally, his voice rich, firm, "that lodged in the flesh of mankind there exists a mysterious potential for scientific mommy that . . ." He could not be certain, of course, that he had actually uttered the word; it might have been a loose echo floating idly across his brain. He began again: "How remarkable that lodged . . ." but then he could no longer control himself and it spilled out of him in such a powerful mixing torrent of grief and loss that only the earth itself, deserted suddenly by a massive body of water, could ever have known. "Oh mommy," he said. "Oh mommy, mommy, mommy, don't die . . . Oh mommy, mom, mommy, mom, mommy, mom, mom . . ."

The Gentle Revolutionaries

FRED HUGHES STRETCHED OUT on his king-sized bed at the Cyrano Hotel in West Hollywood and tried, without success, to get back to sleep. The musician in the next room—adhering strictly to the rules—had begun to practice at nine in the morning on the dot—and Fred had been awakened by the sound of deep bass chords, rumbling through the walls. In truth, he didn't mind that much. He had been at the Cyrano for a month—and this was the first time he'd been disturbed by music —unusual in a hotel that catered to recording artists. It seemed fitting that it should happen on the day of his departure.

In an hour, a car was scheduled to pick him up and take him to the Los Angeles Airport. From there, he would fly back to his home on the North Fork of eastern Long Island. He had been living out of a suitcase, picking up an extra shirt or two and some underwear along the way. At home, his house was crowded with furniture. Both his basement and attic were filled with files and the accumulated possessions of a lifetime. His clothing never wore out, so he had several closets that were crammed with suits and sweaters and shirts he never wore. Not to speak of the extra TV sets and TV monitors and all the things that belonged to Melissa and the girls. But at the Cyrano Hotel, he realized that all he needed was in the one suitcase. And in some ways, it would be pleasant to get rid of the rest.

He enjoyed the hotel. In the past, he had stayed at the four-star hotels of Los Angeles, but there was a side of him that had always been drawn to the seedy out-of-the-way establishments. And now he was in one.

Ben Scopius, an old friend and former colleague, now living in Los Angeles, had summoned him to Los Angeles to stage an industrial show for a major building conglomerate. After Ben had made the offer, the subject of accommodations came up and Ben had slipped into the corporate "we."

"We were wondering," he had asked, "how you would feel about staying at the Cyrano Hotel." Fred had never heard of the Cyrano, but he could tell from the hesitation in his friend's voice and the corporate "we" that it was not a first-class operation.

"I can't believe you're asking me to do this," said Fred, pretending to be offended. He then described his first trip to Los Angeles, many years back, when he had been picked up in a limousine, taken to the Beverly Hills Hotel and assigned a two-bedroom bungalow, with a wood-burning fireplace, the finest possible accommodation.

"And now you're asking me to stay at the Cyrano with four hookers and Joey Bishop."

Ben let this comment hang in the air—and it took a while before he realized that Fred was joking. Then the two men laughed, Fred a bit more heartily than Ben. Fred wasn't going to say no to the job on the basis of a hotel accommodation. He had not been getting much work lately. Figure it out. Times were tough—and industrial shows were not high on the list of corporate priorities. And it would be fun to team up with his old friend again. They had enjoyed a modest success on a show Fred had staged some twenty years back, when Ben was someone's assistant.

He liked the hotel immediately. His room had some mustiness to it, but it was spacious and there was a mirrored ceiling above the bed. It was his first mirrored ceiling. The service desk was manned by a tall and powerfully built man who wore a suit jacket and kept his shirt collar open in the Israeli fashion. He had a vacant stare and his hair seemed to have come out all at once, with just a few strands remaining around the ears. His movements were stiff and deliberate and Fred had the feeling that at some point in his life he had been tortured. Though he worked alone, he managed to deliver the newspapers in the morning, pick up and return the laundry and dry-cleaning, fix broken appliances and run the garage in the basement. He was also in charge of security.

Tall black women in spandex outfits lolled about in the lobby, waiting to be interviewed by an MTV executive named Buzz. In the surprisingly cheerful coffee shop, Fred generally ate breakfast at the same time as a tall, gray-haired actor who wore a Shakespeare-in-the-Park team jacket and spoke in a deafening baritone. Never before had Fred heard the order "sausage and eggs" delivered with such clangor and authority. Another coffee-shop regular was an Irish computer salesman who dwelled conversationally on trains he had been traveling on that had been derailed in Belfast. "You're trapped in there," he told Fred. "For as long as five hours. And there's bloody little you can do about it."

There was a sweet little pool and patio area atop the hotel with the best view of Los Angeles Fred had ever seen. The Cyrano was tucked down low on a small residential street in West Hollywood. It would have seemed impossible for its rooftop to throw off such a brilliant multiangled view of the city—but through some engineering miracle, it did.

Few of the Cyrano's guests took advantage of the rooftop facilities although Fred did meet a bearded novelist up there who almost immediately asked him to be the man's houseguest should he ever happen to be in the vicinity of British Columbia. Fred was not the type to drop in on people but he vaguely recalled one of the man's novels and said he just might take him up on his offer. The only rooftop regular was a pale English woman in her fifties who sat primly in the shade, turning the pages of a California guidebook. She managed properties in Manchester and was visiting a sister in Hollywood. She told Fred she had been uneasy about leaving her properties and it was only the excellence of her staff that had emboldened her to make the trip. Her style was exquisitely reserved and Fred enjoyed being exquisitely reserved right back at her. From time to time a neatly dressed black man with dreadlocks and dark glasses would appear on the roof and go from corner to corner, looking out at the city as if he were a sentry.

Once Fred had gotten settled in at the Cyrano, Ben Scopius came by to pick him up and take him to the rehearsal studio they would be using, on the edge of West Hollywood and close to the downtown area. Scopius was far from being a heavy-hitter in the Hollywood sense, but he appeared to have prospered in the twenty years he had lived on the West Coast. He had his own company, Scopius Enterprises, and had carved out a niche for himself in the production of industrial shows.

Ben showed up in an old Mercedes which somehow made him come across as being more affluent that if he had been driving a new one. He was a tall, attractive man, with a full head of charcoal-colored hair, and he was dressed in a suit that was both flashy and conservative. That is to say, it was cut extravagantly in the Armani style, but the color was dark and softly muted. And his jacket was shaped in a manner that played down and was actually flattering to his substantial waistline.

When he got out of the car to greet Fred, he moved with the easy stride of an ex-ballplayer, although to Fred's knowledge he had never played ball. Before the two men shook hands, Ben stopped for a moment to stretch, as if he had strained himself making a difficult catch in the outfield.

As nicely turned out as Ben was, there was something troubling about his mouth. As they drove to the studio, he would try an occasional smile and then quickly raise his hand to his face as if to cancel it out. Ben learned that Fred recently had had a mouthful of implants put in—and they looked it, too. They were evenly spaced, but precariously speared in, like the stakes used to prop up tomato plants. Each time

Ben hit the brakes, Fred expected the implants to fall out in his friend's hands.

Fred asked Ben, who had a second family, what his life was like on the West Coast. Ben said that although he lived in Hollywood, he was not a member of the Hollywood community per se. He had only one friend he could think of who was in the entertainment business—a fellow on the Jay Leno writing team. And though he lived in Hollywood, he appeared to take pride in conducting his life just outside the community and putting his energies into family activities such as Little League. Fred wondered—and he hoped it was without malice—if Ben had ever been invited to be a part of the community. Or had he been determined from the start to come to Hollywood so he could live just outside of it.

Their first order of business at the studio was casting, and in this area, Ben was determined to be hands on. That was fine with Fred who lived on the East Coast and did not know the players. Since they were doing an industrial show, there was little hope of attracting top-flight talent, much less Hollywood stars. They knew they would have to settle for people who were either over the hill or unable to get jobs in movies or TV. Surprisingly, one of the first people to show up for an audition was a Canadian character actor Ben recognized as having been in a hundred movies. Ben was overjoyed at this stroke of good fortune and insisted on hiring him on the spot. "We're deeply honored to have you on our show," Ben told the man. "I can't tell you how much pleasure you've given me down through the years." As it happened, the hiring of the great character actor turned out to be a mistake. He quickly turned surly and remained that way throughout the course of the show, his sour disposition lowering the morale of the company. He seemed to be upset about working in an industrial show, although no one had forced him to come to the audition.

Fred felt sorry for the women who showed up for parts in the chorus line. The auditions were held in a personnel director's office, beneath harsh fluorescent lights. Since the women had been asked to wear shorts, their legs, however well shaped, came across as being purplish and mottled. In the case of those with blemishes or small scars, the effect was ghastly. Fred was attracted to a severe-looking woman in her forties who wore her hair in a bun and had thought of asking her out for a drink, but the image of her pale thin legs and their radiological pallor beneath the lights threw him off.

Ben pushed to have his wife cast in the part of the lead dancer, which surprised Fred since Lisa Scopius was not only overweight, but also getting along in years. Still, Fred wasn't going to challenge his friend on the issue. Ben had thrown him a bone, and not too many had come his way of late. Salted in among the cast and crew were other friends and relatives of Ben's, but here, too, Fred did not feel it was appropriate to register a dissent. All could be considered professionals, to some degree, including Lisa Scopius, whose audition showed her to be peppy and to have decent acting skills.

After the cast had been chosen, Ben sat them down in the studio and thanked them for their patience through the demanding audition process. He said he felt they were a fine group and he had no doubt they would put on a wonderful show. And if the corporate brass liked it, he added, there was a chance that the show might be sent on a goodwill tour to major cities throughout Europe and Asia. This came as a surprise to Fred, since Ben hadn't mentioned it to him. Presumably, Fred would get to go along; this would mean additional income along with a chance to see cities like Bangkok and Hong Kong. Maybe he would get to take his girls along. When Ben had concluded his remarks to the cast, Fred took him aside and asked if the tour was a serious possibility.

"It's a lock," said Ben. "I just didn't want to get the kids too worked up about it."

Buoyed up by the news, Fred plunged into rehearsals with great enthusiasm. But no sooner than he had gotten started than the president of the company turned up, along with several executives, and asked if he might see a quick run-through of the show with the assembled cast. The company president was a stocky, broad-shouldered man who reminded Fred of a walking corporation unto himself. Ben treated him with great respect, but his mouth had actually fallen open at the request. He explained, on Fred's behalf, that the cast had barely had time to be introduced to one another, let alone familiarize themselves with the script—and that Fred hadn't had a chance to work with them. The company president said he understood all that and would factor it in. Fred gamely led the cast through a quickly improvised run-through, at the end of which the company president stood up and, with jowls quivering, walked briskly out of the studio, followed by his associates. Fred was shaken and saw his dream of a global tour go up in smoke. But Ben told him not to be alarmed; he understood the process and felt confident that when the time came, the show would be in great condition and the executive would be proud of it. Fred felt better instantly and had to admire what he thought of as Ben's smooth, West Coast style of management. He felt Ben would have little difficulty being part of the Hollywood community if he ever decided he wanted to go that way.

In the days that followed, Fred noticed that although Ben's specialization was the industrial show, he had something of the impresario about him. The script, which had a jungle theme, called for an antelope, which Fred had always assumed would be a rubberized prop. But Ben insisted it be a live antelope, and had one brought to the studio each day in a van, along with its trainer. Ben was generous in his arrangements for the cast as well and made sure there was a well-supplied snack table adjacent to the set, with mounds of raw vegetables and tasty dips, along with fresh bagels and a vat of cream cheese.

Each day, after rehearsals, Fred returned to the Cyrano, and after showering, changed into the freshly laundered clothing that had been laid out on the bed in cellophane by the slow-moving but thorough man at the service desk. Then he headed for a bar and restaurant he had discovered called Jake's which was located just down the road from the hotel. It was in a gay section of Hollywood but did not appear to have a gay clientele. Fred quickly fell in with a group of regulars that included Hal, a struggling portrait painter from Trinidad who was one of the handsomest men Fred had ever met. Women were drawn to him as if to a magnet, a fact of life that Hal accepted with resignation and no particular joy. One night, as a beautiful young student he had just met nestled against him, he turned to Fred and said: "This is all very nice, but tomorrow morning, when I wake up, I'm going to be just as broke as ever." Another new friend was Jane Ellen, a hooker with a Clara Bow hairdo, who announced her arrival each night by sliding onto a barstool and throwing open her jacket to reveal her latest brightly colored bustier. And there was Jerome, a red-bearded Israeli veteran of the Six-Day War who lived in Los Angeles and traded in diamonds. An attractive man, he claimed to have trouble connecting with women and Fred quickly saw the root of his difficulty. Whenever a woman entered Jake's, he would drape his arm around Fred's shoulders and cry out, in a harsh, combat-ready voice: "Hey, girly. Come over here and we will take you out." Rounding out the little circle was Omar, a cheerful, miniaturized George Foreman look-alike who called him "Brother Fred." Each night Omar would try to stir up interest in a new money-making gadget, a meter, for example, which would register the salt content of a steak when plunged into its center. And a new wine-opener which Fred felt was much too complex in its operation. He suggested as much after watching Omar struggle through dozens of maneuvers in the opening of a Chianti bottle.

"That's all right, Brother Fred," said Omar, unfazed. "Lookaheer and watch me do it again."

There was no telling who was liable to show up at Jake's. One of Fred's favorites was a curly-headed man who would nurse a beer at one end of the bar and suddenly punch his chest, throw back his head and in an anguished voice cry out: "I'm a guy." Fred met a proud and beautiful Kuwaiti woman who could not tell him much about her country, since her English was limited. But where else could he meet a woman from Kuwait? And one night, someone pointed to the actor Tony Curtis, just as he was walking through the exit door.

Jake's, his new friends, the sense of adventure each night, all this was a far cry from Fred's situation on the North Fork of eastern Long Island, where, in truth, he had no friends at all. He and Melissa had moved out of New York City to get away from bad influences, drugs, alcohol, the fast pace—and they had succeeded. But ten years had passed and it was as if they had been cured of a disease but were afraid to leave the hospital. Melissa had been a friend, and Fred felt she was the only one he needed—but theirs was a story out of a nineties' textbook. One day Melissa, at age forty, had decided to return to school and get her master's degree in Business Administration. Fred was happy for her and helped out by taking the girls to school each morning. Soon he was packing lunches for them, doing the dishes, shopping and seeing to it that dinner was on the table each night. All right out of the textbook. He enjoyed it, and if there was any resentment on his part, he was unaware of it. After Melissa was graduated, she quickly signed on as an administrator at the local hospital . . . and she began to slip away from him. She went to work at six in the morning, came home late at night, and after eating the dinner that Fred had prepared, she went in to her study to pore over position papers. Once in a while, late at night, they made love in a pleasurable but perfunctory way. So Fred's life became one of housework, books, filmed cassettes and not much else. No wonder he came to life at the Cyrano Hotel and at the Hollywood rehearsal hall and with his new friends at Jake's.

One night, Ben Scopius invited Fred to dinner at a restaurant that was right on the edge, but not really in the Hollywood orbit. Ben often had dinner there with the friend who was on Jay Leno's writing team. Ben had brought along his wife Lisa which surprised Fred since he had been led to believe they were going to have a bachelor dinner. But he took the minor setback in stride. Ben appeared to be an important and highly respected customer and they were seated by the maitre d' with great ceremony at an excellent table. It was difficult to tell who the other customers were. Probably other producers of industrial shows and maybe some of Leno's people. The menu for the most part was made up of thin little gourmet pizzas which suited Fred just fine since he didn't really want to stuff himself. About halfway along in the meal, Lisa began to berate Ben, saying he was an awful husband to his first wife and had been an awful husband to her.

"Let's face it, Ben," she said, "down deep, you do not like women."

The attack came out of nowhere and was not, as far as Fred could judge, brought on by excessive drinking. Fred was embarrassed for Ben and thought it was wildly inappropriate for the attack to be made in front of a family friend. On the other hand, maybe she needed the protection of Fred's presence to be able to say these things at all. During the verbal abuse, Ben kept his head lowered and let the assault rain down on him without rebuttal. When it petered out, he raised his head and tapped at his mouth as if to poke back a few of the precariously staked-in implants. The dinner continued in a desultory fashion and then actually picked up a bit in time for the dessert course. But Fred felt that he had seen another side of life out there on the edge of the Hollywood community.

And one night at Jake's, as he was talking to Omar, he felt a screen of fragrant hair brush lightly against his face. The young woman on the barstool beside him turned and apologized and Fred said it was quite all right. He began to talk to her which annoyed Omar who said he had wanted Fred to meet a friend of his named "Baby." Omar pointed her out, across the bar, and Fred concluded that she was no baby. So he turned back to the woman on the barstool who said she was in banking. She spoke in generalities—there was much more to Los Angeles than met the eye—but she was fresh and friendly and from time to time she would shake loose her great hair as if she had stepped out of a pool. Fred had always been faithful to Melissa, but on this night, his yearning was so great that he would have been willing to have an affair with this relative stranger. She said she was about to try living with an engineer from Washington State and could not bring herself to go back to the hotel with Fred. But they agreed to take a walk. They left the crowded bar, and in the street outside, she said she liked to do subtle things. In a nearby parking lot, he kissed her and let the back of his hand brush against her nipples. She kissed his neck and let her fingertips graze the front of his trousers. They agreed, vaguely, to meet the next night for dinner.

But the following day, during rehearsals, the Rodney King verdict was announced and the rioting began in downtown Los Angeles. The construction company that was sponsoring Fred's show sent some security guards to the rehearsal hall, since some of the fires and the looting seemed to be lapping over into the studio area. Fred didn't know about those security guards. The head man had a Buffalo Bill moustache and carried a Magnum slung low on his hip. His eyes seemed detached from their proper mechanisms and Fred wasn't sure what it would be like to have this man spraying off rounds. And Fred himself felt in no personal danger. During the Korean War, he had bailed out of a burning C-47 and hadn't felt particularly upset about it until later on when he got a bad case of the shakes. The cast held up nicely, too, although the mood in the studio was tense. Ben Scopius's wife, Lisa, did not help matters. She would leave the studio and return with alarming bulletins, such as: "They're at Fairfax now." Ben Scopius himself was busy putting the finishing touches on another industrial show in the Valley. But he was in phone contact and suggested that the cast be dismissed on the early side. He also said that if any member of the cast, in all good conscience, felt a need to leave immediately, that individual was free to do so.

Fred passed this message along to the cast, wrapping himself around Ben's rich "in all good conscience" phrase and adding a touch of his own: there would be no recriminations toward any of the good conscience people who decided to leave before the end of rehearsals. Later in the day, when the first city-wide curfew in Los Angeles history had been announced, Fred laid in a bag of groceries and headed back to the Cyrano. From his tiny balcony, he could smell the fires and look out at the destruction. To his everlasting shame, the only loss he felt was that he would not be able to go down to Jake's and see his friends. Most of them were black, and that's one of the things he liked about the place—the easy commingling of black and white people. There was no such thing on the eastern tip of Long Island, no such place.

He settled in and for hours and hours he watched the local television coverage of the rioting. There was no need to watch as much of it as he did, but he could not stop, afraid he might miss something . . . even though it was pretty much all of a piece. No doubt the King verdict had triggered the riots, but Fred felt that the underlying cause of the carnage was a statistic he'd read some weeks before—that during the eighties some 70 per cent of the accumulated wealth had gone to less than 1 per cent of the population. The people he watched on the news had nothing to lose. Why shouldn't they riot. What puzzled him is why they would want to shoot themselves in the foot. Why weren't they burning houses in the estate section of Beverly Hills? That would effect change overnight. It occurred to him that America, or at least its entrenched powers, had been blessed with gentle revolutionaries.

Fred called his wife that first night to tell her he was all right. She told him he was lucky to be where he was and not in San Francisco. "You should see what's going on there," she said. He told her he could see and smell the fires from his room and cited some statistics to prove that Los Angeles, riot-wise, was in much worse shape than San Francisco, but she wouldn't buy it. So he wasn't even going to get credit for being in the most riot-torn city. It was the kind of thing about her that infuriated him—but also made him love her.

It was announced that the curfew would be kept in force for three or four more days and Fred did not see how he was going to survive, cooped up at the Cyrano for that length of time. His only choice, he felt, was to call upon his inner resources. And that's how he described it, too, later on, in recounting the experience. "I called upon my inner resources." He gave up smoking and threw together a program of calisthenics which he did each morning on the rooftop of the Cyrano. He caught up with the novels of Ford Madox Ford which he had fortunately taken along with him. And he continued to monitor the riots on television, keeping the set on at all times as if he were an anchorman. He did this until he realized the obvious, that it was depressing him.

After the guard came in, and the curfew was lifted, Ben addressed the cast at the Hollywood rehearsal hall. He told them he was proud of them for hanging tough during the riots and that he remained confident that they were going to put on a show that would set the standard for industrial shows for years to come. Though the mood of the cast had been edgy and dispirited, it changed for the better after Ben's peptalk. "We needed that," Lisa Scopius told Fred. "And if the show is a success, it will be because of that talk he gave."

Fred went back to work with the cast—and after the first rehearsal he felt they were just about ready and would peak on the night of the formal presentation. It would be given before an audience of several hundred sales representatives and their friends and relatives. Fred was right. On the night of the presentation, the cast outdid itself. The singers and dancers performed their hearts out, and the aging Canadian character actor, who had been sulking for weeks, showed why he had enjoyed such a long and illustrious career by infusing a relatively minor role with luminosity. The audience of sales representatives and their relatives stood up and clapped and cheered at the end of the half-hour presentation.

After the show, Ben threw a small party in the dressing room area for the cast and crew, bringing in cold cuts from a delicatessen on Pico which was not part of the Hollywood scene. The company president and several of the top executives popped by to pay their respects. Though the president of the company had stormed out of the early run-through with jowls quivering, he now told Fred and Ben he felt the presentation had come a long way, although he did not think it had the makings of a global tour. Ben had obviously been counting on the tour and when the company president left, he smacked his fist into his palm and said: "Why? Where did we fall short? I just don't get it."

Fred didn't get it either and he was disappointed, too, although not as much as Ben was. There would be some loss of income for him—and for all he knew he might never get another chance to see the great cities of Europe and Asia, but in truth, the only thing that mattered to

him was getting back to see his friends at Jake's. So he slapped together a modest corned beef and coleslaw sandwich and hugged the
key members of the cast. Then he gathered up the gift package of
pâtés and mousses that Ben had given him as an "opening night" gift
and headed for his beloved hangout.

It was a medium-busy night at Jake's. The woman with the hair
wasn't there, but most of the regulars were and someone said that Bob
Evans, the producer, had been in for a drink and left. The piano player
was at his post, playing unabashedly sentimental Vegas tunes and Fred
took a phone call from his friend Jerome, who told him about a new
spot that was opening in the Valley. "My friend is the owner," said the
former tank commander, "and there will be plenty of chicks." Fred
said he might very well join his Israeli friend, but knew he lacked the
energy to do so.

Something about Jake's was a beat off. Omar turned up, looking
fresh and scrubbed, and scolded Fred for not having said hello to his
friend "Baby" some nights before. Fred apologized and by way of making amends offered Omar the package of pâtés and mousses he had
been given by Ben as his opening night gift. Omar said fine, let's go get
them, and Fred said he would leave them at the desk for Omar to pick
up the next morning. But Omar wanted to follow Fred's car with his
own and get them immediately. Fred said he didn't want to split up the
evening that way, and the two men had a mild argument over how long
cans of pâté and mousses could last without refrigeration. "Not long,"
said Baby, joining in. But it seemed to Fred they were arguing about
something else. Jane Ellen came in, took her usual seat and threw back
her jacket to reveal a new crimson-colored bustier with black ruffles.
But she quickly became morose and complained about the increasing
reluctance of customers to pay her two-hundred-dollar fee.

"They should pay a thousand dollars just to have *dinner* with me, for
Christ's sakes."

Fred agreed and then struck up a conversation with a pretty young
film student, but his heart wasn't in it, so he paid the check and left.

As he waited for his car, Hal, the handsome portrait artist from
Trinidad, came up beside him.

"What's wrong?" said Hal. "You were doing pretty well in there."

"I couldn't get into it," said Fred.

"Neither could I," said Hal.

Then he looked up at the moon and his eyes got wet. "Oh man," he
said, "those riots just about tore my heart out."

"I know," said Fred.

And there in the driveway, the two men hugged each other hard
enough to break a bone.

*   *   *

In bed the next morning, Fred looked at his reflection in the overhead mirror and wondered if Omar had picked up the gift packages of mousses and pâté he had left with the receptionist the night before. And then he thought about staying another night. It would be fun to have one more breakfast in the cheerful coffee shop. And to sit around the lobby and watch the passing parade. There were four teen-aged girls with team jackets and albino hair who had checked in the day before. They hung around the phone and communicated with one another by breaking into MTV dance steps. Wouldn't he like to know their story.

And he would get a chance to go back to Jake's. After twenty-four hours, maybe whatever it was that was wrong had been corrected. There would have been time for Omar to sample the pâtés and mousses Fred had left for him and maybe this would put the two men on a better footing, with Omar trying to interest him in another gadget. And maybe Fred would invest in it this time. Would that wipe him out? And maybe the girl with the hair would come back and they would do some more subtle things together. And if not her, someone equally intriguing. Jane Ellen would have had time to cheer up and his friend Hal would probably be back resignedly accepting the affections of beautiful women he had just met. It would be fun to feel Jerome's arm around his shoulders and to hear the tank commander holler out harsh and unacceptable propositions at newly arriving women and then wonder why they didn't run up and throw their arms around him.

Melissa wouldn't care. She had her work and might even welcome another night of not having to see to it that Fred was occupied. And to listen again to how he had missed out on life. The girls would make a fuss, but by the time he got home, they'd be away on a sleep-over anyway.

But what would another night mean. It would only drag out the process of leaving. His bags were packed, and a man from Ben's car service was on his way to take him to the airport. It was a small, dependable service, rarely used by those in the Hollywood community. So he checked the closets, took a last look at the room that had been his home for a month and then headed down the hall to the sluggish but functional elevator of the Cyrano Hotel.

Any way you sliced it—it was time to go back to his loved ones.

The Golden Years

HALE AND FIT AT SIXTY—except possibly for his hips—Drexler was worried sick about his age. Every now and then he'd catch a glimpse of his reflection in the mirror of a singles bar and marvel at how out of place he looked. He thought of touching up his gray hair with Just for Men and decided he would try it when he was out of town where no one knew him. Everyone else used it, why not Drexler. His work as an illustrator fell off and he began to pick up code words. His drawings had become "lazy." They weren't "hip" enough. This from an art director who was only a few years younger than Drexler but was careful to affect the grunge look, and to wear an earring.

Slowly, Drexler pulled back into himself. A widower, he lived alone in a draughty one-bedroom apartment on the West Side with a decent view and not much else. One by one, his friends began to disappear. One walked into the sea at Westhampton and never came back. Another, despite great wealth, was being maintained on antidepressant pills and lacked the will to go to dinner. Drexler broke off contact with a third who'd made a random and unforgivable remark. "Your best work is behind you." Drexler knew this. But did he have to hear it from an old and trusted friend.

Virtually unemployed, Drexler slipped by on a modest pension. As a young man in Paris, he'd bought some Kandinsky drawings when the artist was unknown. Whenever Drexler was strapped for funds, he'd sell one off. In his sparsely furnished apartment, he spun away the days chain-smoking Nat Sherman cigaratillos, reading books on slavery—his favorite subject—and wondering how many years he had left. His father had passed away at seventy-five, so he figured he had another fifteen to play around with. Surely there was more to life than this, but who was there to help him?

As a young man, he'd suffered tremendously when his first wife left him for a limo driver. On that occasion, he'd been helped by a certain Otto Granger, a psychiatrist he saw on and off for several years. Drexler still remembered Granger's self-effacing chuckle, his habit of swallowing before he spoke, his hawklike alertness when Drexler said something Granger felt was significant. Once, Drexler had recalled his shock and confusion as a boy when he saw his mother naked in a shower, with no penis.

"Are you *sure?*" Granger had asked, leaning forward and scribbling furiously in a notepad. "It isn't something you read, is it?"

With Granger's help, Drexler had gotten through the crisis. But thirty years had passed. Granger was a man in his forties then. He might not even be alive now.

One particularly bleak and hollow morning, Drexler looked up Granger in the phone book and saw that he was listed at his old address. He called up the doctor, introduced himself and was pleased to learn that Granger remembered him.

"The artist," the doctor recalled . . ." with an extreme sensitivity to violence."

"That's me," said Drexler. "I'd like to see you—if you're still practicing."

"Of course I'm practicing," said Granger with a hint of snappishness. "When can you come in?"

The two men arranged an appointment, and when Drexler hung up, he took some satisfaction in his having reached out to help himself. He expected the call alone to make him feel better, but it didn't. After all, what could Granger do for him, get him a job? Make him feel ten years younger?

Granger had continued to practice in the same office—a huge, musty space in the Gramercy Park area, with a complex arrangement of entrances and exits, to assure anonymity for his patients. On the day of the appointment, Drexler took a seat in the waiting room and remembered that Granger had lived in an apartment adjoining the office. When Drexler first consulted him, the psychiatrist had a young and pretty wife who flitted back and forth through the corridors. Drexler had been jealous of Granger's marriage (which he assumed was a happy one) since his own was about to end in disaster. But years had gone by. It was possible that Granger had lost his wife and lived alone like Drexler.

After a brief wait, Granger came out and Drexler was shocked by what he saw. Still slender, the doctor walked with a limp and his body was twisted like a corkscrew. He had only a few hairs left on his head and maybe a tooth or two. But his eyes still sparkled and he greeted Drexler with that same engaging chuckle.

"Come in, come in," he said, laying a bony hand on Drexler's shoulder, leading him into the office and showing him to a chair opposite his.

After both men had regarded each other with quiet affection, Drexler was the first to speak. On the assumption that the old man was hard of hearing, he leaned forward, pronouncing each word slowly and distinctly as if he were talking to a foreigner.

"It's been a long time," said Drexler. "How've you been?"

The question, he quickly realized, was ridiculous since, in a sense, the old man's crippled appearance had already supplied the answer.

"Not bad," said Granger, who seemed puzzled by Drexler's exaggerated lip movements. "What brings you here?"

"I'm here," said Drexler, returning to a more normal speaking style, "because of a concern about my age."

"You are?" said Granger, who cocked his head in surprise. Getting up from his chair, he limped over to a bookcase, pulled out a scholarly work on commercial artists and showed Drexler a section that had been thrown over to a listing of his achievements. Drexler had been unaware the book existed, and the effect of it was cheering, although, he suspected, not to the extent that Granger thought it might be.

"You've had quite a career," said Granger, returning to his chair, and looking at Drexler with pride.

"Maybe," said Drexler, "but it's been a little bumpy lately."

As if to refresh his memory, Granger said, "Let's see . . . you had a flighty and theatrical mother, your dad wasn't around very much . . . and there was a brother who was killed in the war."

"Never a day goes by that I don't think of Larry," said Drexler, wiping away a tear, and at the same time amazed at Granger's sharp recall of his background. It was true he might have had a look at Drexler's file, but still, he spoke now without notes—and the performance was impressive. Drexler began to unburden himself, and though nothing substantive seemed to be accomplished in the hour that followed, he felt comforted, as if he were having a reunion with an old friend. At his end, Granger, for the most part, chuckled and shrugged at Drexler's concerns, which was also comforting. And remarkably, as the hour wore on, the years seemed to drop away from the old man; for all practical purposes, he became the Granger that Drexler had known decades before. Only once did he lean forward in the sudden hawklike style. It was when Drexler told of his internal struggle over whether to apply Just for Men.

"You're not *trying* to act young, are you?" he asked sharply.

"Of course not," said Drexler, who drew back as if he'd been accused of being a child molester.

At the end of the hour, Granger asked if Drexler would like to see him again.

"I'm not sure," said Drexler. "I'd like to think about it."

As he got to his feet, it occurred to him that the old man's practice, like his body, had withered away; he wondered if he should make an appointment, just to throw him some business. But before he could make his decision, Granger once again put a bony hand on his shoulder and led him through the complex series of entrances and exits to the elevator.

In the days that followed, Drexler didn't feel better and he didn't feel worse. He continued along the same path, doing a few hip exercises, pressing ahead with the reading of his slavery books, and rarely leaving his apartment. And then one day, out of nowhere, an assignment came through. It was at one-third his usual fee but he snapped it up nonetheless. At least he'd be working again.

"Pour your heart out on this one," said the art director. "We've got to get you back to where you were."

Buoyed up by this turn of events, Drexler went to a cocktail party and met a black model with a single name—Taneysha—who appeared to be attracted to him. Tall and thin as a reed, she was a single mom who lived with her five-year-old daughter in New Jersey. Drexler began to date her, traveling to the neighboring state twice a week. They would take her daughter, also tall and reed-thin, to a Chinese restaurant for dinner, then return to her condo and listen to tribal music. As Drexler concentrated on the complex rhythms, Taneysha flexed her arms and thighs to show that she was not only thin but strong. One night, when the child was asleep, they made love. After a long layoff in the romance department, Drexler feared that he might not be able to get an erection, but Taneysha was a great kisser and he came through beautifully.

Drexler felt his life had turned around and wondered if the visit to Granger had anything to do with it. One comment stuck in his mind: "You just won't let go," the doctor had said, shaking his head in wonderment. At the time, Drexler hadn't been sure what he meant, but clearly he'd let go anyway.

Drexler stopped looking in the mirror twenty times a day and forgot about his hip exercises. He bought some new sweaters, leased a Mercury Cougar and traveled to Connecticut to gamble at the Indian reservation. No longer did he sit around trying to figure out how many years he had left.

Then one day, Taneysha suddenly, and unaccountably lost interest in him.

"I'm thinking about spending more time in D.C.," she said vaguely, then refused to take his calls. Drexler couldn't understand what he'd done wrong. She'd seen the shelves of books on slavery in his apartment. Maybe she had taken this the wrong way. Soon afterward, the art director returned his work with the comment that it was "unfocused" although he did plan to make the payment. "I'm sorry," the art director had said, and there was something in his tone that indicated to Granger that it was to be his last assignment.

Refusing to fall apart, Drexler screwed up his courage and went to the opening of a new bar and restaurant, owned by another illustrator. When Drexler arrived, the place was crowded with people in their twenties. From a distance, the owner spotted Drexler and shouted: "Here comes the alter kocker."

Drexler pretended he didn't hear the man—and stayed around for a drink and a few hors d'oeuvres—but the remark burned in his brain.

Having tasted work and romance, then been rejected in both, Drexler, in a sense, was worse off than before. His hips ached and he began to chain-smoke again and to check his face repeatedly in the mirror for new wrinkles. All traces of sunshine were gone. The horizon was solid gray.

Predictably, he considered ringing up Granger again. The man had helped him out before. Why couldn't he do it again? He thought of the ingratiating chuckle, the mischievous light in his eyes, Granger's fierce honesty and the surprising clarity of his mind. The fee was modest. How could Drexler possibly go wrong by seeing him. But then he remembered the corkscrewed body, the thin tuft of hair on his balding head, the two or three teeth and the no doubt decaying breath—and decided against a visit.

Clearly he needed to see a younger man.

The War Criminal

ONE DAY MESSINGER BROKE his rule about not going to local cocktail parties and found out his psychiatrist was an ex-Nazi. It was an evening that had been slightly off center from the beginning. Arriving early, he ordered two drinks from the bartender who served them up with a wink and said: "How's your wife's arse?" Messinger thought this was strange behavior on the part of the hired help and brought it to the attention of the host who said: "He's actually a cellist and he's all we could get." A little later, one of the guests put on a Western Union cap and went up and down the halls, in and out of each of the rooms, hollering: "Telegram for Phil Messinger, telegram for Phil Messinger." He tried to ignore the man, but soon all eyes were on him and he felt he had no choice but to walk up to the fellow and say: "All right, I'll take it."

The man, not really that drunk, said: "One dollar and fifteen cents, please," and Messinger went along, handing him the money.

"It's from the President," said the man, reading from a piece of paper. It says:

> GO HOME AND CHANGE YOUR UNDERWEAR
> IT HAS HOLES IN IT.

The host came up quickly behind Messinger and said: "Don't let him get to you. He's got some dull job in flexible packaging."

Searching for a safe haven, Messinger joined a group of women in the kitchen, one of whom was giving her views on interior design.

"When I walk into a room," she said, "I like it to say 'Howdy' to me."

Messinger surprised himself by saying: "And I like a room to keep its mouth shut."

He was evidently still smarting from the underwear telegram. The woman seemed to perspire suddenly. Toweling herself down with a dishrag, she said: "Oh, you're the one who goes to Dr. Newald. Do you mind about his being an ex-Nazi?"

Although it had been a strangely tilted evening, spilling over with

bad behavior, Messinger believed the woman totally. Still, quite naturally, he resented her passing on the information in such a casual manner and said: "You know this for sure about Newald, is that it?"

"Yes."

"And you're just standing here at a party telling me about it?"

"Um hm."

"You're quite a sensitive person."

Although to the best of his knowledge he hadn't picked it for that
reason, Messinger lived in an area that was heavily favored by psychiatrists as a place of residence. The streets were crammed with psychiatric homes; as a result, the community seemed to have an odd, quizzical
tone to it. Arguments rarely raged, questions were answered in only
the most tentative way and casual street chitchat was carried on in a
warily relaxed manner. Strangers, passing on the street, seemed to do
rapid-fire thumbnail sum-ups of one another. In the supermarket,
bearded Jungians strolled the dessert aisle, pulling out all stops in their
fantasized disrobing of the teenage checkout girls, at the same time
smiling beatifically and congratulating themselves on their adjustment
to the demands of everyday family life. One day Messinger saw a
woman trip and fall against the out-of-town letter slot at the post office. A cool man in emergencies, he scooped her up and drove her to a
nearby hospital. With blood pumping from her scalp, the woman held
the torn cleavage of her dress together in a most feminine manner and
said: "I guess I must have directed some of my aggressive tendencies
toward myself." On still another occasion, Messinger stopped a poorly
dressed Puerto Rican and asked him if he knew of anyone in the area
who wanted to do floor shellacking for excellent pay. The man chuckled and said he could not be of any help. Later, Messinger was told the
fellow was a neurologist, world renowned for his work on upper-class
teens who wet their beds in defiance of wealth and privilege.

In a curious way, Messinger did not feel in the least bit put upon by
the psychiatric currents in the air. A store window designer by trade, he
felt his own status elevated by all the doctors in the area. Then, too,
their presence seemed a protection against terrifying things happening
to him and to his family. If indeed there were a calamity, he pictured
the doctors gathering round it, analyzing it, somehow making it mute
and removing its fangs. He was happy, nonetheless, that Newald lived
many miles away and sympathized with patients in town who ran the
daily risk of bumping into their analysts over a tuna and rye, or perhaps having to shower with them at the local health club.

*   *   *

Messinger found himself curiously unaffected by the ex-Nazi disclosure and wondered, happily, if he had not become spiritually exhausted. Someone he admired a great deal was a young retired poet who sat each night at a bar in the city, a shawl wrapped around his neck, drinking Spanish brandy and playing solitaire. He seemed to do nothing else at all with his life and when Messinger asked a musician about him one night, he was told: "Victor's spiritually exhausted." Messinger found this romantic and attractive and felt a little sad about his own spirit which, in its darkest moments, always struck him as remaining peppy. Now, perhaps, it had caved in. He had been seeing Dr. Newald for three years and was not clear on what stage of treatment he was in. The visits had become mechanical, like morning shaves. He knew only that he was a far different fellow from the one who—three years before—was convinced he was about to be surgically unzipped from head to toe, as if he were a duffel bag. And worried about a tumor; although Messinger himself was a bundle of weakness, he was convinced that the growth, ironically, would be brawny and willful, the first tough thing about him. One day, falling apart at the seams, he had pressed himself against the glass of one of his window displays and considered marching through it. Then, thinking better of this notion, he had walked into a building nearby which, as it turned out, was the embassy of a fresh new African nation. Messinger asked the receptionist if she knew of a psychiatrist; as if it were the most frequently asked question at her desk, she referred him to Newald across the street. A casual recommendation, but not necessarily a bad one. Messinger seemed to receive all the major news of his life in a casual manner. The night of his father's death, he had been unable to get a good telephone connection to the hospital; after asking him to redeposit his dime, it was the operator who took over and told him his father was gone. A bakery clerk had inadvertently told him his mother was sleeping with a Pakistani and now, quite casually, it was an interior designer who passed along the news of Newald's Hitlerian background. He was angry at her, but not particularly at Newald.

Though he knew and cared little about the analytical process, Messinger did have one firm view on the subject—it mattered little to him whether the doctor was a sex pervert, a homicidal maniac, a nine-time loser in the divorce courts or a keeper of tarantulas—all that counted was the quality of what went on between him and his patient in the privacy of his office. On one occasion, Messinger's town was shaken by the news of a voyeuristic psychiatrist, out for a thrill, who had tripped on a building ledge and tumbled nine stories below to his death. It was on everyone's mind, yet so chilling were its implications to the psychiatrist-packed community that few dared speak of it. Without bothering to introduce the subject, Messinger leaned across his backyard fence one day and told a neighbor, "Yes, but if he came back from the dead tomorrow, I wouldn't hesitate to see him for treatment."

In one sense, Newald's Third Reich background fit neatly into Messinger's view, and for the first two sessions after the news, almost smugly he failed to say a word about the perhaps gossipy revelation. In truth, just before the second visit, he did take a good look at Newald and try to imagine him in a jackbooted Wehrmacht uniform. Newald was a small pudgy man with slightly simian features who looked as though he might have been born on the Sino-Soviet border. Additionally, he spoke with a slightly tough-guy Lower East Side accent and it was difficult picturing him in uniform; after some effort, Messinger did manage to slip him into one. Still, he made no mention of the decorator's accusation; indeed, he took wide detours around any references that had the slightest inference of post-war guilt to them. Messinger had to admit nonetheless that it was in the air, not so much because he was one to go about in a festering—and profitless—rage over Nazi crimes, but more because it was there, something unspoken between them; he could not ignore it totally any more than he could overlook a splinter, no matter how microscopic in size. Before the third session, he found himself looking at Newald's office paintings, attractively troubled and dreamlike, and wondering whether they were not the work of young Germans of the new breed, embarking on their own road, petulant and snappish about references to their country's past. Midway along in this third session, Messinger struck pay dirt with a line of thinking about an uncle who'd always seemed to be innocent but now turned out to have an awful lot to do with blocking Messinger's development. Instead of barreling through to new insights, he suddenly veered off and said: "I heard at a party that you're an ex-Nazi." Newald said nothing. The sound of the air purifier seemed louder than before. After a few beats, almost as though the real reason he had stopped talking was to blow his nose, Messinger continued his previous monologue.

Evidently, Newald saw the accusation as being so ridiculous it did not even warrant comment. The following day, Messinger, relieved, had every intention of tunneling deeper into the strange influence of his uncle on his own bottled-up personality. But just as if a highway trooper had flagged him over to the side, he found himself kicking off the session by bringing up once again Newald's possible membership in the Nazi Party.

"Even if it's true, I like to think I'm tough enough to just sail right on with our relationship. But I *would* like to get it out on the table. Nine chances out of ten, it's cocktail-party gossip. I insulted the woman and she probably wanted to get back at me with something mean. Anyway, what's the deal? Yes or no, because I really think I'm on to something with my uncle."

Newald remained silent and Messinger, after a moment or so, said: "All right, I'll accept that," and with some difficulty continued, although he had become terribly aware of a pungent new smell in the office, appealing and disturbing at the same time. Had it been left over by the last patient? If she was attractive, Messinger felt he would be able to lie back and enjoy it. If not, he wanted no part of it. Midway through the session, Messinger said he was a little disturbed by the smell.

"It's a new cologne I'm wearing," said Newald.

Messinger immediately leaped up from the couch, an extraordinary move considering he hadn't done it before in three years, and said: "You'll answer that, but you won't say anything about Nazis."

He sat on the couch, but did not lie down, holding his feet slightly above the rug as though there were alligators swimming about. Newald, totally visible now, seemed small and homely; he was guilty of a dozen fashion blunders and Messinger was able to see immediately the advantage of lying with his back to him.

"It's quite true, you know," said Newald.

"It is?" said Messinger, who hadn't counted on receiving the news in a face-to-face confrontation.

"We've never had any secrets up until now," said Newald in a gentle, bordering on the sweet, tone, "and I don't believe in having this one."

"Well, what's the deal," said Messinger, wanting to lie down again, but embarrassed about doing so, "a screw-up and when you found out what they were doing, you left the party immediately?"

"No," said Newald. "I must be honest with you. I suppose that I more or less knew what was going on and I didn't do anything about it. I just stayed."

"Christ," said Messinger. "There are probably dozens of guys like you in practice all over the country."

"Not dozens," said Newald, snatching more and more of the ground from beneath Messinger's feet. "A few."

Messinger suggested that Newald was probably in some piddling kind of administrative work and when the doctor assured him that this was so, he felt he had finally scored a point. Newald then told a somewhat routine story about his training and indoctrination, one that Messinger, a World War II and Hitler's-Rise-to-Power buff, found entirely familiar and not enlivened in the slightest by Newald's listless, formal way with an anecdote. Almost as though he were doing a routine civil service check, Messinger asked Newald if he had ever killed anyone.

"One," said Newald, holding up a finger. He said that he had been an orderly in a prisoner's hospital at the time and had been put in charge of an apparatus that was designed to keep serious post-surgery patients alive.

"There were some controls. A knob, particularly, that had to be turned regularly. At one point, I could not bring myself to turn it and, perhaps as a result, the man perished. He was old and feeble and probably would have died anyway, but I don't excuse myself. It was murder by negligence."

Consciously making a grave face—as if he were the doctor—Messinger asked if the man was a Jew.

"I don't know," said Newald. "He was a Nazi prisoner. He may have been a Polish officer. I must say that a fair and prudent guess would be that, yes, he was a Jew. It was not an issue as far as I was concerned. To my recollection, I remember being hypnotized by the power I had to grant life and death and found the temptation to kill him irresistible."

"So that's about it, eh?"

"That's about it," said Newald, softly, looking straight into Messinger's eyes. "I've repented, studied hard, spent more than twenty-five years trying to atone for my misdeed. Speaking quite truthfully, I suppose it's one reason why I've cultivated this Lower East Side accent of mine."

"I'm glad you brought that up," said Messinger. "I'd always wondered about it. But that's the whole story?"

"Every word."

"No gold fillings, no Jewish babies, nothing like that?"

"Nothing at all like that."

"I'm not going to go to another party and hear about a little death camp you ran on the side?"

"No, Mr. Messinger."

"I guess my worst story for some reason is the Jewish boxer one. They got him to put on the gloves and then the German commander put on a pair, except that he kept a revolver in one of them. When the Jewish guy put his hands up to fight, the German shot him through the head. It's amazing that of all the horrors—and believe me, I've read about 'em all—that's the one that keeps haunting me."

"I've told you everything."

"Well, good," said Messinger, briskly snapping his legs up in front of him and glad to be back on the couch again. "Just so long as it's out in the open. I'd like to get back to my uncle. The thing I remember about him is that every time he came to our house, he always had his hands on Mom's shoulders."

Pitched Out

ABOUT HALFWAY ALONG in the meeting, Harry Towns could tell it was not going to work out. The network executives were polite, attentive. They even threw in an encouraging chuckle here and there. The woman with the man's name leaned forward, as if she were right on the edge of excitement. But the executive who was known as the Inquisitor didn't ask any questions. He kept his eyes lowered and scribbled notes. In the corridor, the agent said he felt it had "gone well." Yes, the executives had the power to okay the show then and there, but sometimes they didn't. Sometimes they wanted to kick it around "internally." As it turned out, Harry was right—the executives had just been going through the motions.

He had been pitching a show in which the main character was a dog. He used that as an example of how low he had sunk. "A dog show," he had told a friend. "It's come to that." But he had gotten to like that dog show. He imagined himself doing five years' worth of it and never getting tired of the sucker. As it turned out, the network had a similar show in development. One with a famous dog. That meant he had made the trip for nothing. Two and a half hours to the airport, a couple more sitting on the ground, then five in the air. Not to speak of getting up for the meeting. He hadn't gone to one for a while, so naturally he was rusty. He had to remember to be focused but also a little casual, so as not to give the impression that it was life or death for him.

He had taken six months off to write his famous Spanish Armada play. Famous around his house. The way screenwriters are always going to write a novel someday, he was always going to write a play. He had gotten a few months ahead and finally decided to call his own bluff. The trouble was that the British and the Spanish never really went at each other. They stayed out of each other's range until a storm tore up the Spanish fleet. So it wasn't inherently dramatic. He thought he would jump in and see if he could drum up a little conflict along the way—but he hadn't succeeded. Meanwhile his accountant had called and told him he'd better hurry up and get a payday. If he wanted to keep his house. The accountant had been a little detached. There was a possibility that the fucking accountant might drop him. How would that look?

And now he had to take the trip back—with nothing to show for it. He would call Julie and tell her about it and she'd be cheerful, telling him that something else would come up, it always did. But maybe it wouldn't this time.

It wasn't anyone's fault. These things happened. The networks were secretive about their projects. They probably wanted to see if his notion was different enough from the one they had to justify a go-ahead. It wasn't as if the trip could have been headed off.

He drove back to the hotel feeling bone tired. He had heard people say they felt every one of their years. It was his turn to feel every one of his, plus a few more. They had put him in a hotel of their choice, not his, and he had gone along with it. What was so important about a hotel room? For a quick hit. He told himself it was nice to look out the window and see L.A. from a different angle—but he was aware every second that it was their hotel, not his.

He thought of calling Matty, who would take him to Spago, or Sid, who would take him wherever he wanted to go. They were powerful men. Industry survivors. They had weathered the trends and could always get something going. You could call them at the last second and they wouldn't stand on ceremony. If either was free, he'd say so. Harry could get himself seen that way. He was tired at the moment, but he looked good. He had his own kind of tan, an East Coast tan, and though he had gotten a late start at it, he had become a tennis fanatic. So he had a tennis waist, too, or at least the start of one. There may have been some talk that he was a doper. He had reason to believe that a certain producer had spread that around. Because he had picked up the man and his wife and danced them around a disco. The two of them, off the ground and in his arms. A little error of judgment. Also, there was the new concern about your age. If you were past forty, you were in trouble. You had to come to meetings with a young guy who would act as a beard. And was Harry ever past forty. Cruising along, as he said, in his fifties. What the hell, he was fifty-seven. If he showed up with Matty or Sid, a deal would come up, right on the spot. A studio executive would recognize him and ask him to come by. Or a retired agent would shuffle over with a project—like a punch-drunk fighter answering a bell. And there would be something to it too. He had seen it happen. But not lately.

He had a few notions, too, and had intended to see if any of them would fly—as long as he was in L.A.—but the meeting had stolen his energy. He was pitched out.

He called Julie and told her about the setback and, just as he anticipated, she was cheerful and told him not to worry about it. The thing to do was to go out and have a great time his last night in L.A. Her response was predictable, but what was he complaining about? He had been with some gloombombs and should have known better.

Harry knew a handsome woman in L.A. and had a feeling that he could probably catch her in for dinner. But it had been several years since he had last seen her, and she'd had time to store up some new defeats. He didn't feel he could take them on right now. Then, too, they might get something going, and he would have to fly back feeling awful.

He decided he needed a little home cooking, so to speak, and ended up calling Travis, the one friend he had in L.A. who wasn't in show business. Not that he was entirely pure. Travis liked the fact that Harry had his name on a couple of big pictures. And he was ready to sign over his house to any woman with even the slightest connection to the entertainment world. Someone who'd been on "Gilligan's Island." Or even an old girlfriend of Hefner's. That part of his life hadn't gone well.

But everything else had. Travis had come to L.A. some twenty years back—as a pharmacist with shaky credentials—and had proceeded to make a ton of money. Not right off the bat but eventually. And not as a pharmacist but in business deals. Leases, franchises, buy-outs. All of it with a distinctive L.A. stamp to it. Once he had sat with Harry in a darkened car and told him he could make a lot of money for him "offshore." Harry had listened politely, but he had let it go by. That kind of thing had nothing to do with him. Maybe because of the darkened car.

He had a lot of numbers for Travis, but the one he dialed was a central station manned by an assistant whose style was whipped and deferential, even over the phone. He knew who Harry was and how much pleasure Travis got out of the dinners and would see to it that his employer got the message. They set up a date for nine-thirty at the Palm. Harry felt confident that Travis would be there. You could call him at the last minute and usually he'd be available. Not in the way that Matty or Sid would be. With all the money Travis had made, he hadn't been able to get anything substantial going in his personal life. His was a sad kind of availability.

Harry had a minor matter to take care of before dinner. An agent had called and said he wanted him as a client. In the past several years Harry had been represented by a colossal agency, a kind of General Motors, and it hadn't worked out. The arrangement was too vague. He had been warned about the impersonality of such groups, and sure enough, there wasn't a single individual he could really get his hands on. The agent who called said he was just such an individual. So Harry said what the hell, he'd have a drink with him.

The agent certainly looked like a good agent. He had wavy hair and a great mustache. Harry thought he recognized the look from a TV show, one that was slanted demographically toward folks in their thirties, but it still looked good on him. Harry had a double Gibson and began to think it might be nice to have a handsome fellow representing him, one with a nice demographic look about him. And the agent certainly was eager enough. He said he was small but that he would work his ass off. They were joined by a woman colleague. She said she handled the "classy" side of the group's clients, which presumably would include Harry. And she would work her ass off too. So now there were two people willing to work their asses off for him. Harry was starting to figure what the hell, he wasn't going anywhere with the other gang, when the fellow made the remark. He knew about Megan, Towns's four-year-old daughter. He had a five-year-old son.

"If I had you as a client," he said, "my son would always have a little chippy waiting for him back East."

And that was that. Harry said he would think about it when he got back home, but he had already thought about it. No chippy stuff.

Harry was that way. He had canceled out a business manager when the fellow said Towns would be given a "pishy little allowance." Actually Harry had been prepared to allow him one "pishy," but after the second one, it was case closed. He knew what the business manager meant. Walking-around money. But don't call it "pishy."

Travis had him paged at the bar of the Palm and said it was all right about dinner but that he might be a little late. Harry told him not to worry about it, to take his time. They were easy with each other now. Usually Travis tried to fool him on the phone with a Yiddish accent or a Spanish one, but he had dropped that. The accents were getting too easy to pick off.

After waiting at the bar for half an hour, Harry was sorry he had told Travis to take his time. He was ready to eat tables and chairs. Maybe they were being too easy with each other. He looked at the caricatures of celebrities on the wall. When the Palm had first opened, the owner had asked him for his picture and he had never gotten around to sending him one. Now he was sorry he hadn't taken him up on it. At times like this he would be able to look at a caricature of himself on the wall. And the owner had never asked him again.

There were two women at the bar. Harry heard them say they were from Cincinnati. They weren't major leaguers—just two women from Cincinnati. Normally he wouldn't have thought of them that way—not anymore—but this was Hollywood. He shouldered his way into the conversation, telling them he was waiting for a friend who was finishing up a little brain surgery. He had been living in the country for a while, away from the bars, and he was aware that his remarks were strained. But they put up with the intrusion, and by the time Travis arrived, the women were curious about him, even when they found out he wasn't a brain surgeon. Travis fell all over them, giving them every one of his numbers. It was as if he had just gotten out of prison and hadn't seen a woman in years. Harry saw that it was useless to try to pry him away, so he went up ahead to their table and got started with a shrimp cocktail, thinking maybe he had missed his profession.

By the time Travis joined him, the crowd had begun to thin out and they had to rush to get served. Harry ordered veal parmigiana, an unusual call in a steak house, but that's what he was in the mood for. He noticed that Travis dressed differently now. For years he had gone with what Harry thought of as a hairdresser look, the old kind of hairdresser, with his shirt cut low to the waist and heavy chains and white shoes with lifts in them and tassels. He'd worn a lot of orange. And he had come up with an odd color for his hair, one that hadn't quite worked out. But someone had gotten hold of him and told him to lighten up. He wore a soft linen suit and had let his hair get a little gray and comfortable-looking. He seemed less prickly too.

Since they didn't see each other too often, they were able to get a good clean bead on one another. Normally it was Travis who was up against it. Travis, with the sister who freaked out and lived in Cuba. Travis, with the father who surfaced after thirty years and threatened to kill his mother if she didn't take him back. Travis's women. The short, rudderless one with the great body. Should he let her do a split-beaver shot for a skin magazine? It was the first time Towns had ever heard anyone say *split-beaver.* Or Travis's niece, would you believe? She had packed up her children and left her husband for Travis. Was she intelligent enough for him? Or the Polish model who had a roomful of furs but didn't seem to have a visible means of support. Could he trust her? With his credit cards?

Travis couldn't figure out where he went wrong with women. He had once taken a psychiatrist along on a date to see how he interacted with them. An L.A. solution. Harry had introduced Julie to Travis, who immediately perceived her as being a certain kind of parochial-school girl he remembered from his childhood. A type that had nothing to do with her. Nonetheless, he had flown at her with angry theological arguments—the Catholics against the Jews. Later, when Harry suggested that he had acted poorly, Travis had been shocked. He thought he had been charming. So Harry knew about Travis and women.

He would listen to Travis's adventures and try to throw out a helpful comment, at the same time trying not to be smug about it. This was difficult since Travis was rolling around like a loose cannon and Harry was seeing things from the safe compound in which he lived with Julie and Megan. But the work stopped coming and Julie had started to knock them back, and he was so uneasy that he couldn't even enjoy his daughter. So this time around it was Harry's turn to unload.

He told Travis about the trip and how he had come up empty. And how the dice had been running cold for him. About the age thing in Hollywood. And how he couldn't seem to get anything going. He had the credits, and as he was fond of pointing out, they didn't put your name up there because you were Jewish. But it didn't seem to matter. He was perceived as someone who couldn't bring a script over the top. And to an extent it was true. But what was wrong with getting them in sight of the goal line? He had been doing that for years and hadn't had a complaint. But it was different now. They wanted fellows who could take them all the way. He could do that, too, but they weren't giving him a chance. Or who knows, maybe it was the dope rap. Harry didn't use much these days, but he had used a lot back then, used it the night he had picked up the producer and his wife and waltzed them around the disco. The producer had a resigned little pout on his face as he and his wife were whisked off the ground, and who could blame him for being pissed off? He was known as an amoral little prick, but who knows, maybe the fucker had some dignity. Who could blame him for passing it around that Harry was a doper?

When Harry's veal parmigiana came out, it didn't appear to have any veal in it. Or maybe the veal had dissolved in the sauce. It had been that kind of trip. While Harry was deciding whether to send it back or just mop up the parmigiana part with bread, Travis took a quick turn. He was wondering if he should part company with a business associate. He had given the fellow thousands of dollars on ventures that kept going down the drain. He didn't mind that part. "I'm making so much money, anyway," he said. But the fellow kept putting him down. Travis had his eye on a girl, someone who had once done a "Family Ties." The fellow had told him face it, what would a girl in her twenties see in someone like Travis? Harry picked that one off easily. He told Travis that by definition he shouldn't have anyone in his life who put him down. And then he jumped in quickly and got started on the house, how much it meant to him with the peach trees, and how he would feel if he had to sell it and move Julie and Megan up to Vermont somewhere. He admitted he would be embarrassed about it. He and Travis had known each other since college. The clock was ticking. They could get naked with each other.

"Why didn't you come to me?" Travis asked. "How is anyone supposed to know you're in trouble if you don't ask?"

"I wouldn't be much good at that," said Towns.

But why wouldn't he? For one thing, he didn't know if the offer was meant to be a loan or a gift. He couldn't take a gift, could he? And if it was a loan, what if he didn't pay it back in time? Travis's father had been in the rackets, connected with one of the smaller casinos in Vegas. They had found him eventually under a piano in the lounge, and Travis had to go out to identify the body. So the father was dead. But he probably had associates. You could say that this was Travis, not his father, but Harry remembered his friend in the darkened car whispering about offshore stuff. Also, he had seen some types moving quietly around Travis's house in the hills. Irritable men wearing Arrow shirts and ties in the hot sun. Not official hard noses, but worse in a way.

But that wasn't it. For all he knew, it was a straightforward offer, from the heart and with no strings. What reason did he have to doubt this? It was more a question of Harry not wanting to turn over the wheel. He had to be the one to bring the ball down, pick up the check. He had a few dollars out on the street. He liked to say that: "I have some money on the street." In truth it wasn't much—fifties, hundreds. But he was the one who passed it out. How would it look if he started taking? How would it look if he had to move to Vermont?

At school neither of them had much money, but it was Harry who had bought milk shakes for his skinny friend. Later he was a screenwriter with his name on a couple of big pictures. Travis boasted about having gone to school with him. How would it look if he took money from Travis, who was shorter than he was? Always, it was how would it look.

So he let the offer slide. He had been in trouble before. Something always came up. Fuck the age thing. Could anyone match his original conceptions? When he was on target? Let them enjoy their youth. One of these days he was going to grab one of them and say: "Congratulations on your youth."

He let Travis pick up the check. It was the least he could do. And they went out on the street. Travis was in wonderful condition if you liked that kind of shape. Real tight and drawn. He hit balls every day of his life. He'd gotten up to ten hours a day once until he realized he was having a nervous breakdown. But for the moment, in the streetlight, bent over, with his shoulders bunched up tight, he had the skull of a little old man.

Harry was fading, but Travis wanted to keep going. He was almost cranky about it. He didn't get much of a chance to see his pal and he wanted to milk the occasion. Harry had a sign over his desk that read, SUCK IT UP, one that he had started to ignore. He just couldn't suck it up anymore. But he did, one more time, and agreed to go down the street

to the Mexican place that was still open and have a beer. Travis had an
open Corniche waiting. He paid the attendant a few dollars to keep
watching it, and then the girls came pouring out of the Troubadour.
They had their hair chopped off and slanted six different ways to nowhere, and their clothes were black and netted and expensively forlorn,
but it was them, all right, the same gang that had stopped him cold
years back when he first came out to Hollywood and thought he was
the only one ever to get a fruit bowl sent up to his room at the Wil-
shire. As usual, they were mismatched with pale men carrying attaché
cases, but they were the cream and they had the kind of undeniable
beauty that you simply couldn't be casual about no matter who you
were and what coast you were from. He looked around and quite
frankly couldn't spot a single one who'd be incapable of slipping past
that fence he'd built around himself when he first met Julie—so as not
to mess things up. All it would take was the inclination.

"Oh, Jesus Christ," said Harry. "Will you just look at them."

"I can't," said Travis, with a pop singer's heartbreak in his voice. "It's
too painful."

"For Christ's sake," said Harry. "Show them the Corniche. You can
get laid just on that."

Travis had his first laugh of the evening, and Harry put an arm
around his friend's shoulders. Travis put an arm around Harry Towns's
waist. A famous first and fuck the sentimentality. They just stood there
marveling at the girls, and Harry asked his friend what he would say to
fifty thousand.

"Where do I send it?" asked Travis.

"Hey, that's right," said Harry. "You don't even have my address."

They stayed fixed on the girls, watching them dance in place as they
waited for their cars, some of them using the Troubadour's awning
poles as a ballet bar. Harry knew that there were still some adventures
up ahead.

"Oh, yeah," he could hear a friend in the theater say. "Blindness,
impotence. I can hardly wait." But that was his friend in the theater. It
wasn't Harry Towns. Take the next morning, for example. He'd get up,
have a full breakfast, check the trades, then fly back to his family and
get set to see what it was like on the receiving end.

Notes

"The Subversive," "When You're Excused, You're Excused," "The Good Time," "Mr. Prinzo's Breakthrough," "The Canning of Mother Dean," and "The Little Ball" appeared in *Far From the City of Class*, The Frommer-Pasmantier Publishing Corporation, 1963.

"Brazzaville Teen-ager," "Black Angels," "A Change of Plan," "The Interview," and "The Scientist" originally appeared in Esquire.

"Far From the City of Class" originally appeared in Mademoiselle.

"The Partners," "Lady," and "Back to Back" appeared in *About Harry Towns*, The Atlantic Monthly Press, 1990.

"The Man They Threw Out of Jets" originally appeared in the Antioch Review.

"Detroit Abe," "Business is Business," "Living Together," and "The War Criminal" appeared in *Let's Hear It for a Beautiful Guy*, Donald I. Fine, Inc., 1984.

"The Mourner," "23 Pat O'Brien Movies," "The Icing on the Cake," "The Gent," "The Investor," and "For Your Viewing Entertainment," originally appeared in Playboy.

"The Hero," "The Humiliation," "The Holiday Celebrators" (published as "A Rose for Moss"), "The Operator," "The Death Table," and "The Neighbors" originally appeared in Cavalier.

"The Mission" originally appeared in the Saturday Evening Post.

"The Enemy" originally appeared in the Transatlantic Review.

"Wonderful Golden Rule Days" and "Let's Hear It for a Beautiful Guy" originally appeared in The New Yorker.

"Post Time" originally appeared in The Twilight Zone Magazine.

"An Ironic Yetta Montana" originally appeared in Rolling Stone.

"Our Lady of the Lockers" originally appeared in New York Magazine.

"The Trip" originally appeared in Commentary.

"Marching Through Delaware" originally appeared in Cosmopolitan.

"Show Biz Connections" originally appeared in *Lonesome Monsters*, published by Lancer Books.

"The Night Boxing Ended" originally appeared in the Gentleman's Quarterly.

"Yes, We Have No Ritchard" originally appeared in The Magazine of Fantasy and Science Fiction.

"Pitched Out" appeared in *The Current Climate*, The Atlantic Monthly Press, 1989.